JADE

JADE

Gwen Davis

WARNER BOOKS

A Time Warner Company

Warner Books, Inc., 666 Fifth Avenue, New York, NY 10103

W A Time Warner Company

Printed in the United States of America
First printing: May 1991
10 9 8 7 6 5 4 3 2 1

Library of Congress Cataloging-in-Publication Data

Davis, Gwen.
  Jade : a novel / by Gwen Davis.
    p.   cm.
  ISBN 0-446-51584-1
  I. Title.
PS3554.A9346J3   1991
813'.54—dc20   90-39347
                                              CIP

Designed by Giorgetta Bell McRee

For Owen Laster

ACKNOWLEDGMENTS

This is a work of fiction. But, like many novels, it is also threaded with truth, real experiences, information, ideas and insights I was fortunate enough to have access to, through friends. I am particularly indebted to Lieutenant Edward M. Fortner, Officer in charge of Communications, San Francisco Police Department, a writer in his own right. Thanks also to Superintendent David Evans of the Royal Hong Kong Police, Detective Inspector Phillip Fraser, head of Vice in Wanchai, Melinda Parsons of the Hong Kong Government Information Service, her associate Mark Pinkstone, Ernest Beyl, Gerrie Pitt of the Mandarin Oriental, Hong Kong, Khun Pornsri Luphaoboon of the Oriental, Bangkok, May Law and Ralph-Peter Jentes of the Grand Hyatt, Hong Kong, Lyle Connelly, and all the gracious people who were such a help to me at the Hong Kong Tourist Bureau.

My gratitude also to Mary Peterson, who taught me the dread language of computers, Nicholas Prior, Katherine Mihoc, Dr. Matthew Naythons, Georgs Kolesnikovs, Wolfgang Rohde, Craig Wolfson, Paul Temple, Deb Brandt, and especially Leslie Keenan, who restored my faith in working editors. Affectionate thanks to Sandra Burton, who told me to do it for Hong Kong, Jack Kornfeld, who told me I could do it, and Nansey Neiman, who insisted I take an extra year to do it right. I hope I have.

The author.

THE PHOENIX IS A FEMALE
RISING OUT OF HER OWN ASHES
SHEDDING BAD EXPERIENCE
LIKE A TIRED SKIN
REJUVENATED BY THE HOPE
THAT SOMETHING BETTER IS COMING
SHE CREATES THAT POSSIBILITY
AND SO, MORE OFTEN THAN NOT
SOMETHING BETTER COMES.

DAO TSIM

BOOK ONE

◆

THE PEAK

ONE

◆

Because they were young, their bodies were beautiful. Even under
the grotesque circumstances, even with the grim details the autopsies
would later reveal, at first discovery, there was more a sense of the
erotic than the dark pornography of death. The girl's head was
between the boy's legs. She was naked, on her haunches, the
peachlike curve of her buttocks settling gracefully back against her
calves, ankles and still roseate toes underlining, like the lesser-known
paintings of Corbeau, the sweet crack of her ass.

A local European walking his dog on Black's Link came upon
them early in the morning, beneath a secluded, heavily leafed banyan
tree, a strangler fig curling upstart branches at its base. Even the
trees had mystery to them, Clement Leslie could not help thinking.
He had been a policeman in Hong Kong for over twenty years, and
the romanticism of the colony still held him. Banyan: the tree under
which Buddha had found his Enlightenment. Strangler figs: growing
on the strength of the parent tree until they became strong enough to
choke their progenitors. All the ugliness of a place the soul knew was
greedy and lusty, carved from the human underbelly, and all the
terrible beauty.

The banyan tree where the couple was murdered grew just
below the Peak, that part of Hong Kong that was aptly named.
Happy Valley, the low-lying sector of the island, had been a

3

euphemism, Clement understood clearly. More accurately, camouflage, a verbal hoax so Chinese laborers and indigents who lived there
wouldn't be constantly reminded of the malaria and other diseases
that flourished in the marshes, the swamp the area really was.
Drainage, physical improvements over the years had made it habit-
able, safe. There were places in it that were now actually "fashionable":
the Royal Jockey Club of Hong Kong, the official racetrack, was dead
in its midst. But nothing took away the irony, the cruel sham
flimflammed on the poor, through language, the best weapon of the
Brits. It embarrassed Clement sometimes that a tongue he loved so
much, one that had given rise to Shakespeare, could also be used for
so many lies.

The dead teenagers were from British families. The boy's father
was a prominent banker, the girl's mother—her parents were divorced—
the colony's leading jewelry designer, specializing in jade. The
Chinese regarded jade as lucky, and had elevated the price even
before Maggie Evans's pieces became so trendily sought after. Her
shops and showcase were part of the designated tours arranged by
luxury ships that stopped in the harbor long enough for their
passengers to feel they had seen Hong Kong, although mostly what
they saw were stores. Little arcades with open counters on the way
back from the main marketplace served as a kind of decompression
chamber for those who had what Clement called "Rapture of the
Spending," so they wouldn't, like divers who had come up too
rapidly from the deep, have burst bubbles in their brains.

There were Maggie Evans boutiques in the Landmark in Hong
Kong, Shangri-La, and the Regent Hotel, Kowloon side. The last
important murder, still fresh in people's minds, had been that of a
Malaysian financier, who'd been part of a huge kiting scandal, a
$2.5-billion public company that turned out to have no assets but its
overeager investors' money. His body had been carried, chopped up,
in a suitcase, from the Regent Hotel. Because of that tenuous thread,
Police Superintendent Leslie's young assistant had put a watch on the
Regent, thinking that perhaps certain glorious locales inspired people
to murder, as Venice inspired people to a more serviceable passion.
But he was very young, Clement thought, and even more of a secret

romanticist than his boss. Still, Clement let him do his surveillance, though he knew there would turn out to be no connection.

The murdered girl, Elizabeth Heather Evans—called "Betsy" by her parents, known as "Wisp" to her friends, for the gentle way she spoke—was eighteen at the time of her death, a year older than David Palmer-Smith. He'd been a grade behind her at Kensington Academy, an expensive private establishment for young colonials. The Brits still considered themselves that, though it was a long time since Hong Kong had been colonized, and increasingly closer to that day in 1997 when it was to be turned over to the Chinese. The general apprehension and anxiety generated by that prospect was momentarily forgotten in the furor over the murder, giving the inhabitants of Hong Kong something present and comfortingly sensational to focus on, as a man waiting to find out if the biopsy is malignant can be distracted by a cut finger.

So ripped was the Gweilo community—white eyes, according to the local jargon—by the scandal and horror, that the sadness of the death of two healthy, handsome young people seemed swept aside. Sex among the Europeans was not as it was among the Chinese, Clement knew firsthand. The Asians considered all Westerners pro-miscuous, even when they weren't two young people making love on a hillside. Chinese regarded men-women relationships as a partner-ship, accepting philandering as long as it didn't impact on the family. A decent man, if he could afford it, paid for it. Signs in the streets of Hong Kong and Kowloon told where prostitutes were available, usually just a few feet from the sign. A single girl for sale on premises without a protector was no offense, either by law, or according to the local ethic. Certainly Clement made no judgment, or for that matter, arrests. A superintendent saved his attention for important matters, and, as important as the heart was to him, he didn't confuse it with genitals. Or, at least he had spent most of his adult years trying not to.

Still, he knew all the rules, official and unofficial: two or more women at a location made a bona fide brothel. On Jaffe Road, windows with green trim meant prostitute. The Hong Kong Classi-fied had fourteen pages devoted to "Massage," including full-page ads, drawings of ice cream cones, with "Little Girl" printed in the midst of the confection, and a slogan that read "Everything nice, that's what our little girls are made of." Clement sometimes thumbed through the yellow pages late at night as a kind of soporific, when he hadn't drunk enough to be unconscious, and there wasn't any woman in his life pretending to care about or be accessible to him. So he would read them and smile and try to dull his brain enough to make him go to sleep, and not let the thought enter his head that perhaps his interest wasn't that detached, that it might be easier buying it.

In addition to the Massage section, there were fifteen pages of Escort Services, featuring pictures of the girls, sloe-eyed, smiling, ready. Besides what was offered in the Classified, one of Hong Kong's most profitable enterprises was a club called Volvo's. Five hundred Mamasans were in attendance, waitresses, receptionists with walkie-talkies, voice-transmitting the arrival of the customer before he got to the bottom of the escalator, where his projected favorite types would be already on tap. Volvo's had in its employ twelve hundred of these "hostesses" working the flashily light-bulbed disco bar, a neoned expanse that covered seventy thousand square feet. There were individual VIP rooms, where Clement was always welcome as the guest of the manager, who also ran an expensive playground for children.

According to the gentleman, which he very much considered himself, as he considered Clement his friend, Volvo's serviced fifteen hundred customers and took in a hundred thousand dollars U.S. nightly. He recounted the figures in a prideful manner, with the same expansive ease with which he greeted the superintendent, offering hospitality. If Clement had enough to drink, as he did more often than not, he accepted, imagining, when drunk, that a hostess who fondled you and seemed genuinely interested was not the same as someone plucked from the classified. The numbers the manager boasted of were accurate, since one room was occupied solely by accountants, working in shifts just to keep up with the figures, which had been given to the Hong Kong Stock Exchange when Volvo's tried to go public. Profits did not include what the girls made during "Happy Hour," the optional foray to a nearby hotel, from which the establishment took what it considered to be a fair cut. They never did that in Clement's case, since he was not allowed to pay. The boss paid the girl himself, and instructed her to go home with Clement, and tell him she was doing it for nothing because of how much she liked him. One of them had revealed that to him, but fortunately he'd been too drunk to remember, because he still liked to think he wasn't desperate enough to buy it.

Sex in Hong Kong was a commodity, patently shameless, in the real meaning of shameless: without any shame. Rather a source of pride, it seemed from the logos in the telephone book, and the manner in which the club had been flogged to the stock exchange. In fact, it was not the immorality of Volvo's that caused it to be turned down as an offering, but that one of its owners, himself an official of the Exchange, had been indicted for insider trading, and manipulation of funds.

But it was a horse of another color, as they said around the Jockey Club, teenagers from good families fucking in the bushes. Scandal in Hong Kong was usually financial, since everyone was leveraged up to their eyeballs, in a city where, if you had no money, you had no face. The measure of the quality of the would-be escapees—the "Brain Drain" that had been leaving Hong Kong since Mrs. Thatcher initiated the agreement to return the colony to China, accelerated by the massacres in Tiananmen Square—was whether they had not only the skills, but the means to relocate. Hong Kong was about money, at least as long as capitalism lasted there. Money is God, they said all the time. People understood greed. Sympathized with it. Were under its spell, as heroines in Brontë novels were to brooding men. One day's races at the Jockey Club with fifty thousand people present meant gate receipts totaling forty million dollars U.S. Although Clement didn't gamble, he appreciated the impressiveness of those figures, and the zeal of those who thought fortunes could be made in a day. Greed was the foundation of the place.

But sex, more properly, belonged in the Yellow Pages, not on the Peak. The Peak was the perch from which the rich and privileged could see all of Hong Kong, the sloping hills down to Victoria Harbor, the Erector Set profligacy of skyscrapers built every which way, crowding the already jammed landscape below with new and chromier designs, twin towers, octagons and obelisks, mirrored exteriors flashing back sun at the already blazing day. Nobody had stopped building, just because of the fear that gripped the colony about the future, about a government that could not be counted on to keep its word that Hong Kong would stay capitalist for fifty years. Jackhammers hadn't stopped splintering the never-would-be silence. Silence was more ominous than death to the Chinese, carrying with it the message that no one was making money. So building continued, even though there were no guarantees of what they were building for, structures with no sense to them. Building codes had no restrictions, unlike sexual ethics. A Chinese father would have beaten his daughter had she taken a lover as Betsy had done. The availability of prostitutes in Hong Kong was in large part so that no one would debauch a good girl.

So Clement could feel Elizabeth Heather Evans being dismissed as a spirit by a large part of the congregation assembled at Saint John's Cathedral, even as her body was laid to rest. While the reverend spoke of the light that had been extinguished, Clement stood at the rear, watching people shifting uncomfortably on the wooden benches. He could read through the back of their heads to the thoughts inside, of how very improper it all was. Young and fair of countenance as Betsy and David had been, they had lusted. Filthy as was the crime committed against them, Clement was sure the message in the minds of many was that their sexuality had brought the evil on them.

The Bible stand supporting the text from which the minister read was a bronze eagle with outspread wings, metal feathers buttressing the oversized volume. The flowers that nearly obscured the vast altar were mostly pink and yellow, so it looked the colors of a baby shower. Because of the circumstances surrounding the deaths, and the condition of the bodies, both coffins were closed. Above the finely carved walnut caskets fluttered low-hanging wood-bladed fans, *whoosh*ing through the pauses in the minister's words like sighs. Slowly revolving shadows from the blades lent a Maughamian air to the proceedings, ghosts of a better time, when both the Empire and its authors had true weight. As a lover of literature and his country, Clement mourned the mounting ineffectuality of both.

But he also mourned the children. Though he had known

neither of them, he had a passing acquaintance with the girl's mother. Hong Kong was a small town, and Maggie was in her way a celebrity, very much in evidence, larger than life. But larger than death? He looked at the back of her sweat-darkened yellow hair, and wondered how she would survive it. Wondered how he himself would have survived the death of the child he'd never had, who might have been the same age, and gone to Kensington Academy, if a policeman could have afforded it.

Through the stained glass window to the southeast the May morning sunlight streamed, illuminating Christ calming the waters; in the left panel of the triptych stood a British seaman, on the right, two sampans and a barefoot woman in a coolie hat. Along the dark-wood walls hung crests on painted shields, pigment flaking and darkened, with the great names of England: Wakefield, Derby, Manchester, Bradford, Coventry, Truro. In spite of the fans and the early morning hour, the heat was already oppressive, the humidity wilting even those not seemingly devastated by the events. Clement could see Maggie's shoulder blades through the wet back of her blouse.

The cathedral was unusually full. Even Sunday services were mainly conducted in the chapel to the front, so that the few faithful, and possibly God, would not be made uncomfortable by the small numbers. But there was an impressive turnout for this funeral. Almost everyone in the European community did business or socialized with at least one of the parents. Nearly all of them had children themselves. Those who had gone to school with Betsy and David sat in shocked silence, white-faced, white-knuckled, beside their elders.

Clement saw the pale, thin-fingered hand of Nicholas Evans, the girl's father, move along the back of the wooden bench and come to a comforting rest on his ex-wife's shoulders. She shrugged him off, brushed the place where his hand had been with a gesture of annoyance, as though it had been an insect. What if they had stayed together? Clement wondered. Would the girl still be alive? He had seen them all those afternoons in the Clipper Lounge of the Mandarin Hotel, looking so much the stylish, perfect colonial family, sipping their high tea, Maggie pouring, the girl devouring the tiny sandwiches, Maggie playfully slapping her hand at the un-Englishness of a zesty appetite. Had that been a charade, how pleased with their life they seemed? How very comfortable with the elegance of afternoon tea in that glittering, crystal-cascaded lobby they'd looked. How long-limbed and stylish Maggie had appeared, so at ease with her new, great success. Never had there been on her face any of the loathing expressed in that one dismissing gesture of brushing the comforting hand away. And on the girl's face—Betsy's beautiful face, so like an unlined cookie-cutter version of Maggie's own pale oval—complete contentment with the setting, the sandwiches, the life that she had. What if her parents had never been divorced? Would she have been taking tea that fatal afternoon, instead of making furtive love on the hillside? Was her sexual indulgence more than the loosed blood of adolescence, hunger that could no longer be satisfied by sandwiches? Was it a reaction to her family's coming apart?

Even as the thoughts went through his head, Clement under-stood what a moralist he was, what a man out of his time, soon to be out of his place. Had he married, which he still was surprised he never had, he would never have dared divorce, one of the reasons why, he supposed, he had never married. There were covenants man made between himself and God, as he made agreements with his Queen. When you served, you served, faithfully and forever. No matter how the hand on your shoulder came to repel you.

After the service, Maggie stood in the courtyard beside Nicholas, a look on her face of distracted commitment, her body at curious angles, half moving in toward his, half leaning away, as though she were trying at once to be with him and escape him. The mourners passed in straggling groups, giving their sorry good wishes. Clement could hear the homilies. From the limbs of the huge banyan tree linear roots grew, thin lengths of wood spiraling toward the earth, by the great stone wall where the mourners were grouped. Orchids curled around the trunks of the larger trees, a leech species that seemed to grow with them. Behind Maggie were lavender jacaranda and coco yam, names as succulent and exotic as the place, the very lushness of the setting an argument disputing death. What if she'd stayed with her husband? Clement wondered again. Maybe then none of this suffocating sorrow, the cloying heat, the so-called comforting words, would have had to be endured.

On the small hill behind the gray wall was a strangler fig of the same variety that flowered where they'd found the couple. The family of the boy stood near it, the ashen color on their lips more lifeless than the dead limbs of the parent tree. They were dowdier and sadder than the Evans pair, the woman a wash of withered middle age that had not sought to preserve even a vestige of its youth, as if dyeing gray hair or brightening a cheek would be presumptuous, the false vanity scorned by the puritanical. She had gone through a struggle at the mortician's, part of which Clement had witnessed, as to whether or not to close the casket. The hideous evidence of the murder weapon had been eliminated: a pencil had been removed from the boy's eye. But the eyeball had collapsed, and the mortician had been forced to stuff the eye with cotton so one eye wouldn't look flat, while the other was round. The lid had been sewn shut. In spite of the mortician's skill, the stitches still showed. The skin cut ear to ear at the back of the head to flap up and over for the autopsy exposing the brain, penetrated by the murder weapon, had been deftly put back in place. But the bruises on the dead boy's face were more extensive than those on the girl's, dark blue on the kind of white English skin that seemed always to be blushing, mottling red in the slightest cold, a complexion that in girls would have been called peaches and cream. His hair was darker by shades than Betsy's flaxen curls, a tawny, muddy yellow. His pigmentation and the assault on it, despite the cleverness of the undertaker, had forced the decision to give him his ultimate privacy.

Classmates of Betsy's were shaking Maggie's hand now, dully offering words of consolation, tears in their eyes, noses reddened from weeping. An older woman moved in close to Maggie, looking into her eyes with the intense sincerity of strangers who thought they were friends. "You have to go on, dear," she said.

"Why?" asked Maggie.

The sky was a deceptively cool blue, cloudless in spite of the rains that would fall by afternoon, flooding the gutters, sotting the earth. That had been a problem for the undertaker as well, Clement knew, cleansing the earth from the two young faces. Only the back of Betsy's body had been unsullied, except for what was inside. The police report was still incomplete, but even the full details available had not been passed on to the parents, partly because there was still much Clement himself didn't know. But the mud, at least, had served to capture some very good footprints.

He saw Maggie notice him, lean away, as though she were shocked, even offended to see him there. Only the color of her clothes and the slack-jawed sorrow on her face signaled the dire nature of the receiving line: from the brightness of the day and the smell of the flowers, the well-wishers might have been congratulating her on her daughter's wedding. Her shoulders collapsed inward at the sight of the policeman, as though someone had struck her in the chest. She seemed to try to shrink into what little there were of shadows.

He moved toward the line, stood in it, held out his hand, and felt hers against his palm, clammy, so light and slender he wondered how she could carry the weight of the carved jade ring on her index finger. "I'm surprised to see you here, Superintendent," she said, in a tone edged with weariness, a husky voice that had lost its strength, and sounded now like a rasp. "What's the etiquette for funerals? Are guests like death, able to come whether or not they're invited?"

"Thank you very much for coming," Nicholas said, quickly offering his hand. He wore plain, wire-rimmed glasses that were coming back into fashion again, but seemed a man who didn't care if he was fashionable, and so had probably worn them all along. The shadow of the banyan tree fell across the upper half of his thin, sharp-cheeked face, so the lenses were darkened, and Clement couldn't see the eyes behind them. He could, however, make out his own reflection, the slightly heavy face, wattled with the sad truths of life, the deep-set, bagged dark eyes. It was the visage of a good-looking bassett hound, somber with the knowledge that consolation calls were no consolation. "Do you know anything yet?" Nicholas asked him.

"This is hardly the place, Nicholas," Maggie said, a look of disdain pulling at her already downturned mouth.

"I just assumed if the police were here . . ."

"Well, don't assume." Her voice was etched with the practiced acid of twenty years of quarrels. "Stop always assuming."

Clement was embarrassed, as though he had inadvertently

eavesdropped on their intimacy, or lack of it; as if he had caught them at a dinner at which he wasn't welcome. Funerals always made him uncomfortable and awkward. He attended as few as he could, unless they were those of close friends. There'd been more of those than he'd cared to count in recent times: funerals of confreres younger than his own forty-nine summers, dead often as not from drink and too much good living, the riptide that flowed under this lake of luxury. People were so easily seduced by the hedonism available in sunny locales with dearths of real allegiances. Unless, like the Superintendent himself, you really loved the Queen, and would have been willing to die for her if you had the choice.

He was, by his own burly nature, a true colonial, with fewer and fewer locales left where he could serve. And serve his Queen he did, usually with a heart bursting with conviction. But the death of these two children wrenched a place in his belly that went deeper than duty, and made him wish he had chosen another profession. Still, he had had no choice but to attend this gray event, in case he could pick up some intelligence. To more or less trim his grizzled beard, put drops in his whiskey-reddened eyes, and come to this churchyard, blasted with melancholy sunshine. Even in the midst of death, as the minister had put it, people were in the midst of life. In Maggie's case, from the look of her, whether or not they wanted to be.

"Will you join us at the flat, Superintendent Leslie?" Nicholas said. "We're having people over."

"Must we go on with this?" Maggie snapped. "I want to be by myself."

"Thank you," Clement said, the words directed at Nicholas, deliberately ignoring Maggie's petulance, forgiving it. "I have to get back to headquarters."

"You'll let us know as soon as you find out anything?" Nicholas asked.

"Of course," said Clement, and moved off into the shade, no relief from the heat and humidity under that canopy of trees. Only a little mercy from the glare. But more mercy than the two young people had been shown. A lot more mercy than that.

Behind him, Maggie murmured, "I hate all these people. This is just another party for them."

"You can't possibly believe that," Nicholas was saying.

"My dear," said a woman in black, "you must know how sorry I am."

"You hardly knew her," said Maggie.

"She doesn't know what she's saying," Nicholas said.

"I know exactly what I'm saying."

"Do you?"

"I suppose not," said Maggie, and started to cry.

Clement could see her from the corner of his eye, slipping into the awkwardly offered circle of Nicholas's arm. He pressed her to his thin chest. "My poor baby," he said.

She pushed him away. "I'm not your 'baby.' I haven't been for a long time, and I never will be again."

"I wasn't talking about you," Nicholas said, and started to weep more pitifully than she had.

It was too painful for Clement to watch. As accustomed as he was to being the observer, as much a part of his duty as it was to perceive, even pry, he had the feeling he was peering into someone's window. A funeral Peeping Tom, spying on their grief, more intimate than sex. Though it might be his job, sometimes watching was more than he could stand.

He averted his eyes, a kind of modesty he might have shown if someone flattered him, which not many had done. Looking to the heavens he had spent so much time and effort struggling to believe in, he saw what was high in the tree.

An open umbrella. White, with sad little hearts all over it. At least they looked like hearts. It wasn't until they got it to the lab that they found out how much of the design was blood.

TWO

♦

Outside the plane window, the sky was ablaze with neon. Chinese characters danced up the sides of buildings. Bright red and blue and yellow lights reflected on the glassy surface of Victoria Harbor, flashing Yashica and Samsung, signaling adventure at discount. Claire had spent the last year trying to redefine "adventure" for herself, canvassing her friends for a fresh definition. She knew it involved some degree of risk. An adventure, one friend said, is something that you don't know how it will turn out. Well, she had no idea how this would turn out, but the only element of risk, as she could see it at the moment, was whether or not the plane would crash into the buildings on all sides of it. Nothing else was at stake, really, besides her life.

The wings of the plane seemed to brush by the windows of apartment houses, inches away from laundry lines, like a process shot in a movie where the plane was badly superimposed, too close to the scenery. On a roof not far below—a few hundred feet, really, it looked like—was the huge painted legend, TURN RIGHT. Was that an instruction for the plane? Was Hong Kong so folksy and frontiersy that buildings had signs on their roofs to tell the navigator what to do, and a pilot could pick up his clean underwear on his way into the airport? She wondered if a machine as giant as this one had ever been pulled from the sky tangled in someone's shorts, as the jet had gone down in Long Island from starlings' being sucked into its engine.

The pert, pretty flight attendant collected the last of the glasses, and Claire gave hers back, suppressing the impulse to find out where the woman was staying in Hong Kong. She had been kind during the flight, not the official, efficient kindness of airline training, crisp along the edges, like the uniforms, but a genuine warmth that spoke of humanity, in a world where, often as not, there was nobody home. Claire could feel little pulls of attachment, a reluctance to let the stewardess pass too easily out of her life. The feeling cropped up often lately, something between affection and anguish at the thought of losing someone. Even leaving Abercrombie and Fitch in Beverly Hills, where a salesman had shown her a massage table and been unusually pleasant about it, had seemed a rupture, making her go back to shake his hand and say goodbye to him.

All things recently seemed to be endings, so it was important for her to go through a ceremony of farewell. The truth, as she understood it now, was that you never knew when it might be the last time you saw someone, or whether anybody would come into your life again.

She was afraid that her heart would stay empty. That nobody would ever love her, that her husband hadn't loved her as much as he said, or he wouldn't have died. It was not a rational feeling, she was aware of that. She dismissed the thought as crazy even as she had it, remembering how hard he had struggled—how hard both of them had struggled to keep him alive. But the speed with which he had vanished, first from his own wasting body, then from their bed, then from the world, had sent her into shock. Fortress that he had been to her, big, beefy, warm-hearted wall between her and the world, she was left feeling that she had no skin.

Judith Taylor had come through, as Judith always came through, with an invitation to Hong Kong, where she was now Bureau Chief of *Elan* magazine. She had been very clear, as Judith was unfailingly clear, of what the procedure was to be: what airline Claire was to take, and when; what door she should pass through once the plane landed; and what would be waiting for her there. Nothing sentimental, no prospects for a fantasy, nor even a definition of adventure. Claire hadn't asked Judith for that, one of the few friends she didn't bother in that particular word search. Judith had said there would be a man in an orange jacket waiting on the other side of the doorway with GREETING marked on it. "No s," Judith said with her unerring accuracy, a hint of humor in her tone, as if she didn't have to explain how constant was the struggle for Asians in Hong Kong to get the English right.

Claire had friends all over the world, the finest of them Judith; it was absurd to think life would be emptier if she didn't keep up contact with a stewardess. For a moment Claire understood how inappropriate it was to become attached to strangers, to try to transform them too quickly into friends. So at the door, all she said to the young woman was thank you, and goodbye, even as the words thickened with what was in her throat.

She moved through passport regulations, feeling an unexpected rush of freedom: a place she'd never been with Charley. Anywhere else she'd gone to try to feel better was prickled with recollection, because they'd been there together. Making her cry because she remembered, no matter what a good time they'd been having, how much he really hated to travel, how much more he'd like to be home. That he had only done it for her, because the last thing Charley wanted was adventure. Even the times they'd gone to visit Judith in whatever outpost the magazine had assigned her, he'd done it only as a concession to love.

Claire collected her bags, carted them through customs, moving toward the door marked GREETING, smiling at the language encased in red lettering. It lifted her, like a wave from an enthusiastic host. Barren as the terminal was in actuality, with illuminated yellow signs, freshly painted flat white colors giving off a certain futuristic seediness after the dazzle of the landing, she felt strangely welcome. She scanned the waiting crowds for Judith, bright, efficient Judith, who had joined the ranks of the magazine as some did a religious order, forswearing any personal life when the organization called. Filling her life with impeccable detail, as some would restful moments, her job, her training, having become the arc of her personality: a clear, detached way of looking at the world.

The air was oppressively heavy and humid in spite of air conditioning. Claire could see no one in the whole terminal with a jacket on. No known face beaconed to her, except her own, in a mirror over the concession stand, heart-shaped, open, innocence stubbornly clinging to features softening into middle age. Her chocolate eyes were still eager as a child's, little dots of sweetness that had somehow survived the hard edge of the business she was in, the place she lived, the inarguable truth that life was short, and, most of the time, not exactly fair.

Familiar shoulders slouched over the counter of the concession stand: Judith in her semibroken executive posture, head slightly bowed, the weary stance of one who'd risen, through merit, in the corporate world. Finally promoted to a place that proved women were wanted and even preferred on occasion in jobs once reserved for men, she still had to work twice as hard. She was correcting copy even as she ate her sandwich. Claire could see her numbly nourishing herself, not even tasting, her angular, intelligent face furrowed with concern, evaluating the story she had culled and written, making sure it wasn't either favorable or confrontational, but just how things were. Neutral. Judith's way, even without the policy of the magazine.

Claire moved up behind her, suppressing her own natural enthusiasm, fighting back the impulse to hug. Partly she didn't want to startle this woman, whom she could not describe really as her "best" friend, since that expression carried with it the air of high school neediness that Judith had long ago left behind, probably even before high school. "Favorite friend" would be precise, exact, as Judith was. But besides that wish not to jar her, Claire also understood that physical affection was inappropriate. Fond as Judith was of her, she simply was not demonstrative. And although unfailingly kind to friends, opening her home, her head, and her resources to them, she rarely uncommittedly opened her heart. Not that it wasn't full, Claire understood, but it was private.

All these qualities, Claire supposed, added up to making Judith the perfect reporter: her sharp sense of observation, her natural reticence. She also looked deceptively average, not so tall as to stand out in a crowd, not round enough to be thought voluptuous, so she didn't intimidate men even as she attracted them, which seemed to be the case when women combined sexuality with brains. To cover whatever she had of secret assets, she dressed inconspicuously but neatly, usually in something wrinkle-free and tailored, like her point of view.

"Judith?"

"Oh, there you are," she said, swallowing, without lifting her eyes, still fixed on the page in front of her. Even the moment carried with it priorities, as if she could not begin the welcome task of socializing with a friend until she had finished the job of correcting copy. At last she looked up, and caught Claire squarely with her sharp, no-nonsense gaze. "Greeting!" she said, and smiled.

Her eyes moved almost imperceptibly past Claire, as though she were expecting someone else to be right behind her. For a moment Claire imagined that he was, and turned to see if Charley wasn't really with her, if the whole thing hadn't been a terrible dream, the way it still seemed to her a lot of the time. If his disappearance wasn't just a joke he'd played on her, because that was his favorite thing, making her laugh. Making her break with relief because life was never as serious as she took it. Only this time it was. This time there was no changing it into a joke. Because if he could have been there for anyone besides Claire and the children, he would have been there for Judith. Judith who had always recognized what a rare breed he was, a caring, funny, masculine man comfortable in the company of women, no matter how bright they were.

The drive along the waterfront filled Claire with the same kind of excitement as the landing, without the sense of personal peril. Everything was spectacle: buildings topped with two-story-high signs advertising restaurants. SING-ALONG CLUB, said one, giving her the impulse to sing along, which she started doing. "Some day we'll go places, new lands and new faces . . ." Claire sang.

"Is that one of yours?" Judith asked.

"Yip Harburg. My favorite lyricist. But I'm honored by the confusion."

The neighborhood where Judith kept an apartment—Claire couldn't think of it as where Judith lived, there being such a tentative quality to her activities, as if they existed a week at a time, like the publication she worked for—was in Mid-Levels, the high-priced rental area just below Victoria Peak. As the car wound round the heavily foliated curves, Judith tour-guided in a soft voice. The locale was occupied mainly by Europeans, she said, which meant anyone white-skinned. Chinese working for European firms, including those who'd gone to Harvard, which an amazing number of them had, could not afford Mid-Levels' prices. Even men laboring in the same banks as Judith's neighbors were not paid equal salaries, although they might have identical jobs.

Judith's voice got even lower. "Asians are the women of Hong Kong," she said.

The walls of her apartment were hung with mammoth French theater posters, from the city of her last bureau post: mustachioed melodrama, the wronged woman cowering in a shadow, holding her child, while just beyond the doorway, the villain who'd undone her married another. It touched Claire in a particular way, Judith's Parisian past transported to Hong Kong, because it had taken her friend until nearly the end of her five-year stint in the City of Lights to take full advantage of being there, so busy had she been with the daily demands of the magazine. Not until she knew she was being transferred to Hong Kong did Judith even buy a couturier suit. Just as she'd trailed her California furniture with her to Paris, now she had shifted her Parisian decor to Hong Kong, not having the time or inclination to furnish the place anew.

The spreads on the beds in the guest room were the same ones that had covered the beds in Paris where Claire had gone to visit Judith with Charley. It was Charley who had more or less picked out Hong Kong as her next base. In the summer of '81 she'd been offered Beirut. "No," he had said. "You can't go any place Claire and I don't want to come to visit you." So when Lebanon exploded and Judith wasn't there, Charley announced he had saved her life. The spreads on the beds were a little too evocative for Claire: memory pulled at her throat.

Souvenirs of Paris filled the walls, Aristide Bruant looking superior to the rest of Lautrec's bar figures, with the splash of Hong Kong outside the sliding glass doors. The city might have been just another spectacular wall hanging, one Judith might not even notice until the time came to move on to the next locale, when she realized she couldn't pack it up and take it with her. Wherever Judith was, it seemed to Claire the adornment for her present was the past, as if the only attention she could pay to what was actually happening was in the stories she wrote. Maybe her whole life was to be motion recollected in tranquillity. Providing she ever got any.

The study had been made into a working newsroom, complete with fax, desk computer, 9600 baud modem, with a dedicated line, Judith explained, so she could communicate easily with other news offices. The whole idiom of the computer world was alienating, giving vague feelings of nausea to Claire, who considered high tech just another encroachment on the humanity that was disappearing anyway. But she listened with affected interest as Judith pointed it all out to her. The far side of the study had all the equipment of a darkroom: darkroom trays, stop bath and fixer, easel, negative enlarger, curtains to close, and safe light in amber.

"Charley would have loved this," Claire said. "When he was having such a tough time getting work, and he was looking for other careers, we took photography courses at Beverly High. Night classes for adults. We both got pretty good."

There were balconies at the end of the living room and outside both bedrooms, facing down to the harbor glittering below, like an orgy of fireflies. Claire was already infatuated, as if you could put your arms around a place. Even from the window of her bathroom she could see the lights. The mirror on the medicine cabinet above the sink, opened at the angle it was, reflected them, as she set her toiletries inside. Not until she'd finished did she see that she'd put everything on the left, still leaving room for Charley's things in the other half. A startled cry escaped her.

How long did it go on, anguish provoked by memory? How many habits of companionship were there that a person wasn't even aware of, sending little pricks of pain into the heart? Charley had been so unmistakably present, so big, so there for her. "They had a lot of words for that big guy," he would joke about himself, like a sportscaster; the phrase now seemed to hang in the air, a jovial epitaph. He'd seemed like an easygoing knight, interceding between her and the dragons: failure, rejection, her mother's anger. Warming her against the cold, real and imagined. An artist set her soul on a plate, for people to see and taste and—one hoped—be nourished by. So it cut to the core when the offering was ignored or rejected. Charley always told her not to take it personally when a work failed to sell, when a performance artist gave less than a song deserved, a distributor failed to get it around, a radio station to play it. But it was hard not to take it personally, when what was held out was yourself. Always at those moments he had been there, rubbing her back, stroking her ego. Telling her she was the best, that the world just hadn't caught up with her.

Now he was gone, her partner, her lover, her audience. Sharer of the agonies, as well as the joys and the medicine cabinet. How many tiny torments were there, a found piece of paper with his handwriting on it, a cuff link at the back of a drawer? She had stopped looking at the desk in the corner of her living room where the silver-framed pictures of the family were, because to see his face, the proud puff of barrel chest, strong, protecting hands on shoulders of the then-little children, was too painful for her. How many wounds were there that you couldn't see, splinters in the spirit, events that weren't that dramatic, which, when recalled, were as cutting as knives? Privation that made itself felt when you still made room for him, only he wasn't there.

"Are you all right?" Judith was in the doorway of the bathroom, concern softening her angular face.

"I'm fine," Claire said. "I'll be fine."

"I'm glad you came to Hong Kong," Judith said, and, surprisingly, embraced her. "We'll show you a good time."

In the darkness of early morning, the neon lights of the harbor were out. Samsung did not reflect red against the water, as if anyone up that late could not possibly have the energy to buy. Only one sign, green, still reflected on the water: Carlsberg beer. For the diehards, or drinkhards, who could still bend an elbow, late as it was, or early.

Claire looked at the clock: 3:40 A.M. The Carlsberg sign went out. An endtime for drinkers. But still the lights of Kowloon gleamed upward in perpendicular slashes against the curved line of dots outlining the decks, the illuminated tracer flow of the mainland stretching to the east. Above it all sparkled a single, low-lying star, summoning the shepherds, she supposed, to the Bethlehem of business.

Claire was not sure whether it was jet lag or loss that urged her into wakefulness. Since Charley's death, sleep had been elusive, in spite of the torpor she was swallowed by, a lingering inertia that, for a long time, made her unable to get out of bed. She had collapsed for a while into flannel sheets, making her whole bed into kind of a comforting nightgown. As if fabric, the gentle, warming cloth of childhood, could piece her shattered feelings back together.

She had a fear of self-pity that was almost as strong as some people's fear of death. Death, she understood now firsthand, was a definite ending. Self-pity appeared to be infinite. That she might be justified in feeling sorry for herself did not excuse her, in her own eyes. Charley was the one to feel sorry for, all that he was missing, all he had suffered through. Still, she could not forgive him for leaving her, or imagine ever being able to sleep again through the night, without arms around her.

A single tiny boat, lit with a green light, glided through the glassy black of the harbor, iridescence mirrored in the water below. She stared out the glass for what had to be hours. To the right of the balcony the first pink light of morning began to soften the sky. The darkness opposite melted into the gray hills of Kowloon. And the single star that had lain over the cradle of night revealed itself as a light, a nipple on the breast of a mountain reclining like a well-endowed odalisque on the chaise that was the harbor.

Something between wonder at where she was and exhaustion, the wish that her grieving could be left behind, overcame Claire. She put her arms around herself, rocking the upper half of her body, feeling the pressure of the soft skin of her inner arms against her breasts. Nobody had touched her but herself in all the time since the funeral. Nobody had given her comfort after the mourners, who hadn't really embraced her as much as held her while pushing her off, distancing her with their own unwillingness to face mortality. Charley had been the biggest, the strongest, the most jovial, and, in his group, the youngest. His death had come as an affront to all of them. Her presence had become an unwelcome reminder. Invitations had gone the way of hugs.

And she who had always feared being alone, being abandoned, was both. There was nothing to be more afraid of, except self-pity.

Still, she tried to needle herself out of it, as Charley would have done, a little pinprick of humor so she wouldn't take herself so seriously. "Aren't you having a terrible life," she said. "Claire of the Orient."

She lay back on the pillows. "You'd love it here, Charley," she murmured, and tried to swallow the anger that bubbled up inside the sorrow.

THREE

♦

The umbrella in the tree outside the cathedral had belonged to David Palmer-Smith, the murdered boy. Not enough, Clement thought, a world in which people desecrated churches. Now they desecrated funerals. That already awful occasion, the burial of the two sexually assaulted teenagers, had been given the final obscenity of the bloodstained umbrella. A part of the assault, lab technicians had determined.

The boy's mother had swooned at the sight of the upturned, opened parasol, shaft and handle pointed at the sky. There was calculated insult in the gesture, not just the horror of the murder anymore. Nothing that could be put down to homicidal impulse.

Homicide and murder were two different crimes in Hong Kong. Murder had intent in it; homicide could happen in the course of another crime. In either event, somebody was dead. But it had been the Superintendent's hope—if you could have hope in this kind of rank crime—that there might not have been premeditation. That it was the result of some bestial urge.

But there was nothing spontaneous in the placement of the umbrella. Whoever had set it in the tree had had to determine where the funeral would be held, and when. Though almost all important rituals of the Anglican community took place at Saint John's, a number of the colonials were Catholic, and celebrated their joys and sorrows up the road at Saint Joseph's. So the perpetrator had to go to some trouble to make sure this would not go unmarked. Someone with the intelligence to check out that both families were Church of England. The resourcefulness to call to verify the time and date of the service. Someone with the physical prowess to climb a tree, and place the umbrella there.

"No sign of his shoes, sir," said Andrew, Clement's assistant, as they went over the crime scene for the sixth time. Even all these days after the murders, the place made Clement queasy. The view was perfect, the setting bucolic. He could see where two young lovers would have been drawn to it as a trysting place, lush as it was with mossy grass and leafy trees. Branches swept the ground, offering what must have seemed to them protection, a lacy screen between their heat and the heat outside. Worried about nothing but the unreliability of the weather, in its way reliable, sure to bring an unexpected rainstorm at some point every afternoon. Days that began cloudless were the rule, with only the humidity offering a hint of what would be coming. Bright blue skies harbored not a clue of the torrential rains that would sweep the place by tea time. Not a clue. Even as he heard the phrase in his mind, Clement wondered if that would be the motif for everything.

"We've recovered all the rest of their clothes. Hung very neatly in the tree they were," said Andrew.

"You found *her* shoes?"

"Sandals, yessir."

"And forensics made a cast of the footprints in the mud?"

"Several good ones, Superintendent. Quite deep. As though whoever was there was watching for a time."

No question the lovers had been using the locale awhile. Carved into the bark of a tall, thick-trunked banyan, the words running sideways, double-rowed, was BETSY IS EXQUISITE. Clement could imagine the time and effort the boy had put into making the letters equal size, the careful strokes, the evened edges. He could visualize David's laboring, passing up the easily spelled PRETTY or even BEAUTIFUL. Exquisite. Something so heart-rending about the word. A description doctors used when pain was too sharp to bear. And the final pathos of her name, the sweet, young name, sounding so vibrant and yellow-haired. More touching because the boy had called her "Betsy," as her parents did, rather than "Wisp," as did her friends at school. There seemed to Clement in that choice an air of protectiveness, as if David would have taken care of her, if only he could have.

In a city where vice was part of the entertainment industry, Clement supposed, as a policeman in the Criminal Investigation Division, he should have developed a thicker skin. Crime, like the architecture, went every which way. Pornography flourished, its more well crafted examples bringing prices as high as, sometimes higher than, legitimate art. Petty crimes, which comprised most of Hong Kong's offenses, went mainly unreported. Organized crime was ruled by the Triads, who were to Asia what the Mafia was to Italy and the United States, mythic and overblown, their doings beyond ordinary comprehension. Their members went on ax rampages, leaving twenty-eight dead in their wake in a hotel in Macau, for instance. There was little that could be done about them. The courts were ineffectual. Triads were too powerful, impenetrable ranks led by histrionic bosses who called themselves names like "Dragon Head." But that part of the venal slate aside, considering how poxed with human weakness the island was, there weren't too many murders. A hundred a year, perhaps. Little consolation, the "reasonable" statistics, to the two young lovers.

"We have casts of young Palmer-Smith's feet as well, in case we find the shoes," Andrew was saying. "Made before they closed the box on him."

How eager he was, Clement noted. Had he himself ever been that energetic, even when he was young? Then there had been a whole future of law and order ahead of him in Hong Kong. He'd come there in the middle sixties, just before the riots that nearly tore the island apart, when anything even vaguely official had come under police jurisdiction. The pressure on the department had been overwhelming, with ambulances, fire engines, customs, even the judiciary adding to the burden. Finally responsibilities had been subdivided. But even now, into the nineties, it was tricky being a policeman, a combination of detective work and athletics. Warrants had to be executed with mercurial speed, brought before magistrates within forty-eight hours, or the deadliest criminal could get out on bail. And in Hong Kong, a man could disappear forever. So it rather amused Clement, all this ambition on the part of a lad who had no future, really. How far could a young man rise by 1997? And then, where would he go?

Clement himself had made plans to retire to Manila, where women were hungrier than anywhere else, their needs hotter than the climate, fueled by economics. No middle class in the Philippines. Only the rich or the desperate. Much as he disliked the idea of himself as an exploiter, his own romanticism was anathema to him. So he tried to view his search for a small-wristed companion who would honor him as a pragmatic one now that he was growing older. Faithful as well as yielding, she would be, lacking so much that his presence would be a godsend, his wishes all that mattered.

As far as he was aware, he was not a lonely man. There were too many distractions in the course of a day for him to be conscious of the emptiness. Too many books to be read, not enough time left to him on the planet to be able to digest even a portion of the thoughts for which he had appetite. Too many good bottles of bonded whiskey. Only rarely, when he felt sexual longings so keenly as to sense the despair beneath them, did he dig down deep enough to feel the isolation, the hunger for connection.

He did not trust his body anymore. It had started to let him down in subtle ways, now that he was almost fifty. Though he stood slightly over six feet tall, there was a certain defeat to his posture, the stance of a man who wasn't sure when the bad news might fall on him. He didn't mind that his hair was graying: that, people considered "distinguished." Threaded in his dark beard, white gave him an authority police work hadn't been enough to do. No matter how much or how often people said they respected the law, and wanted him as friend, they looked at him as if he were in a rearview mirror, and they had been speeding.

The rest of it, the loss of energy, the surprising shortness of breath climbing the familiar, hilly side streets, was an insult to him, like treachery on the part of someone trusted. He was used to being disappointed by women. The eyes, he knew from reading William Blake, were the windows of the soul, and his own, in spite of being brown and opaque, were a little too open. He had finally gotten wise enough to see betrayal coming, but still invited it in, when it wore perfume.

But he wasn't used to letting himself down, and there was no one else to take to task for what was happening to him physically. Still, he wasn't one who whined. His pockets were full enough of cash, since there hadn't been any wife or children to spend it on. But uncertainty was now the coin of the realm. Besides the pedestrian facts, the pensions worked for that might now never be delivered, no one knew what the overall picture would be. Whether Hong Kong had a real future. It was impossible to believe anymore the Chinese promise to let the island remain capitalist for the next fifty years once they took over. On June 5, 1989, the day after the slaughter in Tiananmen Square, the line for visas outside the American consulate had been a mile and a half long, the tail of the line curving around Garden Road to meet its head. Everyone not in love with Hong Kong, and even most who were, was trying to get out, too realistic to delude themselves that it could continue unchanged.

Palmists and diviners of all descriptions proliferated in doorways, cashing in on the unsettled times that lay ahead. None of the uncertainty had put a crimp in business. Apartments were still as costly as they'd ever been. A hotel more lavish than any yet seen in Hong Kong—the Grand Hyatt—with atriumed lobby and colossal black marble columns so impressive Palladio would have felt diminished—had been built to the tune of a hundred million U.S., in spite of warnings that tourism would fall off. It was as if the actual killing in China had triggered a greater desperation for the financial one, while Hong Kong was still Hong Kong.

Among the locals, passports were as money had once been, the focus of longing. Women grew misty-eyed in the presence of men with other nationalities. All most Hong Kong Belongers had were papers the British had given them that were no good anywhere, especially in England. Sixty percent of the population had United Kingdom passports that gave them no rights of abode. So anyone with money was making plans to leave or had already left for Australia and Canada, where good workers were welcome. South

Africa was recruiting Chinese professionals, offering them "honorary white status" as a hedge against apartheid.

Fung shui lights glowed in every Hong Kong window, a softly red consecration to the luck people believed governed everything. Businesses, banks included, never opened without a geomancer, checking the directions of doors and windows, making sure they faced the right way: back to the mountain, face to the sea, so luck could come in, even as the populace fled. The Central Police Station, though continuing to be run by the British, had its back door where its front door had been originally, with a *Fung shui* light to appease and put at ease the Chinese police on the staff. In the Inquiry Room, a great lacquered painting of the wiser gods, dark-red-faced and horned, scowled their blessings onto men not smart enough to find all the answers.

Ten psychics had been in touch with the station saying they could tell what happened on the Peak. Clement knew better than to discount their information. He had his own personal fortune-teller, an old man in an apartment above Nathan Road, Kowloon side, who read palms and faces and threw the sticks. A man could not spend half a lifetime in Britain's last Asian colony without doffing his hat to the invisible. Forensics, an open door for informers, and attention to the crime scene could yield only so much.

"There's some cigarette stubs, sir," Andrew said, bringing him back to reality. "Pretty grotty from the rain."

"Do we know if the victims smoked?"

"Palmer-Smith's mother barely seems to be able to remember if her boy had shoes on, much less what kind of shoes, she's in such a state."

"Check with Betsy's mother," Clement said. He noted in the back of his mind what he had called the girl, as if he were part of the family, personally fond of her. As if it might have been his loss, too. Was it so sad for him that he'd never had a child? Was that an unfulfilled dream? Why were human beings more aware of unsatisfied longings when it was too late to gratify them? "Women notice things like that about their daughter's boyfriends. Looking for things to be annoyed about."

Two men from the Advanced Technology Unit of the Identification Bureau were poking around the earth beneath the banyan tree where the two young people had died. Over Andrew's shoulder, Clement could see them sifting through strangler fig and mossy fern, searching for literal shreds of evidence, clothing threads that might have been left by the assailants. Everything belonging to Betsy had now been recovered, including her purse, a jaunty little shoulder bag with a pocket diary in it, filled with *thé dansant* dates and debutante parties, weekend pleasure junk cruises and lunches that would have an empty seat at them now. Also inside were a monthly pass for the Star Ferry, and a multiple-ride magnetic ticket for the MTR, the rapid transit system, an impressive network of underground subways that ran from Hong Kong Central to the tip of the New Territories. Her money was intact. But missing were her student identity card and possibly her passport. No one knew if she had been carrying it with her. "Did you ask Mrs. Evans if she's found her daughter's passport?"

"She says she wasn't up to looking for it," Andrew said.

"Well, ask her again. And while you're at it, find out if the boy smoked." Clement looked past the men from ATU, and saw a woman making her way under the barrier. "Excuse me," he said, and started toward her. "You'll have to get back there."

"Oh, I'm sorry." She looked around with a show of naïveté that did not go with the lively, sharp expression in her eyes, the sunglasses set rakishly atop her reddish hair. There was a pencil poked behind her ear, notepad in her left hand, ballpoint ready in her right. "I didn't realize this was off-limits."

"What do you think the barriers are for?"

"I thought there was probably building going on," she said, smiling.

A little kittenish it looked to Clement, that smile, when really she seemed more like a cat. Shrewd, with a lot of intelligence behind her expression. And crafty, really, in her excuse. Everywhere in Hong Kong there was jackhammering, an unremitting tearing-up of streets, roadways, hillsides, subterranean walkways, bridges, the constant cacophony of hardhat enterprise. According to the inadequate number of psychiatrists who practiced in the colony, sixty altogether, one for every ninety-four thousand people, the number one irritant that went toward making Hong Kong the most stressful city in the world was noise pollution. Pounding away at construction sites, the rattle of jackhammers sounded even on Sunday mornings, their nettling only a small part of the noise continuum. Cabdrivers listened to radios beamed in on constant, annoying chatter, not music. People talked into cellular telephones waiting on lines in taxi queues, in hotel lobbies, even in the movies, as if success were equated with prattle. There was about it all an air of exhibitionism, a raincoated mentality that flashed private parts of action.

So her excuse was not too farfetched, although Clement recognized it as feeble. "You're a reporter?"

"Judith Taylor." She held out her hand. "*Elan* magazine."

"Everything we had to tell reporters was said at the press conference." He took her hand even while he remonstrated with her, noting how small it was, tiny-boned, like an Oriental's. "Superintendent Leslie. If you have questions, you can call my office." He gave her his card, Chinese-lettered version of his name and number on the back.

"Isn't there some piece of information you can give me that the others don't have?"

"Absolutely not." He let go her hand, and moved his own, in a no-nonsense way to her shoulder, urging her back toward the barrier.

"How many assailants were there?"

"We're not sure yet."

"I heard there were two types of semen besides the dead boy's."

He tried not to look at her with the dismay he felt, an old-fashioned reluctance to hear clinical words from the lips of women, no matter how much a transition to tough the world had encouraged them to make. "The postmortem report will be given to the press in due time."

"I haven't got due time. The magazine closes tomorrow."

"It'll have to close with whatever you've got so far."

"You don't understand," she said, pleading, slightly teacherly. "New York's not that interested in Hong Kong. I have to send them some sexy detail so they'll run the story."

"We'll survive if they don't. And I would consider the word 'sexy' the most heartless one you could use in connection with this case."

Judith reddened. "It wasn't meant the way it sounds. In journalese, sexy means something that warrants a headline."

"I appreciate the education."

"I'm sorry," she said, and held out her card, a slightly begging tone in her voice, as though she were genuinely abashed. "I didn't mean to offend you."

He took the card, turned it over. Nothing in Chinese characters on the back. The security of a national mentality that still believed it could exist without accommodating other people's customs, even in their own countries.

"Will you call me?"

"I'll have someone inform you when the next press pool is."

"Please." Her sharp, angular face seemed to soften, even as her hazel eyes looked hard into his. "I don't think this is just another murder."

"Really?"

"I covered the Manson case, and this gives me the same kind of feeling. That it's not about murderous passion. That it's about something else."

In spite of how he felt about reporters, and women who could say hard words without their tongues breaking off, he was impressed. How easy men were, really, he could not help noting about himself. All a woman had to do to seem compatibly clever, the kind of brightness that did not put a man off, was to have the same opinion as his own. "Maybe I *will* call," he said, putting her card in the pocket of his safari suit.

FOUR

◆

When Claire first saw James Bingham, he was coming at her on a slant, the way Cary Grant might have at the height of his charming audacity. James's dark hair was slick with the rain that had started so unexpectedly, except that he should have known to expect it, being a longtime resident of Hong Kong. A light red stripe, also at a slant, gave a jauntiness to his navy blue tie, an echo of the way he moved and stood. His shoulders were very broad, exercised and muscular from rugby and sailing. His pin-striped blue gabardine, tailored as well as it was, Hong Kong being the capital of quick sartorial splendor, showed his body off to its best advantage. Claire tried not to seem to appraise him, but did not succeed. She had been waiting for Judith in the Captain's Bar of the Mandarin Hotel for over half an hour, and had practiced looking composed for as long as she could, before her eyes wandered, and met his.

He walked toward the bar stool on which she sat, and leaned toward her, smiling. His smile was only a little less irresistible than the rest of him, not quite as spontaneous as the amusement in his bright blue eyes.

"You oughtn't to look at a man like that," he said.

He smelled of Drakkar. It was a light, unmistakably masculine cologne she'd given Charley once. He'd never worn it, preferring to smell like himself, fresh from the shower. The fragrance gave her a little buzz. "Like what?"

"So . . . honest. An unscrupulous man could take advantage of such a look."

"Are you unscrupulous?"

"This is Hong Kong. I couldn't survive if I weren't."

Certain men in the world were dangerous. A truth about women, Claire perceived, was that the most vulnerable of them were usually drawn to the men who could do them the most damage, the very willingness of the woman to be victim making her a magnet. Certainly this one had all the standard equipment for a marauder, the looks, and in a quick exchange, the easy charm. But just in case it wasn't all out there for her to see, he had announced himself as unprincipled. She felt a literal pull.

"Fortunately, I'm just passing through," she said.

"But you will stay long enough to get in trouble?"

"How long does it take?"

"If you move quickly, which everyone does in Hong Kong, you can do it right away. James Bingham." He held out his hand, as perfectly manicured as the rest of him, a school ring on his third finger.

"Claire Black," she said, aware of the warmth of his palm.

"How long have you been in the Orient?"

"I just arrived."

"One must be in Asia as though one had never been anywhere else. It's all about mystery and deception. You would do well to develop those things."

"And you want to help me."

"I certainly do." He offered his arm. She slid from the bar stool and took it.

A few feet away from the couch in the corner where Claire and James settled, a woman sat. She had a certain radiance, not an easy thing to perceive in the Captain's Bar, with its deliberately dark lighting. The level of the lights undercut any hint of garishness, no matter how intense or aggressive the level of business going on. It was the subtlety of the room that drew people to it, like the hotel itself, repeatedly voted the best in the world by the bankers who stopped there. All Asia had the distinction of being staffed by people who, in the words of an Englishman who hoped he didn't sound bigoted, "weren't afraid to serve." But at the Mandarin you picked up a glass, and the ring it left on the table was gone by the time you put it down again. The miracle was you never even saw anyone wiping it away. It was this invisibility that gave such a feeling of comfort and security, addicting people to the hotel like the opium trade that had long ago started Hong Kong. The entire ambience of the place seemed to offer a setting for errors that could be made without anyone's seeing, cleaned up before they could be reported in the *South China Morning Post.*

The woman on the black leather couch was not exactly invisible. The gold of her hair picked up the sheen of the occasional brass ornaments on the wall, so there was about her almost an aura, in spite of the muted lighting. She sat directly beneath a matted, oversized ink drawing of the Grand Saint Lundi, a chubby little dwarf straddling a case of ale, bottle in his hand, halo around his head. But his light shone less interestingly than hers. Her elegant legs were crossed, the point of one Maud Frizon high-heeled shoe digging into the back of her shapely calf, sending her slender body into a continuum of curves. Everything about her looked delicately rounded, rarefied, preened, up to the long arch of her neck, with its teardrop diamond on a slender chain against her tanned throat.

There was something touching about the simplicity of the stone, as obviously costly as it was, like the woman who wore it. Her clothes were so patently designer that the labels might have been on the outside, dress by Karl Lagerfeld, bag by Chanel. In a city where so much was counterfeit, particularly clothes, with every arcade and alleyway honeycombed with tailors who could copy the best designs in a matter of hours, the original stamp of her wardrobe was unmistakable. She wore it effortlessly, as though she had no time for vanity, that beauty and privilege were something she had been born to, and so made no fuss about. Her body was tight, her sleeked-back hair even tighter against the sides of her impressive skull, emphasizing the high, slanting cheekbones, a renegade trace of Cherokee in the otherwise Anglo-Saxon face. Her jaw was square and strong, but with little hollows in it, rivulets of softness. And her eyes were yellow-green, a cat's eyes, so wide-set as to appear almost at the sides of her face, like wraparound glasses.

Everyone else seemed to be watching for someone, or, if they were already with someone, waiting for the deal to be on the table, which, since it was lunchtime, featured roast beef. Huge slabs of meat on gold-and-white Royal Doulton bone china were set everywhere, table, bar, bar stools, the quick businessman's lunch that was a feature of this particular room. More straight to the point than the Clipper Club buffet, or the quiet, time-consuming elegance of the Man Wah restaurant on the top floor. The blonde seemed out of place in the wolfing-down atmosphere, as if everything about her should have time to unfold, including time itself. But it was the very fact of her being out of place that increased her attractiveness. Everyone wondered who she was.

Her name was Erica Thorr. The bartender knew what her name was, as he knew the names of everyone staying in the hotel, for even a day. But he did not share the information with the many men who asked, taking his cue from the woman herself, who seemed deliberately unavailable. Whenever anyone invited her for a drink, or approached her, she thanked them without exactly looking at them, the huge wraparoundish eyes fanning downward, weighted with thick, lightly mascaraed lashes. And she always said no.

"If she's not looking for any action, what's she doing alone in this bar?" asked an overweight Texan, who'd been turned down. The room was heavily air-conditioned, but he was still sweating.

"Maybe she wants a drink," said the bartender.

"Hard to believe, a woman that looks like that, on her own."

"Here for two weeks now," the bartender said. "Never with anyone." He wiped up the ring left by the man's glass.

"I'd like to do a little offshore drilling in that," said the Texan.

A page moved through the bar, pulling a thick rope that sounded a bell on top of the blackboard he carried, calling out the name chalked on its surface. Heads turned. Erica's was not one of them. It was as if she weren't waiting for anyone, or anticipating anyone's trying to find her. The last seemed particularly strange to those who had become Erica watchers. She wasn't that young a woman. Estimates over the two weeks she had been at the Mandarin were from her mid-thirties to her early forties. So it seemed impossible for her to have no history, an ex-husband or husbands, a child, an abandoned or abandoning lover. Or, as the new fantasies went, a great corporation of which she was the head. Someone had to want to be in touch with her.

Yet she appeared suspended from any real connection, neither wanting nor expecting, not moving toward anything, or away from something. Just being there. Perhaps the only one in Hong Kong who was.

Everyone had his eye on something else: the merger, the bargain, the potential husband, the quick deal, and lately, the mainland Chinese. What had always been a city on the edge, emotionally and geographically, now sat under the blade of a guillotine. There was only so much time left to make fortunes, mold destinies, escape. Since its start Hong Kong had been a short-term place, its mood suicidal or euphoric, depending on the state of the economy. Passions, quickly ignited, were extinguished just as fast. No one had an attention span. Nothing had ever stayed except the British, and now they were gearing up to go. In a blatantly stressed-out, overcrowded city, filled with people desperate for the last chance, or in the case of the Hong Kong Belongers, the only chance, Erica Thorr sat like a silken beacon of calm, signaling to no one, content to be alone.

It was a lively bar, full of hustle, women in costly, graceful dresses, men on lavish expense accounts. There was about it the air of an English pub, the easy camaraderie of those so sophisticated they could afford to seem simple. But for all their apparent ease, everyone was restless, hoping for something. Hong Kong had always been a roller coaster, its population, both tourist and resident, charged up on adrenaline, addicted to speed—the speed with which fortunes could be made, clothing could be copied, people could move (if you didn't count the pedestrian clog-up on Queens Road at lunch hour). Teachers of Buddhist philosophy said the trouble with people was that they thought they had time. So they lived their lives without an awareness of their mortality, the true connectedness to life that that awareness brings, treating every moment as precious. But the people of Hong Kong knew their lifespan had a limit. That everything would end in 1997. That the movie would be over, and the audience would have to get up and leave the theater, and the Chinese would come in and clean up the popcorn. Or force someone else to.

So there was a consciousness that existed nowhere else, people quite literally on the edge. Of an island, of an era. Of a penchant for self-indulgence that had survived unmodified in a world struggling for enlightenment, political freedom, concern for other human beings. A selfish, self-serving civilization that jangled the nerves while appearing to offer everything that soothed them. Like nicotine, jarring while the addict convinced himself it calmed.

Hong Kong was a fix. Everyone who lived there understood that. Those who passed through could rarely do so without hungering to return. No one was peaceful in the whole of the place, not even the professional purveyors of peace. The clergy were nervous about where the road would lead before the one that went to heaven.

So Erica Thorr, tranquil in the middle of all the action, gave off an air of spiritual independence as conspicuous as her beauty. None of the men in the bar could take his eyes off her.

Except for James Bingham. It charmed Claire that such a handsome man, several years her junior, riveted by her, wasn't looking past her at the blonde. Even with her back to Erica, Claire could feel her allure. Having spent most of her adult life in Beverly Hills, Claire was used to people who never really looked at each other. Men whose eyes were forever wandering because somebody more important might be coming in. Women who had learned their desperation from the men they followed, allied themselves with, envied, married, had eyes of an equally jumpy nature. The inattentive tic was not restricted to public arenas. Claire's old agent, Louise Felder, always telling ribald tales on herself, had regaled one Hollywood party with a short comic saga of an unnamed movie star, whose eyes had darted wildly about the bedroom even while they were at it, as if, as Louise had put it, "he might be missing his chance to fuck someone more influential."

So to feel the steadfast intensity of James Bingham's gaze fixed on her, in spite of the gorgeous woman who sat nearby, touched

Claire in a very basic way: proof that she could hold a young man's attention; giving her a moment when she was not being abandoned. Pretty as she was, in her brunette, valentine-faced way, she knew she was no competition for the sleek-haired siren behind her. Lush and full of life as Claire might have been, she had an adolescent's lack of self-assurance. *Adolescence* was the operative word again; the uneasy emotions of that time period earthquaked up in her, from the upheaval of losing Charley. Everything he had reinforced in her in the way of confidence had disappeared, the maturity come from his love, vanished. She was thrust back into the anxious teenager she'd been, viscerally foolish, rocky once again, now that the man who had made her feel sure of herself, and of him, was gone.

So James Bingham, with his fine features, lively light behind eyes that seemed beaming in directly on her, made her disproportionately happy. As if life could offer a second rescue from a woman's most superficial panic, giving her a belated invitation to the prom.

She could see over the tops of his lightly tinted glasses, pulled slightly downward toward his well-chiseled nose so he could study her better. His eyes were clear, and very sharp blue, shining with laughter at the tales he was telling on himself. Doting grandmother, public school education at Uppingham. "Upmarket from Eton," he assured her. "We just don't get near the publicity."

His smell held the promise of protection, male crannies you could crawl into, where nobody could get to you, to harm. A friend of hers, another widow, had told Claire not to be afraid to begin enjoying things she wouldn't have been able to if her husband had been around. Having a partner always entailed compromise. Charley had never liked perfume on her, just as he'd always told her not to wear hats, that she didn't have a "hat face." Somewhere slightly past the fog of the funeral, she'd gone out and bought a Garboesque hat, covering the sadness of her eyes, she thought, but in a strange way, defying him, now that he had let her down by leaving. So, a little spurt of resentment at his never having worn the Drakkar she'd given him mixed with her pleasure at the smell of it on James. It was a penetrating smell, moving through her nostrils to her brain. She felt intoxicated. Perhaps, she thought, it was only her privation, her loneliness that made him seem so attractive. She tried to bring her reason into focus, see him feature by feature as he was, look through the charm of his dialogue to check for substance. But it was too much work; she relaxed into the ease of just enjoying him, the comfort of being in the company of a barrel-chested handsome man.

The page, with his small, clanging bell and blackboard, moved through the bar, calling her name. James raised his hand and snapped the air commandingly. "Over here," he said. "The lady."

"Call for you, madam," the bellman said, showing her to the phone by the bar.

"There's been a murder," Judith said, on her end of the telephone. "I've got to try and write it up. I won't be able to meet you."

To Claire's surprise, she felt almost elated. Whenever anybody canceled anything lately, even an appointment she hadn't wanted, she felt a pang, an echo of betrayal, a smaller version of the kind of wrench that she felt when she thought about Charley's dying. She had always seemed so self-sufficient to the world; it surprised her how dependent she really had become, on other people, even on appointments. The prospect of anything other than her own company seemed a balm to her, sunlight on the horizon. So to have the person she cared for the most in the world, Judith, whom she loved in a different way from anyone else, with respect, deference, honor, to have Judith cancel and feel glad about it was amazing. "That's perfectly all right," Claire said, and meant it.

"What will you do?"

"I've met somebody... interesting," Claire said.

"One day in Hong Kong," said Judith. "I should leave my social life to you."

When Claire returned to the table, there was a Chinese man sitting with James. He seemed young, which could have been deceptive, as most Chinese men, except for the very old, appeared young, their faces hairless, skin never weathered. His collar was a little too perfectly starched, his suit almost too well tailored, as his manner seemed overly polished. He was on his feet before James, at her returning. She waited for James to introduce them, but he said nothing.

"My friend's been held up at the office," Claire said. "She won't be free till this evening."

"Outstanding!" James reached into his pocket, signaling for the check with his other hand. "I shall take you on a tour of the town."

The Chinese man smiled at her, his eyes expressionless. There was a curious symmetry to his smile, as though that, too, had been custom tailored. He looked at James, waiting. When no introduction was forthcoming, he reached into his breast pocket. "I am Anthony Go," he said, holding out his business card.

She started to reach for it, but James stepped between them. "We have to be going," he said. And taking her arm, handing a hundred-dollar Hong Kong bank note to the waiter, he hurried her out of there.

FIVE

◆

Semen had been found in the girl's throat, lungs, mouth, and passages into her nose, which had, according to the coroner, been squeezed shut. Bruises on the neck indicated she had died by strangulation. The boy apparently had been held down, the pencil shoved hard into his eyeball, penetrating his brain. His penis had been engorged. Those who liked to dwell on such morbid matters— and there were plenty of them around—argued that his member might have been stiff because men often become tumescent when death was a shock. Hanged and crucified victims were often depicted in art with erections, though only the California sculptor Baker had dared to do so with Christ.

Two other specimens of semen, besides David Palmer-Smith's, had been found in the girl's vagina, and in her rectum. The sphincter was badly torn. She had been raped twice and sodomized before the final sexual posture. The pathology report was enough to make the most ascetic of men, which Superintendent Clement Leslie was not, drink in the daytime.

Still, there was not much that could start him off at his desk in the morning sucking on whiskey. Occasionally, when a woman made him feel brokenhearted—his least favorite, most self-indulgent word— he would drink at lunch, and allow himself an afternoon of wallowing. And when a friend died too young, as they always seemed to lately, their ages close to his own, he would go to their wakes, and plow himself under with Glenfiddich and reminiscences. But drinking in the daytime was not a habit he had fallen into, certainly not in the office. Still he understood what was making him do it this morning, looking at the report in his hand.

As inured as he should have been to violence, and the words associated with violence, it still made him sick with shock to see such things on the page. Probably it was because there was something about the written word that had more weight for him than even the sight of murder and mayhem. Once he had been in a restaurant so liquid with slaughter that the policemen present couldn't keep their footing because of the amount of bodily fluids on the tile. Repellent as it had been to witness the actual scene, it had been the written report of the Triad revenge shooting that had actually made him sick to his stomach.

It was the same way for him with pornography. He did not consider himself a prude, although he knew that at heart he was a sentimental man, old-fashioned, usually fancying himself at least a little caught by the women he made love to, not a particularly masculine characteristic. But he needed that, in a way, to really enjoy the act, as base as it was, as animal, as comic as it was if you weren't involved. Or even if you were. He needed that romantic overlay, to coin a phrase, of emotion and feeling to celebrate fully what he was engaged in, telling himself more often than not that he was in love, so he wouldn't put it down to simple rutting. Not notice how very like the other creatures in nature man was, not that different from hippopotamuses and praying mantises in this aspect, really, except for the kissing, the thirst for nipples, the techniques of touch. Intercourse was universal, across the line of creation, although of course videos of beetles fucking didn't sell.

As with violence, movies of the act didn't really bother him. They were not his style—he preferred to watch old Fred Astaire movies, epitomizing as they did a kind of dispassionate grace that, in its way, reminded him of the once Empire he served. But porno movies didn't go against his grain. He certainly didn't like them, but he didn't see where they hurt anybody, any more than the magazines he supposed kept deviates off the streets, jerking off in their beds, where they belonged. He understood of sex that it was often about loneliness, that people desperate for communion tried to fill up their emptiness with what was easily attainable. Just as those who were hungry for love overate. So it was okay with him if those who felt isolated relieved their longings by looking at pornography.

There had just been a raid by the vice squad in Wanchai led by the young idealistic inspector, who'd rounded up forty-five thousand obscene comic books. The idea of obscene comic books made Clement laugh, especially once he'd looked at a few and seen the women's genitals whited out by a printer of obviously tender sensibilities.

But reading pornography, seeing it in words, offended him. He supposed, when he thought about it, that it was because of his love of language. Men had only so many words in them, so many ideas they could absorb and communicate in a lifetime. So many books they could peruse or lose themselves in that could lift them, instruct them, illuminate their souls, or, in the case of light reading, distract them. Everything didn't have to be literature: it was enough that men read. But to waste the eyes and the intellect, no matter how low on the scale, reading filth, made Clement testy. Still, he made no attempt to cross over into cleaning up pornography, leaving that to the earnest young men in Wanchai.

Most crimes were compartmentalized in Hong Kong. His job was to eradicate the real dangers transferred to Central. The Peak police station was ill run and seedy: the Black's Link murder had come down to him. Murder was always vile. But in this case it seemed so seamy it made him sick to his soul.

"We have the rest of the technology unit's report, Superintendent," Andrew said from the doorway. "The footprints under the tree are some kind of sneaker tread."

"Palmer-Smith's?"

"Not likely. His mother finally remembered what shoes he was wearing. His favorite pair. Kind of a spectator shoe. The sneaker tread's not the same size as the cast of his foot. As for the blood on the umbrella—"

Clement waved the information away. "I already know that part of it." He put his fingers over his eyes, as though not looking could alter the report in front of him. "What made you join the police force, Andrew?"

"Ad in the paper back home, sir. Three years in an exotic place. Five months' holiday at the end of it. Twenty-five percent of your three years' salary as a bonus. Hard to turn that down, when you're bored with the job you have."

"For me it was a way to serve my Queen. Doesn't seem like that right now. Some days I hate being a policeman."

Andrew looked disinterested, just this side of uncomfortable, as he always did when Clement said anything open or personal. The Brits as a rule didn't like information that might be connected to the heart, as if fearful they might inadvertently tap a vein that had blood in it. Not that Clement didn't revere his own kind, but he understood them.

"Some reporter called before you came in," Andrew said. "Judith Taylor her name was. That must be a great job. Rounding up the sordid facts without having to get involved."

"No one says you have to get involved. You could stay detached, like I am." Clement poured more whiskey into his glass. "Did she say what she wanted?"

"She asked for you to call her back. You also got a call from your *Fung shui* man."

"Dao Tsim? What did he have to say?"

"Disregard any tip it was Triads."

"Did we get any tips it was?"

"We always get tips it's Triads. You can't have posters outside the Star Ferry with teenage boys holding knives to people's throats, and a sign that says 'Report any Triad trouble,' without someone reporting Triad trouble. But Dao Tsim says it wasn't them on Black's Link."

"I already know that."

"How?"

"This isn't about crime as we know it. Certainly not organized crime."

"You don't have any idea who did it, but you know what it's about. You should go into business with Dao Tsim."

"Maybe I should." Clement put the pathologist's report back on the desk. "The news would be better. Love will find you. You will go on a long journey. Your bad debts will be repaid."

"What if they're not?"

"Nobody ever killed a psychic because their life didn't work out."

"Maybe they should. It would be an interesting case. Not guilty by reason of false information. A crime of psychic passion. Double nonsense."

Clement looked at him curiously. "You don't believe in passion?"

"A man loses what he is, when he gets carried away."

"What's so bad about that?"

"I don't like the idea of losing who I am. I keep control over my passions."

"You're a better man than I am."

"Thank you, sir."

"I don't know that it's anything to be grateful for," Clement said.

She could not even begin to look for Betsy's passport. It made Maggie crazy to go into her daughter's room, set her body literally to shaking. Howls that were subhuman, bestial, came from her throat, bellows of sorrow at the sight of Betsy's canopied bed. Flaxen-haired dolls, looking so much like the girl who had been too attached to them to let them go in the wake of her blossoming maturity, still waited for her organizing touch. Earrings glittered in a saucer on the vanity table, as though at any moment she might whirl in, and set them into the holes in her delicate lobes, making them dull in light of her personal sparkle.

Betsy's death was God's way of punishing Maggie, she was sure. Not so much for losing faith in Him, which she had, as for her desire, the lust that had raged in her since her divorce. A jealous

God they said. How right they were. But why would He even have wanted her, the way she looked now?

She could see herself coming at herself from every wall of her black marbled bathroom, inlaid with mirrors at slants, slashing the pitch like little jabs of lightning. A lot of her time since the funeral had been spent in there, sitting on the toilet, wanting to flush herself down it like the filth she knew she was, wishing she had the courage to slash her wrists, to splash her tainted blood into the sink, and make a package of the two of them, mother and daughter. Her sexy deco powder room. She'd designed it especially so she could pick up some hunk at one of the clubs, and do him in there, catching obscene glimpses of herself, at all those interesting angles.

Had Betsy heard? She wasn't stupid, only innocent. Or at least so it had seemed. Certainly she had known what was going on with her mother and men. Maggie had made halfhearted stabs at discretion, waiting till the girl was asleep to bring men home, never letting them be there in the morning. Still, Betsy must have known. Heard the thrusting tattoo of bed against wall, the orgasmic groans of the men, the moans Maggie couldn't contain in herself, she was so relieved still to have wet feelings, cocks that could get hard for her.

What had it done to her daughter, the petty vanity, the fear of growing old? Sending Maggie on a rampage of promiscuity after the divorce, deluding herself that it was a celebration of freedom. Freedom. A curious name for sickness in the hips, a surfeit of uncontrollable passion. For which God had punished her, she was sure, even though she no longer believed in Him.

She understood, even as she tried to wash the salt from its caked place beneath her swollen eyes, that part of her grieving was for herself. For the woman who never thought about anything terrible happening to her, except getting old. Betsy had been her resurrection, her immortality, her youth, in a softer, rounder-hipped version. Betsy, the spun-gold Snow White Maggie would stand beside in front of the mirror, mockingly asking if she was still the fairest in the land, knowing the answer in advance, pretending to like it. To love the unlined face, the wide cornflower eyes with not even a hint of a wrinkle beneath them. Acting as though she were pleased that the heads of men turned more quickly now in her daughter's direction than they did hers, as once they had done, in the days when she had been too prudish, too caught in establishing her art, to feel what was really going on inside her. To catch the look in their eyes, and respond.

The truth, the terrible truth, was that deep inside she'd resented her daughter's freshness, coveted the effortlessness of beauty that was just about being young. No tricks of makeup or hair, no clever way of dressing, no manipulative smile, a movement of lips to flash still excellent teeth, a hint of tongue behind them. No worldwide reputation of talent and success to balance out the weight of breasts that were no longer high. Youth the only showcase youth needed; no glass sarcophagus for brilliant designs in jade. Jade. Not just a mineral for carving into gemstones, but also a worthless woman. Jade by a jade, it should have read on Maggie Evans's designs.

She heard the bell, persistent, the rapping on the door. In the days since the funeral she hadn't been answering the phone. A few times the police had come to her apartment, with their annoying insistence on picking up details. What further details did they need to determine who had killed her daughter? Maggie had killed her daughter, with her self-absorbed sensuality. Her obsession with sex. Her lust. She'd hardly been able to think about anything else. Never had she cared so much about sex as when she was afraid it would be taken away from her. Like a woman who'd never loved a man as desperately as when he was leaving.

"You have to take estrogen," her gynecologist had said, "or your vagina will shrivel." Where did they learn how to speak to women, these men who had gone so long to school?

Her vagina would shrivel. She had to put aside her fears about cancer of the breast, shut her ears to the arguments that still went on, and take the hormone. No one in the world could guarantee its safety, but what did it matter? The risks were not as great as the potential loss. Her breasts were treated like slabs of meat, anyway, every time she had a mammogram. Pressed so flat they became pancake paps, like the hideous pictures of aging African women in *National Geographic*. Such was the tenderness displayed to breasts in the world of medicine. What was the gamble, really, in comparison to "your vagina will shrivel"?

She had weeping memories of the youth she now saw as wasted. Wondered why she hadn't let the boys who had tried to touch her between her legs have her, there and then. Saw them in fantasy as less awkward than they were, recollected breath that smelled sweet now, instead of rank as it had been. She had waited for and married a man with the passion of a flounder, and the belly to match, been faithful to him, until the divorce. What if she died before she was properly fucked, and often?

She had never even learned to flutter her eyelashes, or play the coquette. Innocence had been genuine when she was a girl; now she was too old, too much in a hurry to feign it. Her eyes sought out men's crotches as men once-overed women, their looks taking in buttocks and breasts. Only one part of a man's anatomy interested Maggie. Dreary weekends, when she panicked that nothing was on her plate, she flew to the Philippines and watched the little brown men in the sex shows, shoving their impressive penises into spread-eagled women. She struggled for the sight of the sweet round rings, the touching little ridge, like a crown on a simple, balding, foresty king, rhythmically disappearing. Always there was someone else watching who was alone, as excited by the display as she was. They would end up together, for a "cuddle" as she called it, making it sound friendlier than it was. Sometimes they robbed her while she was sleeping.

Her body was still in good shape, if she didn't check too closely the inner part of her upper arms, the slight sag at the bottom of her buttocks. She had managed to stay slender. She danced almost nightly, like a madwoman really, frenetic, possessed. Her skin was as soft as it ever was, lubricated with costly creams. She gave herself freely, fearlessly to strangers who might have hurt her, her only fear not getting laid. Not being fuckable. But there were worse things than not being wanted, weren't there?

Betsy had found them. Betsy had suffered for her sins, a different kind of crucifixion. Had they spread-eagled her, like the women in the sex shows? Had they pierced her? Maggie was crazy to know the details of the autopsy, as reluctant as the Superintendent was to reveal them to her. Who was he to spare her ugliness, when she had brought it about? Who was he to try to protect her from the punishment she deserved?

She answered the doorbell now. Two young policemen stood at the threshold, one of them Cantonese. He was obviously new to the corps, not quite tall enough for the old regulations, one of the inductees under the new sets of restrictions, lowered, like the height requirements, to allow for more Chinese. Automatically, her eyes moved to the fabric below his gunbelt. What was the characteristic of Asian cocks? She hadn't had that many Orientals, really, if you didn't count the porn star. But he had been magnificently endowed. This one looked puny.

Her eyes moved to the young British officer. Brits were rarely a turn-on for her, partly because of her sexual history with Nicholas, but also because they were usually uncircumcised. What she loved was a fine, thick, circumcised cock, waving its desire at her. Or the exotic one if it had to have a foreskin, the Mongol she'd met on the train to Tibet, who'd shoved it into her without a word of foreplay, sometime in the freezing Himalayan night.

"Yes?" she said now to the two police.

"We haven't been able to reach you on the phone," the young Englishman said. "The Superintendent is quite anxious to know if you've found your daughter's passport."

"What difference would it make?"

"It's something we can look for if it's missing."

"You can look for it even if it isn't missing. You can go into her room and bloody well look for it yourself if it's so important." She started crying. "I can't go in there."

He put his arm around her. To her surprise, she smelled him. A little prick of interest started through her nose, at the light, boyish scent of his cologne. Lavender, or something simple and country, like he probably was. She breathed him in deeply, inhaling him, the scent of male. A cock to tether herself to.

She leaned back and looked at him. He had very pale eyes, almost crystal in their lightness. His jaw was firm. His nose was cracked in the middle, so the bottom half was more on the left side of his face than the right. She looked down at his pants. He dressed to the left.

How hideous she was. How incorrigible and disgusting. Even in the midst of death we are in the midst of life, the minister had said at her daughter's funeral. Even in the midst of rape and sodomy and murder, we are in the midst of getting laid, she could hear filtering through her brain. But her distaste at herself, her remorse, didn't stop her.

"Maybe you can come later tonight," she said to him very softly now. "And I can show you where to look for it."

SIX

◆

The fortune-teller that Clement relied on was a *Fung shui* man named Dao Tsim. He lived in an apartment above Nathan Road. Though well into his nineties—how far in, no one was exactly sure—Dao Tsim was both energetic and calm. Anger, worry, and fear, he told his clients all the time, did nothing to make things better.

Neutral and balanced, he guided his customers through their anxieties and impatience. What was coming to them was coming to them, he always said. Trying to hurry it along served no purpose but to make them irritated. Irritation was as unproductive as expectations, which always led to disappointments.

"Why do you tell us what the future holds, if you don't want us to have expectations?" said Hin Lap-Kui, a little round woman who'd come for her monthly reading of the sticks.

"Because knowing what will be, you can relax," he said. "Stop trying to control, and you will have a happy life."

"If we get to Vancouver," she said.

"You will get to Vancouver. Just don't irritate yourself about when." He had a very long beard that was still black, though the decades had made it sparse. A round red satin hat came to the edge of his curiously unwrinkled forehead. Only some dark freckles of age indicated how long he had lived. Those seemed less blemishes than

53

spots which in women might be called beauty marks, but in his case signaled wisdom.

"We must get there soon," she said. "We must build a new life for our children."

"You will get there when you get there," said Dao Tsim.

From the doorway, Dao Tsim's great-grandson Chen watched his ancient relative do his fortune-telling. He was in no way spying: Hin Lap-Kui liked him, and always invited him to sit beside her while the old man read the sticks. But there was a certain immodesty, a lack of discretion, in her parading her destiny in front of him. He preferred watching from a slight distance.

From where he stood, he could take in the whole picture. The still noble set of the old man's proud shoulders, the one black hair that grew from the mole on Dao Tsim's cheek, long as his beard, coarse, like a wire, a supposed good luck omen that Chinese coveted. The room was decorated in red: brocade wall hangings, red silk cover and pillows on the rosewood bed. On an altar to the front of the room was a round metal prayer tub filled with sand, burning incense. A red *Fung shui* light was set into the carved shrine in the wall, beside candles in red hurricane lamps. At the table to the front of the low, cushioned bed, Hin Lap-Kui knelt, her hands holding the cylinder filled with fortune sticks, those that had not fallen out with her shaking one free. Dao Tsim sat at the other end of the table, kneeling on his soft prayer mat, easing the pressure on his knees.

The spectacle of his great-grandfather in his powerful role as seer always touched Chen. He regarded Dao Tsim with the same awe he did the history of Hong Kong. In truth, it was a fitting parallel, since the chronicle of their family was nearly an exact record of the island. Dao Tsim's own grandfather had been born in 1842, the year Great Britain had been given dominion over Hong Kong. "A barren island with hardly a house on it," Chen remembered Lord Palmersten's quote from school.

As indifferent a student as Chen was, the history of his homeland had captured his full attention. Even in the face of the explanations that were being given, he still could not understand why the British were leaving, when they'd been given the island in "perpetuity." The word was one of those English words he could not pronounce, making him stutter not only in his mouth but in his brain, as cold as the word was. As cold as the fact that it now wasn't true; they weren't standing by their promise.

Dao himself had been born in 1898, or sometime around that year, so long ago the records had been lost. That had been the year the New Territories and outlying islands had been added onto the treaty. The ninety-nine-year lease that would expire in 1997, taking along with it Hong Kong and Kowloon.

"Shouldn't we leave as soon as we can?" Hin Lap-Kui was asking Dao. 'What if the Chinese come in before the agreed time?"

"They won't," said Dao.

"How can we believe anything they say? How can we even pretend to believe they will keep their promise to leave Hong Kong capitalist?"

"Maybe they will."

"And maybe they won't shoot their own people. And maybe they won't arrest the refugees who ran away from them. And maybe our children will be as safe to ask for freedom as their children were."

"Maybe."

"What do the sticks say?"

"I don't waste the sticks on politics. I use them only for truth."

"Politics has truth in it."

"Politics is a game. There is no truth in games."

The round, energetic woman got to her feet, bored. Chen showed her to the door.

"Always remember that as a way to rid yourself of people," Dao said, as his great-grandson returned. "They are never so eager to leave as when the discussion stops being about them."

Chen smiled, and sat near his great-grandfather's feet. "Tell me my history," he said.

"You know it as well as I do. Maybe better."

"I like to hear you tell it." There was something reassuring about tales told in his great-grandfather's voice. Like longevity itself. A feeling of what was eternal, things you could count on, without promises being taken back.

"Your mother was born in 1941. Two days before the Japanese conquered Hong Kong."

"On Christmas day," said Chen, his black eyes bright. Although annoyed at Christians for failing to practice their philosophy, he did enjoy their holidays.

"I, my wife, my son, his wife, and their daughter, your mother..."—Dao stared off, the one heavy layer of skin on his face, the webbing at the corners of his eyes, like a valance—"... all were interned for the duration of the war. With only your mother and me left alive at the end of it."

"When you were freed by the British."

"Good men," said Dao.

"Then why are they leaving us?"

"It is the agreement. The lease is up."

"Hong Kong was not a lease. It was given in... perpetuity." His tongue stumbled over the word.

"But it cannot be held when they give up the rest, that was only leased."

"Why did they have to have the New Territories? Why weren't they satisfied with just Hong Kong?"

"Greed is a given in human nature."

"So they are not such 'good men.'"

"Even the best of men has greed in him. Only with effort do we overcome our shadow side."

"I like my shadows," said Chen. "I welcome them. Someplace to hide when the Chinese come."

"Maybe you'll be gone from here."

"With what money? You need to have fortunes for the places that will take us. Or great skills. I have no skills; no time to learn them. And you are so virtuous, you were never greedy, so there is no money."

"Your sister will help you."

"My sister," said Chen, contemptuously.

"She is your blood."

"A blood she would gladly open her veins and spill out if she thought a transfusion would make her white. British."

"That is because of love."

"Don't call it love, what she has with that yellow-haired fop."

Dao looked up, startled. "Where do you learn such words?"

Chen smiled, self-satisfied. "From old movies. We watch them at our club. 'Fop.' That's a good one, yes? *The Scarlet Pimpernel.* Leslie Howard, he is our second favorite, after Fred Astaire." Chen got up from the floor, and did a few slow, sliding taps around the room, arms extended. "Grace," he said. "Style. You have it or you don't."

"Well, it's nice to see you're trying for it," said a young woman from the doorway. She smiled at Dao, bowed her head slightly, over pointed hands, touching palms, lips to the edges of the fingertips, in a gesture of respect. "Great-grandfather."

Dao brightened visibly. "Kip!" he said. With great effort, he started to lift himself to his feet.

"Please. Don't get up for me." She moved to the place on the floor beside him, threw her arms gently around his neck, kissed the weathered cheek.

"I am too long in one position," he said, and with her help, got to his feet. "Better I do not lock into it."

"To what do we owe the pleasure?" said Chen. "Did the computer break down, or the fop throw you out?"

"Don't be jealous," said Kip. "One day someone will want you."

"Many want me already. But unlike some, I am discriminating."

"I didn't come here to fight, Chen." She helped Dao to the bed, the slowness of her movements synchronizing with his. Her knees bowed slightly outward, almost imperceptibly, giving her well-rounded, muscular calves an extra tension, making them seem more shapely, stretching the tendons behind her thighs as she moved, squeezing her buttock cheeks into circular mounds beneath the tight turquoise *chungsam.*

Chen caught a flash of purple bruise on her inner thigh. "Do you save all your fights for Peter?"

"I don't wish to discuss him with you," she said, easing her great-grandfather into a sitting position on the bed. She leaned over to kiss him. He took her face between his hands and stared into it, cupping the subtle point of her chin in his parchmentlike hands.

"But who should you tell, if not your family, when a man is beating you?" Chen asked.

She turned, her black eyes fierce. They were unusual eyes, long, narrow, clear, and beautiful. Dao Tsim had said once she had the eyes of a phoenix, the classic eyes of a mythic bird with boundless vision. They separated her well-shaped brows from her aristocratic nose, their beauty for the moment obscured by the anger in them. "He has never laid a hand on me."

"Really? Then what's that on your thigh?"

"I fell. They put a waterfall in our office building, and the escalator steps got wet."

"Excellent! You can sue! Isn't the building owned by the great Jardine's, where your lover is such an important man?"

"He is only a fund manager."

"*Only* a fund manager. I remember you bragging that at his age he was *already* a fund manager. You made it sound very impressive."

"It is very impressive. But I would not look to him for compensation for a little accident."

"You would not look to him for compensation for anything. Not for your love, or your pride, or your honor."

Dao looked from one to the other of them, his face a mask of sorrow. "Why do you do this to your sister?"

"She does it to herself. She does it to herself and so to all of us."

"I do not sell my honor. Or my love. Or my pride."

"How about barter?" said Chen.

"You are to stop this," Dao said, tears misting his eyes.

"Tell her. Tell her to stop."

"She is a grown woman," Dao said. "It is a new world."

"Where she cannot afford to have self-respect, because what she needs is a passport."

"Enough," said Dao. "Leave us."

"Gladly," said Chen. He slammed the outer door to the apartment as he went into the hall.

"I am so sorry," the old man said.

"You have nothing to apologize for."

"I don't apologize. I am just sad."

"He'll grow out of it," said Kip. "He's still a teenager, after all."

"I am not only sad about him. I'm sad about you."

"But there's nothing to be sad about!" she said, and smiled. "I came to give you good news." She opened her purse, an oversized black leather sack, and reached behind the papers she was carrying. Taking out a bundle secured with elastic bands, she handed it to Dao.

"What's this?"

"I've gotten a raise," she said.

"Money?"

"I was saving it for what my American co-workers call a rainy day. But now I won't need it."

"Why are you giving it to me?"

"I want to help take care of you, the way you took care of me."

"I can manage for myself. And your brother. I thought when you said good news you were going to tell me you were leaving him."

"Why are all the men in my family so hardheaded?"

"All the men in your family are only two left. We owe it to you to try to protect you. Young as your brother is, he is sometimes smarter than you. We know about this man you waste yourself on. He will never want you the way you need to be wanted. He will never make you part of his life."

"I am part of his life."

"You are his concubine. He wants no yellow babies to go to Eton."

"He loves me." Tears welled in her eyes.

"Then keep this for your passage to England, when he takes you there as his bride." He thrust the packet of money toward her. "Keep it for the clothes you will need, when he invites you to meet his mother."

A little choke of nervousness caught her. She reached inside her purse for a handkerchief. "As a matter of fact"—she wiped her eyes—"his mother is coming next month. I'm so scared."

She melted in his vision back into the little girl he had raised, a flutter of the eye before, it seemed to Dao. His arms reached for her. "What have you got to be afraid of? She's the one who should be afraid." He hugged her as hard as his strength allowed. "How can she possibly be a match for you?"

"Isn't James like Charley?" Claire asked Judith, that night at the Foreign Correspondents Club. It was a dark place, oak-paneled and weathered, walls hung with yellowing news stories blown up and framed, awards to its members, pictures of the year, from years that were long gone, like the journalists themselves, killed covering the battles. Vietnamese civilians waded through torrential rivers, sobbing with loss and confusion. Downstairs a giant television screen flashed the continuous news from CNN, while members at the bar ordered drinks that were still bought with scrip, cheaper than any drinks in Hong Kong, the only whiskey in town that was subsidized—by whom, no one was quite sure. Against the wall a teletype machine ticked off the details of stories for those who still preferred print. Upstairs, well-dressed women discussed over semitasteless food, the one dull meal in town, what headhunters had tapped their husbands for better corporate positions.

"Doesn't he remind you of Charley?" Claire asked Judith again.

"He reminds me of Charley in that they're both big and good-looking and that's *all*." Judith spoke crisply, allowing for no misinterpretation. So much of her job was what she called "damage control," making sure no misinformation got into the magazine, it had leaked over into her personal appraisals. The ingenue expression on Claire's face, the eagerness, the flush of girlish happiness on the far-from-girlish cheek, genuinely worried Judith.

She was a woman who saw things with absolute clarity, probably the main reason she and Claire were friends. In spite of how bright Claire was, she was often muddled, her perceptions altered by how she wanted things to be. But she was smart enough to know that about herself, and kept Judith as a litmus test, the friend she ran everything by to check out how things really were. It was a kind of blind respect, charged with affection, that made Judith uncomfortable. Judith had little time for love, either of the romantic or friendship kind. But it touched her in spite of herself, how fond of her Claire was. She appreciated being appreciated, even though her schedule allowed for little besides the magazine. Being as clear as she was, she saw the lack of balance in herself, and was grateful that someone cared for her enough not to see her as askew.

So she studied James as she might have a politician, looked for the hidden agenda. Watched him coming back to their table from the telephone, noted the broadness of shoulder, the slightly cocky stance. He was handsome, no question about it, and extremely charming. Wasn't it the natural position of women to be occasionally head over heels? Wasn't it perhaps a failing in her, that she always had her feet on the ground?

"My chum Kenneth will be joining us at the disco," James sat down. "It'll make it more fun, the four of us."

"Disco," Judith said. "The very word sets my teeth on edge. I'm the wrong generation."

"Nonsense. You're as young as Claire."

"Don't say anything or I'll kick you under the table," Claire said.

"She has rather sensational legs for a journalist, I must say. What do you do to keep them so shapely, if you don't dance?"

"I stalk hypocrisy."

"Dancing takes less of a toll, I'd wager. And you'll like Kenneth. He's a chum of mine from Uppingham."

"Slightly upmarket from Eton," Claire quoted him. "But they don't get near the publicity."

"Probably because of the school song." He turned to Claire. "Maybe you could write us a new one. 'On, Uppingham,' or something like that. But your services probably come very high."

"I could make a sacrifice," said Claire.

"No, you couldn't," said Judith, and ate her prawn.

"Undoubtedly I could raise a goodly sum from the Uppingham expatriate community. We have quite a few here in the Orient."

"In banking, like you are?" Judith asked, wondering if she should run a check on him in the morning, right after she interviewed the man who had found the bodies on Black's Link. There were too many things Superintendent Leslie knew that he wasn't even hinting at to Judith, and too few things, she suspected, that James could tell Claire.

"Banking, the law, government, real estate, drugs, white slavery."

Claire laughed.

"She thinks I'm joking."

"Aren't you?" asked Claire.

"Americans are so trusting."

"Some of us are," said Judith.

Later in the club, they all danced. Judith, with her right palm against the sweaty palm of James's friend, Kenneth, tried to be less judgmental. The fact that these men still did what was now being called "touch dancing," a souvenir of softer times, made her kindlier disposed to them. They were both in their middle thirties, she guessed, though her balding escort seemed older. He showed a few signs of depth, something Judith had thus far failed to see in James. Still no man needed to be everything a woman hoped. The more complex the woman, the less likely it was that she would find her match. Perhaps James was just what Claire needed at the moment. Judith could feel her friend's emptiness and pain.

For all her consciously achieved detachment, in a way Judith envied Claire's hunger for affection, sorrowed for all the leftover love she had no outlet for. Twice in her own life, Judith had let herself be ruled by emotion. Been as light-headed as other women were when they believed men's promises. Both times she had been trounced back to reason not by any particular awakening on her part, as by the lie on theirs: that it was going to change, grow, be a commitment.

She knew that her passion for the magazine might have been displaced if either of the men had meant what they said. But now that she was older, it was a moot point. Her thoughts, ambitions, needs, and highs were inextricably bound to her career: the magazine was lover, husband, child, father, and friend. But she remembered the innocent feelings of a younger time, the rush that infatuation could engender. As glad as she was not to be prey to it, she remembered how alive she had felt. So, in a way, she mourned for that a little.

She understood how Claire, who in spite of her seeming independence had always thought in terms of partnership, could so eagerly dive into a pool aflow with romance, no matter how shallow it might be. No one but Charley had known her real vulnerability. In business she had a tough reputation, paraded a harder edge than

Judith. Toughness in women was an acquired trait. Charley had understood how fragile his wife was underneath, and had shielded her. As he'd shielded his children. As he'd shielded everyone except himself, his own marrow-deep compassion, his fear of offending, robbing him of the killer instinct he'd needed to rise in the entertainment business.

Judith knew that at times Claire had hated the marriage. There had been hard moments when things were better for Claire than for him. Sometimes, those moments had stretched into years. It was she who'd become high profile, in a town where people had their profiles fixed. It had never been her intention or dream to be as great a success as her husband, much less a greater one. The situation chewed at the two of them, so they were both supersensitive, defensive. Quick to suspect a slight, which it nearly always was. In Beverly Hills all that counted was deals, not what people were. So they'd been more or less dropped socially, once Charley was out of the business, and Claire hadn't had a hit song for a while.

Judith had watched them weather the difficulties of his long periods of unemployment, had seen his hearty good humor give way to abrasiveness. She'd seen Claire's anxiety at being financially responsible for her family. The feminist movement had come without impacting her awareness. Claire's mother had taught her men were better, and the fact that they weren't made her confused and angry. "Preserve your marriage," Judith had cautioned her, on being transferred out of L.A. It seemed important not only for Claire, but Judith as well. "The high-profile women who have kept their families together and flourished in their careers and stayed feminine can be counted on the finger of one finger."

Claire had listened. Or, at least, it seemed to Judith she had. But Judith wondered how much resentment had smoldered, what guilt there might be at Charley's having died. To see Claire looking so happy, then, to see the lightness on her features, the return of what seemed a carefree heart, pleased Judith. Still, she wished she was not so sure Claire was seducing herself.

She could hear them talking as they brushed by on the dance floor. "I told you, you oughtn't to look at a man like that," James was saying.

"Like what?" Claire asked.

"Like you can see through to his soul."

"Oh, but I can."

"And what's there? Is it black as pitch?"

"Pink. Baby pink."

"Sounds pretty sexy. Maybe it isn't my soul you're looking at."

"I say," said Kenneth to Judith, squeezing her palm with his own sweaty one. "Did you hear that? Why do they get to talk sexy and pink, and all we do is current events?"

"Maybe you should be dancing with them," said Judith.

A woman sitting alone at the bar got up from the luminous stool and started dancing by herself. The whole room was lit in a kind of ultraviolet, so shades of white became an eerie, neon lavender. Her lips appeared black, like the circles beneath her eyes. She was about the same age as Claire and Judith, somewhere around her middle forties. But she dressed very young, and it made her look older, as did the way she wore her hair: gathered in trendy little clumps, held with the beauty parlor clips that had come into recent fashion.

Her eyes were closed, her arms wide and open; she seemed held by a dream lover. There was a pained smile on her tired face, as though she feared an honest expression would crack her makeup. She wore big glass earrings, the same hot pink, translucent as the clips in her hair. Her shoes were a like tone, fluorescent against the flashing lights coming up through the glass-blocked floor. Her dress was black, as were her stockings, and the liner around her wide-set lids. She looked hauntingly familiar to Judith, who couldn't quite place her.

There were not many people on the dance floor. The club was fairly deserted for the moment, or maybe for good, popularity being like the quick killing in Hong Kong. Something that could pass as quickly as it arose. A young couple stubbornly doing the staccato motions of rock and roll inappropriate for the ballad playing were the only other dancers on the floor. The solitary woman, arms around herself now, glided past them, humming louder than the music. Her full lips seemed to be forming words, but no words came out of them. Just the high, nasal soprano of her hum. She stumbled, and bumped against Claire.

"I'm dreadfully sorry." She opened her eyes. They were a gentle, cornflower blue, their softness made more poignant by the contrasting harshness of the eyeliner.

"It's all right," said Claire, and smiled.

"You have a lovely smile," the woman said, trying to smile in return. But her full lips were rubbery, slack at the corners. What seemed an ordinary attempt at camaraderie disintegrated into bathos.

"Excuse me," Judith said. "Aren't you Maggie Evans?"

"Am I?" Maggie looked at her, frowning. "Should I be? What do you think? Would that be awful?"

"I'm Judith Taylor. I did a story on your jewelry last year. *Elan* magazine."

"Oh, yes. I remember."

"What kind of jewelry?" Claire said.

"Ah, it's caught her," said James. "She's in Hong Kong. She must start shopping."

"Jade."

"I'd love to get some jade," said Claire. "I hear it's good luck."

"Not if you design it," said Maggie.

The music stopped. Lights still flashed through transparent white blocks on the floor, alternating with black ones. It was like a giant chessboard on which they stood, pawns in a game nobody was winning. The young couple kept on dancing, even though there was no music.

"I'm sorry about your daughter," Judith said.

"So am I. May I buy you all a drink?"

"I'd love a drink," said Kenneth.

"I have to go home," Judith said.

"There's always time to go home," said Maggie.

"I'd like to see your designs," said Claire, as they moved to the bar.

"Here's my card." Maggie handed it to her. "I'll be in tomorrow, I think. I'm out tonight, aren't I? This isn't just a dream, is it?" She looked around the disco. "So much of what has happened lately seems a bad dream. Is this part of it?"

"Are you all right?" asked Judith.

"Why? Do I seem odd? Perhaps what I need is a dance." She turned to Kenneth. "How about you, sweaty teddy bear?" She put her hand on the back of his neck, touched the fringe of his hair, where it circled his scalp, monkish, the boyish skin of his face, shining, giving the lie to the hair loss. "Would you like to dance with a crazy lady?"

"I should like to have a drink first. I'm not used to brushing up against famous women."

Maggie ordered a bottle of champagne.

"Are we celebrating something?" asked Kenneth.

"Life," said Maggie, lifting her glass. "Because we are some of us still alive." She looked at Judith, as though for confirmation. "Aren't we?"

Her eyes moved to the doorway. She seemed visibly to flinch. Judith followed the line of her vision. Superintendent Leslie was coming in the door.

"Here's someone who can tell us for sure," Maggie said.

"Good evening," he said, half bowing, a gesture that seemed less gallantry to Judith, than a wish to avoid everybody's eyes. Shy men, she had noted, even those who were professional observers as he was, tended to lose their air of scrutiny in social situations. Policeman's eyes that at the crime scene appeared to be taking in everything now seemed watchful in his own behalf. He was a handsome man, Judith thought, in a beat-up way. Like an old leather purse that one couldn't bear to throw away because it had done much service, and had hidden compartments.

He was dressed in a safari suit, tailored carefully to his measure, which included the start of a small paunch. He sucked it in neatly as he resumed standing tall. "Nice to see you," he said, sort of to Judith, not exactly looking into her face, but aiming the words at her.

"Have you got an autopsy report on any of us?" Maggie said. "Or are we still alive?"

"Excuse me?"

"We are toasting life," Maggie said. "You should join us in the toast." She nodded at the bartender for another glass. "I just wanted to make sure we're all really here, that this isn't just part of the dream."

"It feels to me like we're here," James said, and put his arms around Claire from behind, the lower half of his body dancing in against hers a little, to the music that had started again. She leaned her head back against his throat, and half closed her eyes, her mouth opening. Even in the dark of the disco it was possible to see the rise of color in her cheeks.

"Your assistant was supposed to come look for Betsy's passport," Maggie said to Clement. "But he didn't come. I hate it when men don't come. Especially young men. You wouldn't think they'd have any problem."

The bartender filled Clement's glass. "Cheers," he said. His eyes skipped slightly sideways, catching Judith's.

"Whatever you say," said Maggie. "You are the authority." She lifted her glass and clinked it against his. "What's that you're holding? A new kind of stun gun?"

"A cassette," said Clement.

"Pornographic movies, Superintendent?" Maggie asked, wiliness back in her smile now, sharp, the flaccid melancholy pulled in.

"Hardly, Fred Astaire. *Flying Down to Rio.*"

"I wouldn't have picked you as one for nostalgia," Judith said.

"Actually I wasn't," Clement said. "I got pulled into it, more or less, by my young friend here."

The Chinese boy who'd been dancing rock and roll came toward him from the dance floor. He was smiling, his hand outstretched. Clement got up and shook it, and then embraced the boy. How's Great-grandpa?"

"Sharper than the rest of us," the boy said.

"This is Chen." He introduced him to the group, himself shaking hands with those he hadn't met officially, Judith making the introductions. "Here's your tape." He handed it to the boy. "When do I get *Daddy Long Legs?*"

"As soon as the rest of the guys are finished with it."

"I really have to go home," Judith said.

"Was it something I said?" asked Clement.

She shook her head.

"Was it something I didn't say?"

She smiled at him. "Maybe."

"We can fix that."

"Something's going on here," said Maggie, looking from Clement to Judith. She turned and saw Claire and James. "Something's going on there, too. Oh, I hate it when something's going on everywhere but where I am." She put down her glass and held out her arms to Kenneth. "Come, sweaty teddy."

"I'm not a very good dancer," he said.

"I'm stunned to hear it." She took his hand and led him toward the dance floor. "I used to worry about that, you know, when they couldn't dance, or didn't come. Women are so worried about the fellow's needs. So fearful it will make them seem less a woman if he feels less a man. But we have to start worrying about our own needs, finally, don't we? Our turn to dance, isn't it?" Her voice trailed off, as she turned to Kenneth, lifting her arms.

"I must be going," said Judith.

"May I see you home?" asked Clement.

She shook her head. "Thank you anyway. Are you ready?" She turned to Claire.

"I'll take her home," said James.

"Here's a key." Judith gave it to Claire.

"I won't be too late."

"I'm not your mother," said Judith, and wondered why she felt like she was.

SEVEN

◆

The gentleman to whom Claire had not been introduced at the Mandarin bar, Anthony Go, took great pride in introductions. He had just had new business cards made; business cards were the Hong Kong handshake. People whipped them out at the least provocation, exchanging them faster than they could start a smile. Anthony Go's card read: ENTREPRENEUR, in raised lettering under his name. Since the advent of Donald Trump, that had served to wipe out any need for people to explain what they really did. So Anthony Go had felt most thwarted at not being able to hand his card to Claire, and to find out, in return, who she was.

His personal road to the Mandarin that day had been difficult and not well paved. The fact that it was now inlaid with jewels and celebrities pleased him. Jewels he wore with comparative modesty, in the starched cuffs of his shirt. Celebrities he laid out on the deck of his pleasure junk every Sunday, since his advent to prestige, for the world to see and all of Hong Kong to hunger for.

His lavish pleasure junk was no showier than the average yacht in Hong Kong Harbor. It slept twelve, and was maintained full-time with a Chinese skipper at the helm, on duty even when the junk was anchored at the Aberdeen Boat Club. This was in case it was needed, or, since the very word *luxury* meant something not needed, *wanted* by any of Go's associates. These included merchant bankers, restaurateurs, realtors, casino operators, drug dealers, pimps, an occasional stylish murderer, and an obese American novelist who had written a best-selling saga about Triads.

As savage and amoral as Triads were considered, the writer had portrayed them heroically, with great love of family, and with a high code of ethics, albeit their own. Like the business card, the myth created by the novelist had given weight to those who might otherwise be suspect, foremost among them Anthony Go. As a result, the author, MacDonald Chin, was treated royally, carried on a silver tray wherever Triads had power, which was every city in the world where there was a Chinatown.

On the junk this particular Sunday was a syndicate-backed singer whom Chin had defiled in his novel. Journalists and critics who had been less than kind to the singer had been known to have "accidents," sometimes of a permanent nature. So it had been thought that the author might not be long for this world. But the assassins who were fans of the singer were friends of the assassins who were fans of the writer, and between them had agreed to leave everyone alive. Besides, revenge had no end date, became more delicious when it festered. There were those who believed that the order was in for the day after the singer died, for all who had slandered him to follow him to the grave.

He was in Hong Kong to give a concert. His popularity in this part of the world was considerably less than in the United States, which generated the rumor that he was there to launder syndicate money. Anthony Go knew that this was the truth, and was sorry he hadn't asked him first.

Money laundering was the rub, as Hamlet might have put it, had something been rotten in Hong Kong. No matter how rich a man became, beyond his wildest dreams, indeed, the wildest dreams of Imelda Marcos, there was always a downside. Anthony Go owned many businesses heavy in cash to funnel the money through: restaurants, clubs, actual laundries, even a few banks. But there were never enough outlets to handle all the money a respectable Hong Kong merchant-gangster could make. The more respectable he became, as far away from his teenage Triad initiation as a monk was from a Pope, the more Go coveted a bank that was high-powered and British.

He envied that inbred elegance, the snobbery that looked down on everything, including, or perhaps especially, the Hong Kong Chinese. For all their power, Triads were no more emotionally secure than men all over the world, wanting most what didn't want them.

Go's pleasure junk, like those around it, had been carved from an old traditional junk, its hull left intact and refined. The rest was constructed of the best, most modern seagoing machinery. A realtor might have called it magnificently appointed, but that did not begin to describe the details Go himself had supervised. Jade carvings served as pedestals for dining tables on deck and in the saloon. Umbrellas under which guests shaded themselves on deck had poles that glinted back the sunlight with what people assumed was gilt, but was, indeed, real gold. He did not point this out to his guests, a certain modesty balancing what otherwise would be considered ostentation.

Every important banking concern had its own yacht, as did everyone of affluence on the island, except for those who did not care about impressing people, a breed that was hard to find. Gearing down as most international money concerns in Hong Kong were purported to be, as ominous as were the discussions of Taiwan's leading billionaire businessman, Y. C. Wang, moving, European banks, venture capitalists, Japanese investors, and the rest were still operating full tilt. As long as fortunes were to be made, even in one afternoon as they often were, cash was courted. So people were used to being lavishly entertained. Nothing much impressed anymore. Still, with all the profligate spending, the most influential, sought-after man would have welcomed the chance to be invited on Go's yacht this particular morning.

The *Hong Kong Tatler* had announced in its current issue that the singer was coming to town, that his retinue would include the great martial arts star, Johnny Wong. With him was to be the rising young movie actress Henry Wu, and her much publicized agent, Louise Felder, all of them to be entertained by Anthony Go. There had been an absolute scramble for invitations, a greater interest in being on board the yacht than in attending the singer's concert. Go had responded to the sudden flood of would-be friends, regretfully, that the singer wished to keep socializing to a minimum.

That the socializing included Henry Wu was most titillating, giving substance to recent rumors that the singer was having a hard time making love. It was sad scuttlebutt, since he had been the sexual hood ornament of his time, so even people not fond of him grieved for the transience of sexuality. "I hear he can't get it up anymore," said a man who had never really admired him, realizing he couldn't get it up anymore, either.

So the presence of Henry on board, sexual creature that she was, gave people a prurient hope. Henry was an odd name for a woman. Her agent, Louise, a behind-the-scenes person often in front of the scenes, sometimes making them, had assured her the "Wu" would travel. Especially if one considered the nature of her early films, which Louise was trying to help her get out of circulation. As for the "Henry," Louise thought that kind of charming, an attention-getter. Since there had been—longer ago than Louise could believe—a big hit song called "A Boy Named Sue," why couldn't there be a Girl Named Henry? She had sold that thesis to *People* magazine, which considered the idea quite deep, and had done a cover story on Henry, before anyone knew who she was.

They knew who she was now. Besides the ingenious job of promotion Louise had done on what she referred to, affectionately, as her "token Gook," Henry had linked up with Johnny Wong, the most popular male star in Asia. He was a handsome Eurasian, big and dark, but somewhat light in masculine strength. The mantle of Bruce Lee had fallen on him, like a Ringling Brothers' circus tent on a midget in a clown car. In the face of the grieving over the great star's death, people fixated on the closest thing they had as a replacement, unwilling to see Johnny could not fill the idol's shoes, much less his pants. He had a good square set of jaw, clear eyes, and a balletic grace and ease at Tae Kwan Do that seemed to balance out his being less charismatic than his predecessor. He was quite tall, but somewhat wispy, the slight effeminacy giving rise to hints of homosexuality, a criminal offense in Hong Kong. People had a hard time accepting there could be such a thing among the Chinese. Disco Disco had been ruled officially off-limits to the police because it was a gay bar. There had been thirteen deaths from AIDS, officially reported, plus all the ones that weren't, so no one could turn a completely blind eye. But most shaded their vision.

So it came as kind of a starstruck reprieve to Johnny's audience, his being with Henry, or Horny, as she was sometimes known. His fans, all tens of millions of them, became uniformly mad for her, as though she were some kind of carnal Bernadette, offering him, and them, a healing. Several women he hadn't known had committed suicide over him. Everyone understood, for the sake of their memory, how important it was to keep the fantasy going.

Henry lay now on the deck of Go's yacht beside Louise, the two of them shaded by the golden-poled umbrellas, looking enviously at the one person on board taking the sun. Henry had to stay out of it because the Chinese looked down on dark skin; tanned weathered skin belonged to peasants, with low economic status. Louise, successful as she was, liked to consider herself still a peasant, as long as no one else thought it first. She made jokes about her origins at the tables of royalty, just as she told salacious tales about herself in the presence of lechers and prudes. It was her intention to amuse the first, and shock the second, though often she misread her audience and got transposed reactions. In any event she told herself she didn't care anymore what people thought of her. But she was still afraid of her dermatologist.

Her once-honeyed skin had been consigned to his care, in a world where even Michael Jackson got older. As there were celebrity chefs, where there had once been celebrity hairdressers, where, very long ago, there had been gifted artists and writers at the best Hollywood poolsides, now there were celebrity medical specialists working the so-called A parties. She had gone to what she thought was going to be a carefree evening, a Christmas gala glitzed with flocked trees and the Pointer Sisters carrying their Shih Tzus. In the master bedroom she had come across her doctor with his magnifying loop, examining the pores of Gore Vidal. He had turned his enlarged eye on her, and told her to stay out of the sun.

Shade was not Louise's natural exposure. Before she had been anyone, she was at least radiant, struggling for her place in the entertainment sun. The honey blond hair that served as such a contrast to the salty mouth had capped her healthily toasted look, backed up the pouty gold-brown lips, the even-toothed smile. The fact that she'd gotten more than her dream, that the spotlight was always on her now, was no consolation for the irony that being finally who she was, she could no longer look as good as who she was when she wasn't.

"I remember when I used to be all honey brown and everyone wanted to eat me," she mused, her eyes on the sleekly oiled blonde lying facedown on the deck. "Who is she?"

"I hate it when you're interested in other people," Henry said.

Offscreen, her features were unspectacular. Her eyes were more round than angular, giving her history a hint of European invaders, though the high, blunt slant of her cheeks was unmistakably Mongolian. On film, however, she had an electricity she did not possess in life, a magic, a love affair her face had with the camera. She was caressed by it, cosseted by the lens, no matter how quickly shot or flatly lit her movies had been. Even her body looked longer than it was, lither, the almost concavity of her chest giving her a waiflike quality that would have touched Charlie Chaplin, had he lived longer. Louise had a theory that if he had seen Henry, he would have.

All the Orientals on the boat occupied the canopied portion of the upper deck, where a luncheon of pheasant under glass was being laid. The men shied away from the rays of the sun as much as the women did. As the male object of desire in Western lore was tall, dark, and handsome, so was his Chinese counterpart "a fair-faced scholarly-looking man," a phrase from the literature of the Song dynasty, which, to Louise's amazement, Henry had read.

"Don't be jealous, Henry," Louise counseled her. "I have too much energy to devote to one person. The men in my life have always been grateful when I got interested in someone else."

"I am not the men in your life," said Henry, sullenly.

"I could tell that without your saying anything."

Henry touched her breasts, or the lack of them, through the latex of her bathing suit. "You should have let me have the operation."

"You're distinctive the way you are." She indicated her own rather unimpressive bosom. "Although it would have been exciting, getting four for the price of two."

The oiled blonde stretched, her hands reaching up to sunglasses set in the tight coil of her white-gold hair, moving them down to her eyes. She gave kind of a soft animal moan with the stretch, as though it relieved her, although the effect on the men on board seemed quite the opposite.

There was no doubt about it, Louise could see: the woman had true magnetism. She herself, who had tired of faces as a restaurant critic wearied of recipes, found her glance moving again and again to the classic contours of the woman's face, the impressive cheekbones, the extremely wide set of the green-yellow eyes. She wanted to tell her to take off the glasses, so she could look at them again, even closed, the curved arc of the heavily lashed lids as lovely as the eyes themselves.

She enhanced her beauty by seeming unaware of it, not seeking any attention. In all of Louise's history of making stars, those she had created, and those she had bedded, there wasn't one who could get enough attention. In the beginning of her success as an agent, she had had a number of what she was now finally grown-up enough to label "flings," which she had imagined at the time were love affairs, with actors. She hadn't wanted anything from them, not even a climax, grateful just for their company, confusing their narcissism with a correct appraisal of her, that she was really unworthy of a good-looking man's serious regard. Thankful simply for arms around her, kisses bestowed in what seemed like generosity, she took comfort from having her mouth sweetly pressed, sucking on a tender tongue. But even their embraces had boiled down to a kind of vanity practice, a preparation for lips that really mattered, a scene before the camera. The hands that caressed her ears and hair had offered less the affection she was seeking than an urging of her head toward their penises. And always there had been a fight for the mirror afterward, even with the few who said "I love you" while coming.

Women had made her even more disappointed. Those she loved without wanting anything in return, even the one whom she had made into the most important star in the world, had turned on her when their own self-interest came into play. It was always just about them, without Louise even coming in second. Women, she knew now for a fact, could break each other's hearts more effectively than men could. Being open, more trusting, the betrayal went deeper.

To observe this woman then, this softly feline creature lolling around apparently unaware of and unconcerned with the effect she was having on the others on board, felt refreshing to Louise, in a life that no longer seemed it could be refreshed. Henry watched her watching.

"I don't like blondes," she sulked.

"No question she's blond," Louise appraised. Even had her hair been covered, instead of parted in the center and slicked back tight as it was, she would have telegraphed blond. Her black suit looked like it was painted on, slick against her graceful, long-limbed body, square line of straps emphasizing her strong-looking shoulders. She had a swimmer's upper chest, well defined, tanned to a burnished gold, with a teardrop diamond on a fine chain against her throat.

Louise's own throat tightened at the sight of that stone, because someone had doubtless given it to the blonde. Someone had noted how delicate she was, and had gifted her accordingly. No one would ever give such a dainty piece to Louise, cloak her in what was delicate. *Delicate.* Only once had a man even used that word about her, a European actor who'd taken her out for sushi after they'd made love, and said of the yellowtail, "It tastes delicate, like you." She'd come without his even touching her, believing for that moment he could appreciate what was invisible about her. She tried not to feel suicidal when he'd dropped her after she got him a six-picture deal.

Now even the costly gifts that came to her each Christmas from the hangers-on, and the suckers-around, were big and bold, like everyone thought she was. Like she supposed herself she really was, except for her custard heart, so crustily encased.

"I like you, Louise," Henry said, quietly. "But then, you're not a true blonde."

"Have you been fucking my hairdresser?"

"I hate it when you talk like that." The films she had made prior to Louise's discovering her notwithstanding, Henry was very prudish about language.

"How else would you know whether I was a true blonde or not?"

"You don't have a blond attitude."

"And what, pray, is that?"

"Confident."

Louise sat up stiffly in the deck chair, her black hat with its deep, low brim halfway down over her eyes. Her eyes still had a lot of light in them, what her spirit had lost. They were as lively as they'd always been, with little flecks of gold like intelligence kaleidoscoped, never coming to rest. The skin around her lids was not as weighted as that of the contemporaries who hadn't submitted to cosmetic surgery. Good genes had spared her yet having to take that chance. It was always a chance, no matter how simple a procedure everyone said it was, no matter how much Louise liked that other breed of partygoers, plastic surgeons who had married stars, and so sat poolside with the Pointer Sisters. There were still accidents, faces that were on too tight. Louise had a terror of ending up permanently wide-eyed, in an inflexible gape. The expression in her still pretty eyes hardened. "You think I'm not confident?"

"You're cocky. Cocky isn't confident."

"I hate it when you talk like that." Louise got up and went over to the blonde. "I used to get that color, but they told me the sun causes premature aging, which in my case it's too late for."

The blonde raised her head slightly, the muscles of her flat brown belly contracting. She smiled, just wide enough so it didn't seem forced. "Your skin is lovely as it is," she said.

"Don't try to win me," said Louise. "You can probably do sit-ups without straining."

The blonde smiled again. It was a perfect smile, Louise noted, lips not particularly full—thin, really, they looked—but when she smiled alchemy took place around her mouth. It was transformed into something generous, as if a better nature were taking hold of her, and everything of constraint was overruled. She looked open, free, all signs of reticence vanishing.

"Who are you?" Louise asked.

"Erica Thorr."

"I don't mean who are you. I mean, *who are you?*"

"That's all there is."

"Are you an actress?"

"No."

"You could be an actress. Half the women I've handled don't look as good as you do. Make that nine-tenths. I'm Louise Felder."

"You're a talent agent?"

"Agent. Let's not be overly generous. What do you do?"

"What's it like, being an agent?"

Louise heard that Erica had not answered her question, was being evasive about something as simple as what she did. Everybody did something. Even those who did nothing had a cover, some pretend agenda to distract people. It surprised her that Erica would not have said, for example, "I'm a model." Anyone would have believed her, she was so striking. It was easier to lie than to evade. Evasions raised suspicions, whereas lies were the currency in Hong Kong. Nobody even checked them out unless they were going to invest with you, and sometimes not even then, people were so eager to believe.

"Not like it was in the old days," said Louise. "Which don't seem that old to me. When I first came to Hollywood, I mean when I was a kid, at the end of the sixties, there were really 'old days.' The great old days, filled with the ghosts of the founders, those little Munchkins determined to begin a great industry. They thought they were the framers of the Constitution starting a great country. Men who really loved the movies. None of this conglomerate, corporate shit, with Japanese takeovers waiting in the wings to swallow us, like Godzilla.

"We're talking men who were obsessed with film: Harry Cohn, Darryl Zanuck. Not these rocket scientists who run the studios now. Yuppies in their twenties, thirties at the outside, who don't even know who Jack Warner was, much less who he fucked, which is how you made deals in better days. My salad days, I guess you could call them. Now they're arugula."

Erica smiled. "You make yourself sound older than you are."

"You want to marry me?"

"Let's just be good friends."

"That has sexual implications where I come from. Whenever people in Hollywood say 'we're just good friends,' it means they're sleeping together."

"Well, I'm from Philadelphia. All it means there is, let's be good friends."

"Philadelphia," Louise mused. "That's good. The new Grace Kelly. But with breasts."

"I told you, I'm not an actress."

"Neither are plenty who've made it big in movies. I could make some calls . . ."

"No, thanks," said Erica.

"Who are you here with?"

"Nobody in particular. I met Johnny Wong at the hotel, and he invited me. But I'm not with him."

"So you don't belong to anybody."

"I didn't say that," said Erica, and turned over, face on her folded arms.

Her back, Louise saw, was as stunning as her front, tapering down from wide, well-defined shoulders to a tiny waist, curving out again to gently rounded hips. Down the center of her spine nubbed the visible line of her vertebrae, to small, but impressively shaped, firm buttocks. Louise could tell they were firm without having to touch them, the muscles taut, outside the meager cut of the swimsuit panty. It was not Louise's bent to be attracted to women, although Bunyan Reis, her favorite homosexual friend and client, was always telling her she should permit herself a taste of that when they visited Thailand. Even he who found women's bodies repellent, with all that interior plumbing as he said, enjoyed a good soaping all over with a woman's body as a scrub brush, a featured delight of the Bangkok whorehouses. Still, for all of what Louise liked to consider her depravity, she shied away from even considering that aspect of sex.

Her own sexuality, at midlife, was still a puzzle to her. Men had had her when she was young, and believed her to be as tough as she'd only pretended. It had been "cute," she'd been sure, to have a hard mouth, underneath the too juicy one. Men had been drawn to her then, drawn to her tawny skin and her plump little lips, dripping clever garbage as traditional seductresses oozed honey. She had never really dreamed of being a seductress, only hoped that men would want her. Having learned that innocence was no lure and certainly no protection, she had affected her invulnerable veneer. So men had foraged through her secret places. When they'd burrowed all the way inside her, they'd found out how soft she really was, how eager to defer and depend. She'd become attached to them, and they'd fled. So she'd become as tough as she'd only pretended. Soon the softness vanished completely, even deep inside. A callus grew over the tenderest part of her, so no one would ever touch her again the way they had in the beginning. And for that, she sometimes wept at night.

The last thing she needed was a passionate involvement with a woman. Women had hurt her enough without her ever having made herself physically vulnerable to them. Still, if she were going to be attracted to a woman, she could see, being objective, where it would have been easy with Erica Thorr.

"Why did you have to invite her?" Louise asked Johnny Wong, underlining *her* with a downward sweep of glance taking in Erica Thorr. She said it loudly, so everyone would know, especially Erica, that she was joking.

"I thought there should be more than one gorgeous blonde on board."

"All right. Take it out. I'll do whatever you want."

The group under the canopy laughed. None of them really knew Louise except the singer, but they all knew her reputation. Slatterns were a dime a dozen or less in the Orient, but successful people who talked filth were still a novelty. Some of the guests were slower on the take than Louise's mouth was, and really didn't get what she had said. But knowing how clever she was supposed to be, and outrageous, they laughed anyway.

"I hate it when you talk like that," said Henry.

"Well, at least I only talk, dear," said Louise, and moved close to her protégée, so she could speak without being overheard. "It wasn't Lulu who made all those movies we must try to get out of circulation." It didn't please her to be unkind to Henry, but people wanting her to be other than she was rankled her. This was who she was, wasn't it? She'd read all the articles about herself, culled them for content, in case the writers had a good bead on her. She thought her personality appeared solidified: effective, funny, arrogant, and loved by the people who kissed the air near her cheeks. She also believed the pieces that considered her despicable, even while threatening to sue over them, telling her lawyers not to dignify such fluff by actually bringing an action. "As long as they spell my name right," she always said, quoting Tallulah or some other bitch who'd been bigger than life, as Louise supposed she was. What was life, really, for her to be bigger than it? A series of disappointments. Smart as she was, she was still not smart enough not to be disappointed. Lately, though, she expected the worst, so was rarely let down.

"I'm not interested in sex with you," said Johnny to Louise, responding to her gibe that she would do whatever he wanted. He wore a light cloak over his naked shoulders, a sleek throw of silk the same wheat color as his tights. He loosed it from his neck, and got to his feet, and did a few Tae Kwan Do moves very slowly, with exceptional calm.

"Is that to make me feel sorry?" Louise said. There was a remarkable grace to his movements, but grace had never been what she was seeking, neither in the way people carried themselves, nor the way they behaved with her. Grace she considered *goyishe*, one of those high-born things in Episcopals who went to ballet schools when they were children, instead of wondering why their mothers didn't love them, as Jews did.

"It's not to make *you* feel anything," said Johnny. "It's to clear my head. Because there *is* something I want."

"I'm all ears," said Louise. "And a little cellulite."

"I would like you to package Henry and me in a picture together."

"You say you stepped in *what?*" said Louise. She turned to look at Henry, her eyes filled with accusation.

Henry got up and went to the opposite side of the ship, staring out at the other boats, avoiding Louise's obvious pique. Around the yacht as it glided in the direction of Lantau, the port was as busy as the streets of Hong Kong, thick with merchant shipping vessels. Flat-bellied freighters sat low in the water, with the weight of the cargo they carried. Counterpointing all of it was the spirited bustle of the Star Ferry, on its way from Hong Kong to Kowloon. Alongside the yacht skidded high-masted, antique sailing ships, the seagoing toys of those who could afford them. Motorboats, junks, and sampans slid by, crowded with families and dogs. Henry bowed her head slightly, in case any of them were hers.

She had lived her childhood on sampans. All she had known, and thought she would know, were sampans, as the rest of her family accepted that that was their life. It had not occurred to her to think in terms of a future that would be any different or better, until her great-granduncle read her sticks, when she was twelve, and told her she would grow up to be a great film star. It was as if she had awakened at that moment, hearing words that said she would move through the highest circles. She had not understood what that meant at the time, but did not think it would prophesy her making a porno about a high-flying circus act, which she had also done. Rather did she imagine it might surround her with luxury and beautiful people, as her present life was doing, finally. The interim adventures, the foray into lewd movies, she had more or less sleepwalked through, like the floors Cinderella had to scrub before her time came to go to the ball. She had done what she had done to get out of what she had been, simply following her path. The Chinese were nothing if not pragmatic.

But Louise was more pragmatic than the hardest Hong Kong merchant. So Henry was full of anxiety about what her reaction would be to what Johnny had suggested. Henry's mother and three sisters were living in houses bought with what she had made from stag films. But she would have to become a very great star indeed to take care of the whole family.

There were so many of them. She loved them all. Relatives all up and down the harbor, some as far away as the islands outside the New Territories, and Lantau. Prized them more than the virtue she hadn't considered really at stake in what she was doing, since virtue was meaning well, loyalty to family, and not hurting anybody. Henry had been very clever about that, declining to participate in bondage-and-domination scenarios, refusing to even listen to stories that her employers sometimes did snuff films. Horror to her had become the poverty, the seediness they didn't even know was seedy, a day's catch of fish in the middle of living quarters. Now, in addition to just getting them off the sampans and putting them in real homes, once her only ambition, there was a panic to get them out of Hong Kong.

Nobody trusted the Chinese. Nobody expected them to keep their promises. They were already threatening to renege on what they had agreed to in their treaty with Mrs. Thatcher. Taking pictures of Hong Kong people who protested their methods, writing down their names. How could Henry make enough money, even with Louise handling her career, even with the salaries a star could negotiate eventually, to relocate all her family in time? The only relative she had who was really capable of supporting herself in another culture was her second cousin Kip, Dao Tsim's great-granddaughter. She, at least, understood computers, worked with them. Great-granduncle was too old to relocate, didn't really want to, feeling that his life was the life of Hong Kong, his history the same as the island's. Chen, Kip's brother, was too ornery and not educated enough to make his own future. Out of all the family, Kip was the only one who might be able to save herself, to survive on her own, if her British lover refused to marry her.

Most women in Hong Kong had only that alternative: to marry a lover with a solid passport. None of Henry's family, except for Kip, could even count that possibility. All the rest of them needed help, political connections. It was not enough just to have money without some influence to pull them to another place. Success for Henry, no matter how great, or how fast, could never take care of all of it. And for that she needed the backing of Triads. Johnny Wong had that connection.

"I'd like you to package the two of us in a movie," Johnny said, again.

"I didn't know you were a comedian," said Louise.

Henry recognized the tone. It was Louise on the hard edge, voice stripped of honey, contempt Brillo-ing its surface. Henry had heard that timbre a time or two, and shuddered for those it was being directed at: an executive peeled of his power, who had looked down on Louise when she first came to Hollywood, now needing a favor; an old lover who'd cast her aside coming to her for a job. Henry had been present at a couple of those occasions, the seemingly informal meeting in the Polo Lounge at the Beverly Hills Hotel, which Louise had likened to Yalta, with palm fronds. Henry's soul had contracted as it never had when she made the pornos, because she had never allowed herself to feel really present, really a part of them. But she felt a genuine part of Louise, had a stake of true affection in her. So she hated to witness how full of contempt Louise could be. How distaste curled the still appealing mouth, when what Louise worried about all the time was lines around her lips. Why didn't Westerners realize how much more destructive to beauty scorn was than age?

"We'd be very good together," Johnny said.

"It's taken me two years of constant campaigning and hard work to make Henry white." She spoke to him peremptorily, as

though he were not very bright. "To make them see her in Hollywood
as good for a role designed for a Caucasian. A Mel Gibson co-star."
Her mouth moued into a pout, a leftover from the surly little girl
who'd had so much affection to give, which no one was willing to
receive. Now she became sullen not when men let her down, which
she'd finally concluded they could not help doing, but when talent
tried to take a hand in dealmaking. "If I put her with you, she'd be
back where she was before I started. Why would I want to do that?"

"My last picture grossed a billion dollars."

"Hong Kong dollars," said Louise.

"It's still a lot of money. There are more Chinese in the world
than anyone else. They all want to go to the movies."

"But what do I have to gain? How much laundry do I need
done?"

At that moment Anthony Go appeared from the galley, and
overheard. His face clouded over, darkened. "You repeated to her
what I told you?" he asked Johnny hoarsely.

Louise spoke a little too quickly, her mouth, as usual, a few
beats ahead of her brain. "I said laundry, not laundering." It wasn't
until the words fell out, and she saw how furious Anthony Go
looked, that she realized what she'd said. When she'd been a little
girl, her favorite fairy tale had been about the two princesses: one,
whose lips dripped diamonds as she spoke, the other, whose mouth
had belched forth toads. Louise had always tried to identify with the
first princess, but her habits of speech had made her the second.
"Oops," she said now.

She tried for her sweet, naughty, little girl smile, so long
inappropriate, but always in reserve. Anthony Go was clearly not
charmed. She could tell that, as Henry could. Henry had turned to
face them, was watching him anxiously, her hands gripping the
railing behind her. Go looked even stiffer than his natural bearing
and overstarched collar allowed. Whatever pretended overlay of ease
there had been in his yachting gear vanished. Anger played across his
face.

"Why Anthony, you look pissed," Louise said. "What happened
to inscrutable?" On a roll, Louise was unable to stop herself. She had
no real fear in her. Go was obviously a crook, for all his too-perfect

tailoring, his idealized life-style, in the jargon of the *Hong Kong Tatler*, which someone had given her to read. But she had known crooks before, in their Hollywood, white-collar version. She imagined that society in the bustling commercial port of Hong Kong was not that different from L.A., where the more publicized a criminal you were, the more celebrated you became. She had been at parties featuring both John Dean and John DeLorean, their presence guaranteeing it being an "A." Being friendly with her town's—in her words—"top scumbags" had done her nothing but good. Still, her main traffic with organized crime had been supplying several key players for *The Godfather*. But like method actors who learned to live their roles, Louise had crossed over the line into believing she understood evil simply by casting it.

Henry knew better. "I think it would be fun," she said quickly, "doing a picture with Johnny." Go was a contained man, as most Chinese were contained, rarely showing emotion. That he was allowing his fury with Louise to come through made Henry genuinely afraid. She giggled, half out of nervousness, half trying to lighten the atmosphere, to take it back to show business, where people only rooted for each other to fail, not to die.

"You thought it would be fun to suck dick swinging from a trapeze," Louise said.

"No, I didn't," said Henry, genuinely offended. "They didn't even have that scene in the script when I agreed to do it."

"They had a *script?*" Louise asked.

"I have succeeded in rounding up and destroying all but one copy of that particular movie," said Johnny Wong. "The one I can't get my hands on, that's in Mr. Go's office."

"I see," said Louise.

"Do you?" asked Anthony Go.

She sank back down into a deck chair, aware, finally, that a great deal was going on that she was not prepared for. Go moved around and over her, shadowing out the sun more than even the umbrella she sat under.

"They tell me that you are most clever and influential, Miss Felder. But perhaps you do not understand how important it is to all of us in the Chinese film industry that Johnny begins making films that are significant in the West."

"I wasn't aware that you were in the movie business," she said.

"I am in many businesses. I am in any business I choose to be."

"I see," said Louise.

"He must have a co-star acceptable to European audiences."

"Henry has no following in Europe."

"By Europe we mean all white people. Including Americans. We know what a favorite Henry is becoming in the United States. So it would be excellent if they could co-star together. Perhaps I could offer you some inducement to help that happen, as I offered her."

"Like what?"

"Shares in our company. The company that will be partnered in a joint venture to capitalize the movie Johnny has in mind."

"That's conflict of interest," said Louise. "I'm only amoral, not unethical."

"I'm sure we can think of something to tempt you." Anthony Go straightened his shirt, and stepped back underneath the canopy, his smile brightening, broadening, like a car being shifted into gear, as he moved toward the singer and his retinue.

"Well, I'm sure you can't," Louise called after him.

Johnny Wong got up from his chair and squatted next to hers, his knee poking at the side of her chair. "How about if he lets you live?" he said very softly.

A white-jacketed waiter struck a brass gong. "Luncheon is served."

BOOK TWO

◆

MID-LEVELS

EIGHT

◆

Wen she interviewed the man who had been walking his dog on Black's Link, Judith found out about the position of the bodies, and the pencil. Superintendent Leslie had stubbornly refused to give her even a glimpse of the postmortem report. In the absence of an actual suspect or suspects, there was no way to know what would happen in a trial, whether the pathologist would be called, whether the defense would challenge the results of his findings, whether the report would even be entered as evidence. All these explanations he gave to her. But she put it down to simple stubbornness, unwillingness to help. The few seamy details she knew from journalistic gossip hardly prepared her for what the witness had to say.

"I don't like talking about it any more than you enjoy hearing," the man said. He was Scottish, a strain of conqueror powerful in Hong Kong since the original colonizing. Life hadn't been hard on him. He was still a good-looking man at sixty-four, slightly bent in the shoulders, but otherwise fit, from walking his dog, a black Labrador that sat now at his slippered feet. The dog had its watery eyes on Judith, as if he would interview her in exchange. Ask questions why a woman should sit in such a respectable setting, stuffed furniture covered in gingham, poking for details of fellatio and murder.

The Scot's wife had died a few years before, a fact he told Judith at the start of the interview, apologizing for the cheerlessness of the place. He'd been reluctant to meet with her, arguing that everything he'd had to say, he'd told the police. But she'd managed to persuade him.

"I suppose I should offer you some tea," he said now, tight-lipped. He crossed his knees, making a halfhearted gesture of readiness to get up, hands on the faded lace loosely covering the arms of the flower print chair.

"That's all right. I doubt I could drink anything."

"I've lived here since I was twenty, and I never imagined that people could do that to each other."

"You mean the murder, or the sex?"

His eyes narrowed, as he searched her for sarcasm. "You're American, aren't you?"

"It wasn't anything national, I'm just interested in what exactly you meant."

"I meant the murder, of course." He shifted, impatiently.

"You take long walks around here often?"

"Several times a day. Angus is a territorial old man." He patted the dog. "He likes to mark his trees."

"Did you ever see them around before, that young couple?"

"I make it a point not to pry. If something's going on, unless it's my business, I stay away from it."

"I appreciate that. But did you ever see them before?"

"I might have."

"The parents are offering a reward for any information."

"I'm a Scot. That's supposed to excite me?"

"I wasn't suggesting that. But this is a particularly frustrating case. It's got to be very hard on them, losing their children, and being so in the dark."

"Are you making a pun?"

"A pun?"

"The boy being blinded . . ."

"Blinded?"

"That thing in his eye. I didn't know what it was, at first. Took me a bit of time to see it was an eraser. Just the end of it. What you get on a pencil." He shuddered. "They must have shoved it right into his eye."

"Good God."

"The papers just said he was stabbed with a sharp instrument."

"That's all they told us," said Judith.

"I suppose he was using it to do his homework."

"You saw them doing homework, then?"

"A few times. And other things."

"Making love?"

"I told you. I make it a point not to pry."

"Still, if you passed by there often, and they were there, you might have seen what they were doing."

"I have little time enough at my age to take in all there is in the world that's decent. Must less what's disgusting."

"I see," Judith said. "Did you notice anyone else around watching?"

"I wasn't watching."

"Did you ever observe anyone else who might have been?"

"No."

"Anyone hanging around who doesn't live near here?"

"Am I suppose to know everyone who lives here?"

"Well, it's a special neighborhood, the Peak. Hong Kong is a pretty small town. Walking as much as you do, you must know your neighbors."

"I mind my own business," he said, and ate a mint from the dish beside the chair, crunching it into the silence. The dog looked up at him. "They aren't good for you, Angus," he said and, realizing, held out the small round crystal dish to Judith.

"No, thank you. So did you notice anyone you knew to be strangers?"

"Some construction workers, but this is Hong Kong. There are always construction workers."

"Chinese?"

"Europeans don't have to do that kind of work."

"Were they there the afternoon of the murder?"

"I don't recall. I'm not even sure I walked down that far the afternoon they were killed. It was the next morning I found them, remember."

"So there was no one else watching them make love that day?"

He slid out of his slippers, started putting on his shoes. "If you'll excuse me, it's time for Angus's walk."

The dog began barking excitedly at the word. "Yes, yes, my friend. That's what I said."

"Do you mind if I walk with you?"

"As a matter of fact"—he tied his laces—"I do. I like being with my dog." He got up and went for the long leather leash hanging on the back of the front door, the dog nipping at his heels, following behind him.

The slickness of Hong Kong was evident even in its real estate brochures. The descriptions inside them, like the paper they were printed on, were high quality, glossy, and a little slippery.

Even the windows where Wolf, Simpson & Co. had its office were characterized as "high performance," as if the building had to match what was expected of the employees.

Kip had lived all her life in Hong Kong, but she was still dazzled by her city, enthralled by her workplace, as she walked to it. The granite-and-glass overpass connecting the waterfront of Central, linking ferry piers, bus depot, Mass Transit Railway, and various real estate developments of Hong Kong Land glittered as brightly as everything else. The ceiling of the footbridge network was tinted with silvery metallic stripes, seamed down the middle like a road divider. People streaming in both directions observed the unwritten rules of that particular road, driving their bodies at a coolly frenzied pace, staying to the side on which their traffic moved, as though they were in lanes. In spite of the crowds, they stayed respectful of each other, very much in a hurry to get where they were going, but seldom colliding. The pavement on which they walked was remarkably unlittered, renegade sunlight between the rush of feet illuminating bits of mica in the asphalt. So there was, even in that literally pedestrian place, a serving of flash.

Flash was the key, hypnotizing Kip, as it did everyone under the spell of Hong Kong. On the other side of the walkway from the Mandarin Hotel on Connaught Road was Exchange Square, where she worked, three sparkling glass-and-stainless-steel towers rising like a mirrored fortress. In the basement of Number One was the New Unified Hong Kong Stock Exchange, which guarded its operations with military secrecy. Security guards outside its doors stopped everyone who had no authorization to be there. Two secretaries inside barred the way of even those who did. No less vigilant were the watchdogs who managed the American Club on the top floor of the tower of Number Two, permitting no photographs, circumspect about visitors.

Kip knew that firsthand—it was her only dance with audacity, the one un-Oriental thing about her. Now and then she would go upstairs and use the ladies' room of the American Club, just to prove she could. It involved changing elevators, and her whole approach to life, setting aside training and attitude, not being deferential, forcing herself to be bold. Better than bold, actually impudent. That is, it would have seemed impudent, had she been caught. But she never was.

The ladies' room was more beautiful than the lobbies of most deluxe hotels she had walked through, dazzled, as glittering in its decor as the bars where Peter would take her, when he was being grandiose. Treating her as though she belonged among the Gweilos. As if he were proud to have her along, not just suffering her company in public, because he needed what she did for him in private. She would think of him, as she always thought of him, and a rush of heat would come up in her that was not so much about making love as anger, when she faced realistically how little he cared for her. When the fury became insupportable, she would go upstairs to the ladies' room, touch her cheek against the rose granite walls and Carrara marble to cool herself down. Turn the taps on the gold fixtures that ushered the water into the gold sinks, and splash some bracing liquid against her face. Each toilet stall was fitted with a deco light, in a soft shade of bronze neon. Taking her calm from the gentle luxury, she would urinate. Peeing on privilege, relieving her rage at how inequitable it was.

Alert as the lookouts were, they never stopped her. The first time she'd gone there, dressed in her business-suit best, she had assumed the bold air of one who belonged. She'd seen their eyes appraising her, watching them make the decision to let her go by. The second time—she'd been for lunch with Peter, who was meeting an American friend—she had smiled at the managers as though they were old friends of hers. Ever since, they'd been suitably confused, probably assuming she was a member. One of the rich Chinese who could afford to buy a membership as costly as a seat on the exchange downstairs.

It was a fix for her, that ladies' room, a shot of both richness and defiance. Making her understand that on the inside, at least, she was not as acquiescent as Peter thought she was.

Moving onto the escalator from the ground-floor entrance hall, she planned on going there just before lunchtime, when the Gweilos hadn't gathered, so it would be hers alone. A ladies' room for one whom white-skinned men considered less than worthy of being treated like a lady. Taking comfort from her but giving none.

The escalator up to the plaza was capped by a rotunda with gleaming lights. On either side of the moving stairs was a walled mosaic of yellow-brown rocks, through which flatly flowed a gentle stream of water. She felt an insistent press against her back, surprising, annoying. People in Hong Kong understood by nature how crowded the place was, and went to great effort not to touch, except in unavoidably congested times. Living with Peter in Mid-Levels, Kip could walk to work, making her way down the mazes of steps twisting like secrets into the streets of Central. So she never had to ride the MTR or Star Ferry at the height of the scramble, and be caught in the crush. Even the crush was usually polite, without fingers poking, as was happening now. She turned, irritated.

Behind her stood her brother. He took the finger from her back, pointing it at the flow cascading along the wall to the left. "Is that the famous waterfall that caused you to slip?"

"Give me a break, Chen," Kip said.

"You should have said that to the waterfall."

"What are you doing here?"

"Great-grandfather wanted me to come. He's worried about you."

"There's nothing to worry about."

"Try telling that to someone who can see into the future," the boy said.

They reached the landing. Early morning light, slightly hazy, silvered the floor-to-ceiling windows of the foyer, grayed the mirrored columns around the circular gazebo, rising three stories high. Trees, like dancers on the reflecting platinum floor, stretched toward the ceiling, trunks arching out of square patches of bare earth. The harbor beyond the glass fronting the foyer was alive with boats: steamers and ships of commerce, the ferry on its way from Kowloon to the terminal jammed with workers, sampans and fishing boats returning with their sunrise catch, slated for market. Rings of metal chains looped on posts between the metallic columns, protected the vista like guards at a museum.

"Nice," said Chen, looking around, obviously impressed in spite of himself. "Is this where you and Johnny Jardine will have your wedding reception?" he added, naming him sarcastically.

"Go home." Kip's heels clicked on the polished floors as she hurried toward the bank of elevators.

He quickened his pace. "What is there about home that I should find so wonderful? It isn't enough to hold *you*. Not what it *is*, not the thought of what it *means*, what your *family* means, what *pride* means."

"Then get a job," Kip said. "Do something to use up your energy besides drive me crazy."

"What kind of job?" he said. "I don't have the training or talent of my brilliant sister. I don't like computers."

"You don't like anything that requires discipline or effort. All you want to do is watch your stupid movies."

"Stupid?" He stepped back, as though she had struck him. "Stupid? They don't hurt you. They make you feel good. Not small and worthless."

"Nothing I do makes me feel small and worthless."

"What about what is *done* to you?"

Her face darkened. She pressed the call button. "What do you know about what is done to me? He does nothing to me but make me happy."

"Very happy," said Chen. "I can see by the corners of your mouth how happy you are. Great-grandfather did your *I-ching*. He said you are given no nourishment, and that is why you are pulled down at the corners of your mouth."

"He is a superstitious old man."

"He is wiser than anyone you know. Certainly wiser than that yellow-haired fop who treats you as his whore."

She turned and slapped him. The rest who were waiting at the elevators lowered their eyes, except for an American woman, who raised them, and caught the red fingermarks against his cheek.

Tears stung Kip's eyes. "I never thought . . ."—she faltered—"I never thought I'd hate my own brother."

"It isn't me you should hate," he said, very softly. "Hate the one who taught you what hate is. What prejudice is. By his country's fine example." He turned and walked away.

In the cubicle next to Kip sat Earnest, the name he'd given himself in English, easy to pronounce and appropriate for him. She was surprised he'd taken off his jacket. The office was completely air-conditioned, as were all the new buildings in Hong Kong, the oppressive humidity transformed into an almost liquid chill. He was a totally formal young man; she'd never seen him not in a suit and tie. Intense already, at eight o'clock in the morning, he burrowed into his end of the project they'd been assigned: working out a technology to help people get to work faster in Taipei. Taiwan was building an underground railway transit network to alleviate traffic problems in that crowded city, and a new computer system had just been introduced to handle administrative engineering, planning control, document service, personnel, accounting, and payroll for the project. Wolf, Simpson & Co. had been retained to design it.

He looked up for a moment, and smiled at her through the glass. She turned on her computer. He tapped in "Good Morning."

She mouthed "good morning" to him, and started working on her assignment, designing a program for data processing. From time to time she would look at the clock. The day crawled by. As she was leaving the office, Ernest stepped out into the hallway.

"Good evening," he said.
"I'm late," said Kip.
"It's good to see you, too." He smiled.

The apartment where Kip lived with Peter Sansome was on Conduit Road, in Mid-Levels. Cabdrivers, who, almost without exception spoke little English, responded to the directive "Conducto" in Cantonese. They whirled passengers to their destinations around a series of curves, across narrow concrete bridges, past small grocery stores carrying goods that appealed mainly to British appetites: barley water, digestive biscuits. The rents were quite high in the buildings along Conduit, where balconies fronted a view of the harbor. So except for the occasional local boy who had gone to Harvard and become a headhunter, the most disgraceful career a Hong Kong banker's son could turn to, there were few Chinese.

Kip was the sole Hong Kong Belonger in her building. She did not consider herself officially there, although Peter did allow her to have her name on the mailbox, and had the phone listed in her name. She was not quite sure this was a courtesy as much as a way he had of fielding calls from his soon-to-be ex-wife, who could reach him only at his office, since she didn't have his home phone number. The almost ex-wife knew about Kip, although Peter didn't tell her Kip's name. But he'd told her he was living with someone, a Chinese girl. Kip had overheard their conversations, as he assured his ex-wife there was no point in coming, it was over between them. He told her repeatedly. It was not as if Kip eavesdropped. He always placed the calls when Kip could hear, making it a point to take her hand and lead her to the bed and stretch her out beside him and fondle her while he got his wife on the line. He stroked her with his fingers, moving the tips of them down her throat and around her nipples while his voice stroked Valerie over the very-long-distance lines. He was always gentle with the woman in England, just as he was gentle with Kip, at least while he was talking to someone else. At some point he would take her hand, usually just after Valerie started crying, and put it on his zipper. She knew what to do after that.

He had her beside him when he made phone calls to any

woman. It was his way, he explained, of showing her he was faithful, even while being interested in other females. He was, after all, a man, just a *tad* past his sexual prime, having turned thirty the previous spring. But he jogged every morning and it gave him the energy of an eighteen-year-old, as she could see, he pointed out, by how hard he got, how fast, the moment her fingers went around him.

Surely she could not expect him not to be interested in other women with the amount of juice he had, which she could clearly attest to with the expertness of her stroke. He promised in spite of how unfaithful he might wish to be, he would stay sexually steadfast. At least for as long as it was good between them, which he assured her it was. Which he evidenced it was, especially when it was mouth instead of hand that she moved down on him, tongue and lips that performed the service. Trying to distract him from the voice on the other end of the line, which, ultimately, she managed to do, at least just before his climax, when he would say to the woman: "Oh, do forgive me, I've got a call on my other line." Or, "There's something coming in on my fax."

Always he would sign off with a "cheerio," just before he shot his stream, and remembered who he was really with. That it was some kind of subtle form of torture was not lost on Kip. She'd accused him of that once, using phone calls to other women to torment her. He'd seemed genuinely offended.

"Would you rather I'd call them behind your back?" he'd asked her. He had very blond hair, silky and sweeping, so it fell down over his eye. He was constantly pushing it back with his long-fingered hand, a hand much larger than most men's, almost large enough to accommodate his cock, though he preferred leaving that to Kip. At least when she was home.

The gesture of sweeping his hair away from his eyes seemed at once annoyed and imperious, two attitudes that, in Kip's estimation, characterized a great many Brits. She never expressed that opinion however, loving him as she did. Passionately. Sentimentally. Though what she could find to be sentimental about realistically escaped her. Still, she understood that sentiment had little to do with realism. Peter had explained that to her once, when he'd done his little favorite thing with the scarves. "Men are realistic," he'd told her, knotting. "They deal from their brains. Initiate. Women are reactive. They respond. Emotion. That's sentimental . . . as I have a tendency to be when I'm with you, beloved," he'd whispered, whisking silk over her tip.

His nose was very sharp, a chiseled nose, fine and thin at the bridge, whittled at the end. It was a nose that might have seemed imposing were it not part of an otherwise supple face, slightly fleshy in spite of careful diet and exercise. His eyes were heavily lidded, almost lashless, soft, as in a Flemish painting. With a chin rounded like a cherub, and skin to match, he looked the very picture of innocence. The outrage of his expression when she accused him of being unfair with her underlined what he assured her was his straightforward way of dealing. "Would you rather I'd call them from the office, so you wouldn't know?"

"I'd rather you wouldn't call them."

"But you know exactly where I stand. I've never been other than honest."

"I'd rather you'd be less honest and more faithful."

"I am faithful. I just like to talk to them."

"What would you do if I talked to other men?"

"Why, I would be delighted. You should make an outside life for yourself. You're wrong to be so dependent on me."

"But I love you," said Kip.

"And I love you," said Peter. "What underwear have you got on?"

When she came home from the office this day, she was already nervous about being late. Peter had given her the scenario for this particular evening before she'd left for work. He was fastidious about punctuality. She saw his umbrella, wet with souvenired rain from that afternoon's downpour, leaning against the wall of the entrance hall next to the elevator, a small puddle collecting around it. It was a typical British umbrella, big and black and ready for a tour around Hyde Park, half a world away. She felt a little spurt of fondness for his tribal customs, even as she fought anxiety at his probable reaction to her tardiness. But he was not waiting for her as she unlocked the door, not standing there glowering as she half expected to find him. The door to his study was ajar. She could see his socks as he stretched his feet onto the ottoman by his brown leather chair. He did not speak at the sound of the door closing, so she hurried inside her room to change.

The school uniform was hanging on the back of the closet door where he'd told her it would be, back from the cleaners, immaculate again, no sign of the thick crusty stain that had been on the stripe of the tie, white blouse and navy skirt fresh. She slipped out of her *chungsam* and put on the new black lingerie he'd laid out on the bed. Closing the buttons on the blouse, tight so her breasts would be flattened beneath it, she pulled the skirt on. The hem fell just below her panties, several inches above her knees. Knotting the striped tie, she reached into the closet for the navy blue jacket with the school emblem sewn onto the pocket. She put on white knee socks, and laced up her brown shoes. Then, pinning her hair back with flat barrettes, she took a deep breath, and went in to his study.

He had his shoes back on. He sat in the chair, smoking a pipe, a copy of the *Asian Wall Street Journal* opened across his lap. He did not look up as she entered the room.

"Good afternoon, sir," she said, and did a little curtsy.

"Good afternoon." He closed the paper and looked up at her. Smoke from the pipe made his soft face look even softer, obscuring the twinkle in his eyes. "Were you a good girl today?"

"I think so, sir."

"Well, don't you *know*? School is where we go to *know* things."

"I'm not as smart as I should be, sir."

"Well, you'd know if you'd done anything naughty, wouldn't you?"

"Yes, sir."

"Have you done anything naughty?"

"Not yet, sir."

"Would you like to?"

"Oh, yes, sir, please."

"Very well," he said, and set aside the paper. She reached for the buckle of his belt. "The shoes," he said. "Start with the shoes."

"Yes, sir. Excuse me, sir." She knelt at his feet and started unlacing his shoes. Her fingers were shaking.

"Take your time. No rush."

"Thank you, sir." She slipped off first one shoe, then the other. Then the socks. She pulled his toes, stroking them one by one, rubbing a stretched-out finger between them.

"That was very well done."

"Thank you, sir."

"You don't have to be bright because you're very good with your hands."

"I'm glad, sir."

"Almost as good as the little girls in Bangkok. Now you may do what you wanted to do before."

"Oh, can I, sir?"

"May I. You mustn't forget your lessons, good little schoolgirl that you are."

"May I, sir?"

"You may."

She could feel his eyes watching her as she opened his belt. The clasp caught in her fingers. There was already a thick bulge in his pants, straining the zipper as she eased it downward. She put her fingers just inside so the metal wouldn't catch his skin. He seemed to be smiling with approval, but she couldn't see clearly through the smoke.

"You're a very good girl."

"Oh, no, I'm not, sir. I want to do dreadful things."

"You do?"

"Oh, very much, sir."

"Well, go ahead then."

"You won't tell my mother?"

"You may be sure of that," he said, "or my mother either."

She reached inside his boxer shorts, sprung him free. His erection was enormous.

"Did you do that?"

"I think so, sir."

"Well, what are you going to do about it?"

"This, sir," she said, sticking out her tongue, pointing it downward like a shaft. "That is, if you'll permit me."

"Oh, very well," he said and, raising his buttocks in the air, slid his trousers and shorts off, onto the floor.

"Too hard," he said, after a moment.

"Sorry, sir," she murmured, as best she could. She gave herself over to it completely, loving the texture of him against her tongue, the pressure inside her cheeks, the feeling of him swelling in her mouth. It was all he gave her of power.

"Now," he said, and took her under the armpits, and raised her onto the chair, so she straddled him.

"But my underwear, sir."

"Underwear?" His cock bobbed, massive. "Have you got on your little schoolgirl panties?"

"Not exactly, sir."

"What have you got on, then?"

She stood up on the chair, her feet planted on either side of his knees, and raised her skirt. He gave a little gasp.

"Oh what a wicked bitch you are."

"Thank you, sir," she said.

He ran his fingers around the tight elastic band, reached inside it. "We'd better take these off. You could get into a lot of trouble wearing black lace panties."

"I hope so, sir," she said.

He brought her down very hard on top of him, ramming her, without even touching her first. But she was already wet.

"Open your blouse."

She started to take it off, riding him.

"Leave it on," he wheezed. "Just unbutton your blouse."

She did. He put his hand inside the black lace of her brassiere and squeezed her nipple, shuddered, shouted over his orgasm, a bellow that shook the frames of the French doors to the balcony. She fell against his chest, kissed his neck, struggled for his mouth.

He pulled away from her and smiled. "You're a good little pervert."

"I'm not a pervert!"

"Of course you are. Why would you do this if you weren't a pervert?"

"I love you."

"How can you love a pervert, unless you're a pervert?"

"Are you sure that's what you are?"

"I'm sure that's what we both are, beloved." He kissed her lightly on the lips. "Otherwise, how could we possibly have such a good time?"

It was a question that riddled her sleeping, when she could sleep. In the darkness, she raised herself up on one elbow beside him, stared down into his perfect English face, so boyish, so fair. So free of mischief. Or was it? Caught as he was in dreaming, angelic with the moonlight beaming in on him, he seemed to have a smile on his face. She wondered if it was satisfaction. Or was it just the slightest bit of a sneer, mocking? Because depravity was its own reward, just as much as virtue.

NINE

♦

Tripping her way down concrete steps zigzagging through the streets in Mid-Levels, Claire arrived at Queens Road, Central. It seemed to her the brightest and happiest day of her life. The streets were clogged with double-decker red buses, taxicabs, limousines, an occasional tourist-laden rickshaw. Sounds assaulted her ears like overeager, abrasive kisses: air brakes, metallic squeals, horns. All of it enlivened her, as the kisses would have a teenager who knew nothing of technique, but everything about loneliness.

Having spent most of her adolescent life fearful that no one would ever love her, her young adult life learning that being loved could create as many problems as it solved, Claire faltered on the threshold of middle age trying to cope with her feelings of abandonment. When Charley had gotten sick, it had never occurred to either of them that the illness could be grave. Fear in Beverly Hills, where they lived, was about failure, about money. Claire had labeled their community "The Capital of *Schadenfreude*," a German word that meant joy in other people's disasters. As all the world had been a stage for Shakespeare, in Los Angeles all the world was a restaurant—most particularly Spago, a glittering, noisy, celebrity-studded eatery where only success was served, and then, with very small portions.

When the diagnosis came up cancer, she had gone into a kind of sleepwalk. The word alone struck such terror into the mind and body that holistic practitioners believed the sound of it hastened the dying process. Charley was so big and hearty. Like most anxious men in their forties in a high-stress society, he'd been waiting for his heart attack. To be struck with a degenerative illness seemed an insult to him: he took great personal offense. Just as he had been impeccable in his personal habits, looking always as though he'd just stepped out of the shower, he'd been an example of good health, appearing younger, stronger than his contemporaries.

Once the initial shock was over, like the hard worker she was, Claire had rallied out of her stupor to become an expert on the disease. On-the-job training, Charley had called it, sort of laughing. It seemed to be the on-the-job training for everyone, including the doctors, the disease was so mysterious. No one had sure answers. Oncologists were burned out from losing patients. It seemed to Claire nobody told the whole truth because they didn't want to say there was nothing they could do. They put Charley through the conventional chemical therapies, and after he was sickened past the point where he could continue, admitted the treatment wouldn't have saved him anyway.

So Claire got on the phone to Bermuda and Germany, where there were experimental so-called cures, and smuggled in Italian drugs that supposedly enhanced the immune system. None of it did much good, except to give him hope, and a respite from the poisons. He lasted eleven weeks, from diagnosis to death. She lay in his arms and sang to him of crystal streams and lavender mountains, made daydreams into songs, as she stroked him, and put his hands on her breasts, so she'd remember the feel of them.

She sang to him of ministering angels, all the love she felt, all the love they felt for each other, which came as a comforting surprise. They'd known they had passion and anger and forgiveness, but neither of them had ever imagined how deep it went. He would curl her hair with what was left of the strength in his fingers, and tell her she was the best, the most beautiful, the sweetest, the most gifted. And she would say, as she'd said her whole life to praise, still not sure, "Do you really think so?" And he would say, "Yes. But then, I'm on drugs."

Even at the end he gave her laughter, along with the rest of it. She understood finally what it meant to love with the soul. So she was sure she had written the last of her songs. Charley had been more than support for her, he had been a creative buttress, reinforcing her shaky self-esteem. His validation had stirred her creative fires. When his light went out, she was sure that hers had, too. That her gifts had gone with him, along with all there was in the world of unconditional loyalty and masculine affection.

A singer friend made an album of the music Claire had written for Charley. Claire was sure that had been her swan song, as well as his—that inspiration was dead in her. Walking through Central now, with the feel of James Bingham's mouth still on her lips, the taste of him on her tongue, she could feel little pings of joy, like a triangle in a symphony orchestra, starting in a corner of her spirit. Pieces of melody sounded. She wondered if it was song coming back, or life coming back. She was aware of the shiny straight black hair on the heads bobbing in front of her, the press of bodies around her, the remarkable absence of offensive odors, considering how hot and humid it was. Instead came the delicious redolence of herbs from open doorways, a smell like salt from butchered ducks hanging darkly crisped, upside down in glassed-in storefronts, looking curiously appetizing, except for their bills.

It had been so long since she'd felt a part of a place. Beverly Hills had been an agony for her, bringing up all her worst fears about herself, that she wasn't good enough, that people judged instead of cared. All of it had been intensified by the anguish it had caused Charley, the constant reminder of the success he hadn't had. She'd tried to get him to move, but he'd stubbornly clung to the environs, honoring the system that rejected him, instead of himself. "Where would we go?" he'd asked her, and she'd answered, "Anywhere." And now, that was where she was.

Strangely at home, curiously free, in this place where there were no real ties, no connection to or recollection of Charley. Fitzgerald had said there were no second acts in American lives, but he had never been a widow. Nor, to the best of Claire's knowledge, had he ever been in Hong Kong.

Far away—how far away exactly was it? Geography had been her worst subject—were her realities. The children, tethering her to earth as they'd once been tethered inside her, were mercifully in the hands of the housekeeper, a woman Claire knew she could count on. Also on the scene was Claire's mother, who'd flown in from Washington. ("On her broom?" Claire's son had asked.) Considering that the boy and girl were well into their teens, it had taken Claire long enough to trust her mother to be a grandmother. "Anyone would think I didn't like children," Evelyn had said, waiting for Claire to say that was the truth, which both of them knew. But Claire, for once, hadn't risen to the bait.

There was a break on the right side of the street, in between the narrow sidewalks, a tiny alleyway bordered with stalls, lined with rolls of shimmering satins, thick bolts of gabardines. WING-ON STREET, it read on the building that sided it. Moving out of the flow of pedestrian traffic, she entered the alley, pausing for a moment at the top of the slight incline to take it all in. Colors blazed at her, a Chinese Arabian night, silken sails that could carry her into any adventure. Judith had given her the name of a tailor in Kowloon who could make up clothes for her. Pulled, magnetized, she moved down the alleyway, smiling at the waiting hawkers. "Silk, lady?" asked bony Chinese in rolled-up shirt sleeves, cigarettes dangling from their mouths. "Looking for silk?"

"Love," she said, sure they would not understand. "I'm looking for love."

The Star Ferry carried her across the harbor to the second half of her enterprise. Laden with plastic bags filled with yards of fabric, she crossed the glistening waters, wondering if there was anything in Hong Kong that did not shine. Water everywhere, all over the world, but none with this intense a sparkle. She wondered if it was because her eyes were more open than they'd been before she understood how quickly life could be taken away. Or was it that gloom lifted, sharpened what was bright?

Sea gulls shrieked above her head. Warm winds threaded through her hair. She leaned out the window at the prow of the boat, smiling with a sense of familiarity at the huge neon signs she had seen from Judith's balcony, as though, close up, by day, they were friends with whom she'd been out dancing the night before. Behind her glittered Hong Kong side, with its total absence of city planning, no architectural overview, a raucous work of high-tech art, slick with mirrored finishes, silver and deep satiny brown. As the ferry came nearer to Kowloon side, she saw the clock tower that once signaled the finish of the trans-Siberian railroad trip from Europe. Near it stood the recently constructed domed space museum, its exterior a dull, white plaster. Just beyond the ferry landing sloped the new gray-stone art museum, which, according to Judith, was designed to be shaped like a butterfly, its most controversial feature the total absence of windows. City architects who'd been assigned the projects had announced that art should be its own distraction. As the building was to house painting exhibitions, they wanted no competition from the view. These were the same men who had designed many of the city's public toilets. To Claire it looked less like a butterfly than a ski jump for the suicidal. The most spectacular city view in the world and men had elected to block it out.

In front of her lay the jumble of Kowloon, with its electronic advertisements, flashing even by day. Street vendors held out ties to her. "One hundred percent silk," they promised.

She stopped for a moment, tempted. It had been a long time since she'd bought a gift for a man. Her son was not yet out of his awkward time, still classifiable as a boy. "Why don't you save this for someone with bad taste?" he'd say when she bought him a shirt, with what she earnestly hoped was only a facet of adolescent perversity.

"I'd get the red one," said a familiar voice. "Unless he's a banker, or the last conservative gay."

She turned and saw Louise Felder. "My God, what are you doing here?"

"My god had nothing to do with it, as Mae West might have said, if she couldn't get laid in California and had to come all the way to Hong Kong."

There was an awkward pause between them. It was Claire who leaned in for a kiss.

"I would have called," said Louise. "But death gives me gas."

"I forgive you," said Claire.

"Don't forgive me. You make me feel guilty. It's one of the

reasons I had to drop you as a client." They started to walk toward Nathan Road.

"I loved your last songs. I bought Kerry's tape and played it all the time in my car, and made a vow I was going to drive over and see you, but I just couldn't do it. I just couldn't face you. What could I say? What can I say now?"

"Hello is good," said Claire.

"How old was he?"

"Forty-four."

"Younger than I am," said Louise. "Though we won't say by how much lest they do another piece on me in the *National Enquirer*. Look at that building." She nodded her head toward the space museum across from the Peninsula Hotel. "It looks like the nuclear reactor at San Onofre." She turned and indicated the green Bentleys parked around the fountains in the forecourt of the hotel. "These poor bastards are just trying to keep up a front. Who would stay here with that view?"

"Why are you here besides that it makes me feel good to see you?"

"I have a client. Why would you be happy to see me? What's the matter with you? How could he die like that? God, I hate getting old."

"You're not old."

"Trust me," said Louise. "Remember how we used to worry about getting fat? Fat seems kind of adorable now. Fat you can always get thin. But old, you can never get young."

She took a deep breath, sighed almost, although what it sounded more like was a little rush of despair. "What kind of a world is this? Remember how young we all were? Desperate for fame. Love? Well, you, at least, found it.

"That's why I couldn't call or come. I didn't know what to say. I was so afraid. Because if this happens to the people who found love, what about the ones who never did? I would have had to face all these things in myself, and say them to you. And . . ." She swallowed, hard. "I don't know how to keep up conversations when they have real content."

She stopped, turned, and looked at Claire. Her eyes, strangely, had stayed exactly the same, filled with mischief and the promise of something true, little darts of yellow light in their brown, like sincerity hiding behind sham. "But I remember. . ."—there were tears in them, suddenly—"I remember how funny he was. And how sweet. And I remember. . . how much he loved you." She turned and bolted into the entrance of the Peninsula.

For a moment Claire started to go after her. It was Louise's M.O., always, to end conversations when she wanted to end them, to flee, to hang up the phone, to turn away. Claire understood it was true, what her once closest friend had explained: she didn't know what to say. In the past, Claire had been as tenacious in that friendship as she'd been in other aspects of her life, refusing to let Louise escape, calling her back, writing her notes. But every time they'd caught up with each other after Louise had dropped the curtain, it was more than anticlimax. There had been a brick wall. Finally, Louise had shut her out completely, terminating her as a client, refusing to take her calls, closing her out as a friend.

Now, for the first time in any of their encounters, Claire chose not to pursue. It was a difficult action for her, against her nature. But she'd been suffused with self-help books, given by well-meaning friends during Charley's illness, on how to let go. They had been some comfort to her; she'd tried to learn from them. Not until she'd realized there was nothing she could do to keep Charley with her had she been able to ease him lovingly and with grace into death. So she realized she had no choice with Louise. You couldn't keep someone in your life who didn't want to be in it, any more than you could make someone live who was dying. The only alchemy in the world, the only true transformation, was in yourself.

Even knowing that, she was filled with regret and loneliness, wishing Louise hadn't run away. Hefting her plastic sacks heavy with folded silk prints for blouses, phosphorescent fabrics for evening dresses, Claire turned the corner onto Nathan Road. Evening dresses. She echoed the phrase in her mind. In Beverly Hills, unless you were part of the tinsel and glitter the way Louise was, more accurately, sequins and bugle beads, there were hardly any nights you could consider "evenings," much less occasions on which to dress for them. But Claire was caught in Hong Kong's compulsivity, the conviction, along with an adrenaline rush, that because things were less expensive than in a place where ordinarily you wouldn't buy them, it was important to buy them even if you had no use for them. A way of making money, really, in a city where the illusion flourished that letting milk spill out of a pot meant you would always have something to drink.

On the way to meet James Bingham for lunch at the Regent Hotel, Kowloon side, she bought him the tie. According to some psychotherapists, too much giving was really a way of controlling, and although Claire could see the possible truth of that assertion, it made her happy to give presents. It lifted her that there was once again a man to give them to. She picked out the red tie, as Louise had suggested, trying not to think about Louise. A grieving mind became obsessive, tried to figure out how it could change the unchangeable.

She held the tie out to James as he rose to greet her. "You shouldn't have," he said, beaming, convincing her she should have, no matter what therapists said.

"I shall put it on this instant." He loosened his own tie, holding the new one in the twist of his fingers. Around them in the lobby of the Regent, with its panoramic floor-to-ceiling windows, hotel-wide, people chattered and drank and marveled at the view the government architect who'd designed the museum had obliterated. Just outside a woman in a sampan poled her way past the luxury she had no time to see.

"Outstanding," James said, puffing out his chest, the newly knotted tie in place for her approval. "Excellent taste."

"It looks like you."

"How sweet you are." He put his hand on hers.

She could feel the hairs on the tops of her arms move.

After lunch, he took her back across the harbor to the market at Wanchai. Ancient cobblestones bulged beneath their feet. Old women in gray clothes squatted close to their stalls, selling meats and cakes and knives and machetes, carving pineapples into pagodas.

Cages at the base of gray wooden stands held penned-up ferrets. Open vats with snakes, curling in water, flanked caged frogs scaling the sides of their bamboo pens. The streets were unwashed, the smell from the reptiles slightly rank. And yet, with it all, there was about the place an air of the erotic.

Claire wondered if it was in her, not the atmosphere; if sex, like beauty, was in the eyes—or in this case, the thighs—of the beholder. She had let James kiss her repeatedly the night before, but only kiss her, as if she were the queen of a widow's prom. It was too soon, she was sure, too fast, to let it go any further, protecting a virtue outdated and very far away. Was Charley really gone? Was it long enough? Would he be ashamed of the heat that had given him such pride when it was for him?

What she longed for, she was sure, more than sex, was affection. What she missed more than someone inside her was the comfort of touch. During his illness, a close friend, a smart woman, had sent Claire a masseuse, as a gift, to keep her body together so she wouldn't fall ill with Charley, as partners of those with mortal diseases too often did. After he died, the masseuse had given Claire an oil called Auraglow, soothing, smelling deliciously of almonds. She'd told Claire to use it at least once a week, to "acknowledge" her breasts. But Claire could not rub it on her nipples without weeping. It wasn't fingers she wanted, not just her own touch, but the feel of that masculine hand: the warm, slightly downy presence, that even when gentle, weighed slightly heavy on the chest. Charley had loved her breasts, not just acknowledged them. He had stroked them and sucked them and marveled at them, how full they were, how lush, how high, in spite of their weight, and the two children. Just the sight of her breasts had been enough to arouse him. Now, when she showered or dressed, she averted her eyes from her own nudity, for fear she would remember how he'd feasted on her body.

She had a fine carnal appetite. But now she felt less hunger for the wanton than the sweet communion of skin. The warmth of flesh. It did not even have to come with caring, she felt so empty.

James put his arm carelessly on her shoulder. A tremor went through her, at the unaccustomed pressure between neck and collar-bone, a familiarity she had forgotten. For all her yearning for the hand on her breast, lips on her mouth, a congress of tongues, this went deeper. It was so routine, so commonplace and filled with friendliness, she had not even remembered it till she felt it again: male companionship. She moved into his touch, turned her cheek toward the back of his hand, felt the light coating of hair against her face. And ached. Ached for how good it felt, so different from sex and yet so much a part of it, that informal male touch to which she'd become so accustomed, but had forgotten, until he reached for her.

They walked for a while like that, through Wanchai Market. A woman scoring pineapple with a knife that was more properly a small machete, cut swiftly with diagonal strokes, carving it into a tower, offered them a taste.

"You have to take it or she'll be offended," he said.

The sweetness dripped from Claire's lips. He wiped it with his mouth, drinking her overflow. "You have to take it, or I'll be offended," he whispered.

"What made you come to Hong Kong?" she asked, when she could speak, trying not to believe it was destiny, a gift from the universe to her.

"I opened a local branch of my father's business." They started walking again.

"Is he a banker, too?"

"I never said I was a banker. I said I was in banking."

"What exactly do you do?"

"I'm a pirate."

"I like unusual occupations."

"Not so unusual in Hong Kong." He guided her around a woman sweeping the street in front of her stall. "How do you write your songs? Tinkle them out at the old eighty-eight?"

"I sing them. I hear them in my head. I go for walks and sing. The only one walking in Beverly Hills, besides the Mexican maids. People use their cars to go to the corner mailbox."

"Beverly Hills. Everybody's dream."

"Everybody's dream," she said, trying not to let the irony sound.

"And you just walk around there singing your heart out?"

"Not anymore. I haven't written any music since Charley died. Tell me about your wife."

"She was vain and shallow."

"Why did you marry her?"

"I was a bit vain and shallow myself."

"And young," Claire said. "You're still so young."

He stopped walking, and turned her toward him, placed the fleshy mound at the base of his thumb against her jaw. She could feel the pulse in his wrist on her throat, turned her head, opened her mouth to taste him.

"You're *so* sweet," he said, kissing her. Something went through her like grief. Nobody had ever known how sweet she was except Charley. Her mother had called her wicked. Her friends had thought her clever. But only Charley had marked how sweet she was. He'd actually called her "sweet." Tears sprung to her eyes, because it was more than a kiss that was happening. It was recognition, appreciation, all that had been missing.

He kissed her again. A sigh came out of her. That, of course, she had remembered, longed for, tasted the night before: another's mouth. His was lightly coated with mint, the candy he'd popped between her lips and his at the end of the meal, little bursts of pineapple around the edges, so he tasted fruity and slightly sharp all at once. Behind the flavor was his warmth, dancing against her tongue, drawing her in with a subtle suction. She wanted to be part of him, fill him up with what was empty in her.

"We better go somewhere," he whispered.

"We are somewhere," she said.

"Don't be smart, now. I already know you're smart. It's the rest I have to find out."

They went back to his apartment, in Mid-Levels, on Robinson Road. It was a young apartment, as he was young, disorganized, with the flung-about decor of youth. But she did not see it clearly; she saw only him, how beautiful he was. He took her clothes off slowly, as though they were petals on a flower, sipped her in layers, like a stingless bee. And she opened to him as a flower would, the gazania that bloomed in Southern California, spreading in the sun, petals straining toward the light, and the heat.

He took his time. He touched her everywhere. Stroked every inch of her, even the hollows behind her knees. Caressing her with both sides of his hands, he trailed her nipple with the soft buff of his nails. She was almost screaming.

His mouth was on her mouth. She all but drank his tongue, so greedy and anxious was she to suck him in. "Easy," he whispered. "No biting. I know how hungry you are."

And she was ashamed because she was so eager. Eager and transparent. Then apology vanished, and all she had a sense of was him. His becoming part of her. Comforting the deprivation. Every young man who had passed her by. The young Adonis who'd ignored her at the prom. Indifferent, irresistible boys who never knew what she had to offer. Those who had seen, maybe for a moment, before they'd thrown her away. She was the girl she'd been so long before, when nobody cared. As nobody had ever cared until Charley carved her from her amorphous clay, into the lovely, accomplished, desirable woman she'd become, except in her own imagination.

In her arms was the love she'd missed as a teenager. She was young again, loss and grief and confusion generating their own fountain of youth, spitting her back out into the world with all her experience peeled away. She was once more the ungainly, unlovely adolescent her mother had promised would be unloved forever. But present now, filling her with heat, the old, longed-for completeness, was the beautiful lost lover she'd never had, along with the one she had had who'd left so unexpectedly. Passions remembered. Passions forgotten. And some she'd never realized.

Gratefully she clung to him, gently clawing at him, trying not to devour him with her mouth. Weeping as she raised her hips to welcome him. Becoming a part of his rhythm.

He plunged all the way inside her, and she was full again. Full as she had been hollow. And she came with the force of a Sousa marching band, loud and clear, with a lot of brass.

"Outstanding," said James, and kissed her.

TEN

◆

"But what does it mean exactly?" Louise asked. She was seated at Dao Tsim's feet on the floor of his roseate room, incense sweetly suffusing her nostrils. She tried to tell herself the whole thing was ridiculous, indeed had told Henry all the way there that it was foolish to go for a reading. Louise didn't believe in such things, she insisted, no matter how much she would have liked to represent Shirley MacLaine.

Henry, however, could be just as stubborn as Louise. And just as proud, her pride stemming oddly from the same place as that of most Westerners: her own insecurity. Dao Tsim was her only aristocratic relative, and she wanted to parade him to Louise. At the same time, she needed to show Louise to him, so he'd see that his prophesy was being fulfilled: that Henry would become a major film star, and the filthy part of her life was over. Her brain, which was far from small, had been conveniently asleep. A kind of self-hypnosis had taken over during the porno filming. A preoccupation with goals had distracted her attention from what she was actually doing. She had been in the grip of the little girl who had her fortune told, assured she would glitter as brightly as the stars in the heavens. Or brighter. Success was more tangible than astronomy, and so more relevant in Hong Kong.

Now they waited, the two women, for the mystical pronouncements of the impressive ancient. Little as Louise believed, or believed she believed, there was a certain breathlessness in waiting, a tendency to gulp and hold the inhalation in. Dao had charted the year of her birth, which she had lied about initially, but the year she had given him made her born in the year of the Snake, and it was a little too symbolic for her. She had decided to trust him, and Henry, too, swearing them to secrecy. The truth had made her a Dog, which she supposed she could handle, though she would have preferred being a Cock, so she could tell everyone back in Beverly Hills. Better to be one than need one, she was already rehearsing as a wisecrack. But Dog would have to do, especially since knowing the accurate year, Dao complimented her on having all her own teeth, something she found at once ingenuous and offensive.

He had already told her what her good years had been. They were too long ago to please her. Seeing them written down like that, she realized she should have taken advantage of her youth, instead of barreling through it. On her way to what? She had achieved everything she'd dreamed of achieving, except for the one thing she'd never really dared believe could come to her. Her accomplishment, like a jackpot that had been won by the player immediately before, had yielded up only what she'd put in. Cynicism. Comedy, with an undercoat of despair. Affection that was, at its core, loveless.

"What it means," Dao Tsim was saying in answer to her question, "is that you must take advantage of the here and now. This is the best year for you since 1964."

"When I wasn't even born yet," Louise said, and smiled her cutesy smile, which had worked so well that long-ago winter. At least she'd thought it was working, till the man she'd loved betrayed her.

"There is a Pig waiting for you."

"I'm not surprised."

"He means a man born in the year of the Pig," Henry explained. "That goes well with a Dog."

"Almost as well as a Rabbit," said Dao Tsim.

"I couldn't handle a Rabbit." Louise shifted her legs, which she had underneath her, in a position of half kneeling. She felt embarrassed at how worshipful it must look, as if any minute "Lifestyles of the Rich and Famous" might burst through the doors and discover her not being skeptical. "Andre Sherman said I would eat my young," she said, mentioning the promoter who'd dazzled and deceived her, as he had everyone, including himself. Where was he now? Probably a part of the stadium where Jimmy Hoffa was chopped up and cornerstoned. "Imagine if I had a lover who was a Rabbit."

"A Rabbit can be very strong," said Dao Tsim. "Gentleness doesn't mean weakness."

"It does where I live."

"Maybe you should leave that place," Dao said to his great-grandniece.

"It's all right," said Louise. "I'll protect her."

"You would do well to protect yourself," said Dao Tsim. "Although the Pig will be glad to do it for you. You will meet him on a boat."

"Don't give me any false expectations."

"All expectations are false," said Dao Tsim.

"He has a weird philosophy for a fortune-teller," said Henry. The doorbell rang. Henry got to her feet. "I'll answer it, Po-po."

He nodded his thanks, and turned his attention back to Louise's chart. "This is the turning point for you."

"I helped put together that package."

"Why do you talk so fast?" Dao Tsim asked. "And about things that have no meaning? Are you afraid people won't find you interesting if you don't have a history?" He lit his pipe. Pungent tobacco smoke rose from the ivory bowl, half obscuring the wizened gaze.

"I happen to be one of the most fascinating women of my generation," she said hotly. "Don't you read *Lear's*? I'll send you a subscription."

"I want no gifts from you."

"And I don't want any from you," she said, wondering why she was so upset. Her feet were asleep under her, and she was sorry she had ever agreed to come. She had no wish to insult the old man, but she was angry at him, and Henry, and everybody who shoveled hope. Hope was the thing with feathers, according to Emily Dickinson, but according to Louise, Hope was just another movie star whose day was over.

"Why so irritated?"

"Who's irritated? I didn't want to come here. Why do I need you telling me what my good years were? I know what my good years were, and believe me they weren't as hot as Liz Smith reported."

"Another actress?"

"A gossip columnist. Where've you been living, on the moon?" She reddened. "I'm sorry. I don't mean to be rude. It's just . . ." She felt tears in her eyes, which stunned her, even as they stung her lids. "I hate it that someone makes me think things can change. I spent the whole first half of my life believing things could change, and they never did, not the way I wanted them to. I put so much into it, into these people, and none of them care. None of the parties are as much fun as they sound, when you know there'll be no one taking you home who really gives a shit. Excuse me. Castles are cold. Down comforters don't give you real comfort.

"But neither does believing there's something good waiting. Because that's all over for me. It was never there." She wiped her nose with her sleeve. "My mother would be so embarrassed that I still don't carry Kleenex. She didn't raise me to be sentimental. Just to clean up after myself."

"Will you be much longer?" Henry said from the doorway.

"It's over," said Louise, and tried to stand up, but she couldn't feel her legs. "I hate it when poor circulation ruins an exit."

"It's your friend the Superintendent," said Henry.

"Tell him I will only be a few minutes."

"Don't wait on my account," said Louise, stretching her legs out, massaging them.

"You can come in," Henry said.

"Good morning," said Clement Leslie. "Forgive me. I didn't mean to interrupt." He was wearing a safari suit, curiously crisp in the wilting heat, khaki pockets buttoned sharply over his chest. His posture made him look bigger than he was, a certain brave, soldierly stance having become a part of his bearing. "I thought you never did readings in the morning."

"You were correct," said Dao Tsim. "But this is a very special woman. My great-grandniece's Hollywood agent."

"Louise Felder," she said, and held out her hand. "Forgive me for not getting up, but I'm auditioning for the part of Freud's patient. The one with hysterical paralysis."

"I saw that movie," said Clement.

"I'm so glad. I was beginning to think I was in 'The Twilight Zone.'"

"Detective Superintendent Leslie." He shook her hand.

"James Robertson Justice."

"I beg your pardon?"

"The British actor. The one with the gravelly voice. That's who could play you, if he were still alive. Do you know if he's still alive?"

"I'm afraid I don't."

"I'll put in a call to London. But even if he is, he'd be too old to play you. Maybe we can get Anthony Hopkins to grow a beard." She shifted onto her knees. "I think it's coming back," she said. "Would you help me up?"

He leaned over and put his hand under her elbow, raised her to her feet. "Is that all right?"

"I can walk! I can walk! It was my father! He abused me! Or did I abuse him? I can't remember. Do you remember that part of the plot?"

"I only remember Montgomery Clift and Larry Parks."

"Larry Parks," Louise said, and touched Clement's cheek. "You're my kind of guy. Naturally I was just an infant at the time of *The Jolson Story.* But I saw it on television. I don't suppose you're a Pig?"

"We don't call policemen that in Hong Kong."

"I mean your birth year. Not that I believe in that sort of thing."

"I'm a Dragon," said Clement.

"Not good for you," said Henry.

"You're in no position to judge," said Louise, and handed Clement her card. "Let me know if you'd like to do character parts when the Chinese take over."

"I'll be long gone," said Clement.

"Maybe so will character parts. Maybe there'll be nothing left but violence and cartoons and Japanese monsters and Dolby stereo. But call me anyway, if you get to L.A." She hobbled out of the room.

"Good to see you, Henry," said Clement, as the girl followed after. He waited till he heard the door close. "What's a Hollywood agent doing in Hong Kong?"

"I told you," Dao Tsim said. "She represents my great-grandniece."

"Are they going to make a movie here?"

"Perhaps. Henry said something about a film with Johnny Wong."

"I heard he was trying to change his image. But that seems a little extreme."

Dao Tsim lowered his eyes. "Henry does not do that kind of movie anymore."

It had been suggested by Henry's agent that the interview be conducted on a sampan. For Judith it seemed a pleasant enough prospect, if a little slight, a piece on Henry Wu. Unaware of Henry's earlier films, all Judith was familiar with was the pitch: Henry Wu, Hong Kong's first major international movie star. The interesting part of being Bureau Chief in her present post was that all stories, from assassinations and coups in neighboring countries to the murder on Black's Link, fell onto Judith's plate. So she got to write not only hard news, finance, and the arts, but also about the occasional ditsy starlet passing through.

Walking through Central now, on her way to the port, Judith noted how filtered the day looked, the strangely golden aura of the Orient. It softened what was sharp, made hazy what was blunt. She wondered if it would do that for her, half hoped what she had spent a lifetime refining could be messed up a little. Something in her longed to be spontaneous, riotous, foolish.

As she neared the waterfront, she could see Henry's group already assembled, the tiny actress in a flame-colored pantsuit, blazing against the day, an exotic bird, the opposite of puff-chested. Louise Felder, whom Judith knew from reputation, and had met a few times at parties in L.A., wore a black linen greatcoat that came to her ankles, and a coolie hat on her honey-colored hair. Robin, the photographer assigned to the piece, juggled lenses and reflectors.

"Do you think my insurance covers sampans?" he asked Judith, as they made their way down the pier.

"I just had my fortune told," said Louise. "He said I would meet my great love on a boat. Is this it?" She looked at the worn wood of the hull, as a wrinkled Chinese in a faded blue shirt reached out his hand to help her on board. "Is this him?"

"That's my uncle," said Henry.

"How do you feel about me as your aunt?"

"Are regular shoes okay on these boats?" Robin asked, as he jumped on board the sampan, balancing the sudden motion with his arms and several lenses.

Garbage floated in the water on all sides of the sampan. Judith was aware of the smell. *Hong Kong* was supposed to mean "fragrant harbor." She wondered how long ago that had ceased being the reality. "I don't think you can scar this wood," she said, and stretched out her fingers for Robin's.

A woman cleaning fish in the center of the boat looked at them through heavy lids, saying something in Cantonese. Henry answered her.

"Is she talking about me?" Louise asked. "Am I wearing the wrong outfit?"

"You look great," Henry said.

"Does he think so, my fiancé? Is she furious because I'm so irresistible? Look at him. He can hardly keep his eyes off me. Those are eyes, aren't they?"

"Stop it," Henry said. "People will think you're a bigot."

"Bigots make fun of what they don't understand. I make fun of what I do."

The old man poled them out into the harbor. Around them, the water churned with the motion of other, greater boats, steamships, freighters, the Star Ferry bouncing toward Hong Kong, passing a sister ship on its way back to Kowloon. *Midnight Star. Morning Star. Twilight Star* waited at the dock. Louise could read the names even without her glasses. They were prescription, very smart and Gloria Steinem, although Louise never thought women were better unless they were her clients. The glasses and the admiration for Gloria Steinem, especially her hair, were the closest Louise had come to feminism. She had done a seminar once with a group of high-profile women, among them Betty Friedan, and had been tempted to sign none of them. But she did have some thoughts about their appearances, and how they might help the world a little more easily if they didn't look so sour around the mouth. In her heart of hearts, which she hoped she still had, Louise believed in the superiority of men, because they continued to pass judgment on her, forced her in some subtle way to audition.

The eyeglasses themselves were a source of some discomfort emotionally. Every time Louise put them on, several times daily, she remembered her last appointment with the ophthalmologist who'd prescribed them. He'd diagnosed her "presbyopic." She had been flattered at first by the appraisal, which sounded Protestant to her. But he'd explained that *presby* was a prefix meaning aging, and that the vision she prided herself on, the ability to see movie marquees and read them from as far as six blocks away, was not a sign of her sharpness, but a symptom of getting old. Was her whole life to be like that, sounding interesting, but coming up empty?

"Where were you born?" Judith, notebook open, pen poised, was asking Henry.

"The Walled City."

"It sounds so mysterious," Louise said, exaggerating the movements of her lips as she repeated the name. "Walled City. Like the Forbidden City in China. Filled with lust and romance and shots by Bertolucci."

"Most people never get out."

"How did you?" asked Judith.

"My parents bought a sampan from their cousins. I didn't know what to do when I first hit the air. When you're born in a place, you think that's how the world is. You don't notice things like no light. You think rats running through the corridors are a normal part of life."

"Aren't they?" asked Louise. "It sounds like my agency."

"What took you to Hollywood?" Judith asked.

"Johnny Wong's private jet." Henry smiled craftily.

"An old line but a bad one," said Louise. "I brought her to

Hollywood. I found her in Bangkok, if you'll excuse the expression, and flew her to Hollywood for a test."

"I didn't know they gave screen tests anymore," said Judith.

"Who said it was a screen test?"

Later, when the photographer was taking pictures of the old woman cooking the fish in the center of the sampan, and Judith was out of earshot, Louise cornered Henry. "Why would you bring in that lie about Johnny Wong?"

"You don't know what you're messing with," said Henry. "You don't go against Anthony Go."

"It's a joke," said Louise. "A road-company Mikado Mafioso. What can he do to me?"

"Plenty. I have to protect you."

"Stop protecting me. The way you protect me is to become a big star. The way you become a big star is not by dragging some fag Karate Kid into a movie with you."

"You two look plenty intense." Judith made her way toward them.

"Well, it is intense," Louise said. "We're talking about how touching it is for Henry, being born in the slums, growing up on a sampan like this one. And now here she is, with the salary she makes for one picture enough to bail out a platoon of her relatives."

"Only if you make a deal with the right person," said Henry.

"The singular magic of movies," said Louise, unheeding, "making stars out of those who came from the slums. I remember once I was in New York, in a gorgeous town house, at a party for Tony Curtis. He was looking out the window. There were tears in his eyes. And he said, 'My father used to have a tailor shop three blocks from here. If only he could have lived to see this day.'"

"Who's Tony Curtis?" asked Henry.

Louise got to her feet, rolling her eyes heavenward, as though giving up her own particular ghost, the ghost of movies past. "I've outlived my usefulness," she cried, and feigned jumping overboard. But, the sampan was not constructed for sudden gestures, no matter how sardonic or inspired. The movement tipped the boat, and catapulted her into the water.

"Oh, God, save her!" Henry screamed, and kept on screaming.

"Throw her a rope!" Judith said.

"Life preserver!" cried Robin, trying several words in Cantonese before the fisherman understood. He took a life preserver from a pile of ropes, and threw it toward Louise. Robin stripped off his shirt and shoes and was about to jump in, when Louise, flailing in the water, managed to grab hold of the life preserver. They hauled her back to the boat, and with some effort, lifted her on board.

The long black coat, sotted, clung to her frame. "I spent a fortune for this coat," she sputtered. "I hope they don't see this at Lane Crawford."

"Are you all right?" asked Judith.

"I just did it to liven up the interview." She looked at Robin and smiled. "You look cute without a shirt. Were you going to save me?"

"I guess."

"Nobody ever wanted to save me. They're always looking for me to save them. Would you like to be a star?"

He handed her a towel the old man gave him. "Not particularly."

"They all say that in the beginning. Before you do it for them, before they do it to you." Louise wiped her face, and her tongue. "Has anyone ever died from swallowing this water? How polluted is it?"

"Well," said Judith, "besides what's dumped from the ships, and the sewage, and the garbage from the junks and sampans..."

Louise held up her hand. "I'd rather not know. Anyway, it doesn't matter. I've lived long enough." In spite of the brightness of the day and the strangely glistening effect her dousing gave her, little beads of water clinging to her hair and her cheeks, casting her back to a certain newly washed innocence, something dark was in her face.

"You mustn't say that," said Henry, with genuine concern.

"But it's true. I've been around too long. Past my time, my span, my memories of *Photoplay*. I've outlived any real usefulness. Certainly to myself. Not to mention Tony Curtis."

"It's only Tony Curtis," said Judith, smiling. "Don't take it so seriously. Not as if it were Cary Grant."

"Who's Cary Grant?" asked Henry.

Louise got up, threw off the towel, and jumped back into the water. It seemed as good a joke as she had ever made, since she was a strong swimmer. But the current was powerful, there was a swell from a passing yacht, and she was carried very quickly into its wake.

Thrashing around and sputtering, calling out obscenities, Louise made a sorrowful spectacle. "Help! Somebody!" Henry screamed.

The yacht changed its course. Sailors on its deck shouted to each other, as a white-haired man in a captain's hat noisily supervised them. He called out instructions in a language unknown on the sampan. But the words were sharp, audible through the air.

The sailors on the yacht pulled Louise from the water. They could be seen hovering around her, offering her blankets, drinks, towels. Through it all, Louise's mouth was going, as the man in the captain's hat toweled off her hair.

Eventually the yacht was maneuvered alongside the sampan. Her shoes still on and squeaking loudly, Louise descended the ladder on the side of the yacht. Reaching out for Robin's extended arms, she came back to her group.

It was not in Henry's nature to worry unnecessarily. But for the rest of the interview, she felt slightly unsettled, wondering if there wasn't something actually suicidal in Louise's seeming joke. Perhaps something flat-out suicidal in her behavior with Anthony Go. She had said herself that she'd lived too long. Her actions seemed to support that conviction.

When the interview was concluded, and they were all safely back on the dock, Henry tried to shake off the shadowy feelings. Walking through the lit underpass that would take them back to the hotel, she studied Louise's posture, the shoulders bent slightly forward, as though she were still on her way to somewhere, but didn't really want to go. It was then, in the neon-flared subterranean dark, that Henry noticed the man who seemed to be following them.

ELEVEN

◆

The Landmark in Central, where Maggie Evans had one of her boutiques, was quintessentially Hong Kong. Connected to the Mandarin Hotel, Prince's Building, Alexandra House, the Rapid Transit station, and any number of other places that could bring it commerce, by a network of overground and underground walkways, the Landmark had a glitter that would have made the eyes salivate, had they the right juices. Its façade was simple enough, concrete and ordinary-sized windows, but inside was a deep vortex, with dancing fountains, trees, open cafés, and shops at the base of escalators that seemed more a descent into another world than a lower floor. Swarovski crystal had an exhibition in the midst of the floor, hypnotically alive with a giant crystal Christmas tree, set up months before Christmas. Vast numbers of locals stood transfixed, gazing at the prisms, on their faces a look of rapt devotion.

They ringed round the ropes guarding the tree from touch, a kind of stubborn hunger on their faces, mouths set in subtly belligerent pouts, looking into the light refracting through the jewellike surfaces. Unlikely as it was that any of those so caught could afford even one of the smaller pieces showcased in the display, crystal teddy bears, pyramids, clustered grapes—much less the tree—they stood rooted, dazzled. The tree itself was four-tiered, on bands like antebellum hoop petticoats, swooping upward to a five-pointed star. Near its base swirled and spurted the indoor fountain, lit from beneath, like an echo of the crystals, spherical where they were sharp and angled. People sat around the edge of the fountain like summer picnickers outdoors, taking their lunch, sipping from soft drink cans. Children in American-style baseball jackets stared through the strings of octagonal crystals, at what was, in their imaginations, waiting beneath the tree. Presents that might have been there, were they Christians and rich.

There were rows of people, well behaved, oddly quiet for Chinese, as if that much outrageous splendor inspired awe. Claire, who stood looking at them, saw it as curiosity, already considering herself an expert on their behavior, fond of them as she was. They had too much dignity to stare at jewels in windows, or gawk at limousines painted pink, lined with matching upholstery and matching women, the profound excess that characterized this most seductive of cities. But somehow the tree was so dazzling, it overpowered their usually affected indifference, as when Prince Charles and Princess Diana had visited their last colony at the end of the eighties. In spite of the fact that Hong Kong had been virtually abandoned by the Brits, the Royals at least had made a show of caring. So crowds gathered reverentially wherever the couple made its appearances, offering constancy and flowers, as if nothing had changed, or ever would. As if Charles were not shorter than people imagined, his stature, like the paternalism of his country, more stately in people's concept of it than in fact.

Claire did not for a moment imagine that she was any less mesmerized than those who stood around the tree. She was captured, not just by the place, but by the feelings that were coming back to life in her. Mornings she awakened with joy made disproportionate by the lifting weight of her sorrow, a euphoria that came from being sure prayers could be answered, even when she hadn't dared pray. Her first thought on waking was of James. Her body jangled with electricity at the sight of him beside her, once she got over her initial surprise that he was still there. Happiness for her now was instantly suspect, triggering dread. Often she had been roused from sleep in recent times not remembering Charley was dead, before being jolted into the reality of the empty pillow next to her. So to think of James on waking, and to find he had not disappeared, abandoned her, died, run away, was an early morning high. She would rush to brush her teeth before he was conscious, so her mouth would be ready to receive him, and his kisses could suffocate the words of love she found springboarding to her tongue. Infatuated as she was, out of control in her emotions, she had the sense not to speak her feelings, and frighten him. Men could not deal with romantic fervor as women could. It was only their own desires they had sympathy for, and let themselves be driven by. Anything that smacked of sentiment, particularly too soon, they fled. Even knowing that, she still had to swallow her ardor, which seemed to have a life of its own. Involuntarily it swelled in her throat. But instead of speaking, she translated all the words she didn't dare express into a sexual gusto James marveled at, delighted in, comfortable as men were with passion it was their intention to inspire. As long as things were physical, the male of the species seemed at ease, provided he believed it was he who had initiated the move.

Making her way across the sparkling arcade, Claire looked in the men's boutiques, pausing at the window of Gianni Versace. She couldn't wait to give James things. Besides the tie she'd bought him, she'd already gifted him with shirts and a Members Only jacket that was probably a rip-off. It was bright blue, the color of his eyes, and made him look even younger than his thirty-four years. She wondered if she wouldn't have been wiser to give it to her son. But generosity, like lust, bubbled out of her, uncontrolled. It was such a joy to have someone to give to again, whether it was gifts, or her body.

"Ciao, hello!" Maggie called out from the other side of the fountain. "Are you coming to see me?"

"I am," said Claire. She had stopped being surprised at bumping into people. Cosmopolitan as it seemed, Hong Kong was really very small.

"*Favoloso!* Fabulous!" Maggie clicked past the crowd, her high heels a clattering tattoo on the floor, loud enough to break through the *whoosh* of the water, the cascading murmur of conversations on other levels. "I was just going to do some bookkeeping, and I prayed something would happen to distract me. I so hate anything real, like numbers." She looked into Claire's face, her own cornflower blue eyes sparkling like the crystals, the jets of the fountain. "Are you the answer to my prayer?"

"I doubt it."

"How humble. Americans aren't usually that modest, are they?" She looped her hand through Claire's arm, and pulled her gently toward her boutique. "Or perhaps they're simply not spiritual, so they don't like to be the answer to someone's prayer. Do you want to see my jade?"

"That's why I came."

"No, it's only why you *think* you came. The real reason why you came is because I need a friend." She squeezed Claire's arm. "I can't be friends with anyone I already know, because they're too full of pity and scorn. We're fresh to each other, so we can see each other as we are this minute, without any of our luggage, the personal tragedies. Do you have a personal tragedy?"

"If I tell you, it will be luggage."

"How smart you are!" Maggie turned and faced her. "Not just another pretty face, as they say in your country."

The boutique had pale cream satin draping its walls. A ridge of black leather went around the crown moulding, finishing it off, just below the ceiling, so it seemed very like the jewel boxes her pieces were packaged in. There were glass display cases in front of all three walls, filled with carvings, necklaces, rings, two attentive Chinese salesgirls stationed behind them. One went to get Claire the tea Maggie had ordered on entering the shop. The other pulled up a Louis XV stool upholstered in beige velvet for Claire to sit on as she looked at the jade.

"You should have apple green," said Maggie. "You're summer. I can tell that just by looking at you. You have a slight bluish tinge to your skin."

"How flattering," Claire said.

"Oh, no, that's the best undertone. You'll look better in my jewelry than I would. I'm spring. It sounds lovely, but we don't have the range and choice you do. Here." She took out a pair of earrings. "These look like you."

"They're a little big," said Claire.

"Your face is still very young. You should wear big, like teenagers do." And she herself, she might have added, but didn't. Her cheeks were framed with outsized multicolored glass that seemed to cover her entire ears. "Plenty of time later on to get conservative. After all, he's young, isn't he? That gorgeous man you were with the other night. Where did you find him?" She bit her lower lip, and a streak of dark scarlet appeared on her front tooth. "Or is it none of my business?"

"You have lipstick on your tooth."

"You really like me, or you wouldn't tell me." Maggie leaned over and kissed Claire's cheek, rubbed off the dark lipstick smear she'd left on her skin. "I'm so glad. I thought maybe I put you off. Forty percent."

"Excuse me?"

"I'll give you forty percent off. That's what I do for very old friends, and I like you better than any of them." She smiled like a child, then pulled back her lips, leaning over a mirror on the counter. "Doesn't that half make me look like a victim of Jack the Ripper." She wiped the lipstick off and moved the mirror in front of Claire. "Aren't they lovely on you?"

The earrings were in the shape of leaves, bright green, with a scattering of tiny diamonds, like dew. "How much?"

"Four thousand."

"Hong Kong?"

"U.S."

"That's more than I want to spend."

"But darling, everything's more than we want to spend. They'd be six thousand for anyone else, who wasn't as dear to me as you are."

A big, beefy man entered the shop, setting off the bells that marked arrivals. Maggie looked up, and over, and down, taking in his entire measure with a glance that frisked him as a policeman would for guns. Her interest in Claire seemed to evaporate as her energy moved in the man's direction. "Ciao, hello!" she said, coming around the counter, a wave of her perfume enveloping the front of the shop.

"Hi," he said, with a thick Texas accent. "This the place been recommended for jewelry?" He pronounced it "jool-ry."

"I would hope so."

"I'm looking for something special," he said.

"That's all we have."

He peered into the display window inset in the front wall, holding necklaces on plaster throats, thick cords of jade beads twisted and held with diamond clasps. "What would you recommend?"

"Who is it for, and how much do you want to spend?"

"The most aloof lady I ever seen, and I don't care."

"What fun!" said Maggie. "Does she have pierced ears?"

"I don't know."

"And you don't care about price?"

"That's right."

"Well, what here appeals to you, besides the two of us?" She smiled a flirting smile that he was not interested in.

"Maybe a necklace," he said. "She has a gorgeous chest. How much is that one there?"

"Six hundred thousand," Maggie said.

"What is that U.S.?"

"About eighty thousand."

He whistled.

"Jade is very precious," Maggie said. "My designs are bought all over the world; I deal with only the best quality. You can go to the jade market if you want to, and get something cheap."

"Hey, I'm not looking to fight with you," he said. "I was just surprised."

"Well, yes, if you don't know how high the prices have gone, I suppose it can be a bit of a shock. But then . . . the right woman is worth it, don't you think?"

"I'm not sure she's the right woman."

"Then you better take your time," said Maggie. "You wouldn't want to make the wrong investment, would you?"

"You're not a very good salesman."

"I don't have to be. My jewelry sells itself."

"Be seeing you," the Texan said, and left.

"Don't you care if he buys?" Claire asked.

"I care if *you* buy, *preziosa*. It's not about money to me. It's about my art enhancing beauty. Are you going to take these?" She touched one of the earrings.

"I haven't accomplished anything for a long time; I don't deserve a reward."

"You're alive, aren't you? To be alive, and not be hurting anyone, and make someone else feel good, the way you do me? That's an achievement. I'll let you have them for three. That's my cost."

"I don't know. . ."

"You don't have to know. *I* know." She took Claire's face between her hands. "You look absolutely lovely. They suit you. You must have them. I'll buy lunch."

"We'll go Dutch."

"Where do you suppose that expression came from? Do you have traveler's checks?"

"Yes."

"If you give me traveler's checks and I don't have to pay the charge card people, I can let you have another seven percent off. And I'll buy dinner as well."

"I'm busy for dinner."

"He is *gorgeous*," said Maggie, and started writing up the sales slip. "What a lucky woman you are. A beau like that, and a new friend like me. Dutch. I've had several Dutchmen and I've never seen one of them rush to pay his share of anything."

They lunched at the Culture Club, a private Japanese restaurant upstairs in a building in Central. The sushi bar was occupied end to end by Japanese businessmen, eating raw fish and chain-smoking. Maggie asked for a table in the corner, and sat Claire beside her, facing the sushi bar, so she could observe the action.

"They're the same with women as they are in business." Maggie tilted her head in the direction of the counter. "Devouring. Industrious. But willing to pay for what they're swallowing up. They'd give a woman a hundred thousand a year for her company. Designer clothes, first-class transportation, the best hotels. Limousines. Still, I don't like the idea of being an indentured servant, do you? And all that cigarette smoke!" Maggie waved it away, as if it were in front of her face instead of at the sushi bar. "Besides, I'm not young enough. They like their women young. But you still look young. Even more so, now that you have the right earrings."

"My husband gave me these," Claire said, looking inside the box Maggie had given her, to put her old earrings in.

"Well, they're pretty enough, but they are small. Still, diamonds are lovely, whatever their size. He must love you very much."

"He did. He's dead."

"I hate death." Maggie's mouth hardened, and she looked away. She seemed not to be there for a while. The waiter came, and she looked as though his arrival had made her remember where she was, and order.

"How old was your husband?" she asked Claire, after the waiter was gone.

"Forty-four."

"I bet he never did a mean thing to anyone."

"He might have lived longer if he had."

"Isn't that the rotten truth," said Maggie. "How can anyone believe in God?"

"I don't think it has anything to do with God. It's people who let each other down."

"What a sweet spirit you have. I suppose it must come from someplace. Still, how can you look at who it is that suffers in this world, and who gets away with murder, and think there's anything benign out there?"

"Nobody ever said it would be fair."

"Well." Maggie exhaled deeply, breath *whoosh*ing out of her like a bellows, with more to give out than take in. "If God did exist, She would be lucky to have you on Her side." She smiled a crooked smile. "What an illusion, yes? Women give each other such airs these days, as though we had a real chance of being in charge. It's better to have illusions about men. The one you were with the other night, for example. He isn't real, is he?"

"He seems real enough."

"*Senti*, listen. This is Hong Kong, darling. You mustn't believe appearances, since that's all there are."

A Japanese businessman at the sushi bar lifted his sake cup, smiling at Maggie. She seemed surprised, visibly taken aback at his attention, her shoulders moving toward the cloth of the banquette, as though she'd been struck, but by a tender blow. She lowered her eyes, and smiled a curling smile that twisted her unhappy mouth into Cheshire corners. "Don't look now, *amore*, love, but I think we've made a conquest."

The man at the bar said something to the waiter, pointed at Maggie. In a moment, the jacketed steward was at their table. "The gentleman wishes to offer you a sake."

"Is that all?" Maggie said. "I was expecting something more in the way of a contract. A takeover. Still, I suppose sake will have to do for starters." She nodded toward their benefactor, his cup raised once again in the air. He wore the dark blue suit that seemed to be the uniform of all the men at the bar. On his flattish nose sat the oversized, modish glasses that also seemed to be their standard, along with cigarettes, held either in the corners of their mouths, or cupped in the hand with which they weren't eating.

"Maybe he's more complex than the rest of them. Maybe he's been lifted from their ranks by intelligence and sensitivity, and likes older women. Maybe his Mars is trining my Venus." She sat up straighter. "I've never really wanted a Japanese, although I did have one Korean. It was very boom-boom. Straight to the point. Sometimes I do get such a yen for subtlety. But then . . ." She paused, for not even a moment. "What's subtle about a yen?" She giggled, pleased with herself, raised her water glass to him, and smiled her peculiar smile, as if her face had not settled on whether it was experiencing pleasure or pain.

A light patina of lavender colored the hollow beneath her eyes, a moist run of the liner around her lids, appearing in the harsh lighting of the restaurant like broken veins. She was still a remarkably good-looking woman, Claire thought, the unhappiness on her face notwithstanding. Her cheekbones were high, siding a finely whittled nose. Her chin had an appealing cleft. Only the mouth, with its pull of misery at the edges, took away from the overall prettiness. She applied lipstick constantly throughout the lunch, after every few bites, glossing and then blotting off the too-purplish color. Her mouth appeared mauve, dull in the garish light.

Hong Kong was lit mostly with neon, inside apartment houses and restaurants. The Chinese liked it because it was cheap and bright. At night Hong Kong's buildings were fluorescent against the sky, so that ordinary film not even set for time exposure took pictures of the skyline, so incandescent was it. That was partly what had so moved Claire on first coming into the city. It was as if the cheap effulgence could bring her out of her personal darkness. But the lighting in the restaurant was cruel to Maggie, and Claire wished she knew her well enough to tell her not to wear such blue colors, making her mouth appear mauve, pallid next to her milky skin.

After a few sakes had been proffered, and the businessman's card, he sent over what appeared to be his lieutenant. "Mr. Takahashi presents his compliments," said the young Japanese. "He says that it will surely rain. Fortunately he has his limousine outside. It will be his privilege to take you anywhere you want to go."

"Mardi Gras in Rio," said Maggie. "But of course it is the wrong season."

"I will tell him." The young man bowed, and walked away.

"*Delizioso*, delicious!" Maggie clapped her hands, leaned over conspiratorially. "A rich and powerful admirer. It's about time!"

"How do you know what he is?"

She fingered his business card. "Raised lettering. Video cassette business. Soaring yen. Bribery and corruption in government. What more could anyone ask for?"

"Love."

"How sweet you are."

"Don't you think love is important?"

"Important? It's vital! I rank it right up there with God. All that we hope for, and nonexistent. It's about fun, darling. Don't get serious with this boy. He'll break your heart."

Mr. Takahashi appeared beside their table. "My assistant informs me you would like to go to Rio."

"I was joking," Maggie said.

"I have a plane."

"Seriously? All he promised was a limousine."

"With your permission?" He pulled over a chair. "Miss . . . ?"

"Maggie." She held out her hand.

He took it and bowed over it. "Kisaburo."

"Is that your name? Because if not, it's the end of our relationship. I don't do animals."

"Kisaburo Takahashi," he said, and sat down.

"How fortunate that you come into my life today, Kissy." Maggie touched his cheek. "One day earlier and I would still have been in mourning."

"Has somebody died?"

"Faith," she said. "Decency. Everything we believed in."

"I'm sorry."

"Not your fault. Or maybe it is. How well connected are you?"

He looked puzzled.

"Do you have a line on life and death, and who is responsible? Have you got informants?"

"I have to go," Claire said, suddenly embarrassed, anxious. Judith had told her about the murder, and although she hadn't brought it up, not wanting to add to Maggie's misery, there seemed to be some common core of anguish shared without discussing. Grief and loss pulled at the pit of her stomach, even as she tried to imagine it was too much sushi.

"Off to find love, are you?" asked Maggie.

"I may have already found it."

"Oh my dear, *carina*." Maggie touched her hand. "Why so grave, when the grave comes soon enough? Why can't you just have a fling, like me and Kissy?"

"I enjoyed our lunch." Claire got up.

"I owe you a dinner," Maggie said. "Come see me. All the time. This won't last very long." She leaned to her left, and kissed Takahashi lightly on the lips. When she turned again, Claire was nearly at the door. "Ciao, goodbye!" Maggie called out. "I'll be waiting for you."

*   *   *

She was on his lap in the limousine, kissing him, in the rained-on crush of Hong Kong afternoon. Outside the window, teetering on the curb, waiting for the light to change, stood Superintendent Leslie. He looked straight at her, but Kisaburo's head was partly in the way. So maybe he didn't recognize her. She hoped he didn't recognize her. It wouldn't do for the police to think Betsy's mother was a slut.

TWELVE

◆

Like most of the men who were in the Mandarin bar, the Texan stared at Erica Thorr. It had become kind of a game with him, dropping into the place at the unappointed hour, times when he knew from observation she might be there. He had started to follow her to different watering holes: the Champagne Bar at the Grand Hyatt, lit with its three different blues, rings of incandescent light that seemed as mysterious as she was; the lounge of the Regent, fronting the last perfect harbor view from the Kowloon side. No-where she went did she seem to be looking for anything. Everywhere he followed her, he tried not to seem as though he were looking for her. He failed.

He was not used to not getting his way. In the beginning he had invited her for drinks. She had repeatedly declined his invita-tion, always ordering a drink for herself, making sure the bill came to her. In the Mandarin, she signed, adding a room number she would hold her hand over, as if he might have the temerity to peek and follow her there. In truth, he would have, which made her as shrewd as she was beautiful. His kind of woman.

He had put out bribe offers to various bellmen and room clerks during his stay at the hotel, which had now run two weeks longer than he had originally intended. He had phoned his wife in Austin and said he was hot on the trail of an important deal that would determine their future. That was the truth. He wanted her so badly by now that he would have risked his marriage. Having never been turned down, either in business or love, he could not imagine that the hard time would continue. Everybody had a price. Except the goddamn barmen and bellmen at the Mandarin, who seemed to pride themselves on protecting her from him. The stubborn impeachability of the Asian servant class.

A relief doorman had been the only one to buckle, telling Biff Lester where the cab she had taken was going. It was that one he had followed to the Grand Hyatt. The bar there irritated him, sexy as it was, bathed with that sultry blue light, even in daytime. Several times he had thought about renting a room and spiriting her upstairs. Once he had thought about buying the hotel to show her his power. In a city of luxury hotels, the new Grand Hyatt had been buzzed about in the trade as "the Flavor of the Month," its grandeur diminishing all the opulence already existing. Palazzo entrance, circling staircases on either side of the lobby, gave it the air of a European ballroom at many times scale. Black marble columns lifted the eye to the atrium ceiling, seven stories high. As a businessman, the Texan wondered how the chain could possibly recoup the hundred-million-dollar investment by 1997; as a would-be lover he would have eaten the loss to be with her.

The first time he'd followed her, he'd pretended to be surprised that they were in the same place, had greeted her like a friend. She had turned away from him as she always did. But not as pleasantly as she had at the Mandarin. A wrinkle of annoyance had creased her flawless face, at the realization that she was being stalked. He was an awkward man, handsome, but oversized, and his manner of dealing was usually blunt. So once it was obvious she was on to him, there was no way he could pussyfoot around. A woman that sharp, and that gorgeous, knew when someone had her scent.

That's what he was doing now, hunting her. Trying to be subtle, which was not his way. Laying traps that would have worked with a less clever animal. Taking what was already fabled and outrageous, giving it an overlay of romance, which Biff had never known was in his character. He had gone so far as to find the floral consultant for the Hyatt, who did nothing but fill the high, oversized vases around the majestic lobby, at a fee of a million a year. He'd gotten the floral consultant to design a special bouquet for her, at a cost of over five hundred dollars. When it was delivered, he'd tried to follow the bellman to her room. Again, he had failed. She had sent it back to him, which really pissed him off, because she had found out his room number, when he hadn't been able to find out hers.

Once or twice he had waited by the elevator at the Mandarin, hiding behind a column, like a spy. Skulking behind the illuminated crystals siding the wood-paneled walls, bolting into the car after her, just before the doors closed. Trying to start a conversation. But by now she was angry that he was trailing her, and wouldn't speak to him even to turn him down. Wouldn't even look at him, pushing a button that was obviously not even her floor to elude him.

He tried to tell himself at moments when he briefly regained control that it was only quiff. He was one of the richest men in Texas, which, granted, didn't mean as much as it once did, everyone in that state having scaled down their definition of wealth. But it was still something. Plenty, according to his accountants, who had assured him that his kind of money wasn't affected by what everyone else considered a depression. The world was filled with pretty women, not one of whom had ever said no. Biff was accustomed to being appreciated. Unlike a lot of big men who had surprisingly little to offer in the genital department, Biff was in every way superscaled. He was used to their screams of pleasure, even when he didn't prime them. Shit, he had even thought of going down on her, a sexual obeisance he hardly ever performed. His fantasies had already run away with him. He was furious at her. After what he had imagined doing, that was not even his style. She wasn't grateful, creamy with the pleasure he had thought about giving her.

She had a nerve. Bigger than her exceedingly fine ass, in his angry opinion, salted at this particular cocktail hour by a few margaritas. He watched as other men made approaches. It offered a little relief that she turned them down. But not enough. He had a hard-on now from looking at her.

If there was one thing he couldn't stand, it was a cock-teaser. Just by looking the way she did, she played with a man's cock. He was on to her. Eyes fanning downward so modestly, like some fucking geisha, one who didn't want to serve.

"If she doesn't expect people to come on to her, what's she doing in a bar?" he asked the bartender once again, trying not to seem like a man who'd had too much to drink. Not really able to remember that he'd asked the question before.

"Maybe she's thirsty," the bartender said.

"She could drink in her room."

"Maybe she's not an alcoholic."

"You think it makes someone an alcoholic to drink in their room?" Biff asked testily. He had started doing that, late at night, when he thought about how they could be sleeping together instead of alone. Had started drinking himself unconscious, just so it would be day again, and he could start shadowing her.

"Not a good sign to drink alone. Worse in a woman. Especially one that beautiful."

"How long has she been staying here?" He knew of two weeks and a day himself, the day being the one he was supposed to leave, until he'd seen her.

"I'm not a detective."

"Nobody's asking you to give out damaging information. I'm not an agent for the P.R.C."

"The People's Republic of China isn't interested in sex," said the barman.

Biff looked at him through the tequila haze, filtered at the edges by soft light, and people who still smoked. "A hundred U.S. for her room number."

"I can't do that."

"Maybe I want to send her flowers."

"You already did. She sent them back."

"What is this, the nightly news? Does everybody know everything?"

"Just about."

"So how come I can't even find out a room number?"

"Maybe you should get a job at the hotel," said the barman.

"There's got to be some way to get to her," Biff Lester said.

"You'd have to get up pretty early in the morning," said the bartender, in what was the closest anyone had come to giving Biff a hint.

Angry, feeding on his frustration and several gold tequilas, the Texan left the bar. "Mr. Lester?" said a young Chinese, in the uniform of a trainee.

"Yes?"

"That hundred you offered the barman. You still have it?"

"In my pocket."

"I cannot give you her room number. That would be a breach of our policy. But if you like swimming, may I suggest the health club at six-thirty A.M."

Biff gave him the hundred-dollar bill.

To begin with, he was starting to develop a bit of a gut, so he couldn't have her see him in a bathing suit. Not right off. But he was ready for her in the corridor outside the health club when she came at six-thirty in the morning. Not so she could see him, though. He'd changed his room to the twenty-sixth floor. He'd taken a suite between the elevators and the health club, so she'd have to pass him. Six-thirty was pretty early for him, but he hid behind his door like a kid, just straining for a glimpse of her.

Once she was swimming, though, once he climbed the stairs and peered through the glass doors and noted what her routine was, he watched her. She looked taller in the water, long and lithe, the definition in her chest beneath the collarbone as impressive as her high, fine breasts. He loved it when she did the backstroke.

Nobody else was there at that hour of the morning. It didn't take him long to figure out a way to have her, and as often as he wanted. He was on the phone within the hour, after the fifty minutes he'd watched her swim. After he'd looked at her toweling off, bending over, seen the thin slit of latex crawl up into her crotch, and wished that he could do the same.

But everything in its time. The secret here, he understood now, now that he finally had access and knew he could get her on tape, was patience. Patience and the right cameraman, who could set up equipment with discretion. Maybe even underwater.

*   *   *

The barman's opinion to the contrary, the P.R.C. *was* interested in sex. The Chinese had a large financial involvement in Volvo's, the high-priced "hostess" hall, haven for tired businessmen, many of them communists from the mainland who were still merchants in their souls, hedonists in their pants. In addition, there had been a recent crackdown in China on pornography. Those concerned with freedom saw it as a ruse, the government's way of closing in on certain intellectuals. But others who studied the machinations in Beijing—professional "China watchers"—judged the arrest of pornographers as token harassment. After the student massacres in Tiananmen Square, some officials, it was thought, were ashamed of the hard line their government had taken. Having to make a show, they had started closing in on people with no idealistic weight, the sellers of smut. A meaningless offense, really, pornography, in comparison to speaking out.

Like the mainland Chinese, Clement Leslie's interest in pornography was not really what it seemed. The murder on Black's Link had struck him from the start as the kind of death that could have been in a "snuff" film. The dark thought had crossed his mind when he'd seen the positioning of the bodies; it had been reinforced by the postmortem report. Strangulations, semen in the lungs, the boy with his still swollen penis. All of it the kind of appalling sexual detail that fertilized the bottom of the pit, where wallowed those who paid extra to see young women raped and murdered on celluloid. He'd heard chilling tales of moneyed sensation seekers traveling to Chile and Argentina to watch actual filming. Listened to accounts of the rank finales of beautiful sort-of innocents who thought they were going to have genuine movie careers. Heard descriptions of how and where the movies were made. It was a barbarism he'd been convinced could never happen in Hong Kong. Now, he was not so sure.

The appearance of Louise Felder in his city had tripped a wire in Clement's brain. Celebrities, high-powered movers and shakers, came to Hong Kong every day, but most of them didn't stay. He noted Louise was spending real time. Real time was longer than it took to get clothes made by Sam the Tailor in Kowloon, or stones set by

Stephen at Larry's Jewelry in the Landmark. Hong Kong was fast food for the glittering, greedy, irritable people with patience in as short supply as their money was long. He knew that Louise had been on Anthony Go's yacht a few weekends before. There was no need for police informants on that score: Hong Kong was a very small town where gossip was concerned. He was aware of Go's courting of Johnny Wong. What he hadn't known was the professional connection between Johnny and Henry Wu. And her being represented by some Hollywood hotshot. For a policeman, with observer's eyes, Clement didn't have a suspicious mind. But, suddenly, everything was suspect.

There was no doubt that Go, along with his other dirty activities, had trafficked in porno. Triads had their hands in all profits to be made from vice. There were self-styled numbers and color names, like coded military ranks in an army, 426-49, for ordinary criminals, Blue Lantern, 426 Red Pole, 415-White Paper Fin for advisors, Chinese *consiglieri*. The numbers rose to 489 for the top men, Dragon Heads. It was all quite melodramatic and structured, basic and low. What did they want with Johnny Wong? What was the connection with Henry? Was this Louise Felder in town to bring it all together for them? Were the purveyors of porno trying to make it into legitimate films? Or was porno itself going upmarket, moving to the Big Time?

Though he'd never had any personal objections to pornography, the situation was starting to trouble Clement. He could not deal with the thought that movies, for which he had such pristine passion, were going to be corrupted. Not by pornography itself, which was already its own category, but by tainted people moving into an arena he considered sacrosanct. Whores becoming nuns.

So when he got the call that someone had been caught filming a swimmer without her knowledge or consent at the Mandarin, something clicked, disturbingly. He had the feeling it was all linked, in a fashion he couldn't fathom. Seediness coming to the surface of what had always been stylish and beautiful. Including the Mandarin pool.

"Was he a Gweilo?" Clement asked the bartender in the Captain's Bar that afternoon. He had already concluded his official questioning of the security people, and the pool attendant, who'd been in another part of the health club, and claimed he hadn't seen anything. Gossip was the best filter in this pool, Clement had a feeling.

"I work the bar," said the barman, polishing a glass to illustrate.

"But what did you hear? Was he a Gweilo?"

The barman shook his head, lowered his eyes. Like most Hong Kong Chinese, he didn't like it when a villain was one of his own.

"You know anything about him?"

"Only that he got away."

"And nobody saw him in the elevator? That must have been a little conspicuous, someone dripping wet, with an underwater camera."

"Maybe he used the stairs."

"Security said there were no wet footprints. No sign of him."

"If you've talked to security, what do you need with me?"

"Maybe you're smarter than they are. Maybe you have more connections. Maybe you hear more."

"Speak no evil, see no evil, hear no evil."

"How do we know it was evil? Maybe it was just some camera buff getting off on spying on a beautiful woman."

The barman smiled. "Come *on*." He nodded toward the couch in the corner. "Though God knows she is beautiful."

Clement followed the line of the barman's vision, and went over to her. "Miss Thorr?"

"Yes?"

"Superintendent Leslie. May I sit down?"

She nodded.

"Can you tell me exactly what happened this morning?"

"I've already told a number of people. The concierge. Several policemen . . ."

She looked extremely uncomfortable. Clement was used to people being uneasy in his presence. But beautiful women had a serenity of their own that went with their slender bodies and the ease of their breathing, a quiet security that made them even more attractive to men than they already were. So it surprised him a little how unsettled she seemed, even with what had occurred.

"I thought it was just someone else in the swimming pool. I get in a kind of trance when I swim. It wasn't until he came up practically between my legs that I saw the camera. I screamed. He jumped out of the pool and ran."

"You didn't recognize him?"

"He had a mask on. A diver's mask. And a tank." She shuddered. "What kind of creeps are out there?"

"An endless variety," said Clement, and gave her his card. "Will you call me if anything happens?"

"Like what?" She looked a little pale, even with her tan, even in the dark, caressing light of the bar.

"Anything that seems out of the ordinary."

"This is Hong Kong," she said. "That's all there is."

She was not doing a very good job of seeming sanguine, and she knew it. All day long, she had had a hard time staying inside her own skin. Her aura of peace, like her wardrobe, was something that had been acquired. She'd felt edgy all day, literally jumpy, wondering if she should call Philadelphia to alert the Syndicate to what had happened.

She herself wasn't sure what exactly had happened. But she knew it wasn't innocent. Could someone know what she was up to? She felt frightened and guilty. Not that there was anything to feel guilty about, she assured herself. At least, not yet. She had never done anything to hurt anyone. The Syndicate had convinced her their plan was harmless. And it was certainly brilliant, there could be no arguing that.

But she was not a secure woman, in spite of the picture she presented. Doubt and anxiety gnawed at her, as they had from the moment her husband had left her for another woman. She had pulled herself together by a daily, devotional ritual of swimming, clearing her head, molding her body, strengthening her calves in the bargain. It had restored her, really. Better than restored her. Made her what she had never been before. Swimming had become a drug for her, a positive addiction, reshaping her destiny as it reshaped her arms. It was what she had been doing when the Syndicate found her, in the health club where she worked as a locker room attendant.

There were women who went there to exercise after charity lunches. Women who went there because they were afraid to go home too early, and start drinking alone. Women who went there because they felt a need for fellowship, outmoded and Quakerish as the word was. Women whose friends dragged them along, so they wouldn't be depressed. Women who went there because it was part of the divorce settlement, membership in the club, when the bastard had just gotten his golden parachute, and was using it to fly on the Concorde to Paris with some doxy a third his age. And these were the women who made up the Syndicate.

There were seven of them in all; they had reached a point in their lives where they'd always imagined they'd be taken care of, rewarded for a lifetime of love and loyalty. Married in the fifties, when their husbands' futures looked bright, they'd been dumped in the eighties, when corporate takeovers and mergers and stock frauds and insider trading had given their men the wealth of Arabian sultans, with matching regard for women. Not one of the wives had received what she regarded as her fair share. Assets were gone in a miracle of camouflage, sequestered in Swiss bank accounts, diverted into secret funds. Actions once inconceivable to the noble young men they'd married, so eager were they to screw their wives, were commonplace now that everybody was older. Too old to capture the heart of another man rich enough to give them the respite they deserved. And then, they'd found Erica swimming.

Because of who they'd been married to, they understood leveraged buyouts. Each of them bought a share in Erica, putting up money for her clothes, her trip to Hong Kong, and her stay at a fine hotel. Like seven little Rumpelstiltskins, they'd spun her straw into gold, her Ann Taylors into Karl Lagerfelds, in exchange for a portion of the wealth of the rich husband she would surely capture. Her air of mystery, her inarguable beauty, together with restyling and wardrobe, would doubtless combine to magnetize a titan. They'd decided he would most likely be found at the Mandarin, since through it passed businessmen from all over the world, who only thought they meant business because they hadn't met the Syndicate.

Till this morning, it had seemed to be going well. Every man who'd seen Erica, it seemed, had approached her. It was reassuring for a woman with shattered self-esteem. Her failure to respond was not aloofness but caution: she'd been instructed to check out the men before starting up with them. Hong Kong had a certain pushy formality; people leaned aggressively into business and relationships, wagging their own credentials. It was as if having carded who they were, with raised lettering, they could do no harm. The names, addresses, company headings, telephone and fax numbers on the card made them easy for Donald Ng to investigate.

Donald Ng was a local variety of Dun & Bradstreet, a financial consultant who could come up with more information than the subject's mother. His name had been given Erica, along with wardrobe, makeup and hair restyling, training in manners and comportment, and the stay at the Mandarin. So far, of all the candidates who had presented themselves and their cards, there had been not a single man who was a single man. Married men were not on Erica's menu.

Adultery was out of bounds for her, and the ladies of the Syndicate. Cynical as life had forced them to become, they had retained respect for other people's marriages, since their husbands had so little for their own. Along with teaching Erica how to pour tea in case the target was an Englishman, they had cautioned her to play fair. At least as fairly as a woman could play when everything about her was a lie, including her posture, tutored in leans and stretches and arcs to stress her curves by the same consultant who'd gilded her behavior.

Everyone advised her to keep her air of silence. It spoke of more intelligence than words could, and with a sweeter voice. Too much was at stake for her to hurt herself by giving out information, as women often did, being at base more honest than men, eager to parade the blamelessness of their lives, one of the first things that made men lose interest.

The entire charade was not just an investment for the Syndicate, but an act of revenge: for a man's not holding a woman as dear as she held him, for waiting to show his true colors until hers had faded.

A group of fallen goddesses, they raised her, Aphrodite on the half-shell, from the sea of disappointment that was their lives.

But great as the plot was, and clever, the morning's adventure had unsettled her, as had the questioning of the Superintendent. She lowered her eyes in the gracefully imperious way she had been taught, so that men would become self-conscious, and know they were dismissed.

"I'll be going then," Clement said, obeying some primordial signal.

She did not look up. He moved toward the door.

Sometimes, when she would be in places long enough that were not her usual turf, Louise would forget who she was. Not her true self, because the sorrow that was her foundation, layering under the gritty humor, stayed with her, reminding her that her cockiness was a sham. So she always remembered she was a phony, in the truest sense of the word: that is, that she was not as others perceived her. But away from film centers, like L.A., London, and Rome, where she couldn't throw her weight around, she would lose what others had come to regard as her identity. At such times she would flounder internally, fearful of something as simple as crossing a street, because the street was unfamiliar, and there was no one who knew her, or thought they knew her, on the other side.

Eventually, if she stayed with the anxiety long enough, a kind of peace would settle on her, as she realized she didn't have to be anybody. That most people in the world weren't anybody, and as long as you didn't have to ride the subway with them, you were fairly safe. She had almost come to that feeling in Hong Kong, a kind of bliss in her closet anonymity. Henry had left her alone much of the time, visiting her family, accepting Louise's dictum that if you'd seen one junk, you'd seen them all.

But abruptly, Bunyan Reis, her beloved (sort of) genius curmudgeon, artist, sculptor, and, when Louise represented him for films, scenic designer, had blown into town on his way to Bangkok. He went there once a year to collect exotic pieces, as he told both strangers and friends, strangers thinking he meant art. Usually Louise was overjoyed to see him, since he was the meanest-spirited man she knew, and the fact that he loved her indicated some light inside her, she was sure. But this particular outing, she felt intruded upon: she had been enjoying her slide into namelessness. To have to rev up into being her so-called self again annoyed her, glad as she was to be in his company, which she understood most of the readers of *W* would have given their Maud Frizons for, not to mention the feet that were in them.

Coming into the bar of the Mandarin, her artificial smile back in place, she aimed the full plasticity of it at Clement Leslie, as he came up the stairs. "Twice in two days!" she exclaimed. "Does that mean it's destiny?"

"It means you're all over everywhere," Clement said.

"And I thought I was being inconspicuous."

"Ha!" scoffed Bunyan, beside her. He was already in his Bangkok best, lightweight silk shirt over poplin pants, in the pale gray colors he wore at all times, in all climates, but in different weights and fabrics. In Montreux he sported heavy wool turtlenecks, in New York, silk suits and ties. All over the world the same pearly tones hung in closets he couldn't wait to come out of, dressed to the teeth, in a matching hue. He had plump little fingers, and fat wide feet, which, even though he was small, seemed disproportionately little, as though he were wearing children's shoes.

"Bunyan Reis," said Louise, "this is Police Superintendent..." She could not seem to remember.

"Clement Leslie." He held out his hand. "I'm a great admirer of your work."

"And I yours," said Bunyan. "But I wish you would do it in uniform."

"At a certain level we no longer have to wear them."

"At a certain level nobody has to wear anything," said Bunyan. "That doesn't mean they shouldn't keep up an illusion."

"What illusion is that?"

"Authority. Service. If the sun *must* set on the British Empire, we ought to at least have a glimpse of its ass."

"Will you join us for a drink, Superintendent?" Louise asked, feeling oddly more kindred to him than she did to Bunyan.

"I'm afraid I can't."

"Have I offended you?" asked Bunyan.

"It would take more than that to offend me."

"Oh, good. I have a lot more than that." He studied Leslie with pale, hooded eyes. "Come. Join us. I'll do a sketch for you on the tablecloth, like Toulouse-Lautrec."

"They don't have tablecloths."

"On a napkin then. I'm not as pricey, or as short, but I could be. The Japanese have started to collect me, and we do shrink as we age, don't you know."

"Sorry," said Clement, fingers to his temple, saluting Bunyan as he left. "Maybe another time."

"Oh, I hate it when people go when I want them to stay," Bunyan pouted.

"Why did you beg him like that?" Louise weaved her way around the low tables, past the frosted black-and-white chess pieces on the Lucite room divider.

"I liked him."

"I'd die before I'd ever beg anyone for anything," Louise said, shutting out of her mind the men she'd pleaded with not to leave her, lobotomizing the pain. "You ought to forget about men and collect more interesting women. Here, I have one for you," she said, spotting Erica, heading for the couch where she was seated. "Erica! May we join you?"

"I have to make a phone call," Erica said, getting up, moving past her. "Excuse me."

"Was it anything I said?" Louise looked after her.

"Everything," said Bunyan, sitting down. "We are not getting our hearts' desire today."

"You can forget about the Superintendent."

"How can you be sure?" He turned to the waiter. "An icy martini and a perfect Manhattan."

"I'd like to make her a star." Louise reached into the bowl of nuts, sorting out cashews with her long red fingernails.

"You want her?"

"Only as a client."

"Why? Men have been such a disappointment for you. Why don't you try women?"

"Why don't you?"

"I'm not looking for the same things you are. Affection. Comfort."

"That's not what I want," crunched Louise.

"Isn't it funny how I don't believe you," said Bunyan.

Erica waited until it was nine in the morning in Philadelphia before she made her call. It was not a very good connection. There was an echo on the line, so she could hear her own voice coming back at her, shaking. "Mrs. Rittenhauser? It's Erica Thorr." She swallowed. "I think someone may be on to me."

THIRTEEN

◆

It was not as if he meant to be giving Judith information. That he could even be interested in a journalist gave Clement pause. A friend of his had had an affair with a woman reporter. Clement had asked him, when it was over, what he would do if he ever fell in love with someone like that again, and he'd said, "Cut off my genitals."

He did not consider Judith hard, although he understood, realistically, that she had to be tough to have the job she did, hold it, and do it well. But he was used to soft women, passive ones, Orientals whose only function seemed to be to please. To have this willful, spirited feminine, in his life threw him off balance. He wanted to be smart for her, prove things to her, aspects of his personality that he thought he'd gotten rid of as a child.

All she really wanted from him, he was sure, were pieces of the puzzle, facts about the case. She was not above velvetizing her glance or her voice, trailing her fingers over his hand when they had met for coffee, and she asked him questions. He had struggled not to answer her.

It had become a kind of game with him, resisting her. Treating her as he would any other reporter, or at least trying to. But he had given her a heavy hint that he would be spending the evening at Hot Gossip, a trendy club in Kowloon where young colonials discoed. And he had sort of let it slip that he'd received a tip that someone there might have information about the killers of Betsy Evans and David Palmer-Smith.

So he sat now, in the neoned bar, little curved lightning jags of fuchsia punctuating the darkness, in between the wall-mounted TV screens flashing rock videos. The crowd was a mix of Europeans and the young, punkish Hong Kong set, Belonger teenagers who wanted to be Trendy Brits, or at least what they thought were Trendy Brits, scarlet stripes in their hair and dinosaur backs down the center of their 'dos. Since the decision had come over from England that fifty thousand heads of household were to be given domain in the United Kingdom, there had been a certain modified sigh of relief in the colony. Anxious as everyone still was about the future, panicky that the choice would not include them, there was a new optimism that it could be. There was also an optimism about democracy's coming to China, in view of the collapse of communism in Europe. That the Chinese had taken an even harder line, and kept the news of Europe from their people, seemed beside the point, when it came to castle-building. Hardnosed and pragmatic as Hong Kong people were, they were gamblers, and gamblers were always up for a dream.

Fifty thousand out of five and a half million. What gamblers they really were, to imagine the odds might be in their favor. Two hundred twenty-five thousand Hong Kongers in Britain at the outside, for those heads of household who could take their families along. Like the forced return of Vietnamese refugees to the tyranny they had fled, certain actions of Her Majesty's government appalled Clement. But what choice had they had, really, with the colony already so overcrowded. At least, that was what he tried to tell himself. It was easier to order another drink.

Leather-clad young people, metal-belted, studs in their boots, diamonds in their noses, leaned in toward each other across hot pink tablecloths in the dining area. Clement wondered who in the world could find that look attractive, but they all seemed to have opposites. Mostly this evening they seemed to be Chinese, teenagers emulating their young British peers, showing respect with spray-glued hair, saying that there was nothing they wanted to be so much as young Brits, even those whose parents could not bear to look at them.

Whoever it was who had called him did not approach him.

Clement felt quite conspicuous by the bar, even without uniform, his age marking him clearly out of place, the intensity of his eyes checking out the crowd labeling him not the usual visitor. He moved toward the circular staircase down to the basement, carrying his drink with him, loud music from the disco pulsing up as he descended.

There were mirrors everywhere, and pink lights fighting the strobes illuminating the gyrations of the dancers. Cheap silk flowers in fish tanks bordered the seating area, gray benches with fabric faded by the artificial light. By the bar, black lacquer bar chairs upholstered with the same sad, faded fabric semicircled high tables, legs squaring deep impressions in the turquoise carpet. Everywhere were artificial flowers, bogus palms. Fake cascading bouhinia, the signature flower of Hong Kong, edged a poster of *Ghostbusters*. Pinball machines and pin spots sent out dashes of light.

The disc jockey, a handsome young European—blond, tall—had a diamond in his left ear. Clement tried to remember if that was the one for gay or straight. He waited until the break, and approached him, telling him immediately who he was, and that he was there on official business lest the young man think he'd read his earring wrong.

"Did you know this young man?" He showed him a photo of David Palmer-Smith.

"That's the murdered boy, isn't it? Didn't know him. Saw him around, though." There was a slight overlay of Dutch around the edges of the boy's accent.

"Came here often?"

"Often enough so I remember."

"Who did he hang out with?"

"Chinese, mostly. You notice that, because usually Europeans stick with their own."

"And her?" Clement held out a photo of Betsy.

"They were together a lot, far as I saw. But they stopped coming a while before the murder."

Clement thanked him, and went back upstairs.

Judith was waiting by the maître d's stand. Her face seemed actually to brighten up at the sight of him. Clement tried not to take it too personally. It was, after all, enemy turf, this garish land of the young. He assumed she would have been relieved to make contact with any ally.

"Well, Superintendent," she said, smiling at him, reaching for his hand.

"I don't think we better sit together," he said, rather abruptly. "My informant won't come around if he sees I'm with someone."

"Oh, okay," she said, brightly. "You can tell me what he says."

"That would be violating the ethics of the investigation."

"Then why did you tell me you'd be here?"

"I don't remember telling you," he said. "Maybe you ought to sit over there." He nodded toward an empty booth.

She sat. He sat in the one next to her. "We've got to stop meeting like this," she said in a loud whisper.

"I'm sorry I can't be more sociable." His back was to her. "If I weren't on duty I could tell you you were looking particularly lovely tonight."

"I didn't even have a chance to go home and change. It's good you're working because I don't like compliments."

"Of course you like them. You probably just don't know how to handle them."

"Nobody likes a man who's *too* insightful."

"Except a woman who's smart enough."

"That would let *me* out," she said.

"False modesty. I never would have guessed."

By the bar, two darkly dressed couples snaked to the music coming from the TV's, crotches sliding up and down each other's crotches, like cats rubbing up against scratching posts. For all the open animalism of their movements, there seemed very little sensuality in it to Clement, because of the detached air they had, the undertow of listlessness that carried away any feeling of electricity.

"You think they're on drugs?" Judith murmured.

"Some of them, sure. But I think the main drug is their age. They get very high on contempt."

A young man, dressed in black waders, broke from the foursome, and started toward Clement's booth. The black boots that came all the way up his hips were cut out around the crotch, and belted at the waist, one continual line of animal hide that cloaked his prominent genitals like parentheses. He wore a Western shirt with studs around the pockets, and a scarf at his throat. "Superintendent?" he asked, leaning over.

"Sit down."

"I heard there was a reward." He slid into the booth.

"Several rewards," Clement said.

"I also hear you been questioning mainly Europeans." The young man himself was Chinese.

The truth was, Clement had interviewed only white associates of the brutalized couple. He tried to tell himself it was because he was doing what was logical, that only Europeans attended their school, only Europeans were their peers. But the truth was he leaned over backward, always, to avoid any hints of racism. And the murder was so ugly he was hoping in his heart that it had nothing to do with any Chinese. "How did you hear that?" he asked.

"You haven't talked to anyone I know."

"Did you know the Evans girl, or the Palmer-Smith fellow?"

"Not me, personally. But I saw them around. They hung out sometimes with some buddies of mine."

"What are their names?"

"Why don't you just go hang out at 1997?" the boy said, naming a disco on the Hong Kong side. "People like to talk. They have a hard time shutting up. But I'm not one of them."

"Can you just tell me what you heard?"

"Some Chinese kids been bragging they been into a white girl."

"Their names?"

"I don't like being a stool pigeon," the boy said. "You got your own ears." He handed Clement a piece of paper. "Here's my name and address when you find them. For the reward."

"You have no moral objections to getting it?"

"My family wants to move to Singapore," he said. "You need money to convince them in Singapore how glad they'll be to get you."

"Did you hear?" Clement asked Judith, as they walked along the harborfront by the Regent Hotel. It was a well-lighted cement walkway, glitter zigzagging through the asphalt like an echo of the

luster on the water. The outside of the skyscrapers, silvered by a
waning moon, made Hong Kong shine, an even brighter spectacle by
night than it was by day, windows lit with the harsh fluorescence
preferred by the Chinese. The heavy scent of flowers blooming long
past their season, like women who had come late to love, mixed with
the slightly acrid smell of fish and garbage on the water. There was
still summer in the air, though it was well into autumn. The moist
heat slightly frizzed Judith's hair, making him want to reach over
and touch the little fringe of girlishness around her forehead, to
comfort her back into the fragility he was sure she'd had once, before
she'd learned to stand on her own two feet so staunchly.

"Not everything."

"Good. That would have been a complete violation of ethics,
eavesdropping on an official conversation."

"Is that so unusual, a Chinese man having a white woman?"

"Quite. It's common the other way around. Normal. Brilliant,
really, the only thing to do for a white man who has any sense, to
want an Oriental woman."

He could feel her stiffen, which he supposed was his intent.
Nothing turned white women off so easily as telling them how much
you cared for Orientals. But in this case, being truthful with
himself, he knew he was hoping to challenge her, make her decide to
want him.

"Why would they brag about it, if it might implicate them in a
murder?"

"Pride. Some people think it's quite an achievement, having a
white woman."

He stopped for a moment, and turned her toward him, examining her face with his eyes. She looked embarrassed, as though the
moment was a little too real for her. He reached and touched the
light curl the humidity had coaxed from her hair, pushing it behind
her ear. Taking the pencil that was lodged there, he put it in her
hand, and moved in as though to kiss her.

"Why didn't you tell me about the pencil?" she said.

"What?"

"The only thing about you that's less than truthful is the
smoke screen you throw around this murder."

"That's my job, for God's sake. It's more important to get the murderer than to tell you things. Although I'm sure from your point of view justice means less than getting the story."

"You could have told me about the pencil Palmer-Smith was stabbed in the eye with."

"How did you find that out?"

"From the man who found the body."

"Are you going to print it?"

"I don't think you understand. The magazine isn't all that interested in Hong Kong. This is my personal obsession."

"Why?"

"I don't know. Why do people get obsessed? I just think there's something going on here that's deeper and wider than we think, than it looks. The whole ritual nature of the killing, vile as it was. Using a pencil, the way the Manson people used a fork. I can't shake the feeling it's the same. In some strange way, it's the same."

"Will you keep it quiet about the pencil? If someone comes in and confesses, the pencil is our only way to know it's true, to make sure we've got the right man."

"How could they kill him with a pencil?"

"They must have held him down. Hammered it in. Didn't even break the eyeball. Just there in the corner of his eye, shoved into his brain."

He took her home. At her door she held out her hand, but he moved in brusquely, caught her with his lips. "You have a sweet mouth. Imagine what it would be like if you cooperated."

"I don't deal in imagination. I'm a journalist. I see things as they are."

"How are they, in this case?"

"Pointless."

"Why?"

"I'm not looking for a relationship." She started foraging for her keys.

"Well, neither am I. And if I were, I certainly wouldn't want one with a Western woman. A man has to be crazy to want anything but an Oriental." The whiskey was getting to him now, firing his anger, slightly slurring his words. "They know their place."

"Three steps behind?"

"Exactly. Proud of what they're here for. To make life easier for a man."

"What year did you say this was?"

"You just go on being clever. And empty. And lonely."

"I'm not."

"Which?"

"Empty. Lonely. I don't have time."

"Well, the time will come. Faster than you think. But meanwhile, I apologize."

"It was only a kiss."

"That's not what I apologize for. I apologize for forgetting my own tastes, and getting you mixed up with the kind of woman I fancy, just because you have small wrists. I thought they made you feminine."

"I am feminine." She stood on her tiptoes, and set her lips against his, hard.

He did not kiss her back. "Don't think I'm so easy," he said.

"Call me sometime when you haven't had too much to drink."

"Call me sometime when you don't have an answer for everything."
He spoke over his shoulder, not even turning back to look at her.

All the way up in the elevator, Judith tried to tell herself she hadn't lost anything. The Chinese girl who lived in the building was huddled against the back of the car when she got in, her eyes obviously swollen from weeping. The choice Oriental, three steps behind, and men still tore her apart. Judith assumed the tears were because of a man: Hong Kong people were too pragmatic to weep over issues, and family griefs were shared in tight family gatherings. She and Judith had never even really said hello, a modesty on the part of the Chinese, a wish to keep her privacy or Judith's. All they had done was exchange polite smiles, eyes half-averted. Judith wasn't even sure of her name: the British man she lived with had his name on the bell downstairs. So it was certainly not a time for neighborly greetings, even had Judith the wish to be neighborly. The girl struggled to appear smaller, head down, shoulders defeatedly forward as though the posture would make her invisible.

When Judith got to her apartment, Claire was home. Judith was almost surprised to see her: she'd been out every evening. The Filipino *amah*, far from her native land and isolated in the kitchen wing, chattered incessantly when she got Judith's ear, filling it with gossip: *when* Claire had *not* spent the night there, when someone *else* had spent the night in her room, and *then*, not even *in* the night.

"I take it you've been having a good time," Judith said.

"Is that wrong of me, do you think?" Doubt shadowed the edges of Claire's glow. She looked younger than she had when she arrived in Hong Kong, the colorful silks she'd bought and had made into dresses and scarves drifting around her like a change of scenery, lifting her in the same way the trip had. Her skin appeared shining and translucent, the gray-blue tones Judith had noted on Claire's arrival transmuted into pink. The rainbow alchemy of infatuation. "Am I being disloyal?"

For a moment Judith thought Claire meant to her. As if it were something a friend shouldn't do, to blow into an exciting place and land directly in the midst of a romantic adventure, when Judith, who'd lived there for a long time, hadn't had one. Was it an unkind thing to do, so recently back from the cemetery, to be more connected to life than someone in the midst of it? Judith rarely took things personally, even when they were directed at her. It was this detachment that gave her such clarity as a journalist. But, she realized from time to time, it perhaps left something to be desired as a woman. "Disloyal to whom?"

"Charley."

"Charley would want you to be happy."

"Thank you." She let out a great sigh, suspiring over the music coming from Judith's sound system, a piano rhapsody heavy with treacle, being played by Richard Clayderman.

Judith was not usually aware of the identity of performing artists, but Clayderman had just had enormously publicized success at the Hong Kong concert hall, sold out past capacity, cheered to the rafters, all phrases Judith usually paid no attention to. But this particular concert had come as rather an embarrassment to America's most popular singer, who'd filled only a third of the seats the night before, fueling already rampant speculation that he was there to launder money. Recognizing the trills then, Judith wondered why she had the record. She had an aversion to self-indulgence, a loathing for bathos, which in this particular case was so intense as to set the soul on edge. More than her suspicion of people who became too popular, and her dislike for the overdone, she was angry at her supporting kitsch. Particularly as she did not remember buying it. "Where did you find this tape?"

"James bought it for me."

A little moue of distaste formed on Judith's mouth. None of the songs Claire had written were overly sentimental. Soft, sure, often yielding, but with the underlying toughness that characterized the brain of her friend, always redeeming the Silly Putty of her emotions. Her lyrics had a cutting edge, and the music supported them, so the songs were never excessive, which one could hardly say about Clayderman. For James to be leading Claire down the musical garden path to the mawkish disturbed Judith. When discrimination went, so did reason.

Judith understood how judgmental she was being. But as a Brit he had no First Amendment privileges, so she didn't see where she needed to protect his opinion, especially as he was foisting it on Claire. "He has terrible taste."

"In women, you mean?" There was a defensive haughtiness about it, a too-quick retaliation.

"His taste in women is first rate, and you know that."

"I want you to like him."

"I do like him. I just don't like his taste in music. Just because you're interested in someone doesn't mean you have to love everything they love." She was speaking directly to Claire's brain, but she could tell there was interference, like the Chinese jamming the radio during the news of Eastern Europe's shedding communism.

"But you can enjoy what they enjoy." Claire's jaw was set now.

"I remember your complaining about Charley's always watching football. That didn't make you a traitor to him."

"This is music, not the voice of Howard Cosell," Claire said, bristling.

"In my opinion, Howard Cosell's voice was easier to listen to."

"That was because you didn't hear it all the time!" Her face was red now. She heard the anger in her own voice, and sat down abruptly on the couch, silks whirling about her knees, caught in the breeze of her too-quick motion, and pique. "Oh, God, I don't mean to sound like I'm complaining about Charley."

"You're not. You're just being realistic. There's nothing wrong with being realistic, even after someone's dead. It's healthy. Why can't you be realistic about James?"

"I don't want to spoil it," Claire said, the happiness gone from her face, its lines suddenly all going downward, like those of a disappointed child. "He's so much fun."

"Good. That's what you should be having, is fun."

"You don't think it's a problem, that he's younger?"

"It's the fashion. He's perfect."

"You think so, too?"

"I mean, he's perfect for Hong Kong."

"But I'll go home, and he'll be here . . ."

"How lucky can you get? Never to have it peter out. Never to grow tired of each other. Not to have to spend your life listening to Clayderman . . ."

They both laughed. Claire got up from the couch and put her arms around Judith, tentatively. Judith did not move away. "I don't like things to end," Claire said softly.

"But they do. They have to." Judith pulled back slightly, and looked deep into Claire's face, addressing what was wise in it. "Remember when you came to visit me in Paris, and you had that little woolly hat Charley gave you. You wore it all over Paris, and the last morning you were there—"

"I left it on a stall at the market. And I ran back to get it, and it was gone."

"You couldn't stop grieving for the hat. And I told you—"

"It was only for Paris," Claire said, remembering.

"It was only for Paris."

"He's only for Hong Kong?"

"He's only for Hong Kong. Don't try to take him back to Beverly Hills."

"For God's sake, Judith, I've got two children who are still reeling from the death of their father. Do you think for a moment it even crossed my mind to take him home?"

"Yes."

"You know me so well." She went to the French doors leading out to the balcony. Across the harbor, flashing neon lights filled in white stripes on the Kenwood cigarette package, as if in visual counterpoint to the music, the whole of Kowloon a video. "He's so quick, and personable. He'd be such a hit in Beverly Hills. They'd eat up his accent. You know what phonies they are."

"You don't even know what he really does."

"He's a financial consultant."

"Whatever that means. Everybody without real weight in Hong Kong is a consultant."

"But he's smart."

"Smart people fail." She could tell from the sudden abject fall of Claire's shoulders that she was thinking about Charley. Judith hadn't really meant Charley, but the truth was Charley had had a tough time of it in business, and they both knew what a strain it had put on the marriage.

"Well, James isn't going to. He's on the verge of a really big stock deal. If it works, he'll be very rich."

"How much does he need?"

"What?" Claire turned.

"How much money has he asked you for?"

"He hasn't asked me for a penny," Claire said hotly. "I asked *him* if he was looking for investors, and he said he didn't want any money from me."

"He *is* smart."

"You think he's setting me up? You think that's what he's after? You don't think a man like James could be interested in me?" There was as much doubt as anger in her tone, a need for reassurance, as though she had asked those same questions of herself.

"I think any man in the world could be interested in you. You're a pretty, gifted, successful woman. But you're also a widow, and vulnerable. And you're an American. Everyone thinks we're all rich."

"Well, I am rich. A little rich, anyway." She turned back toward the window. "Poor Charley. All his life he struggled for money, and the only way he ever got enough to make us really secure was to die."

"So you're certainly not going to give it to James."

"Of course not." Her voice cracked.

"You're in Hong Kong, Claire. Don't be a target."

"Couldn't someone make a great deal of money here, not just lose? He's a very wealthy young man, from a prominent family. Heir to the title when his father dies."

"Maybe."

"You don't believe he's what he says he is?"

"I don't know what he says he is."

"He doesn't have to say. He's clever, and caring, and extremely well brought up . . ."

"How much did he tell you he needed?"

"Not a penny from me! You're just jealous because I've met somebody wonderful."

"Probably," said Judith.

"Forgive me. Why do we say such things to people we love?"

"Because they're true. Maybe I am jealous. I'd like to be in love."

"Have you ever been?"

Judith hesitated. "It was only for Paris."

In the elevator, James checked his reflection in the bright aluminum stripping that sided the car. Everywhere in Hong Kong there were metallic surfaces so bright one had no need for mirrors. It pleased him that even with encroaching age—thirty-four seemed quite ancient to him—his general appearance had stayed the same. Sailing on Sundays had kept him tan, reinforced the heft of his shoulders, thick from a youth filled with rugby. His shirt collar was tailored precisely to his rather large neck. The fineness of his features balanced the barrel-chestedness, made him look softer than his body was. His overall good looks were enhanced by the perfect proportions of his dark blue suit. He was handsomer than he might have been anywhere else, at a fraction of the price, he could not help realizing.

It was one of the things that made him glad he had been banished to Hong Kong.

The elevator doors opened. "Hold it a minute, can you?" called out a man's voice. "I'm just getting my umbrella."

"It isn't raining," said James. "And the car's going up."

"Dreadfully sorry," the man said, stepping toward the car. "I pushed both buttons. James!" Recognition lit the bland features.

"Peter! I didn't know you lived in this building."

"Do you?" Peter came into the car.

"Just visiting a friend."

"Well, I'll ride up with you. A lady friend, I assume." The doors closed.

"You assume correctly."

"I hope she's rich."

"I'm satisfied that she's white."

"Snobbish of you, really," Peter said. "You have no idea what you're missing."

"How *is* Kip?"

"Heaven itself."

"You're taking her with you back to England?"

"Haven't decided whether I'm going back to England. Jardine's has no plans for cutting back. And even if they did, I should think about staying on and consulting for the Chinese."

"You really believe they're going to encourage capitalism?"

"Of course. They want the money. Just like the rest of us greedy people in Hong Kong."

"Not all of us are here because we're greedy."

"That's right," Peter said. "Living here so long, one forgets about family disgraces." The door opened. "Is this your floor?"

"Yes, it is." James reached back and pressed the lobby button. "I suppose you'll know when you hit bottom."

"Some of us do," said Peter, smiling, as the doors closed.

Inside the apartment, Claire stiffened as she heard the bell ring. "Don't say anything about his deal, will you?" Her voice sounded pleading. "It's confidential. He might not like my having told you."

"Not a word," Judith said, opening the door.

He stood in the doorway, impeccably groomed, immaculate,

bending slightly, as if the arch over the door were too small for him, which it nearly was. He was well over six feet tall, and although the district was populated mainly by Westerners, most of the doors were gauged at Oriental height, so tall men often hit their heads, and got into the habit of listing, as James was now.

"Sorry to be so late," he said, smiling past Judith at Claire. "But my meeting went on a great deal longer than I anticipated." He moved out of the doorway, and took Claire in a casual embrace, kissing her lightly on the lips, as though they had been lovers for a while, and friends for even longer.

"How did it go?"

"Outstanding! Raised all but the last share."

"Are you going to feed me?" Claire said quickly.

"With my own hands. Will you join us, Judith?"

"Another time."

He moved Claire toward the door, his arm around her in a proprietary way, his hand reaching up so his fingers touched her hair. It was all so handsome and friendly and seemingly benign, Judith wondered why it couldn't perhaps be the way Claire perceived it. Maybe there were moments when handsome young men appeared solely for the purpose of adoring, wanting nothing but the love generous women had to give. Maybe there were men who were exactly what they seemed, free of duplicity, so what was on their minds was on their tongues. Maybe truth could come freshly minted, like kisses. Maybe broken hearts could heal, and miracles could happen, and women could find exactly what they wanted, without being torpedoed by their need. And maybe the novels of Henry James were right for their time, but Americans were no longer innocents, to be gulled by clever Europeans, temporarily located in Hong Kong. And maybe love could prevail, and better nature triumph, and justice be meted out to all who deserved it, and people live happily ever after, for a while anyway.

But Judith didn't think so.

FOURTEEN

♦

Having known what love was, Claire was anxious to see it everywhere, falling under a spell she had no awareness she was creating. There was no doubt in her mind that James was a godsend, or, more accurately, a Charley-send. Having loved her as much as he did, having understood, especially at the end, how deep it went, Charley would have wanted her to be happy. So she was quite sure, in the fanciful part of her brain, that James was a gift from him.

James's standing on the brink of the kind of success that always eluded Charley seemed a further link with him, a chance to make right what life had not offered, an opportunity for the first time. They were so alike, she'd convinced herself, in spite of Judith's caution to the contrary. The easy charm, the boyish humor, the great protective barrel chest, a fortress to hide in when all the world felt like an attack by hostile Indians. Even the swagger that Charley had had once seemed a part of James's stance, as he told her about his deal. As Charley had told her about his big chances, before they disappeared on him.

"The stock's going to go through the roof," he told her at dinner. They were at the Golden Bull, a Vietnamese restaurant near the Regent Hotel. A pool just inside the entrance was crowded with carp, their limited movements so chock-a-block that a flip of the tail sent another carp's head out of the water. Around them, tables seemed equally crowded with people, the entire ambience from fish to clientele a mirror of life in Hong Kong. Thatched roofs covered the tables, lending a would-be air of Vietnam, reminding those who could deal with being reminded of all the boat people shipped by the British from detention camps back to the country they had fled. The rest just ate dinner.

James wrapped heavily spiced pieces of beef in crisp lettuce leaves and fed them to her. They ate huge butterflied shrimp and licked each other's fingers. And in between, reluctantly, and always at her urging, he talked about his deal.

"I've got all but the last ten percent of the financing. That's the only hitch. Without that, the whole thing falls apart."

"How much are we talking about?" Claire asked him.

"A million Hong Kong. Anthony Go is longing to lend it to me."

"Anthony Go?"

"The sinister Chinese I wouldn't introduce you to that first day we met. He wants to do me a 'favor,' so he can use my name to open an account at an honorable British bank. Connect with some of my friends."

"What would be the harm in that?"

"Once you get involved with these people, there's no getting away from them, ever. You belong to them."

"*These* people?"

"Triads. Criminals," James said. "Very slick. Very powerful."

"How much money is a million Hong Kong?"

"A hundred and twenty-five thousand U.S."

"I could lend you that," she said, after a moment.

"You shouldn't be so ready to be generous. The wrong man could really take advantage of you."

"You're not the wrong man."

"How can you be sure?"

Naturally there was no answer for that, except her intuition, and how happy he made her. How could he possibly be the wrong man?

In the end, he reluctantly agreed to let her underwrite a bank loan. They went back to his apartment. She called her broker in

Beverly Hills and told him to wire the funds to a correspondent bank in Hong Kong.

"Yes, I'm sure it's okay," Claire said into the phone, as James kissed the ear not pressed to the receiver. "No, I don't need to send you the particulars—there's no time for you to go over them." His lips were on her neck, now, the soft stretch of her throat. "I don't want to sleep on it. I've already slept on it." He kissed the side of her mouth. She turned her face and opened her lips wide to receive him. "And will again," she whispered, and hung up the phone.

Then his fingers were pressing gently against her nipples as his mouth explored her chin, his tongue whisking gingerly over the heart-shaped point of it. And his fingertips traced around the outside of her breasts, following the curve to her armpits, and she could feel him at the softest part of her, the small expanse of skin where chest met arm. And she bit her tongue to keep herself from moaning, then moaned anyway. Because what harm was there in it, as long as she didn't say how she felt. What harm was there in any woman's sighing, as long as she didn't put it into words, when "I love you" also meant "I need you," and frightened men away.

And his hands were all over her, sliding her skirt up between her legs, silk against silk. And he was inside the elastic band of her panties, tracing his center finger along the fold of skin that marked her last external outpost. And then he slid into the slippery place inside.

And she was tearing off his tie, loosening the buttons on the shirt that clung so perfectly to his very broad chest, unbuckling his belt. "I'll do that," he said, and took the rest of his clothes off, dancing on one foot as he slid trousers and shorts free in one swift motion, his erection growing to the rhythm he created as he danced.

She was on her knees, moved by the sight of him, foolishly hopping like a child, nothing of a child in the evidence before her eyes. She slid her tongue along the erect underside of him, up to his tip. He reached beneath her arms, and raised her to her feet. "Don't do that," he whispered, as he lifted her. "You give and give and give. Who gives to you? Why don't you just receive for a while?"

It startled her for a moment. But he curved his arm behind her legs, lifted her, and carried her to the bedroom. Even Charley, big as he was, strong as he was, had never done that without laughing or faltering, pretending to buckle at the knees. Now James swept her quite literally off her feet, and laid her down. And his lips were on her breasts.

And she received.

Clement supposed he was angry at women. He was honest with himself when it came to taking his own emotional temperature. He was incensed, inflamed by Judith's behavior toward him, mortified by the extent of his own interest, and having it rejected. He woke up riled and contentious, unwilling to believe anything but the worst about all of them. So right away he started checking on Maggie Evans.

On a rainy afternoon some days before, he'd seen a limousine go by, with a couple locked in a heated embrace; the woman looked like Maggie. Open-minded as he was sure he was, with his own heavy penchant for Orientals, it had somewhat surprised him to see her with an Asian man. What he had told Judith was the truth: it seldom went the other way. With a high-line, upmarket family like Maggie's, for her to consort with other than her own kind was shocking. In his own mind he knew he sounded like a dowager. But morality was clearly at issue. In the absence of any real information about the murder, hunches were as salient as fingerprints. If there was something sexually suspect about Maggie, he had an obligation to uncover what it was.

It didn't take long. Hong Kong was a small community, with the gossip level of a village. There were a small number of singles bars, popular with the expats: California Club, Causeway Bay. People who prided themselves on being in the know, Canadian Jews who owned restaurants in Kimberly Row, with direct lines to the oddballs and rumormongers, gunrunners and gun dealers, all of them with something to say. But none as clearly or loudly as McCafferty, an Irishman who ran a Middle Eastern restaurant, in fashion with the Brits, as much for the genial prattle of its owner as for its food.

"Of course I know Maggie Evans," he said. Wispy gray hair curled around his pink, lined forehead, like horns, an aging cherub gone over to the side of the demons. The restaurant was not yet open for lunch, but already the smells were rampant, fetid, the too-sweet odor found in hotels where Arabs were encamped, less perfume and body odors than the cooking they did in their rooms.

McCafferty wore a fez near the back of his head, tassel hanging down toward his ear. As he spoke he whisked it away, as though it were a persistent fly. Clement found himself imitating the gesture, the uneasy feeling growing in him as they talked that the place was actually alive with insects. The slow-whirring fans hanging from the ceiling, and artificial palms siding the tables, intensified an atmosphere of seedy desert heat, with echoes of Peter Lorre. "Rice pudding," Clement said aloud. "In Egypt you cannot tell if they're raisins or flies."

"Pardon?" McCafferty said.

"It's a line from a movie. *Five Graves to Cairo*."

"Never heard of it."

"Before you were born."

"Then it must be *really* old."

"Everything's really old," said Clement, a trace of sadness in his voice. "Even Disneyland."

"You were asking about Maggie Evans," McCafferty said, uncomfortable that the small talk was moving away from scandal—always, for him, the dish of the day. "Regular slut she is. Had her myself a time or two."

"Try not to be too gallant."

"I'm not a gentleman, Superintendent, that's accurate. But there's no need when someone isn't a lady. There was nothing personal, you understand, about what happened between us. It would have been anybody with trousers on. Or off."

"Did she dump you?"

"I didn't stay around long enough."

"So you don't have any hard feelings?"

"Feelings aren't what Maggie Evans cares about being hard. She wanted me for her lust. Not for my originality of character."

"You know anyone else she was with?"

"I hardly know anyone she wasn't with. Including Harry Magic."

"The porno star?"

"There's a story they have them on film." McCafferty flipped his fez away from his ear and refilled his small coffee cup from the engraved silver Turkish pot. "More coffee?"

"It's too sweet for me." Clement waved his hand. "Who has the film?"

"Probably Harry has a copy. Very vain about the size of his cock. Watches his own flicks to get a hard-on."

"Where can I find him?"

"Excellent question. No one's seen him around for a couple of months. Baklava?" He held out a plate of the flat, sticky cakes.

"I don't suppose you have rice pudding?"

The bank officer who greeted Claire and James was one of the only women bank directors in Hong Kong. According to a television interview Gloria Steinem had given in the early eighties, if a woman was beautiful and succeeded, word was she had slept her way to the top. If she was ugly, she was successful because she hadn't been able to get a man. Though neither the tape of the interview nor the philosophy of feminism had reached Hong Kong, in the case of Mei Wan Fang there was no doubt the first part of the thesis applied. Beautiful as she was, there was no doubt among the top business people in the community that she had slept with influential board members of the bank. In fact, she had been to bed with none of them, had never used sex to advance herself. Her personal taste ran to women, and, as everyone knew, women had no influence.

Men she turned down imagined she was involved with someone more powerful. Had they known the truth, she would have been socially and professionally pilloried. According to the propaganda, homosexuality did not exist among the Chinese. On Gloucester Road, Disco Disco had been declared off-limits for the police, since men danced with men inside, and the police were not supposed to know. The SIU—the Special Investigation Unit—had been created simply to chase and harass homosexuals among civil servants, weed them out. Police officers found to be homosexuals were dismissed from the force. A suspect police chief inspector, unable to face the embarrassment, had shot himself five times in the head. Five times. It seemed so improbable that the investigation and hearing had lasted longer than the Nuremberg trials. All in all, homosexuality was better left alone, and was rarely charged, although it was legally an offense. Usually it was punished with a fine, and labeled "gross indecency."

The local myth was that in such a sexy city, there could be no alternative bent, one of the reasons there were not many cautions about AIDS. AIDS, like homosexuality, was designated as a problem of the West. The fact that there had been thirteen deaths from it locally by the start of the nineties made it a little hard to hide. But so far neither the disease, nor a gay population in Hong Kong, had been openly acknowledged.

Certainly no one who wasn't intimately involved would have guessed Mei Wan Fang's inclinations. She was a pleasant woman, dissatisfied with no aspect of her life, with the exception of a wish that her bank had offices to compare to the Bank of China Building, designed by I. M. Pei, or the David Foster–designed HongKong Bank. Both buildings offered their own spectacle, although the HongKong Bank was considered the ultimate high-tech architectural masterpiece as well as a flagrant example of capitalistic waste, its cost over 760 million U.S. dollars, more than the Bank of China.

From the inside, Mei's office was as striking as any in either of the other buildings. Bay windows bellied out over Central to offer a 180-degree view of the harbor. The furniture was gray suede and chrome, picking up the color of the water on a bleak day, as this one was. Whitecaps danced across the surface. Shadows of clouds played deep and dark below the waves, as though the clouds were in the harbor, not the sky. All of it comprised a monochromatic marvel, with even the normally bright Star Ferry melding into a shade of gray.

"You're underwriting Mr. Bingham's loan?" Mei asked Claire.

"That's right. My broker should have wired the money."

"You understand we hypothecate it against the loan?"

"I don't really understand the language of business," Claire said, smiling. "I'm an artist."

"If Mr. Bingham fails to pay it back, we tap your account."

"He'll pay it back."

"I wasn't giving an opinion. I was simply explaining the mechanics."

"I appreciate that," said Claire, although she really didn't. The ingenuous comment she had made about failing to comprehend was sincere. She knew she could lose, but didn't expect to.

She was sure the funds she provided for him would be returned. It was more than she could afford to lose—money she considered the children's, minted from Charley's pain. But James wouldn't lose it. His investment in the new computer program, he'd explained, would make him a director of the company. He'd shown her the price of the stock in the paper over the previous week, pointed out how rapidly it was rising. "Whoever gets in on this will make a fortune," he'd said. There was no reason to disbelieve him.

She felt happy in spite of the color of the day, a color that seemed reflected on James's face. He looked quite drawn, his usually vibrant complexion closer now to the hue of the water, as if the clouds passing over the sun obscured his radiance as well. It made Claire sad, because as ignorant as she was about business, she was clear on people, and she understood that James didn't really like using her money. He looked a lot like Charley had looked when things hadn't gone the way he'd hoped, and he'd ended up having to come to her.

"What a woman you are," James said to her now as they left the bank office. He took the check and put it in his billfold, a little worn around the edges, she noted. She remembered a place where there was beautiful leather, and thought she would go there while he was at his office and buy him a new one.

His step was jaunty again, the hand that was through her arm alive with electricity. "What would I have done without you?"

"Every bit as well," she told him, as she'd always told Charley, the words ricocheting in her brain to those earlier times. She could see them both standing taller, James and Charley, present superimposed on the past, men regenerated by her. As she was. As life was. The day seemed very bright around her, suddenly.

*　　*　　*

He had lied to her, of course, but only a little. The rest of the money James said he'd raised did not exist. Still, he had full confidence the stock would perform exactly as the company directors had promised him it would, and he would make the proverbial killing.

"Nothing less than a killing," he said to his chum Kenneth, who had the office next door to the one James pretended to have. He had let Claire walk him to the building, kissing her goodbye at the entrance, telling her the company he was consultant for was extremely strict about not having personal visitors, promising her he would let her see his office one day, buy him a plant, if she insisted. But not this morning.

"I've raised a million Hong Kong." He handed Kenneth the check.

"Forgive me, James, for not being impressed."

It was early in the day, and the air-conditioning was on full, blasting through the white-walled chrome-desked atmosphere, blasting it into a futuristic chill. But still Kenneth was sweating, a light arc of moisture around the fringe of his hair. "This is Hong Kong. Even a million U.S. hardly makes a ripple."

"Buy the stock on a hundred percent margin," James said, his lips tight.

"But my dear friend, you know that's illegal." He looked no more composed at his desk than he had on the dance floor, the night they'd all gone to the club, the perspiration around his monkish head testifying to his struggle to seem at ease. He was a highly successful man, and unequivocally bright. But in spite of privilege and accomplishment, he was still deeply off balance from the simple fact that he was losing his hair. It was no myth, the deep Samsonian principle, that without hair a man was less. Even if his strength wasn't lessened, his self-esteem was. "Nobody would like to see you get rich more than I. On, Uppingham, and all that. But a hundred percent margin . . ."

"Will buy me two million shares."

"But if you lose . . ."

"I won't lose. You've seen the stock moving."

"No question. Something's going on."

"They're going to supply all the schools in China with a

computer and software teaching program. The biggest problem in China is how to get enough teachers."

"They *wish* that was the biggest problem in China."

"We're not discussing politics," said James. "Politics change. The need for education remains. The computer will solve the teacher problem."

"All the teachers in China," Kenneth chortled. "Hard to resist."

"The directors gave me a tip. Shares will double by the end of the month."

"And then you want me to sell?"

"Margin an extra two million."

"Mustn't get greedy."

"My dear Kenneth, this is Hong Kong."

"Forgive me. I lost my head."

Claire waited for him, as they'd agreed, in the bar of the Mandarin. There was a strange elation loose in her now, a familiar feeling of rescue, something she had once not even considered she could do for a man. Her own life had been one of waiting for someone to save her, an attitude she shared with women brought up on fairy tales. When Charley had first come into her life, that was what he had done. Saved her from lack of love, the world's indifference. Making her feel good about herself, her talent, the act of living, which had too often in her troubled, loveless youth seemed more burden than privilege. Only after the babies had become children and his career had foundered, had their situation reversed, and she'd been forced to give him ballast. Much as she'd resented it, on some levels, it gave her control. There was something seductive about weakness in a man, something touching and appealing. It pointed up the lie many of them were choking from having swallowed, that they had to be fearless, and powerful. Vulnerability in a man struck at a woman's tenderest feelings. It also made her what society said she could never be: in charge.

So as attached as she was becoming to James, as giving as she really was, on some level she understood her generosity was a way of controlling, while clinging to him. Already she was planning how she could extend her stay in Hong Kong, was having conversations with her mother, talking her into staying longer with the children.

She sat in the Captain's Bar now, a little high, feeling that rush of potency that women were not supposed to have. She did not want to acknowledge to herself that there had been anything but beneficence in her loan. Though it was true she could not really afford to lose the money, she was sure she could even less afford to lose James. Being young as she was, in spirit, and with her still unevolved feelings of girlishness, and helplessness, she had a hard time thinking of herself as an older woman, no matter what the calendar years were. The thought of her holding on in some unbecoming way to a younger man was repellent to her. Out of the question, really, as well as she had always managed to avoid the cliché. She could not possibly be one of those desiccated creatures so fearful of being unloved they put harpy talons in a man. Especially as vibrant as she was, and looked, as juicy as she felt when she was with him. Still, so far, he'd failed to tell her what his feelings were. And sometimes, in that ashen border between waking and sleeping she was seized with the panic that he might not have any.

"Excuse me," said a sharply dressed Chinese man. "You are the friend of my very good friend James Bingham?"

"That's right," said Claire.

"I am surprised at his bad manners not introducing us." He held out his hand. "Anthony Go."

"Claire Black."

"Yes, I know your name. May I sit with you?" He was already sitting, only his words reticent, deferential. "I understand you were at the bank with him this morning. A widow must be very careful, you know, especially in Hong Kong. Such a woman could be a mark."

"Excuse me, but I don't think that's any of your business."

"Oh, but it is, because I *am* in business. You on the other hand are an artist. A woman who writes songs. You should not go into areas about which you know nothing."

"How do you know so much about me?"

"That's part of my business, too." He smiled, a very white-toothed smile. "Finding out what I need to find out. The British are so genteel. But how gallant are they, really? How gallant is it of Mr. Bingham to borrow money from one so recently bereaved? One who might be considered a target."

"You're no friend of his."

"Oh, but I am. I can afford to have him for a friend. Who but a friend would have offered to lend him a great deal more than the million he took from you? A poor widow."

"I'm not poor."

"By Hong Kong standards you are. Just as Mr. Bingham is. A million doesn't even make him a major player. He's scratching for his opportunity, like so many anxious people. The only thing that gets us what we want is not to be anxious at all. Wouldn't you agree?"

"Go away."

"I'm just trying to warn you. You should be careful who you choose for company."

"Let me start with you." She got up and left the bar.

On a couch against the wall in the Captain's Bar, Peter leaned in close to Kip, not touching her exactly, not soothing her, in spite of the fact that she was crying.

"How can you say I don't love you?" he said, trying to modulate his voice, although it was hard to be heard above the rumble of conversation, speaking as softly as he was. "Don't I give you everything?"

"Everything but what I need," she wept.

"I hate it when you cry in public."

"You hate it when I cry in private."

"That's true. I do. I just wish I didn't have such a soft heart."

"Ha!"

"Are you saying I don't? If I didn't have such a soft heart, you would be out of my life, you little trollop. What do you suppose my mother would think, if she saw what you did to try and hold me?"

"She'd probably think she'd done a very good job of raising you to be a proper British fuck-up."

"Don't you dare use those words! Don't you dare speak like that about my mother." Fury played across his features. "Nothing you can say could possibly make me forgive you."

"I'm wearing the red lace brassiere."

"Well, in that case," said Peter, "I guess we better go home."

In Maggie Evans's boutique at the Landmark, Louise pretended to look at the jade. She was actually interested in it, but her attention drifted to the big, handsome Texan poring over the bracelets. Not that a man that Mitchumesque, well turned out, and obviously wealthy, would be attracted to her. But from some still innocent corner of her brain she looked out with young eyes, and honey skin, and imagined she might have a shot at him. A one-shot, anyway. If he wasn't smitten, that is, which he obviously was, from the prices he was willing to pay.

"And this one?" he was asking Maggie now, holding up apple green circles surrounded by small diamonds, linked with delicate filigree.

"Twenty-seven thousand U.S.," Maggie said.

"You give a discount for cash?"

"Seven percent."

"How about if she doesn't like it? You'll take it back?"

"If she doesn't like it, you can give it to me," Louise said.

The Texan looked up and smiled. He had green-gray eyes, full of humor. "I seen you around the hotel," he said.

"I seen you too," said Louise. "But then you'd be hard to miss."

"What about this?" he said, and held out the bracelet. "You think a woman would like this?"

"Only if she had a wrist."

"Oh, she's got wrists, all right. Pretty delicate, considering what a powerful stroke she's got."

"I don't know if I can handle such intimate details."

"I mean a swimmer's stroke," he said, and kind of chortled. "You're a funny lady."

"Funny doesn't get you bracelets."

"Give her one of these," he said to Maggie, and pointed to a small jade heart. Maggie took it out of the case.

"Are you serious?" Louise said.

"Pretty damn."

To her surprise, Louise found tears springing to her eyes. She turned away, so nobody would see. With his gesture she had realized how long it had been since a man had given her a gift, especially not wanting anything in return. "You're very kind," she said, swallowing. "But I couldn't possibly not accept it."

"I like your spirit." He grinned. "I like the smile. I like the attitude."

They walked back to the hotel together. The heart was on a tiny gold chain the Texan had also bought. "You tell them back wherever you come from—"

"Hollywood."

"I should have guessed. You tell them in Hollywood that you wear that because you caught the eye of a Texan."

"I wish I could have caught more."

"Oh, honey, we could have had some fun. But I'm too fired up." He waved the long box that held the bracelet. "This is *some* woman. She fires me up. She fires me up."

In the ladies' room of the Mandarin, Louise washed her face, tried to take the sorrow from her eyes, looked at herself in the mirror, her focus on the little heart around her neck. Her skin was still pretty, no fine lines or sag in her throat—some genetic miracle, she supposed. She hurried back out to the bar, so Henry wouldn't come in after her. She'd told her about the Texan, and the gift, but tried to hide how shaken she had been by his gesture.

But the Chinese girl seemed to have an intuition as robust as her breasts were flat. "I would've thought you'd be used to presents," she said, as Louise sat back down beside her.

"Well, I am. Trips and cars and houses. But it's been a long time since a man gave me a heart."

"How long?"

"High school," said Louise, trying to remember if her high school love had indeed given her a locket, or she'd only wanted one so badly it had become part of her fantasy scrapbook.

"Well, I have a present for you, too," said Henry, taking a brown paper bag out of her purse.

"What couturier house is that from?"

"My herbalist." Henry handed her a dried flower, in a cellophane packet. "This is Saint John's wort. It protects against evil spirits."

"Miss Felder?" Anthony Go stood in front of them, bowing slightly.

"It doesn't work," said Louise.

"How amusing you are," Go said, pulling up a chair. "The world would be a sadder place without you."

"It certainly would," said Henry, feistily.

"Have you thought any more about my proposal?"

"I have, and I'm not interested."

"Pity."

"I'm interested," said Henry, sitting up straighter. "You come up with the right property, and I'll see that Louise puts it together."

"I'll do no such thing."

"I suppose in a culture where women encourage each other to be obstinate, they lose sight of how vulnerable they are. In the physical sense of vulnerable."

"I see."

"I hope so." He got up, bowed, and left.

"He's not really serious," said Louise. "I mean, what would be the point. You've already agreed to go along with him, in spite of my feelings."

"He doesn't like anyone giving him a hard time."

"Sounds like my first prom date."

"You better take this seriously." Henry took the cellophane packet from Louise, and made a little circle with it in the air, mouthing words Louise could not quite make out.

"You speaking Mandarin or Cantonese?"

"English," Henry said, and recited. "Saint John's wort, scaring from the midnight heath, the witch and goblin with its spicy breath."

"Oh, I feel so much better."

"You'd be surprised how potent some of these things are."

Henry gave her back the cellophane packet, and foraged through the brown paper bag, lifting out a package of twigs and bark. "This makes a tea that puts out the fire in the liver."

"I'd be totally ineffective, if I didn't have a fire in my liver."

"And this . . ." Henry took out an apple.

"But I've never seen one of those before!"

"This is no ordinary apple. This is a divining apple. Sacred to Venus. Friday is Halloween. If you take a burning candle and this apple into a dark room just before midnight, and eat it, while combing your hair in front of a mirror, you will see your future husband. But don't look behind you. As the clock strikes midnight, his face will appear in the mirror. Here." She handed the apple to Louise.

"Why are you giving it to me?"

"Because I think everything would change if you'd fall in love."

"Fall in *what?*"

"You don't fool me, you know. You're not as tough as you pretend."

"I'm tougher."

"I see what happened to you because a man gave you a piece of jade. Your whole shell cracked."

"I was just afraid he wanted to make a movie."

"Try it." Henry kissed her cheek. "I want very much for you to be happy."

"Are you signing with someone else?" Louise asked, mournfully. "They always kiss you just before they go to Creative Artists."

"I care about you, Louise." Henry got up. "See you later."

When Henry had gone, Louise looked around the bar. The Texan saluted her from a stool, where he'd poised himself like a whaler's wife waiting for a ship to return from the sea. His face lit up as Erica Thorr came in.

"Of course. I should have guessed," Louise murmured to herself, and got up. "Is that a bracelet in your pocket," she muttered to him as she passed the bar, "or are you just glad to see her?" She didn't wait for an answer, nor did she greet Erica, so oddly off balance was she, from the heart around her throat, and Henry's incredibly naive suggestion. Love. Good God, when was the last time she'd thought in terms of love?

Still, when she got into the elevator, and the doors closed, leaving her alone, she looked at the apple in her hand. "Sacred to Venus, huh?" she murmured as though it could hear, or Venus could. "Midnight? Halloween? Well, fuck it. It couldn't hurt to try."

In the bar, Biff Lester tried to catch Erica's eye. But her usual aloofness seemed to have evolved into actual hostility. She looked at him directly with a glance so withering all his humor faded, and with it, temporarily at least, his enthusiasm. The bracelet in his pocket pressed against his longing, not just his skin. He had too much invested now to make her out-and-out angry. So he didn't even go over to her, didn't think of offering her the gift. Instead, he went to his room, and ran the tape of her swimming. On a second screen, on the VCR he'd gotten through the same man who'd filmed Erica in the pool, he ran a porno. And while a yellow-haired woman sucked a massive cock onscreen, he stroked his own, and watched Erica's breasts, Erica's waist, Erica's beautiful stretch as she cut through the water, crotch veeing above the camera, and imagined it was Erica's mouth working on him.

FIFTEEN

◆

Although she had stopped going to church on Sunday mornings, Maggie still followed a part of what had been the day's ritual. She would tie up whatever loose ends there were at her office in the Landmark, then walk through the public passageway that constituted the ingenious underpinnings of the HongKong Bank Building and climb the cement steps across the road up to Saint John's Cathedral. At the rise just below the church, hawkers sold imitation leather bags to Filipino maids on their day off, souvenirs of the plastic crafts that did not flourish at home. Sunday was special for the maids, a chance for them to renew their national enthusiasms, tales of love, recollection of family, talk of dependents, husbands included, that they had come to Hong Kong to support. Like cicadas, they chattered from early morning into the evening, a concert of crickets come to their version of the promised land: the last Land of Opportunity. That it was soon to be lost, that the coming of the Chinese might not bring simply an end to fortunes to be made in an afternoon, but salaries to be made in a month, was a tragedy they did not speak of. Tragedy was already a part of their national awareness: a tyranny so jubilantly overthrown, replaced by a democracy that failed. Each of them, no matter how uneducated, had gone through a brief flush of pride at being a woman, with the ascent of Corazon Aquino. Few of them spoke about her anymore, except to note sadly that the job had not been one of a housewife. Mostly they just chirped of happy mindless things in Tagalog, on their way to the special Filipino-language mass at Saint Joseph's, the Catholic church farther up Garden Road.

In the courtyard of Saint John's, Maggie would stop and catch her breath, watching as the ever-dwindling congregation moved inside. She would listen to the cathedral bells, and long to go in. But the betrayal went too deep, God's, as well as her own. She would walk past the massive, open doors, and avert her eyes, as one would at the sight of an old love, with whom it had ended badly.

Some days, she went by way of Hollywood Road in Central. She would stop at the Man Wo Temple, where worship was as garish as the makeup she wore. Ornate dolls, gilded, dressed in red, painted faces staring, cluttered the altar. Incense shaped like hornet's nests, clumps of slowly burning scent, smoldered alongside crowded plates of sweetcakes set out for voracious spirits. The altar itself, in the gold-painted, windowless darkness, was lit with bright red bulbs, and scored with tinsel. A whore's Christmas tree.

Great iron vats held flamingo-red sticks of incense the size of dynamite burning in the sand. A barbecued pig glittered slickly next to pyramids of oranges. Rice paper lanterns painted with landscapes fringed with red. In the next room children in red shorts and white shirts skipped rope and giggled and shouted and sang. For them, at least, religion, like childhood, seemed a celebration. An opportunity to meet together and express some joy at being alive.

"Nearer my God to Thee," Maggie would sing in her mocking, smoky alto voice, a sneer on her face. The vulgarity of the temple, the insult to the simplicity she had always been led to believe was the center of true faith, was a balm to her. Her being there, a fallen Episcopal voice in the ruby darkness, seemed to her a way of mooning God. The whole setting pulled down its pants and waved insolent cheeks in His face, giving Him the tawdriness He deserved, for what He had let happen to Betsy.

It did not occur to Maggie that hunger for what she had forsworn might have led her there. God had abandoned her as surely as He had His more favored Child, proof to her that virtue garnered no better reward than vice. She had turned on any thought of prudence with a vengeance. The forced abstinence of grieving, the chasm of chastity had closed with a clang behind her, along with any lingering wish she had for Heaven. In the past week, she'd been with as many men as there were days. Most of the time she'd been drunk, so she couldn't remember if any of them were good or not. They were all just cocks to her. Circumcised, uncircumcised. Out of their sheaths they were all the same. She preferred penises circumcised, because it made things easier, straighter to the point, the way money did. But money didn't mean much to her anymore, either: she had more than she would ever need, especially now that there was no young girl to educate, plan a future for, gift with a lavish wedding.

In the part of her that still believed God existed, sneakily omnipresent, she hoped He was watching. That He had seen her bypass His tasteful cathedral, and come to this brothel of excess, where she fit in perfectly, His liveliest tart.

Then, she resumed her climb.

Networks of stairs ran beside the roads, meandered like angular rivers through parks thick with trees. Secreted in alleyways, mazes of steps led to the top of Hong Kong.

On this particular Sunday, strong winds had finally snapped the clinging threads of a summer long past its season, and moved the island into fall. Energized by the unexpected briskness of the day, Maggie decided to keep on walking. She moved past her apartment building on Conduit Road, to the stairs leading up to the Peak.

She was still in remarkable shape for her age and excesses, inbred hardiness combining with fierce determination to give her strength for the climb. On other such Sundays, she had made the pilgrimage with Betsy. The two of them packed a picnic basket. Betsy carried it, Maggie walking gaily ahead of her, the parade master. "Hurry up," Maggie would say cheerfully. "What's the matter? Are you getting old?"

Getting to the top, they would spread a light blanket on a flat portion of heavily leafed earth. And they would eat tea sandwiches. Cucumber. Betsy's favorite. Neat triangles of crustless, white bread thick with butter, trimmed with watercress. A tiny bottle of carbonated water for each of them, Betsy's sweet and flavored orange, Maggie's plain.

And she could see the sweet, long neck, with its pink-white skin, Betsy tossing her head backward to drink. Maggie could visualize her muscles as she swallowed, recall how lovely the throat was. And suddenly there were bruises on it, and the marks of cruel hands, the fingers of the mortician trying to cover them. All at once, Maggie was holding the rail and screaming.

Where had she gone, her baby girl, not even ripe for the shadows? Not even dressed for the Netherworld, all wrapped in her prebridal lace. Hardly having tasted life, much less glutted on it, as Maggie had. To have been so viciously slaughtered, caught in an appetite she had only just discovered. Lust was new to her, wasn't it? Little Betsy spun around in Maggie's head, dressed for dancing school, in ballet slippers and tutu, silk cherry blossoms gathering up her hair. And the scream turned to sobs. Maggie stood there, shrieking and trembling, knees collapsing beneath her. She could no longer stay on her feet.

A hand reached out and touched her shoulder. For a moment she imagined it was Betsy, that the whole hideous scenario had been a fantasy. Was God's punishment the grisly illusion that her daughter had died, drowned in semen? That would have been retribution enough: Maggie's lubricity festering in her own brain, giving her nightmares, demonic visions. Maybe God had been truly merciful, and only driven Maggie mad, not taken her child. And it was really Betsy's hand on her shoulder.

But it was a young man's. "Are you all right?" he asked her, standing over her on the stairs.

He was about nineteen, a little older than David, who'd died with Betsy. He had mustard yellow hair, almost brown, but with enough gold in it to catch the glint of the day, all of a silky piece against his brow. His skin was at once lightly tanned and pink in places, as though he'd spent a great deal of time out in the weather, and didn't have the natural protection for it. He was tall, beefy, wide at the shoulder and chest, the kind of young man schoolgirls would titter about, adopting a certain coy maidenly modesty. Except there was nothing maidenly about Maggie. Looking up, she could see his face, all interesting lines and slants, imposing brow, cheekbones angular but already lightly weighted with flesh, as though self-indulgence were waiting just a few steps down the road. His eyes were brown, flecked with gold, filled with concern. His crotch was directly in front of her eyes. She could see his penis. It was thick and long, at a slight right angle to the zipper of his fly, as if the spectacle of her sitting there sobbing had aroused him. Or perhaps he was simply at an age when he needed nothing to arouse him but his own burgeoning sexuality. The answer to a maiden's prayer. Except. Except.

"I'm all right," she said.

"Here." He handed her a handkerchief.

It was quite worn around the edges, but clean and pressed, as if loving hands had ironed it for him, sent him off with the counsel that just because he got hard all the time now was no reason to forget his manners and let his nose run. She could visualize his mother tucking it in his shirt pocket, giving him a pat on his beautiful pecs, avoiding a glance at the sweet handful below. A glance Maggie made no attempt to avoid. What an animal she was. "Thank you. It's so clean. Seems a shame to soil it."

"That's what it's for." He had a genial smile, full-lipped and generous. He sat down on the step beside her.

"Did your mum iron this for you?"

"She's dead." He had an American accent, relaxed, as though he slept a great deal, even when awake.

"I'm sorry."

"Hardly even remember her. They give you clean linen in the navy."

"You're young to be in the navy."

"Been in four years. I lied. Told them I was older than I was, and now I am."

"And you're seeing the world?"

"Yes, ma'am."

"Do you mind not calling me 'ma'am.' It makes me feel old."

"You're not old. You're beautiful."

"What's your name?"

"Christopher."

"Well, Christopher, you're very kind. It's not I who am beautiful. It's you." She reached and touched his face. His skin was

very soft, in spite of the ruddiness, the souvenired days at sea. She
ran her little finger around his lips, felt the dryness at the corners,
the sharp little intake of breath, at her touch.

He turned his face into her palm, kissed the fleshy hollow. It
was not an awkward kiss, despite his youth, but full of giving. It
brushed a juncture at the base of her thumb that a fortune-teller said
was her appetite line. She could feel herself getting moist between
the legs, not so much because she wanted this boy, as that he wanted
her.

"Is it the world you wanted to see, Christopher, or its women?"

"Both."

"Because you have to be careful what women you take up with.
Your mother would have told you that."

"I've been lucky so far."

"Yes? How many women have you had?"

He shrugged his shoulders.

"Tell me about them."

"Island girls mostly."

"Brown skin?"

"Real brown skin."

"Beautiful breasts?"

"Not as beautiful as yours," he said, reaching for her blouse,
palming her nipple. "You're sooo exciting." He kind of hummed the
words, lulling her with them, as though in his travels he had heard
the songs of mermaids, and made their lure a part of his tongue.

"You're very bold, Christopher."

"I don't mean to be, ma— What do I call you if I can't call you
'ma'am'?"

"Demeter."

"Never heard that name before."

"The mother of Persephone. Lost to the underworld. It's a
myth. Except in my case, it's the truth. They've stolen her and taken
her into the darkness. My little girl." Tears started down her face.

He got up and raised her to her feet, put his arms around her,
rocking her gently back and forth, as though they stood on deck on
the rolling sea. "Uh-huh," he murmured, slowly, the nonwords
arock with his easy rhythm. "Uh-huh," he purred.

"Oh, don't pretend you want to console me, and comfort me, like God." She pulled away slightly, her mouth flashing anger, tight lines appearing around it, teeth set hard, row on row, the words seeping from between them like a hiss. "There is no comfort, Christopher. There's only hunger and fucking and what we fool ourselves is pleasure. And then we die. Some of us early." She leaned forward and moved her mouth against his. It was very warm.

He was rocking again, doing his sweet little keening as he kissed her. "Uh-huh," he murmured, kissing. "Uh-huh." Her lips were soothed and fired all at once.

He put his hand inside her blouse, on her breast. He squeezed it, and murmured again, "You're soooo exciting."

"Have you been to Bali?" She pulled away suddenly, business-like, a travel agent, pleasant, perky, with her client facing her across the counter, folders open and extended, filled with pictures of exotic locales.

"We anchored at Jakarta. They didn't give us enough time to go to Bali."

"You must make it a point to get there." She moved his hand in between her legs, slid her skirt up with it, so his fingers were against her, where she was wet. "It's the most beautiful place in the world. Unless you like ruffians. Then the place to go is Tibet. You can't imagine what energy there is in fucking a Tibetan. No subtlety. Such a relief. No conversation. Just hard cocks and slippery cunts. You'll have a wonderful time." His finger moved against her, diddled her clitoris while she talked, as though he'd adapted to the rhythm of her speech, along with the rocking of his personal sea. "But it's terribly cold. You must keep your pants on, and yourself inside them, except when it's inside someone else."

His penis was straining his pants now. She squeezed it. "That must be soooo uncomfortable." She gave the phrase the same lilt he had.

"It is, Demeter."

"Would you like to take it out? You don't have to worry. It won't freeze. This isn't Tibet."

He started to reach for his zipper. She stopped his hand. "I don't think we should stay here." She took his hand and led him round the railing, ducking underneath to a level place of grass and green, across philodendron to coco yam, growing at an angle toward the sun. She pulled him into the midst of it.

"Now!"

He reached for her. "No! Not me! Take care of yourself! Touch yourself!"

He unbuckled his belt, and unzipped his jeans. His erection pulled at the soft cotton of his underwear, stretching it.

"Oh, better take it out of there at once! Something terrible might happen if you don't let it free. Don't you believe in freedom, Christopher?"

"Oh, yes, Demeter."

"Then get those pants off!"

He did, watching her eyes watching him, his penis bobbing as she licked her lips. "Oh, if only I had a mouth that was big enough!" She clapped her hands.

He took his penis in his hand and sort of waved it at her, offering.

"Oh, I couldn't possibly. It's much too big. What a lucky boy you are. Let me see you play with it."

He started to work his fist up and down the shaft, his movements lazy but expert, practiced. He closed his heavy-lidded eyes.

"Oh yes, lovely. You do that like a true magician, Christopher. Transforming yourself from young boy to great man. A *great* man. That must be the loveliest cock in the world."

His motions grew more rhythmic, faster, as his fingers worked to the corona, purple-tipped. He sighed. "Good boy," she murmured, sighing with him. "What a good boy."

He opened his eyes, saw how greedy and shining hers were. A clot of semen burst his tip, and he was grunting, the head of his penis surging, pumping liquid.

"Bravo! Well done!" She moved toward him, his handkerchief extended. "Here, you'll need this back. Wipe yourself off."

"You do it," he said, short of breath. "Touch me."

"Are you mad?" Her mouth set into a sneer. "You think I'd have anything to do with someone so disgusting?"

He bolted toward her, grabbed her by the wrists. His penis was already hardening again. He was very strong.

"Don't be an asshole. I've got a fatal disease."

He let go of her. "AIDS?"

"Life." She ran away from him, back to the stairs, up the winding path. Only when she reached the top did she see she was at Black's Link.

"Oh, God!" She threw herself on the ground. "Why did you make me so vile?" She grasped at the roots of the banyan tree, symbol of long life, at its base the strangler fig, the leech growth that took its strength from the great tree, eventually choking it. "Why did you punish Betsy for my sins?"

She was sobbing now, clutching the green that grew around the tree as if it could give her support, the sustenance that heaven hadn't. She didn't turn as the boy's shadow fell across her.

The Syndicate had assured Erica nobody could possibly know. The women were all from Philadelphia, where Benjamin Franklin had once said that three people could keep a secret if two of them were dead. Profiting from that wisdom, and wishing to prove themselves smarter than men, even the smartest, as old Ben had been, they had taken an oath not only with each other, but with themselves, the only inarguable fidelity. Not one of them had mentioned their plot to anyone except each other, and then, only behind closed doors, carefully checking to make sure there was no one on the other side.

Erica's nervousness was understandable. She was not a sophisticated woman. That was the primary reason they had suggested her persona be cloaked with silence, which always made people seem more interesting than they were. Unsophisticated people had a tendency to take things personally. Sophisticated people often did as well, even with their wider realm of experience, knowing that the universe was filled with carom shots, not necessarily directed at them. The slings and arrows of outrageous fortune. In Erica's case, the Syndicate assured her it had been just some unrelated camera freak in the swimming pool.

So she resumed her daily vigil, and the search that went along with it, without seeming to search. She stood now on the brink, quite literally, her toes hugging the edge of the Mandarin pool, wraparound goggles in place to protect her yellow-green eyes, tight bathing cap guarding her white-gold hair. She cut cleanly into the water with her dive, and paced herself into a calm, persistent crawl. By the end of a few laps she was in her swimmer's peaceful haze. So she was hardly aware of the other body entering the pool, except that she felt the water churning slightly, eventually noting the kick far to the other side.

He was a polite swimmer, observing the undeclared courtesies of those who were serious about their water sports, staying as far away from her as he could. Usually she resented other people in the water. It was the only thing in her life that she could consider her own domain. But there was a certain courtliness in the way he swam, not splashing too much, kicking too hard. When an hour had elapsed, Erica got out of the pool, took her robe, and laid it on the chair where his was placed, looking over her shoulder to make sure he didn't see her. Then she picked up his robe and put it on, reaching into the pocket. She pulled out his room key, noted the number. There was a watch in the pocket as well. A Rolex. Of course, it was Hong Kong, but it looked like the genuine article, had the heft of real gold. She took the key from her own robe pocket and replaced it with his key and watch.

She went back to her room, showered, and waited for a while before dialing the number she had seen on his key. The voice on the other end of the phone was deep, reassuring. "Yes?"

"Hello. This is Melinda, with the *Hong Kong Tatler*. We're having a cocktail party tomorrow evening at the Regent, and we thought you and your wife might like to come."

"That's very kind. But I have no wife."

"Then perhaps you'd like to bring some of your associates from General Motors."

"I would if I were with General Motors. But I'm with Horton-Alexander."

"The power tool people?"

"Venture capital."

"What was your name again?"

"Lockwood Alexander."

"I'm so sorry. They must have given me the wrong room." She hung up the phone.

"He's forty-three," Donald Ng said. "Divorced. The company was formed in 1980 by him and another ace salesman who left Nuveen to start their own arbitrage company. Assets, one billion, sixty million dollars U.S."

"What a nice story," said Erica, and went to buy some new clothes.

As James had anticipated, the stock he'd bought into had climbed. "Well, it's not just a rumor anymore, friend," Kenneth said, over drinks at Someplace Else, a lively singles bar on Nathan Road. There were Tiffany lamps, colorful as the people who clustered underneath them, polished light oak tables, railed off by shiny brass. "It's an open discussion. Speculators are buying heavy, driving up the price." Kenneth's eyes darted about as he spoke, the nervous questing of those who were truly singles. Panic that they wouldn't connect was palpable on their faces, which were spliced with too-eager smiles. Happy Hour might have been better named. "It looks like you're going to do just as you hoped."

"About time," said James.

"Do you intend to pay back the funds?"

"Nothing to pay back. It *was* my father's bank."

"Still, misappropriation . . ."

"I borrowed it, that was all. I had every intention of paying it back. If they hadn't been so fast to accuse, no one would have ever been the wiser. As it was, there was never an official charge. He covered the missing money."

"Then you can offer your profits to the old *père*."

"We no longer speak."

"He didn't understand it was only a loan?"

"He understood almost nothing about me from the time I was a boy," said James. "And even less once his mother left *me* her money." He took a deep swallow of his bitters. "If it were up to my father, I would have been set adrift here with the same prospects as the Vietnamese."

"I for one never believed the stories. You're not complex enough to be dishonest."

"Am I to take that as a compliment?"

"I would," said Kenneth. "What breasts on the one over there. Impressive, don't you think? If you are guilty of any crime, James, it's that you think it's easy to make money."

"But it is. You just have to be in the right place at the right time."

"With the right widow."

"She didn't give me the money."

"I'm sorry to hear that. I quite enjoyed the idea of a chum of mine being a Toyboy."

In truth, James felt nothing like Claire's plaything. She was so obviously infatuated with him, so enamored, he might have said the opposite, that she was there strictly for him, available for his pleasure, the bolstering of his ego, the easing of pleasure in his groin and his brain. No one had been so taken with him since Granny, loving him for his naughtiness, considering it part of his charm, buttering his spirit as Granny used to butter his tea sandwiches at Harrod's, giving him more soft spread than was decent. Claire's feelings for him made him feel powerful. She was so obviously intelligent, he decided perhaps he had underestimated himself. He had no delusions of grandeur, having had nothing in his life but grandeur, before the disgrace. But she gave him delusions of strength.

It pleased him to be able to give to her in return, now that he had money. It made him feel important and substantial to lavish first-class treatment on her. Addicted as he was to the finer things in life, and to ease, whether or not he had earned it, he enjoyed being someone else's great indulgence. But there was enough pride in him that he liked to be able to spoil back a little.

So he took her to pricey discos like Casablanca, where the video ran the looped scene of Bergman and Bogart bidding goodbye at the airport. "But what about us?" "We'll always have Paris." Over and over again, the words were repeated, as James and Claire danced, in between plastic palm trees with jeweled coconuts set in their branches. "But what about us?" Claire would whisper by the circular stairs. He didn't answer. He knew what she wanted was some declaration of love. Even if he had loved her, he wouldn't have allowed himself to give it voice. He understood the game, that the first one who said it lost.

But in a way, he really cared for her. It would have been hard not to, as generous as she was, in every sense of the word. Sexually generous, lavishing on him all her stored-up affection and passion, gifting him in ways he had never expected, or, for that matter, particularly wanted, having spent most of his seductions just trying to get women to open their legs and allow him in. It had not occurred to him that they might want more than the touching and the stroking and the kissing and the fucking: that it was in women to arouse and lavish and spoil in other ways besides overbuttering sandwiches. She would suck his toes and run her tongue up the inside of his leg, making delicate circles behind his knees, take his balls into her mouth and work them with her tongue. It was as mortifying to him as it was exciting. Women were not supposed to be like that. He was, after all, English. Even whores who brought down members of Parliament had never been more than beautiful and seductive, in low-cut dresses and low-cut morality, ripe to be pounced upon. That the female of the species could actually be aggressively sexual, as hungry for it as men were, hungrier even, was not in his ken. Even as the papers were filled with the Japanese sending Chinese refugees back to Beijing, what they were reading with gusto in England were tales of newspaper editors caught in an affair with an Indian beauty accused of being a prostitute. It was scandal that really got the Brits' attention, not politics, or injustice, or even genuine passion. The naughty side of life. Lust, and even genuine passion, in James's mind were not only naughty, but supposed to be the domain of men.

Still, he more or less tolerated Claire's appetite for him, as he had allowed her to underwrite his loan. He closed his eyes and occasionally gritted his teeth, because it went so against his grain. That was to say, he could accept setting her up so she would insist on being there with the money. But he had a harder time taking what he hadn't himself manipulated into being. Once in a while, though, when he gave up control and relaxed into what she was giving, he had no choice but to admit to himself that he really enjoyed it.

Still, he wouldn't say he loved her. Nor would he return her sensual ministrations in quite the same fashion. He regarded them as French, and everyone knew the philosophic difference between Brits and the Froggies. But he was lavish with kisses and the touches that seemed so easily to melt her. And he indulged her romanticism past the hilt, as far as choice of locales. He took her to floating restaurants, garishly lit, ponderous frontages curled with gilt dragons, red light bulbs in their eyes. And while they waited on the platform for the boat that would shuttle them across, he wound her in his arms, and covered her face with kisses.

Because shipboard romance had been so deeply imbedded in the consciousness of young Americans, even before television had turned it to treacle, Claire had hardly ever been able to go on even a motorboat without wishing she were with someone she loved. During the early days of her courtship with Charley, she had sought out his lips on trips as banal as a crossing to Fire Island, when the two of them went to visit friends. Charley had been amused by her amorous yearnings. He understood that her adolescence and young adulthood, unlike his own, had been sorrowfully lacking in passion and sex. Because he loved her, he indulged her on occasion, reluctantly holding hands on the subway, for example, which he himself considered juvenile. His conviction was that all forms of love belonged in the bedroom. Since theirs was quite comfortable, he didn't know why they couldn't save demonstrativeness for an appropriate setting. Kisses, in his estimation, were simply a part of foreplay, not ends in themselves.

James Bingham, however, was able to field the full velocity of Claire's yearnings. He dived into kisses on the Star Ferry as though the two of them were in the South Seas, shortly to be shipwrecked. Though the ride lasted no more than a few minutes, from Hong Kong Island to Kowloon, he would give himself to those moments with a gusto to match her hunger, not only for his lips, but for the arms that had never been around her, all the romantic moments she had missed in her teens. Crossing the harbor was, for Claire, not a commute as it was for the others on board, but a healing. Amiable and crafty and sexy and close to those young feelings as James was, being only twice high school age, instead of three times, like Claire, he was more than happy to cooperate to the best of his ability, which was considerable.

"You're looking particularly lovely tonight," he whispered against her cheeks. He was buoyed by his meeting with Kenneth, pleased that his plan was so on track. In the flash of red and green bulbs strung all around the landing, there was something very young and yielding about the way she smelled, and looked. "All sprightly in your silks."

"I bought this for you," she said, touching the fabric.

"They're going to declare a day of mourning in Hong Kong when you leave town. The merchants will drape their windows in black."

He could see her face grow solemn at the mention of leaving, the corners of her mouth go down heavy with the weight of imagined loss. As much as he was starting to think of himself, after a long period of abasement, a move that had been tantamount to exile, cast adrift with nothing but the family's good name, he was still not prepared to think as much of himself as she did. He could not imagine anyone's leaving to have such a grave effect on him, as the prospect of her being without him seemed to have on her.

"Well, it's not for another six days," she said, obviously trying to lift her own spirits.

"Right. You can do a lot more damage by then. Send a few more children to Vancouver whose parents were the lucky shopkeepers on your route." He kissed her neck, reached down her waistband, moving his hand inside her panties. She strained her face for his kiss.

"Yes?" she said. "Did you say something?"

"You're so warm."

"And?"

"And wet."

"I'm not asking for how I feel. I'm asking how you feel. What you feel."

"Can't you tell? Don't I seem happy?"

"You don't say anything."

"People say too easily. People say, instead of show."

"You're trying to distract me."

"I certainly am. Isn't that what you need? A little distraction?"

"You think that's all this is? That's all you are?"

"Don't try to make it more. We've having a wonderful time. Let it go at that."

"Why do I have to?"

"So when it's over. . ."—he could feel her stiffen—"there won't be anything sad or angry. It will have been a lovely interlude."

"An interlude?"

"That's right."

"When Charley and I made love, he always said 'I love you.' "

"I'm not Charley. You can't make me Charley."

"Don't you love me at all?"

"Do you want me to lie to you?"

"Yes."

They laughed.

She could not discuss the extent of her infatuation with Judith. Besides being sensible and realistic, Judith was usually right. Claire could pretty much gauge in advance what her reaction would be, had already been. In fact, Claire had been avoiding Judith. Her favorite friend in the world, and she had been glad when Judith was too busy to spend time with her.

She got James out early in the morning, before Judith was awake, came home with him late enough so Judith was usually in bed. Her favorite evenings had been those when Judith was overnight in Taipei or Canton. Then Claire could make James dinner, and they would listen to music, and he would bend her backward over the railing of the terrace, with Hong Kong far below, his lips on her throat. Eventually his arm would sweep behind her knees, and shoulders, and he would carry her into the bedroom, taking her on the rug. It was all so spontaneous and erotic she could not imagine it wasn't love. She looked up *romance* in the dictionary, dismissed the first six definitions, which had to do with the literary, and focused on the seventh. *a. Love,* it read. *b. A love affair. c. A strong, usually short-lived attachment or enthusiasm.* Her mind blanked out the *short-lived.*

So caught was she, so needing someone to whom to tell her feelings, she even called her mother, lobotomizing all memory of how little emotional support that woman had provided in her life. "I hate that it's going to be over," Claire said.

"Why does it have to be?"

"He says it's just an interlude."

"Maybe he's just using reverse psychology to trap you, so you'll get really involved."

"I am really involved."

"Take a picture. I want to see what he looks like, this Englishman. What does he do again?"

"He's in finance."

"Perfect. He can manage your money if you're ever a hit again."

"He's only thirty-four."

"Well, that's how old you look. Maybe a *little* older. But we can fix that. There's a doctor in Baltimore . . ."

"It's just for now," Claire repeated what Judith had given her for wisdom. "Soon all it will be is a memory."

"Then make it a *long* memory. Don't come home. The children are fine. Stay as long as you want."

"Really? Should I?"

"Isn't that sweet. You still need your mother's permission."

She watched him sleeping. The light came up gray through the window, softening his sharp features. His nose was perfectly straight, with a chiseled tip; his chin had a cleft in it. Asleep he looked even more the boy; beautiful, guileless, straight brown hair falling onto his high, tanned forehead, lips slightly parted. She heard his snores no more than she accepted he might have flaws, reality playing no part in her observation. Living the fantasy—a beautiful man, an exotic place—she could see less with her eyes open than he did with his closed. Asleep, with the bright blue eyes that gave him so much dash and mischief shut, he looked totally innocent.

A gentle rain was falling. The morning wisped its way into

shadowy lightness. She could see drops on the windows, like tears. Something deeper than longing seized her, rooted more strongly than desire: a tenderness for all men. The beautiful male sharing her pillow. The feisty, handsome son so central to her life, neglected for this time of passion, hardly even brought to mind. The sweet, hearty, cheerful husband she had tried so hard to forget since she'd met James. Had she managed not to think about him? Was that a way of the heart's healing, or selfishness?

She lay down beside James and smelled his hair, more than James's smell. Something generic and hardy, vigorous, played through her nostrils. It was the scent on the sweater Charley had worn before his illness was discovered. She'd kept the sweater in a drawer, so his smell wouldn't escape, long past his dying, after all the clothes were taken away, donated to charity. She'd opened it to the air once in a while, pressed her face in it when she needed his essence. The essence of man. The slightly musky, athletic smell, inoffensive, reassuring. The smell of her little boy's slippers, when he'd still been a little boy. How comforting and would-be brave it was, how different from a woman's. Nothing soft about it, or yielding. Stalwart, really. Strapping. As if it could put its arm around your shoulders and guard you from harm. Offering strength. Protection. She wondered if something different in men's chromosomes gave out the aroma, or women's nostrils perceived it, as a male animal sniffed out the female in heat.

She reached over James to the desk where her camera lay, out of its case, and loaded. Rising to her haunches, she switched on the flash, and focused. She took the picture. He sprang awake, sat half up, startled.

"I'm sorry," she said, still snapping. "I didn't mean to wake you. You looked so peaceful."

"Peaceful must not be your favorite." He put his hands behind his head, appraising her. Annoyed as he tried to seem, his eyes were filled with amusement.

"Would you mind if I stayed an extra week or two?"

"Mind? I'd be enchanted." He turned and reached for the jacket hung neatly on the chair by the desk, fumbled inside, and took out his pocket organizer. Opening it, he checked his calendar. "Why don't you stay even longer than that, and I'll take you to Bangkok?"

"Bangkok," said Judith. "You'll love it. The most exotic city in the world." She was already at work with a large part of her concentration, rearranging notes to the right of her breakfast, sending penciled arrows through the computer printout, as she drank her orange juice.

"Then he isn't only for Hong Kong?"

"Hong Kong. Bangkok. They're all the same. Exotic places."

"He's only for exotic places?"

"That's right."

"Beverly Hills is pretty exotic."

"Only if you don't live there."

"I love you, Judith."

"I appreciate that," Judith said.

After Judith had gone to work, Claire went into the apartment's newsroom. She shut the curtains, and started developing the pictures. James waking. James sitting up, startled. James lying back against bright blue satin pillows, smiling. The background doubly warmed her: they had made an excursion to the market at Stanley, and she'd bought satin sheets, the color of his eyes. It was a romanticism that made her feel both indulgent and indulged: Charley had never given a thought to the look of their bed, the feel of its linens, his only focus the feel of her. There was one last shot of James in shirt and tie, going off to work, before Judith awakened. All of it played out in the developing fluid, a recap of a joyful morning. Made more joyful because she was playing with Judith's things.

Not only had Claire never had a teenage sweetheart, she had never had a roommate. That destiny had moved her halfway around the world to have the brightest one, and in middle age, seemed to her more than a second chance. She was getting all her wishes, on a quarter-century delay.

She watched James's face coming out of the solution. How

beautiful he was, *beau*, as Judith had said. She hung the pictures up to dry.

Outside, it was no longer raining. She went for a walk, becoming more buoyant with each step, her steps turning into a run. And everything that was dead in her, or had felt like it was dead, all that had been weighted with grieving, soul, breasts, belly, and brain, were as though a magic wand had *whoosh*ed across them, shifting, lifting, purifying. Inertia gave way to motion. Despair ballooned into hope.

And it crystallized. And a song came out of her.

SIXTEEN

◆

On Halloween, just before midnight, Louise lit a candle. The entire charade, starting with the candle buying, had been an embarrassment for her. As she went through the strangely colorful shops in the back end of Wanchai, where no one she knew could possibly run into her and observe her, even accidentally, she pretended to be looking for incense. "Do you have that incense that smells like Tea Rose?" she asked one proprietor, a wizened Chinese in a faded black Mao shirt, as though he could understand English. As though she could stand the smell of Tea Rose, a scent so cloyingly sweet it reminded her of days when there were still starlets, hoping to give a whiff of themselves to Sidney Skolsky. "No?" She moved through the dusty shelves, inspecting. "Oh, a candle!" she said. "As long as I'm here, why don't I buy one?"

Once she had been in Shepherd's Market in London with an aging theater columnist, an ardent Anglophile, so in love with the English she couldn't accept the fact that sex shops were there for them, well bred as they were. Disbelievingly the old woman had fingered dildos, stared at walls strapped with leather girdles with teeth in the crotches, blushed at jars labeled "Love Foam." A man putting his hand on a vibrator, testing, had caught his sleeve. And as he stood there ricocheting in place, his quivering voice had cried out, "Can somebody stop this thing?" It was one of Louise's most treasured memories. But fraught with awkwardness as the episode had been, this Hong Kong shop with its candles seemed worse to her, the prospect of being caught there inspiring genuine chagrin. She had longed for publicity in her youth, now there was too much of it. She was forever looking over her shoulder, fearful that the shadows hid a legman for the *National Enquirer*, restaurant fish tanks the lenses of some spy for Geraldo. People were so fascinated with the exploits of celebrities, little realizing most of them felt less celebrated than anxious. "Just because you're paranoid," Louise's dentist had said to her once, drilling, "doesn't mean someone isn't after you."

She had secreted the candle in the bottom of her purse, like something genuinely shameful, worn her darkest sunglasses, and hurried, head down, back to the hotel. The apple she had stored in the refrigerator minibar in her room, checking every evening to make sure no one had thrown it away. Service was almost too good at the Mandarin. Fresh baskets of fruit atop the television cabinet were constantly being changed, as were the drobidium orchids in the tiny thin-necked vases. The apple that Henry had given her, supposedly sacred to Venus, looked no different from the fruit the hotel supplied, except that it had a slight pucker on one side, like a jowly face, to be made into a crabapple doll. It looked inferior to the hotel fruit, so Louise had had some scratches of concern that an industrious houseman might throw it away. But it was still there at cocktail time, behind the white Toblerone, where she'd hidden it.

All through dinner, she felt restless and distracted. It was a lively group, bright, distinctive people, who still couldn't capture her full attention. Part of her agitation, she wanted to think, was because of how hungry she felt, how hungry one seemed always to be in Hong Kong, how many delicious things there were to taste, how dangerously tempting it all was, how fattening.

"Did you go shopping today?" asked the restaurant critic from the *South China Morning Post*.

"Am I in Hong Kong?" asked Louise.

"What'd you get?" asked Henry.

"How slow she is to answer," observed Bunyan Reis, who had himself ordered twenty shirts that afternoon from Sam the Tailor, all in the pale pearl gray that he imagined made him look good. His closets in New York and Paris were already hung with several dozen of the same style and color. But like everyone passing through he'd been caught in the local mass hypnosis, and imagined that spending money, under the circumstances, meant saving it. "Did you buy something sexual?"

"*Vogue* ran an article once that you should never go shopping on an empty stomach," said Louise, eating.

"I'm surprised they didn't say you should never eat on an empty stomach," said Bunyan.

"Oh, they did," said Sylvia Kranet, the senator's wife. "I'm sure they did. It was in their special issue on political wives, especially the anorexic ones. Nancy Reagan always lay down for fifteen minutes before attending a state dinner, and imagined she couldn't eat a thing."

"You're making it up," said Bunyan, giggling.

"I don't think so," said Sylvia. "There's very little one could make up about Nancy Reagan."

Louise looked at her watch. "I'm afraid I have to go."

"But there's still seven more courses," said the restaurant critic.

"I'll have to get by on six. It's been fantastic, Willie, thank you."

"Why are you in such a hurry?" Bunyan said. "There's the first course and the second course, but the best course is inter. . ."

"Stop it." She hit him with her napkin on the bangs of his silvery hair. "Everything isn't about sex."

"That's right. There's also money, don't you know."

"And power," said Sylvia Kranet. "Mustn't forget power."

"I always lie down for fifteen minutes and imagine I don't want any," said Louise.

The candle was white, in a red glass jar, so the shadows it cast were roseate, sultry. She liked how she looked in the mirror, freed from the harshness of electric lights, all soft and unlined again, the oval face with its rounded chin almost vulnerable. Her hair was as honey blond as it had always been, the vats of Vidal Sassoon being able to preserve what time could not. Her eyes were still remarkably wide, an ironic vestige of her long-ago-lost innocence. The expression in them, however, was anything but wide-eyed. Even with no one to stare down but herself, she looked skeptical, and slightly annoyed at the travesty she considered this whole thing to be. Necromancy, for God's sake. Magic. "Sacred to Venus, my ass," she said, aloud, holding the apple in her hand, looking straight at it, challenging.

But she did bite it. What was it exactly Henry had told her? If she ate an apple and lit a candle just before midnight on Halloween, while combing her hair, the face of her future husband would appear in the mirror. Future husband. What a joke. She nearly choked on the piece of apple even as she picked up the comb, and started trailing it through her hair. "Snow fucking White," she murmured.

And yet she felt a presence. The light was flickering and she wasn't sure she could see anything, especially with her glasses off. She'd put them on the dresser, imagining that at such a moment one should be unencumbered by changes, even those modified by modish opticians. Louise as she'd been once, open, eager, ready to believe. Louise with eyes that were still innocent, largely because she couldn't see. But she could sense something. Something in the room. Something in the mirror, starting to appear, in the near distance. As though it were coming from somewhere far away. Childhood? Hope? A vanished dream?

The clock on the ferry building struck midnight. She picked up her glasses and looked through them, without putting them on.

There was a face. Unquestionably a face. Very dark, obscured, but unmistakably a face. It started to come closer.

"I can't believe this," she murmured to herself, excitement welling up in her. She put the glasses on, to see him really clearly.

"Good evening, Miss Felder," said Anthony Go.

For a few minutes, Louise just held her heart, tried to regulate her breathing. Fear, real fear, was something quite new to her. Panic, anxiety, feelings engendered by competition, the roller coaster tracks of show business, falls from grace so precipitous that Andy Warhol's fifteen minutes of fame seemed a lengthy cruise, those were part of her digestive tract. Sickness in the pit of the stomach, when something fell through, or someone didn't want you anymore, that was rejection. That was loss. Painful, but she'd gotten almost used to it.

But to be genuinely afraid, sent into a state of terror by an actual menace, not failure, or unlovedness, was a fresh experience. Louise had an aversion to fresh experiences. Unlike some of her confreres in Southern California, the loose-bolted questers always taking workshops and talking about "growing," Louise had no wish to expand her inner horizons. She had already done and eaten and slept with and felt everything she thought she cared to. Enlightenment to her meant not wanting anything anymore. Not the cessation of desire that some nouveau Buddhists starring in movies and infinite companies of *A Chorus Line* talked about, but a kind of spiritual inertia. She did not have the energy to want more than she'd had, or to have it in a different way. *Lasciate ogni speranza, voi ch'entrate*, Dante had written above the entrance to Hell, according to her former client Zeffirelli. "Abandon all hope, ye who enter." More than hope had been abandoned by Louise at the threshold of Beverly Hills. It was right that the Texan had given her a jade heart, sweet as it seemed, because that was what she had. A spirit so jaded that nothing could jar it awake. Or so she thought.

But she hadn't considered fear. At first, Anthony Go did not say another word. In the flicker of the red-glassed candlelight, he lit a long, gold-tipped cigarette, so the light from the flame of his wooden match was the only other illumination in the room. Then he smiled at her. It was a B-movie smile, arrogant, filled with smugness at how thoroughly he had been able to frighten her.

The tightness in her throat eased slightly, and words came out. "Are you going to kill me?"

"Perhaps," he said, inhaling deeply, blowing the smoke out of his nostrils.

"Well, if you are, please do it quickly. I've already used up my per diem, and this hotel is very expensive."

"It's all just one big joke to you, isn't it?"

"It's not a joke anymore. You made your point. You really scared me."

"You see how accessible you are. How easy it would be."

"But why? Henry already said she'd do your picture."

He took another deep inhale of his cigarette, drew back his lips, and eased the smoke out through his teeth, like a dragon. "You've made things very unpleasant for me. I'm not used to people behaving in such an . . . unfriendly fashion. So now I want more."

"More?"

"I want you to represent my production company."

"I told you, that's conflict of interest. I represent talent."

"I will be talent. Creating and developing properties for motion pictures, as the partner of Johnny Wong. I want you to be my agent."

"How very amusing, as Bette Davis would say. A very talented woman. Difficult, but irresistible. She had the capacity to take what was ordinary and tired, and make it unique and fresh. That's what talent means, Mr. Go. A spark. A sparkle. So you see something or hear something or feel something you've never seen or heard or felt before.

"It isn't particularly joyful work, being an agent. It's a lot like being a truffle pig: you smell out the money. But as degrading and unrewarding as it can be, as ungrateful and disloyal as your clients might end up, because they think, after all, you're *only* an agent, a pimp, a panderer, it has its good side. In my particular case, I've never represented anyone I didn't really believe in. Was sure could do the job."

"I can do the job."

"What job is that? The Lord High Executioner?"

"I understand there is outside the Grauman's Chinese Theater on Hollywood Boulevard a place where the stars put their footprints."

"That was a long time ago. When there were still crowds that gathered for openings, and rafts of stars in limousines, and Hollywood was Hollywood. Not a gathering place for hookers and male hustlers and street people and garbage that made everybody run to Beverly Hills. If you wanted your tootsies in concrete, Mr. Go, I'd say, forget that dream."

"I was thinking more in terms of your mouth. I was thinking

they might take an impression of your mouth in cement, since it seems to me probably all that will be left to remember."

"I was afraid nothing would be remembered at all."

He slid back the glass door that led to the balcony, looked down and across to the ferry building. "Sixteen floors. A long way to fall."

"I've fallen farther." Louise sighed. "To tell you the truth, I'm not so crazy about life. I've run out of laughs, and I hate getting old. I already gave at the office. Whatever you need from me, I can't deliver. And whatever you do to me . . ."—she waved her hand—"I don't really care."

"Not afraid to die?"

"If it was good enough for Grace Kelly, it's good enough for me."

"There are worse things," said Anthony Go, and, handing her his card, he left the room.

Clement was surprised how heavy hearted his nights had become. He tried to tell himself that his quarrel with Judith had had no real effect on him. But he couldn't even drink as carelessly anymore, conscious as he ordered the one drink too many that that was what it was. He hated that she might be right about him.

At the same time, because she had been party to the tip he'd received at Hot Gossip, he wanted it to be wrong. False information. For the first time in his career as a policeman, he went a different route from the one logic indicated, in no hurry to talk to the young Cantonese who danced in the discos. Instead he intensified his questioning of the students from Kensington Academy, where the murdered pair had gone to school. He wanted the killers. But he wanted them not to be Chinese.

He had come to love the people he had superintended in his years in Hong Kong, felt their panic, their sense of abandonment. A part of him tried to believe the government line: that all the mainland Chinese had ever had to do to subdue Hong Kong was shut off the water. That the island was indefensible, even if Great Britain still had its military might. But a popular American cartoonist who published in the *South China Morning Post* said that the British would lie, back down, and waffle on any issue they could. And even as he made excuses for his government, Clement could feel himself lying, backing down and waffling. The bald-faced truth was Mrs. Thatcher had sold her last colony down the river.

Perhaps they seemed nonresistant and resigned, the local population. But most of them were there because they'd fled the mainland. Clement could not imagine their willingly submitting to the very people they'd run away from, whose philosophy they despised, whose word they couldn't believe. How could they be swallowed up without a battle?

"Did you ever watch a python eat a rat?" he asked the bartender at the Holiday Inn. It was the kind of off-the-wall discussion Clement usually started with Nick when he was drunk, which he wasn't this night. He was filling himself with barley water, a cloyingly sweet English drink that reminded him of his childhood, before he'd found out what a release alcohol was, or seemed to be.

"Can't say I have," Nick said. He was a burly man, bigger than Clement, an Australian expatriate married to a Shanghainese. They were the aristocrats of Hong Kong, highest in the pecking order of Chinese. Shanghai had been the great port of China, opening it to traders from all over the world. So a certain internationalism, a sense of sophistication had arisen, which over time had made the people of Shanghai the elite. Shanghainese only respected the opinions of other Shanghainese. It gave Nick a certain cachet to be married to someone from such a fine family of bankers, money traders. She was rich enough that he didn't have to work, but he liked being a bartender.

"Once I saw a rat being put in a python's cage," Clement said. "The python was coiled on a branch above it. The rat didn't see. All of a sudden the rat looked up. The python fixed it. Struck. Grabbed the rat's face, and clamped it. Jaws open . . . hideously wide. Twisted its body around the rat, and squeezed it. The more the rat struggled, the tighter the python gripped. It was like . . . like the struggle hastened the rat's own death. And then the python ate it."

"You sure you don't want a drink?" Nick said.

"Almost sure."

"That's a very upsetting story, especially if you have friends who are rats."

"You think these people will sit still for it?"

"Pythons?"

"1997."

"We'll have to wait and see what happens."

"You can wait. You have Australia to go back to, if it doesn't work out. Everyone who can afford to is emigrating. But what about the average hawker in Mong Kok? You think he'll just allow himself to be swallowed? What if they start gnawing at the bars of the cage?"

"You better have a drink," said Nick.

Not surprisingly, it was harder to sleep without the whiskey. It had been so many years since he'd simply gone to bed instead of stumbled to it, or fallen into it, he'd more or less forgotten what you did. He tried counting sheep, but he didn't like numbers. He liked words. He switched on his bedside lamp and read for a while, but the words only made him think. The more he thought, the more sleepless he became.

What would happen to all of them? The government's piddling concessions seemed to him little more than what the Americans called a Band-Aid. Fifty thousand householders were to be allowed to have domain in Great Britain, the fifty thousand to be selected according to a point system. No one was very clear on what the point system would be. Two hundred twenty-five thousand, if they took their families with them. Two hundred twenty-five thousand out of five and a half million. Workers for the Hong Kong government were applying for dual citizenship to other countries, in case they were not the ones selected, in case the Chinese did not keep their word. But the Chinese had announced that anyone applying for dual citizenship would not be allowed to hold their jobs in the government. What were they to do?

The Chinese had ways of finding out everything. After the Tiananmen Square massacre Hong Kong people had paraded, protested, a million strong. But the Chinese took their pictures, and wrote down their names. All signs of protest disappeared. Hong Kong Belongers were, above all else, practical. So they went back to making money. Politics, conscience, were not practical. Unless China slaughtered people every year, the world would forget. The Chinese were cynical enough to think they could get away with it, and they could.

It was an insoluble problem, and to spend time on it would only keep him awake. He tried to think of pictures. Trees. Rivers flowing. A rush of sweetness came like a kiss from a caring woman. And he thought of Judith. And he stayed awake.

He was exhausted and irritable all the next day, questioning the classmates of Betsy and David. "All right, Damion," he said to a student with magnifying spectacles, his heavily lashed gray eyes three times their normal size. "You were close to Betsy, weren't you?"

The headmaster had given him a study room at Kensington Academy for conducting the questioning. The school had put up resistance to the inquiry, the headmaster insisting that many of the students were so unstrung by the deaths they were in counseling, a very un-British course. To be subjected to an inquisition was more than such sensitive young souls could tolerate. Clement had insisted it was necessary and routine, compromising on conducting the questioning at the school. He had been expecting a cozy, book-lined study. The coldness of the place disappointed him. Comfortable furniture with its stuffing partly exposed carried out what Clement had come to expect from those expat establishments with nothing to prove: it was really only a slight cut above the room where the children would have been questioned at the station house, except for the occasional vase donated by a parent, the flowers picked by a student on the way to school. There were rugs on the floor, distinguishing it from his own headquarters, faded Tabriz carpets that had one flaw. Muslims insisted upon leaving a flaw in their workmanship, since only Allah was perfect. But there were windows here. A great deal of light, as opposed to the close yellow-painted walls of Central Police Station, with their atmosphere of incarceration even for the keepers of the peace.

"We were good chums when we were fifteen," Damion said.

"You weren't friends after that?"

"Not like we were."

"You resented it?"

"No. People change. You go on to new friends."

"But you were angry at Betsy for dropping you."

"She didn't *drop* me. We outgrew each other."

"You weren't jealous of David?"

"Not at all. I got far better grades."

"Didn't mind his being taller, handsomer?"

"Did you know David? He wasn't all that good-looking."

"All the more reason you might have resented his taking Betsy away."

"But he didn't take her away. We just ran out of things to talk about."

"That's all you did was talk?"

"That's all we did."

"You never made love?"

"Certainly not!"

"Did you want to?"

"It never came up," said Damion.

"I say," said the headmaster. "What have you been asking these children. Have you been talking about sex?"

"Just the indicated questions."

"I don't consider it's indicated to ask one of our best scholars if he had intercourse with the Evans girl."

"I was extremely careful not to use that word."

"I think I must insist on there being a parent or some supervising official of the school present. This whole procedure is extremely unorthodox."

"I have no objections."

"Very generous of you, I'm sure."

There was a teacher present for the rest of the afternoon, a small-eyed woman with a heavily veined nose, and thinning, grayish hair. Her lips were pursed so Clement felt her disapproval.

"They went there every afternoon?" he was asking a classmate of

Betsy's, a redheaded girl with freckles so large they might have been painted on.

"They studied together. I don't know if it was always on Black's Link."

"But they were in the habit of going off, the pair of them, every afternoon?"

"As far as I know."

"Did you ever see them go?"

"Yes."

"Did anyone follow them?"

"Nobody I saw."

"Was there anyone who might have been in love with Betsy, besides David?"

"She was very pretty. Everybody liked her."

"No one was jealous? She had no enemies?"

"Enemies?"

"What about David? Did he have enemies?"

"Look here, Superintendent," the teacher said. "I'm not sure these questions are in order. These are children. The most they deal with is teenage rivalry. Petty things. Why would you even put such thoughts in their heads? Why add to the emotional turmoil these children are going through? How long is this going to go on?"

"Till I find out who did it."

But there were complaints when he got back to the station, several phone messages from politicians. Clement didn't return the calls, knowing in advance what they would be about. That wasn't like him either. He was punctilious about returning phone calls, following up leads, even when they led where he didn't want to go. What was happening to him?

He went to visit Dao Tsim, to cool himself off, to try to get back some perspective. "I don't know why I'm doing what I'm doing. I'm not making any real progress on this case," Clement said, as the old man brewed tea. The night was comfortably cool, a freshness in the air, in spite of the too sweet smell of the tea.

"When will you see the woman again?"

"Woman?"

"The reporter. Surely you don't think she's out of your life?"

"Isn't she?"

"Of course not. Why don't you call her? Then perhaps the real reason for your restlessness will be taken care of."

"She doesn't want to see me."

"Of course she does," said Dao Tsim. "As it is, you couldn't find the killers if they stood in front of your face." Outside the window a neon sign flashed red characters onto the night. Carmine shadows played across Dao's sunken cheeks, bathed the softly lit kitchen in its glow. On the other side of the threshold, an old woman waxed the wooden floors, grumbling to herself in Mandarin.

"How long has she worked for you?" Clement asked.

"Too long. I keep telling her the apartment doesn't need that much cleaning. She comes sometimes at night. I threaten not to pay her. She says she will come anyway."

"She's after you," Clement said, smiling.

"She's wasting her time."

"Well, at least you'll have shiny floors. Mine doesn't want me, *or* do cleaning."

There was the sound of a door opening. The old woman sat up on her haunches, and started yelling at whoever had just come in.

"Chen?"

"It's me, Pop."

"Pop. First they bring McDonald's, then Kentucky Colonel. Now I'm 'Pop.'" He raised his voice. "Come in and say hello to an old friend."

Chen came to the door, stepping around the little woman, who continued railing at him, pointing to the floor. "Why is she still working here? I thought you told her we didn't need her anymore."

"She needs us," Dao said.

"Not me. All she does is tell me what a mess I make. Hello, Superintendent."

"Chen." Clement held out his hand, and shook the boy's. "That's what women do. Try to underline how disorganized your life would be without them."

"I like disorganized," said Chen.

"So do I. Let's just keep telling ourselves that, and then we won't be sad when they leave us."

"I'm wiped," Chen said, kissing his grandfather's cheek. "Good night. Good night, Superintendent." Chen left the kitchen, snapping back at the old woman in Mandarin as she raised her fist.

"He's a good boy," Clement said.

"Kind of you to see beyond the hair."

"It's just the age. I spent this afternoon at the expat school questioning the victims' classmates. They have haircuts, too."

"How did it go?"

"I was hard on them."

"Why?"

"I don't want the killers to be Cantonese."

After he left Dao's apartment, Clement went to 1997. Those who didn't know his name and rank, which many of them did, recognized a policeman, even one not in uniform. Besides the official attitude, the square set of shoulders, the restless, observing eyes, there was the pager on his belt, mandatory for those in the CID to wear when on duty.

It was an old bar, opened in a time when there was still some lightheartedness about 1997, a cockiness in the name, as if the changeover wasn't going to bother anybody. But the club seemed very dark to Clement now, partly because of the neon, mirrored deco flash of the newer popular ones, but mostly because there was heaviness implicit in the coming event, like the literally lumbering wood in the decor.

"Did you ever see these two people?" he asked a young couple sitting at the side of the dance floor. There were flashing strobe lights at the entrance to the cave that separated the disco from the bar, jolting the photos in his hand of David and Betsy into an eerie liveliness. The room seemed to Clement more depressed than festive, a melancholy aura around it, like a place that had been condemned. There were not many dancers on the floor, underlining the hollowness of too loud music that held in its sound no real celebration.

The young man said no. The girlish woman he was with averted her eyes, catching his for a moment, before looking away, in what seemed to Clement a kind of signal. She was tiny, even for an

Oriental, with an uncharacteristic fullness of leg, made more obvious by the shortness of her leather skirt and Carmen Miranda-ish sandals, with platform soles and heels nearly four inches high. Her toes were painted a deep blood red, to match her long fingernails and her thinly garish mouth, too wide for the small, round face.

She strained her toes into a point, jiggling her left leg, crossed tightly over the right, but not so tight as to conceal the crotch of her black pantyhose. She subtly nodded in the same direction her toes were pointing, back past the cave, toward the bar.

He went and waited for her there. She was a while in coming. She went straight past him down the steps, not having an easy time of it with her heels and soles as outrageously elevated as they were, kind of rocking her as she walked out the door, into the street. He finished his barley water and followed her outside. She was pressed against the side of a building, the neon sign across the street flashing red into her onyx eyes.

"You're looking for my boyfriend," she said. Her voice was surprisingly husky, smoky, like the sometime stars of old movies who had ruined men's fortunes while seeming to improve them.

"The one you're with tonight?"

"My *old* boyfriend."

"Where can I find him?"

The front door to 1997 opened, sending a wave of conversation out into the oddly silent street. "Wendy?" a young man called.

She pressed Clement back into the shadows. "Come to the Albany apartments at two o'clock," she whispered, and moved past him, steadying herself on the bricks along the wall as she walked.

"I thought you were going to the ladies' room," the boy said, seeing her. "Ernest said you left. Are you mad or something?"

"I just needed some air," said Wendy, and went back inside.

Air. Clement took a deep breath. She wasn't the only one. The Albany. What was a girl like that doing living in the Albany?

"The Albany," he murmured aloud, puzzling it over in his mind. Arguably the most prestigious address in Hong Kong. At the crossroads of the old Peak Road, the original road up the mountain, and Robinson Road, above the Botanical Gardens. Overlooking Government House. The Governor for a neighbor. The Botanical

Gardens for a front lawn. The most palatial apartment block in a city dominated by palatial apartments. With Dame Lydia Dunne, a director of the Swire group, in the penthouse, a woman who had given women and Hong Kong new prestige.

How could a girl like this, with her too short skirt and wobbly shoes and nothing about her that smelled like privilege, be living at the Albany? Neither the clothes nor the makeup had seemed particularly expensive. Trendy, yes, but even the trendy had subtle price tags on it, as did women who traded their favors. No way she was the mistress of someone important, who might have residence there. But sex was a funny thing, and maybe she was into it with some shoe freak, and had tricks he couldn't imagine.

Of course she hadn't said she lived there. But it seemed a fairly odd place to meet at two in the morning if your limousine wasn't driving you home.

He looked at his watch. Another hour and a half. Well, he wouldn't drink to pass the time. Even as he noted that, he felt a slight rush of anger, because he knew why he wasn't drinking, even while he tried to tell himself it was because of the importance of the case. He hated it that a woman was affecting him who didn't care that she was affecting him. Hated to be affected in any way by a woman, much less one who thought she was right, and was. For the first time in a long time he was carrying a gun. Not that he thought there was more danger than usual involved in what he was doing, or that he might need it more. But the rule was you were not to carry a gun if you were going to drink. And the odds were other times he would do just that. Only now he wasn't. The one thing more onerous than a reformed drunk was someone who thought she had the power to reform him. But she hadn't said she wanted to, hadn't shown sufficient interest, really, had she?

He decided to walk to the Albany. What had made the building so desirable as it was, besides the beauty of the locale, was its convenience. Within walking distance of the city, if you liked walking, which Clement remembered, as he started the climb, he really had. Not easy to do, though, with a belly full of whiskey.

He followed the curving sidewalks around Cottontree Drive, up to Robinson Road, feeling the night against his face, cool and humid. A light wind stirred the trees. The moon was in its next-to-fullest phase, only a slight sliver missing, an evening away from total ripeness. Below him, ever farther below him, glowed the fluorescence of Hong Kong, so bright with lights you could take its picture without a flash. Around him was foliage lushly green, slightly luminescent in the darkness, so illuminated was that darkness by the moon, and the occasional streetlamp. A city so gaudy even its nature glittered.

Up the old Peak Road to the secondary road leading down to the Albany he walked, filled with a curious elation. Did he have it in him still to become other than he was, to feel actual physical exultation, a sense of pleasure just at being alive? He knew he was a good man, but he had become slightly bored with himself, as people became inert when they had no prospect of changing things. Was it in him to become part of a transition, instead of just resisting it, resenting it?

He felt almost young as he sighted the portico of the Albany. High above this high portion of the Peak the building towered, majestic, its windows, those that were still alive, softly lit. No neon here, no flashy luminescence, no need for the economical fluorescents. Even privilege had its echelons. This, he supposed, was the peak of the Peak.

He wondered as he started for the entrance, where, exactly, the girl would meet him. Logic dictated the lobby, since she hadn't given him an apartment number. Wendy. He didn't even know her full name.

But he did know her voice. He had noted the slight metallic edge to it, the scrape in her throat, as she spoke. He recognized it as it fell through the air, volume increased to a scream. And he had a long moment to see her, as she hurtled, in the bright moonlight, platform shoes kicking and flailing, toward the cement of the roof over the canopy.

BOOK THREE

◆

CENTRAL

SEVENTEEN

◆

Courage was not Louise's long suit. What she had told Anthony Go was the truth: she had had enough.

It was something past depression. There was a dullness on her spirit now. A quiet ache, because of how old she was. There seemed to be nothing up ahead that had the power to transform.

When she was young, she had had the alchemy of youth. The American dream, that it all could change overnight: instant love, instant recognition, instant table from the headwaiter. But with all the changes that had occurred, with all she had achieved, her life had come up empty. Whatever Go could do to her was not as bad as what life seemed ready to do.

Who was there who had touched her skin to whom it had made a difference? What had she done that had made the world better, or, in the case of those she genuinely loathed, worse? Footprints in the sands of time, as opposed to Grauman's Chinese. Would she have left a mark anywhere? Toted up on the big scoreboard in the sky, all that would remain would be filing cabinets filled with contracts, a few well-told show biz legends, one-liners that would last no longer than the memory of Tony Curtis. There was not much to hang around for, really.

Running into Claire had disturbed her more than she acknowledged even to herself. How would it be to have had love, and lose it, at their time of life? Was it really better to have loved and lost, than never to have loved at all? Or wasn't it worse to be in no position to judge?

But a day went by, and she wasn't dead, and there was a dress she'd seen at Lane Crawford that had seemed too expensive. Too expensive didn't matter now. She decided to go shopping with a gambler's recklessness, ready to lose it all, now that she understood there was nothing really to lose. Since she might not be there when the bills came due, she bought like there was no tomorrow. Maybe there wouldn't be. It gave her a freedom she'd never had.

"I'll have these," she said about shoes and purse, like a little girl in a candy store. "I'll have those," about jeweled buckles that attached to the shoes. "I'll have that," of a gold-strung jade bracelet in Maggie Evans's boutique, that went with the heart around her neck.

"Oh, good," Maggie said. "I'm glad you decided to treat yourself. He was lovely, wasn't he, that Texan. Did you sleep with him?"

"He's interested in someone else."

"They're all interested in someone else. That doesn't mean they won't sleep with you." She slipped the clasp on Louise's wrist, closed the safety catch. "I imagine he must have an enormous penis, his hands are so big."

"We'll never know."

"Speak for yourself, dear," said Maggie.

All through her shopping excursion, Louise had the sense she was being followed. She ducked into doorways to see if she could spot who it was. But the only repeat face she was sure of, in the sea of Chinese, belonged to a European who looked vaguely familiar, a portly man with thick white hair. It made no sense, really, Go's having a Caucasian to do his dirty work.

A limousine moved alongside the curb as she walked. She crossed to the other side, saw that it continued at her pace. Was it charting her footsteps? Did hit men travel in Rolls-Royces? Who could she ask about the technique of Triad wipeouts in Hong Kong, besides Henry? She wouldn't tell Henry what had happened, she didn't want her upset. Upset. How generous she was becoming in her middle years, all that she would have now, thank God. She did not have any wish for her late ones.

At Lane Crawford, she tried on the dress she'd wanted. Dresses were something she hardly ever wore, her main ensemble for business being slacks and shirts and tailored jackets in the style Katharine Hepburn might have sported had she been pushier. Where was the line between Philadelphia staunch and New York aggressive? Was it all in the education, the little fillips of privilege that closed around the words as you spoke, so if a woman had gone to Bryn Mawr and talked marble-mouth she could be classified as feisty instead of ballsy?

The whole puzzle of women's progress had been one to which Louise had paid little attention. She had sprung from her own ambition, unsexed, like Lady Macbeth. Outspoken before it was fashionable for young women—"girls," they were still called at the time—to have any words in their mouths at all. Sharp before it was allowable for women to be as bright as men, much less brighter. Predating active feminism as she had, there had been no philosophy in her rise. Just unfettered hunger for the glory of glitz, such as it was.

But how she would have loved being visibly feminine, like Loretta Young, another star Henry wouldn't know. How it pleased her to waft into the dress she was trying on, as Loretta would have done. Swirling through a doorway, on her way to a garden party filled with goys. Sad that the people and the era that had made Louise want to be glamorous would soon be totally vanished, forgotten, uncommemorated. What would a planet be like with no one on it who remembered Ruth Roman?

The salesgirl started zipping her up. The store, like most establishments in Hong Kong, was more crystal and gilt than its American equivalents, mirrored and clustered with lucite grapes, and workers with plastic smiles, who answered yes to everything, even if they didn't understand. "Ow," said Louise, as the salesgirl caught her skin.

"Oh, I am so terribly sorry."

She was very small. It was intimidating to Louise, all these little women with their toothpick waists and nonexistent bellies, wearing European clothes that were probably size two. She tried not to get angrier than she would have at a clumsy salesgirl in Bloomingdale's. But it wasn't easy. The Chinese loosed the zipper, pinching Louise even more painfully.

"Ow," Louise said again. "Am I bleeding? Has anyone been caught in this zipper who has AIDS?"

"Please, I hope you will excuse me." The young woman lowered her eyes. "I am twice as ashamed. I understand you are a friend of Mr. Anthony Go. Next time I promise to be more careful."

Louise had lunch with Bunyan, and a friend of his, an expatriate writer who'd moved to Lantau Island. She was very hungry, unsettled by what had occurred in the department store. But she ate slowly, understanding that the meal might be her last. "I have to be careful of my table manners. Someone's watching me."

"Someone's watching all of us," the writer said.

"Gordon's found religion," said Bunyan, a pucker of contemptuous amusement on his grayish lips.

"Well, in your case, you're being watched by God. I, on the other hand, am being watched by a hit man."

The two men laughed.

"I wish I was kidding."

"Aren't you?" asked Bunyan. The little beacon of gossip that usually shone in his pale gray eyes, signaling scandal, was temporarily replaced by concern.

"Apparently I offended some bigwig Triad."

"Oh, I love this city!" Bunyan said. "A woman was flung from a window at the Albany where all the elegant people live, including Dame Lydia, don't you know. And no one knows whose window it was. Usually they're found in lightwells, these cast-off lovers. I mean when these people cast someone off, they really cast them off."

"I don't find that funny," said Louise.

"But you have to, sweetheart. I mean, that isn't the half of it. We're talking rumors of sex gangs. Former crown consuls up on charges of conspiring to procure underage girls. Threatening to name names, justices involved with little boys. Orgies. Gay men picking up teenage Aussies in Lan Kwai Fong, found stabbed twenty-two times. Including in the eye."

"And that's only this week," said Gordon.

"No wonder you live here," said Bunyan. "So much material! And they think in New York you moved because of the temples. What a place! I may never leave!"

"Me, neither," said Louise.

"Are you really worried?" asked Bunyan.

Louise took a deep breath. "I wouldn't give myself a thousand dollars to develop this into a screenplay if I were Columbia. How can this be happening to me? I who never offended anyone, but half of Hollywood."

"At least it was the right half," said Bunyan.

Louise dug into her chicken salad, and shrieked as a cockroach ran out of it. "Jesus! Didn't Blake Edwards already do this scene?"

"Is anything wrong?" asked the waiter.

"Not if you're a meateater," said Gordon.

"There was a cockroach in her salad." A faint tinge of color rose in Bunyan's cheeks, so deep it overrode his albino cast, as though the offense had been against him.

"I am so terribly sorry." The waiter took her salad and bowed. "We must see you get better service. We understand you are a friend of Mr. Anthony Go."

After lunch, she went back to the hotel, and found Anthony Go's card. "All right, I get it," she said into the phone. "Your people are everywhere."

"You have no idea."

"I would've thought you'd have more style. Cockroaches are the pits."

"Cockroaches are pretty if you think about some of the things that can happen. Have you ever seen someone get acid thrown in their face?"

"My face is hardly my fortune," she managed to say.

"Still, pain is different from death. No matter how little you care about life . . . to be disfigured . . ."

"Look, there are plenty of agents. All of them hungry. Many of them more unscrupulous than me, I'm stunned to realize. You could find anybody."

"I want you. There is, as you people say, an upside. Besides staying alive and whole."

"Yes?"

"I can promise you protection. The best protection. Nothing will happen to you. I can offer you great wealth. There are concerns I am involved with, assets you cannot even begin to imagine. I will make you part of them. I know you're successful but we're talking riches beyond your wildest dreams . . ."

"You don't know what my wildest dreams were. They didn't have to do with money."

"Whatever you want, I can get you."

"I'd rather represent John Carradine. The way he must look now." She hung up the phone.

All the rest of the day, she saw people in the shadows. Walking along Queen's Road, buying things she didn't even want, slightly unhinged now by the danger that doubtless awaited her, she was conscious of the Rolls limousine moving along the curb. It was being driven very slowly, keeping the same pace she was, accelerating when she did, slowing down when she slowed down. It was a white Silver Cloud, highly conspicuous, even in a city of limousines, with strips and hood ornament that gleamed like precious metal. All at once the rear door of the limousine was flung open in front of her. It blocked her way.

A man in a morning coat stepped from inside. He bowed. "I am Stefan."

"Don't tell me. A friend of Anthony Go's."

"Who?"

"Just know I won't make this easy for you."

"You don't have to make it easy. Count Bassia is prepared to do whatever you like."

"Huh?"

Stefan indicated the man in the backseat. Louise bent over and looked inside. Sitting there, smiling widely, his teeth as agleam as his bright green eyes, was the European who had seemed to be following her that morning.

Up close, she recognized him. "You're the captain of the yacht that rescued me."

"Count Bassia," said Stefan.

The Count reached for her hand, raising himself from the seat, gently pulling her inside. He kissed her hand, half bowing over it, murmuring words in a language she didn't recognize.

"I'm sorry. I don't speak Italian."

"Greek," said Stefan, getting into the jump seat. "It's Greek."

"What did he say?"

The Count began to speak again, with gestures, touching his lips, making waves on the air, moving his fingers toward the sky. "To the ends of the earth," Stefan translated. "To the moon and the islands beyond the moon, where the yachts of dreamers sail."

"But what does that mean?"

"He loves you," said Stefan, smiling.

Now the Texan sat in the bar drinking before lunch. There was a surliness to the way he lifted his glass this day, a deliberate stoking of his own fires. He was due back in Houston. This was taking too much time. Just as he'd never met a woman he couldn't have, he'd never been unable to close a deal to his satisfaction. Even when he had to let it go, which he wasn't about to do with Erica.

He was convinced that a deal was what it was. For all her elegance, the veneer, the costly clothes, the aristocratic curve of neck, the hair pulled back so tight only a true patrician with perfect features could wear it that way, he knew she was no patrician, no aristocrat. She was on the market. He could tell. You could always tell when someone was on the market, like a company that denied it was for sale, but had breakfast meetings with Carl Icahn. It was only a question of determining the price.

The bracelet was in Biff's pocket. He'd spent more and more

time carrying it around, waiting for the right moment. God, she was beautiful. Peering through the soft lighting of the Captain's Bar at the deep, low couch where she sat, he was lifted by the sight of her, as touched by her beauty as fired by it. What if the right moment never came?

He had another martini, a mean drink that gave him more of an edge than his usual margaritas, and decided the moment was up to him, that he would make it happen. He got up from the bar stool and lumbered toward the corner where she sat, choice legs coiled, slightly flattening the shapely calves, nose tilted indifferently, as though she were turning away from him. Imperious, with that flash in her yellow-green eyes. Tiger eyes. Christ, he felt like a schoolboy.

There was another man watching her through wire-rimmed glasses, from a few tables away. Biff felt pissed at him for even looking, as though no one else had a right to study her that seriously. He deliberately moved around to the far side of her table to come between her and the intrusive look, wedging his big legs in the narrow gap.

"Okay. I'm ready to talk turkey."

"I beg your pardon?"

"You made your point, the hard way." He sat down beside her. "That pays double."

"Please go away."

"I got something for you." He put the jewelry box, with its gold paper, on the table.

She did not look at it, or him. "Open it. It's from Maggie Evans. The hot jewelry designer. I checked around. We're talking best in a city loaded with great jewelers . . . Go ahead, don't you want to see the kind of taste I got, besides in women?" When she made no move to reach for it, he tore off the paper himself, fumblingly opened the clasp on the soft red leather box, with its gold-filigreed borders. His big hands were clumsier than usual, because he had been geared up to expect eager eyes. They all liked presents.

He held out the open box. "There's a lot more diamonds than shows straight off. But it's the jade that's really priceless. The Chinks set so much store by it they drive up the price."

She looked at him now, disgust weighting her features, her mouth twisted with distaste. It ate away at her beauty. "Waiter?" she called out.

"Maybe you'd rather have the cash. It cost thirty-seven thousand." He waited. "If it goes well between us, you can have everything in the store." He was sweating now. He wasn't used to selling that hard. "Okay, so you're proud. No woman's that proud. You have your price. We just got to cut the deal."

"Excuse me?" The man with the glasses was in front of the table. He looked slight to the Texan, not very impressive inside the well-tailored suit, young around the jaw, about the Texan's own age, maybe forty-two, forty-three, with eyes that seemed blank behind the wire-rimmed frames. "I thought I heard the lady ask you to leave."

"Stay out of this, Milquetoast."

"Alexander's my name." He held out his hand. "Lockwood Alexander."

"It's Milquetoast to me."

"Won't even shake a fellow's hand?"

"If it'll make you go away." Biff took the extended hand, and winced. His features tightened with the grip. It was a powerful squeeze, a clamp.

The Texan was on his feet, trying to pull his fingers clear. He started to howl. It was a quiet howl, at first, little more than a whine. But it built in pitch, like a coyote's cry, until it turned, high-pitched, into language. "Let go, you son of a bitch!" He tried to strike out with his free fist. But the slighter, shorter man ducked out of the way, all the while still gripping.

"Lemme go, goddammit!"

"If I have your word, Scout's honor, that's what you'll do. Go. Get out of here."

"You miserable pissant," Biff squealed.

"Scout's honor?"

"Okay!"

He released Biff's hand.

"I'll get you for this." Biff scooped up the package. "And you, you whore." Then he was gone.

"Thank you," Erica said.

"Lockwood Alexander." He held out his hand.

She smiled. "Promise you won't hurt me?"

"I won't hurt you," he said, and looked at her in a way that went beyond the promise. Beyond promises most men make to women.

Above reproach as the staff of the Mandarin was, its concierge declining to give the location of brothels to even the most esteemed, high-tipping guest, saying, "I am not that kind of concierge," there were, nonetheless, occasional breeches. A butler on Biff Lester's floor had watched with great curiosity the bringing in of a second television, and two VCRs. Finally, he had given in to temptation, and played the tapes in Biff's machine. A snitch on the kitchen staff told Clement what the butler had seen.

"So he has videotapes of the woman swimming?" Clement asked the third sous-chef.

"And a pornographic movie." He chopped as he answered, giving slanting strokes to the stalks of celery spread before him on the sideboard.

"Well, we can't go after everyone in Hong Kong who has one of those," said Clement, trying to cover his own disappointment that it wasn't, somehow, linked to Anthony Go, some more sinister professionalism, and not just a horny American. He had seen the Texan, or a man he now assumed to be the Texan, in the bar several times, a big, beefy man with a bulldog jaw, hanging somewhat agape at the sight of Erica Thorr.

It amused him a little, really, the truth behind the episode of the uninvited cameraman in the pool, there being so much that was dark and deadly in Hong Kong. Obviously the big man had hired someone to come in and photograph her, so he could have her the only way he could. The whole thing was relatively harmless. Still, it was certainly an illegal invasion of privacy. Clement would have to deal with it, speak to the man. But when he went to his room, Biff Lester was gone. And with him, the tape of Erica.

*   *   *

When she couldn't sleep, which was almost every night now, with the day coming closer that Peter's mother would arrive, a more onerous date to Kip than even 1997, she would go to the window, and look at the sky. With Dao Tsim for a great-grandfather, she was respectful of destiny. She tried to think in terms of the Infinite, that which had spun the stars into their perfect design. She would struggle to see her life as the very small thing it was, not even visible were some souls on those faraway galaxies looking back at her. She tried to release her anguish and longing, to understand that what she was going through did not really matter that much. But it was too much like Peter's attitude to become real philosophy, and instead, intensified her pain.

On this night she dressed again. She did not try to be quiet. Anger was growing in her. It didn't matter if she disturbed him. It seemed to be the only power she had left, annoying him. Except for getting him excited.

"Where are you going?" he said.

"To meet my lover."

"I hope that's the truth. It's the best thing that could happen to you."

"No. The best thing that could happen to *you*."

She slammed out of the apartment, wishing she didn't love him. Wishing she could see him in her heart as she did in her brain: just another callow Englishman, treating her like some island he'd chanced on, on his way to somewhere else, planting a flag in her without any real sense of obligation. Pitcairn. Ascension. Saint Helena. The Caymans. All claimed by the Brits as colonies, inhabitants uniformly excluded from citizenship in the National Act of 1983, along with the people of Hong Kong. Only Gibraltar and the Falklands having their citizenship honored by the Brits. Even the Portuguese, obliged as they were to return Macau to the Chinese in 1999, had made provision for the hundred thousand Macanese to become Portuguese. But the English wanted only white skins in their country. Much as Peter fawned over the texture of her flesh, in their lascivious moments, he wanted that color in his bed. Not in his life.

And still she loved him. Caught in his schoolboy fantasies of lingerie and little girls in uniform, flawed and puerile as he was, she felt she belonged to him. It was a passion she derided in the part of her that was rational, the organized, efficient side, high tech, computer literate. Emotions were the lowest tech. Not tech at all. Not even connected to the brain, she was sure. Or if the brain entered into it at all, it was the soft side, the hemisphere that was creative, inspired, dealing with art, driving itself crazy.

In her middle-of-the-night restlessness, she went to the studio of her uncle, a glassblower. He worked at night, because it was the coolest time. Even in autumn Hong Kong was humid and often sultry. His concentration was better when he was comfortable. How she wished that hers could be the same, that she could find some comfort inside herself that would give her the strength to let Peter go. How she wished there was in her her uncle's capacity to be that patient, working glass through a steady blue flame, till it became molten, easing out what would be a wing, or the bill of a humming-bird.

She knocked at the door, hoping he might pass on to her a tiny portion of his peace. The British could talk all they liked about history and political exigency, but it was they who brought up the lease's expiring, not the Chinese. Conservatives and intellectuals could argue that Mrs. Thatcher had been realistic, but to surrender three and a half million subjects like so many sacks of potatoes to a Communist tyranny defied all decency and honor. And this from the nation who invented the idea of "fair play." The truth was, the Brits had had enough of the island, as Peter had had enough of her.

To her surprise, Dao Tsim answered the door. "Great-grandfather." She bowed. "I did not expect to find you here."

"I couldn't sleep. I came to watch your uncle make glass."

"I, too." She offered her chin for him to cup in his hands, as she always did.

"A man my age doesn't need much sleep. Soon I will sleep forever. Your brother Chen is too busy being a teenager to sleep. But why are you not sleeping?"

She didn't answer.

"How can a clever girl be so foolish?"

"I ask myself that question all the time."

The uncle didn't raise his eyes from the flame. He held a piece of glass with a long-handled, thin-nosed pincers in the flame, nodding his head to acknowledge Kip's presence.

"What's he making?"

"A phoenix. For a wedding cake."

"Has he made the dragon yet?"

Dao pointed with his ancient, long-fingered hand at where it lay. "The male principle."

"Why did they decide to make the female a phoenix?"

"Nobody decided. It just *is*. The phoenix is a female, rising out of her own ashes. Shedding bad experience like a tired skin. Rejuvenated by the hope that something better is coming, she creates that possibility. So more often than not, something better comes."

"You believe that?"

"I know it. Nothing they cannot do once they set their will in motion."

"Nothing?"

"Nothing. The challenge is to choose wisely."

"If we have a choice."

"Everyone has a choice."

"Dragons have choices. I would choose to be a dragon."

"You would rather be a man?"

"It would be easier."

"It only seems so. The phoenix is more powerful than the dragon. She can lift herself."

She put her arms around him, leaned her head on his scrawny shoulder, as they watched. In the blue flame, the phoenix formed.

When Kip got home, Peter was asleep, or pretending to be. She slipped into bed beside him.

"Was he better than I was?"

"In every way. And bigger."

"Good. You deserve that."

"What are you doing?"

"Just checking. Making sure you aren't lying. Trying to excite me with jealousy."

"Please don't touch me."

"You're not even wet."

"He dried me. With his beard."

"You don't like beards."

"His is different. It has spikes in it, like my brother's hair. He sprays it with glue, just like Chen, so it makes hard little spikes that go into my flesh."

"You don't like pain."

"Then why am I with you? I think it must be better when you have it in your body. Then you can feel physically what you're putting yourself through."

"I hate it when women think."

"Including your mother?"

"My mother doesn't think. She has opinions."

"And we know in advance what will be her opinion of me."

"You mustn't take it personally. She's just very British. Scratch a Brit, you'll find a bigot."

"Including you."

"Not in my best moments."

"Don't do that."

"I can't smell him."

"He smelled you. He said 'Fee fie fo fum, I smell the bloodless Englishman.'"

"I am certainly not bloodless."

"No blood. No guts. No passion."

"What do you think this is?"

"Animals get erections. They have no connection to feeling, and neither do you."

"I feel a great deal."

"Bigotry."

"It isn't me personally. It's a national trait. A measure of our own insecurity."

"But it still isn't feeling. Not real feeling."

"Feel this. Feel how deeply I can feel. What I can make you feel."

"I feel nothing."

"I have the evidence. Here. Hard as a little pebble. You're a liar."

"No." She pushed him away and turned her back. "I'm a phoenix."

Clement had had the questionable privilege, in the fall of 1989, to be visiting San Francisco when the earthquake struck. He'd been walking up a hill to the friend's apartment where he was staying, when the earth began to shift, and bricks started cascading into the street. What awed him most, and what nobody mentioned, in the reports and stories that were to be told in the days and weeks that followed, was the sound: a hideous roar, a bellowing, as if some terrible rage in the earth had found voice.

In the same way, what nobody mentioned when a body fell was the sound it made when it landed: the awful crunch of bones breaking, the thud of flesh on concrete, the splat of skin coming open, like the pop of a water-filled balloon, dropped by mischievous children. No mischievous child had sent Wendy hurtling to her death from a high window at the Albany. Though what window it had been, how high the floor, was still unknown to Clement.

There had been only two lights still lit in the front of the building when she'd fallen. Moments after her death he'd been able to question people in those flats, over the powerful objections of the security guard who, stunned as he was by what had just taken place, was still concerned for his job.

Both parties, a middle-aged government official, and a young woman who lived in the apartment just above him, had come to the door in their nightclothes, their faces marked with sleep. No signs of sweat, high color. Nothing that would indicate they had just committed murder. The lights, they each said, had been lamps left on in their living rooms.

"I'll have to question everyone who lives in the front of the building," Clement had told the elevator man, on his way down. Police had just arrived in answer to his call. They were already swarming all over the portico, members of the crime lab taking pictures, the coroner bending over Wendy's body. She was lying faceup, a kind of smile on her face as though pleased it was the back of her head that was spilling its contents on the concrete, and if her face was left intact, she might at least look agreeable.

"Sorry but not at this hour," the elevator man said. "You don't know who these people are that live here."

"One of them's a killer," Clement said.

In the end, he'd agreed to come back in the daytime. No one objected to being questioned, with the exception of a barrister, who didn't like the way Clement's eyes moved around the room.

"Is this an inquiry, or an illegal search?" the man said, keeping a watch on Clement's assistant who was out on the terrace that opened off the living room. The barrister was quite famous in the colony, one of the many hired to represent the perpetrators of a famous financial hoax. At least it was coming to the surface as a hoax; for a while it had been made to look like serious business, investors giving fortunes to a company that, it turned out, wasn't really there.

"I'm an officer of the law," Clement said. "How could it possibly be illegal?"

"I'm a practitioner of the law," the man said. His name was Roger O'Regan, and he was a youngish Irishman, his nose already slightly mottled with drink. His eyes were sharp, though, in spite of the fact that they were not exactly clear. He looked at everything that Clement was looking at, parrying each visual thrust, like a fencer. "I can find some way of making it seem so."

"Is there a balcony off your bedroom?"

"Yes, there is. But no one's been on it."

"The crime lab will determine that. What were you doing at two o'clock in the morning?"

"Sleeping, of course," Roger said.

"Did you know a Miss Wendy Lu?" She had fallen still holding her purse, as though she were on the way to the ladies' room. Her lipstick case had been crushed; the greasy red slightly smeared her identity card.

"I did not."

Clement offered pictures of her, sad little passport photos, four to a strip, the kind people took in booths on the platform of the

MTR, on their way to some embassy where they would apply for emigration. Wendy was on file in the Canadian, Australian, and U.S. embassies, all of which, according to their records, had held out little or no hope. "Did you ever see her in the elevator?"

"How would one know?" He gave the pictures back. "She looks like all the rest of them."

"Nice guy," Clement said to his assistant, Andrew, as the apartment door shut behind them. "One more apartment to go."

"There's nobody home there. Doorman told me. The occupant's out of town. Hasn't been here for months."

"I want to check it anyway."

The drapes were drawn in the empty apartment, the keeping-the-sun-from-fading-the-furniture gesture that always reminded Clement of death. Old people did that, preserving their carpets, missing the life outside their windows, shutting out the sunlight that might energize them, make them forget how old they were, maybe keep them alive awhile longer. There was a musty smell, kind of lemony around the edges, sweet, as though someone had been cooking. He switched on the light.

In the bedroom, in a side table by the perfectly made bed, was a drawer full of chips. "Whoever lives here likes to gamble," Clement said to Andrew, looking at the chips up close. "Paradise Casino, Macau. Anthony Go's place."

All over the apartment were photos, in silver frames, on antique desks, sideboards, Steinway baby grand. "I always admired that," said Clement. "People from fine families who kept their history on display. That was one thing that made me particularly sad about never marrying, never having children. It would have been nice, besides watching them grow, to have them in silver frames."

"I don't think these are quite what you had in mind," said Andrew.

Clement moved to the sideboard. Naked women, spread-legged, smiled at the camera with both their mouths, open lips. Other women sucked their nipples, fingered them. Some, though, were not free to smile, their mouths being otherwise engaged, tongues arrowed toward the center of the huge pair of testicles, or licking them from behind as the man penetrated a bent-over woman. Though the pictures seemed to be of many different women, the man looked to be the same. As in all pornography, cock and balls after a certain scrutiny developed their own characteristics, features, almost like a face. And in case there was any doubt, the man himself was shown, full blown, quite literally in several instances. Naked, he grimaced or luxuriated or watched, as the women performed their ministrations.

He was Chinese, and always at full-staff, his body neatly muscled but slender, not very big, except where it counted most. In one of the photos he was being fellated, at least the tip of him was, by a blond woman who looked to Clement disturbingly familiar. He studied the photo. He found another of the same woman, this time on the man's lap riding his giant rod as he pressed her clitoris with his middle finger. Her back was arched away from the camera, breasts thrust pink-nippled in a paroxysm of pleasure.

"Isn't that Maggie Evans?" Andrew said.

"That's who it is," said Clement.

"But who's the man?"

"Harry Magic. The porno star."

EIGHTEEN

◆

Now their days began together. Now when it was six-thirty in the morning, and the doors to the health club opened, there would be two of them waiting to swim: Erica Thorr and Lockwood Alexander. She had taken to calling him "Lochinvar."

After the initial gallantry that brought them together, the hand-wrestling that drove the Texan to his knees, Lockwood's every gesture had been courteous. He did not seem an easy man: nothing about him was casual, including the way he touched her, or failed to. Having checked him out after spotting him that first day in the pool, she knew he was not married. Having seen him in action she knew he was strong, that the slender package was deceiving. Having dined with him the evening of her rescue, she knew he was courtly, charming, and bright. What she didn't know was why he was waiting to make love to her.

He held her hand during dinner that first night, but only her hand. He took her arm as they crossed the streets, guided her through malls and marketplaces. But never did he press his fingers, or his desires. Or what she hoped with all her energy were his desires.

He was handsomer than she thought when she first saw him, with a good square face, strong chin, and a winning smile he did not give too freely. After dinner he'd taken off his glasses and put them

243

in his pocket, so his blue-gray eyes were fixed on her more acutely, the deep attention farsighted people give to things close up in which they are interested but to which they are somewhat blind. She wondered why he didn't kiss her.

Finally he did. They stood in the moonlight, in Statue Square, boarded by boutiques of the costliest European designers, with their windows lit. It was a sweet kiss, nothing urgent about it, childlike almost. "Will we travel?" he asked, as their mouths parted.

She laughed. "Anywhere you want to go," she said.

The next night he took her to a private club in Happy Valley. They had spoken hardly at all through the first dinner. Now he was full of questions.

"Tell me about yourself," she said, instead of answering, pretending she didn't know anything about him.

"I'm forty-four. I'm in finance. I want to be totally honest with you. And I want you to be totally honest with me."

"Let's not do that," she said, smiling, transforming her cool, blond elegance into sunshine. "Let's be like people used to be when they didn't pour out all their garbage."

"You have garbage?"

"Everybody has garbage. The past is an accumulation of things we don't need. Let's just be here together. Now. Living in the moment."

"Sounds good to me."

"Only one thing we need to know. . ."

"There's no one in my life," he said.

"Or mine."

He smiled, and reached for her hand, tightened his grip in a subtle way, his thumb, forefinger, and middle finger moving up around her thumb. He clasped it, pressing against the fleshy mound at its base, a gentle variation of a brother handshake. Very gentle, and far as it could be from brotherly.

Outside the balcony by which they sat splashed the mercurial splendor of Hong Kong, neon lights, illuminated windows. Some bright red, with *Fung shui* consecrations. Beneath the table, their knees touched, an accident of intimacy, nothing he had engineered. But already she could feel him between her legs, and tried not to want him there. The whole thing had to be slow paced, she understood that, even as she wished she could be in bed with him. It had been over a year since it ended with her husband, and no man had touched her in that time. So she was more than ready. Aside from her obligation to the Syndicate, it felt good to her, the prospect of love with this man, winning him. But men didn't fall in love as women did, because they were vulnerable, or their hearts were ready. Men didn't let themselves be in touch with their hearts. They fell in love because they were manipulated, made to think they couldn't live without a woman who seemed completely capable of living without them.

So she couldn't show her readiness, the eagerness she felt in his presence, the slight acceleration of breath when they were close. During dinner she went into the ladies' room to towel off her face, take some of the heat from her cheeks. There was another woman, quite a bit younger, sitting in front of the mirror, fixing her makeup. "Honeymoons take such a toll," she said.

"I hope so," said Erica.

After dinner he took her back to the hotel, stopping for a moment again, in Statue Square. He put on his glasses. "You're even more beautiful in the moonlight."

"I could stay out of it if it bothers you."

"It does. It really bothers me." He reached for her, drew her close, and kissed the outside of her lips. And then he was kissing the supple inside of them, tasting his way along the edges. "I'd better take you home," he said, and did, leaving her outside her door. "I'll see you at the pool," he said, to her terrible surprise, leaving her.

She threw her clothes onto the chair, angry, irritated. She got into bed. The telephone rang.

"First," he said, at the sound of her voice, his own voice deep, going all the way to her bone, "we take the Amtrak to San Diego. Then we take the light rail across the border to Tijuana, and a bus to Mexicali. Then a train to Guadalajara. About three days there, smelling the roses. Then we take another bus to Puerto Vallarta."

"Are there chickens on it?"

"Of course. Now, here's your job. You have to find the name of the little hotel on the beach, right next to El Set. Maria something

Cantina. Make sure we get the corner room, the one with the bed right next to the balcony, overlooking the ocean. We spend a day or so there, drinking margaritas. Then we take the ferry to Yalapa. We spend five days on the beach drinking each other. Then what we have to decide is whether to come home or keep going."

"Sounds good to me."

"My lips on your lips." He hung up the phone.

She could hardly wait to get up in the morning.

Now they stroked the length of the pool, each of them following their personal rhythm. Her tempo was slower than his, more steady, her long ritual of daily swimming having built up her endurance. She understood that the object of exercise for her was to last, to stretch, to tighten, so there was no particular hurry. She did not feel that way anymore about Lockwood.

She could feel every motion he made in the pool against her body, the surge in the water rocking her slightly, tipping her to the right. His motions lapped against her skin, making her aware of parts of herself she wasn't aware existed. There were sensations of him in her armpits, in between her toes. She was so hungry for him she was short of breath, twenty laps into her swim, when she was used to doing a hundred in a pool this size.

The water was heated to ninety-two degrees, adding to the erotic undertow. No longer was she exercising so much as being carried along in a sexual tide. The pool was mosaicked with a rich, deep blue tile, making it seem like a grotto. Above it was a huge glass skylight through which, backstroking, one could watch the heavens growing light. The same moon that had been such a boon to their evenings was being swallowed by the sky. Now and again he would swim close to her, brush her with his body, a seemingly unintentional gesture that threw her totally off pace.

What exactly was he trying to do? What was his game? Why was he playing a game at all? Just because she was involved in the cleverest con seven smart, bitter women could think of didn't mean she deserved to be toyed with.

She cut underwater in the pool, bored with the stretching and the stroking and the thinking, restless with the drill she put herself through to contain her restlessness. She swam on her back beneath where he swam, moving with his movements a few feet below him, looking up at his body, checking it for proportion, strength, grace. His legs were shapely for a man's, well developed in the calf, thickly muscled through the thigh. His belly was flat, the navel puckered, bathing shorts tapered through the hip and admirably filled. What was the difficulty?

She let herself be carried a little closer to the surface, came up underneath him, her face grazing his nipples. He started in the water, righted himself, and pulled her up in front of him. "Are you all right?" he said. "Did I hurt you?"

"Not yet. I keep waiting."

He smiled, curving his arm around her hips and pulling her to the side of the pool. He sat her on the ladder, both hands on her waist, lifting her as though she were a child. He checked to make sure they were alone, then kissed between her breasts.

"I must taste of chlorine."

"You taste like ambrosia." He kissed her again, in the same place.

"Will we go to heaven?"

"Of course."

"Will we get there by bus or by plane?"

"A glider, I think. We'll leave from Nepal, because that's closest to heaven. The winds are good, and very strong. And then we'll make love on a cloud."

"Why do we have to wait?"

"I didn't want to move too fast. I didn't want to rush you."

"Rush me." She slid from the ladder, and fell against his mouth.

Now she could feel his hand moving along the outside of her body as the water had done, stroking that began on her shoulder and moved down her arm, along her waist, over the curve of her hip to her thigh. And then he stopped behind her knees, and lifted his hand once more to the side of her neck, where the stroking had started, and began again, while with the other hand he held her, pressed her closer, with no greater urgency than he had pressed his suit. They lay that way for what seemed hours. And all the time they kissed, kisses that had no haste to them, no insistence, empty of entreaty. Because both of them knew they were going to get what they wanted.

And sometimes he touched her hair before his hand began again its nightwatchmanly course along her body. She lay on her left side, and he lay on his right. And they breathed with each other's breath, and after a while it became as though they had always been together, and this was not new love at all. Eager as she had been, she was calm now. There was not just passion waiting for her, she understood, but solace. She had never felt anything so kind.

And then his hand moved between them, brushing across the tops of her breasts. And his kisses started persuading. He eased her onto her back, and kissed her aureoles, feathered them with his tongue. And he rubbed against her belly with his hair, silky and thick, and traced back upward till he was at her mouth again. He lifted her hips a little, and with no break in motion, put himself inside her.

And now his kisses had insistence in them, inciting her to move along with him, goading her palate and her tongue, as his tip did the rest of her. And she could feel him on the roof of her mouth, and the roof of her womb, penetrating all her mysteries, making her naked from the inside.

And then he was lifting her and thrusting, and the peace was gone out of him. His face contorted in an expression of rage and grief, as though all the contradictions of man were in that moment: so desperate to be in control, so longing for the control to be taken away. So wanting to be noble, so caught in his animal nature. A cry came out of him, like loss, and he fell against her. She was so touched by him, moved by him, even as she was filled by him, that she broke as he did, but in a different way from any she'd known before. There was, in that moment, not just orgasm, but release. Release from all the anger and disappointment she felt—women felt—because men never cared as much as they did. Or gave as much, or allowed as much, or opened as much, or had to let go as much, or hurt as much when they said goodbye.

*   *   *

They held each other, sent little wet winds into each other's ears, kissed, kisses like awards for a game well played. He started stroking her again, the way he had in the beginning.

"We'll go to Miami," he said after a while. "We won't stay long. Just long enough to pick up our flight to Brazil, by way of Caracas."

"What's in Brazil?" Erica said against his chest. There was a great thatch of hair in the center of it, thicker than the hair on his head, silver in the light of morning making its way through the balcony window. She loved the feel of that hair against her cheek, but it was so abundant she could hardly breathe with her face in it. So she opted for a rest on the side of his chest, where she could breathe him in, but still breathe.

"The Rain Forest."

"Do we have to go by way of Caracas?"

"Not if you don't want to. We'll fly to Rio instead. Stay about three days. Catch a flight to Belém. There's a nonstop from there, or we can touch down in Brasília."

"I'd like that."

"That's what we'll do, then. Maybe a day or two in Brasília. Where the poor look down on the rich. Then it's wheels up to Belém. That's the coast town. We catch a small freighter up the Amazon, jump ship at Manus, hire some native guides. And we explore the Rain Forest. Make love on giant leaves. You mind humidity?"

"Not if we're naked, and we can swim."

"That's what we'll do, is be naked and swim. And make love on a leaf."

"And then what we have to decide is whether to come home or keep going," she said, quoting him.

"Not this time. This time we have to come home. We have to save the Rain Forest. You'll be a great spokesman for the cause. They'll believe you. Because you've slept on the leaves. It won't be some abstract issue of saving the planet, not when they see you. Because you've loved in it. It will be personal. Unique. Powerful."

"You really think we can save it?"

"Of course. In a world full of lies and liars, we found each other. Nothing's impossible."

It was dark. He could not see the shame on her face.

So it was all falling into place, to make a terrible pun at the expense of Wendy Lu. Once it was known that the closed apartment at the Albany belonged to Harry Magic, Clement's whole theory on the case being connected to pornography started to seem less theory than fact. "Find out where Magic's gone," he told Andrew. "Check the airport, passport control."

"Why don't we just ask his friends?"

"Friends?"

"The girls in the silver frames," Andrew said, smiling.

The crime lab had checked Magic's balcony, and found a black thread on the railing. It had turned out to be from the dress worn by Wendy Lu.

Clement called a meeting of the crime unit of the Criminal Investigation Division, gathering them in the briefing room, a grim, yellow-walled windowless place with hard wooden chairs, with a blackboard to the front, giving it the air of a schoolroom, though hardly the Kensington Academy. Present were three chief inspectors, one English, two Chinese; six inspectors, half of them Caucasian; six station sergeants, and twelve sergeants, all Chinese. The last included a few recently promoted recruits, who sat very straight-backed, heads straining toward the ceiling, as though practicing the posture of Zen, or trying to give the lie to the recently lowered height requirements for the force.

Andrew was the only one among those present whose posture was less than crisp. He lounged, blowing bubble gum, chair tilted backward onto its rear legs, propped against the wall to the side of the room.

"Harry Magic is definitely involved," Clement said. "The girl fell from his apartment. She told me I was looking for her old boyfriend. We can safely presume that's who he was."

"The crown prosecutor says we can safely presume nothing," said a young sergeant, new to the force.

"I'm not talking about proving a case in court. Strictly for our own purposes. We'll continue to follow the rest of our leads, such as they are. Let's talk to our informants, and promise them some kind of reward over and above the money."

"They aren't interested in anything else," said Sam Lee, a chief inspector. "It's only you Brits what want the glory."

"I'm not talking glory," said Clement, though he supposed he really was. Looking for honor in the midst of dishonor. Ethics in the waters of a sewer. "If Triads are involved in this—and it could be as high up as Anthony Go—we've got to come up with heavy ammunition to make informers come forward."

"More money," said Andrew, and blew a bubble.

Climbing the stairs that mazed through side streets, greened walks, shop-cluttered alleys; with vendors leaning out of doorways; sweets and gnarled roots and herbs in wooden boxes lined up on stands outside storefronts; Clement felt so much affection for where he lived, he wondered how its underside could be so black. Wondered why there wasn't more you could offer people than money to move them to truth. Why weren't men greedier for the nobler aspects of life? Even fame, which you couldn't exactly offer an informer unless he wanted to get his throat slit, was tied to the material. No one was famous without enjoying material benefits, including the winners of the Nobel. None of them turned their backs on that part of it, really, except perhaps Mother Teresa. Even she undoubtedly was glad to get the money, to take care of her abandoned babies and the starving and the dying.

But why were people spurred into action more easily by their dark side? Anything you really wanted you could get by appealing to human venality. Any one of the seven deadly sins would do the trick: Lust, Envy, Gluttony, Sloth, Greed, Anger, Pride. Why couldn't you lure them with what Saint Paul had called the fruits of the Spirit: Love, Joy, Peace, Goodness, Kindness, Perseverance, Patience, Self-Control? Even running the litany in his head made Clement self-conscious, a kind of syrup oozing around the words themselves, as if knowing what they were made a man less a man. Peace. Peace in Hong Kong, with every breath punctuated by a jackhammer. The most stressful city in the world—and yet one which no one would move away from voluntarily, he didn't think, if there was any way they could stay. Self-control in the capital of excess. Joy in a place that understood only pleasure, where radiance most often meant sequins. Goodness, Kindness, when success was anchored in malice and double-dealing, where money and ideas and designs and information were all stolen with equal ease. Only Perseverance flourished there, and then with gritted teeth, so it was more tenacity and drive than steadfastness, the compulsion that characterized local businessmen, from highest *taipan* to lowliest vendor. Dreaming, as hawkers dreamed these days, of the plastic flower that could make him a billionaire, as it had one of Hong Kong's leading citizens. And now was added a new pressure: *before* 1997. So Patience, the most boring of the fruits, didn't have a chance.

And what of love? Love here was only about desire, wasn't it? Love at its lowest level, exploitative, giving nothing. Wasn't it all tied into his theory about what was behind the murders? Wasn't pornography the underbelly of the arts, as lust was the underbelly of love?

He came to the street in Mid-Levels where the dead boy's parents lived, went through their gate, rang the bell. A Filipino *amah* answered his ring. He could see a woman hovering inside the foyer, like some Gothic heroine long past her prime, all that remained of femininity her frailty.

Middle age and the loss of her son had cut crags in the cheeks of Mrs. Palmer-Smith. Her eyes were sunken, heavy-browed, so she peered from inside herself, like an animal cowering in a cave. "Good afternoon, Superintendent," she said, coming forward, breeding overriding the fear.

"Mrs. Palmer-Smith." He took her hand.

"You have news?" She ushered him inside. Indonesian craft poked from niches, statues half-sequestered in walls. Giant tapestries hung, filled with exotic dancers woven by some artist in Jakarta, where her banker husband had been assigned at an earlier, happier time in his career.

"Nothing concrete," he said, except, he noted silently, for where Wendy Lu had landed. Even the fact that he could make puns in his head bothered him. Maybe he wasn't as good a man as he thought. "That's why I wanted to see you and your husband."

"Alfred will be down in a minute. He's had a hard day at the bank. All this speculation about what's going to happen here has the most dreadful effect on the currency."

"So I would imagine," Clement said.

"Tea?" She lifted a pot from a silver tray on the coffee table in front of her, perching on the edge of her chair, birdlike, the dark colors of her sweater, grays woven through blacks and browns, underscoring the shadows beneath her eyes. She tried to smile. The dim lines between her teeth were more pronounced than the teeth themselves, as though even what was left of her would-be geniality had sunk into gloom.

"Thank you."

"Sugar?"

"Two lumps. And milk, please."

"Whereabouts in England are you from?"

"Blackpool."

"Oh, how nice. Did you play on all the rides when you were little?"

"My father wasn't much for spending money on amusements."

"Pity." She handed him his tea. "Alfred didn't really like to indulge David either. But now he cries about the zoo, you know. The times David wanted to go to the zoo when he was just too busy, or not in the mood."

"That will be enough, Charlotte." Alfred Palmer-Smith stood in the doorway. He was a heavyset man in his fifties, quite tall. He seemed to try to cut the edge of his exhortation with a smile, but it was not as convincing as the anger had been. "I'm sure the Superintendent didn't come here to listen to sentimental stories."

Her hands shook as she poured her husband's tea. Her veins were grayly blue, rising out of her pale hands like mountains on a relief map. There was an unhealthy tint to her skin, closer to her son's after death than the high color of his cheeks in the picture in the frame behind her.

"Have you found them yet?"

"We have some leads. Do you know any teenage clubs David might have frequented?"

"He was a serious student," said Palmer-Smith. "He stayed very close to home."

"But he did love to dance, dear." She held out the cup of tea to her husband, and he took it. "Remember how he'd get all dressed up to go dancing, so natty and Fred Astaire."

Clement looked up.

"He was a great film buff."

"Really?"

"Loved old musicals. A huge fan of Fred Astaire's."

"We have that in common," Clement said, excited for a reason he did not quite understand.

"Had," said Alfred Palmer-Smith.

"He was wearing those shoes, I think . . . at first I couldn't remember. His Fred Astaire spats, he called them. Black and white, wing-tipped, with those smart little perforations. A job to keep clean. David had taps put on them, metal crescents on the tip and heel. Hardship on the floors, they were. Though one doesn't see scuffs on the floor anymore as hardship, any more than an outing to the zoo seems an imposition."

"That will do, Charlotte."

"I'm sorry." She started pouring tea for herself, spilling it on the table. Both men pretended not to notice.

"I've come because, regrettably, I might have to impose on you further. We must rely on our informers. The stakes might be higher than we thought."

"We've offered ten thousand pounds," said Palmer-Smith. "The girl's parents matched it."

"I want to clean this up as quickly as possible," said Clement.

"We must," said Charlotte, wiping up the spill with a crocheted-edge cream color napkin. "Otherwise, it leaves an awful stain."

"Whatever you want," said Palmer-Smith.

"Thank you." Clement got up to go.

"But you haven't finished your tea," said Charlotte.

"I have someplace else I have to be," said Clement.

"How fortunate," said Charlotte, her eyes empty.

"But what possible business of yours could it be if I knew Harry Magic?" Maggie asked.

She was dressed in a white blouse, layered, frilled, as though she were still innocent, from the waist up, anyway. It was very choir-girlish. Clement felt uncomfortable seeing her in it, after the pictures on the sideboard.

"He may have been involved in your daughter's murder."

Her hand shook, as she poured tea. It was almost the same hand as David's mother, Clement observed. No matter what a woman did with her makeup or her clothes, or even plastic surgery, there was no way she could cover the age of her hands. "Sugar?" Maggie asked.

"Two. And milk."

They were in her studio apartment. The appointment having been set for the tea hour, there was no way Clement could be any ruder than he was already going to have to be, and not accept the cup she offered him.

"What makes you think he was involved?"

"The Chinese girl who fell from the Albany the other night was in his apartment. Were you?"

"I beg your pardon?"

"Were you ever in his apartment?"

"Certainly not," said Maggie.

"Then where were the pictures taken?"

"Pictures?"

"I've seen the pictures."

"Oh, dear," said Maggie. "I suppose they're worth a thousand words."

"You had an affair with him."

"I'd hardly call it that. A quickie, perhaps. A very *long* quickie."

"Do you know who distributed his movies?"

"No."

"Did he mention Anthony Go?"

"He mentioned very little. We didn't talk a great deal."

"When was the last time you saw him?"

"The first and only time I saw him."

"When was that?"

"Oh, I can't really remember. Sometime last spring, I think."

"Did he know your daughter?"

"Absolutely not!" Maggie was on her feet, her teacup set noisily on the glass table. "She was a very good girl. You mustn't judge her by her mother. I was a bad mother, a terrible person, but it didn't affect my child. She had no idea."

"Did she go out dancing with David Palmer-Smith?"

"I'm not really sure. A lot of the time she didn't tell me where she was going. But I didn't tell her where I was going, either. Maybe I should have. Not the time with Harry, of course, I shouldn't have told her where I was then, but most of the time. And then she might not have wandered off on her own, going to the Peak with David. What do you think?"

"I don't know."

"I should have taken her to tea that day, and then she'd still be here."

"Nothing's going to change what happened," Clement said kindly. "It wasn't your fault."

"But you don't think she was a bad girl?"

"Certainly not." He set down his cup. "Do you have any idea where Harry Magic might have gone?"

"None. We didn't exactly socialize. *Senti*, listen, you think the money will make him come forward?"

"I'm sorry I had to ask you for more."

"What do I care? Money's the least of it. Though that attitude doesn't fit exactly in Hong Kong, does it? How many times a day do you hear, 'Money is God. Money is God!'" Maggie waved her hands. "But then, God isn't God anymore, so thank God *something* is."

Well, they could tell Maggie all they wanted not to think that way, that it wasn't her fault, that Betsy would have been dead even if her mother hadn't been a whore. But Maggie knew better. After the Superintendent left, she took off all her clothes and stood in front of one of the many mirrors in her bedroom, and hated her body, for what it had done to her child.

What kind of trickster was this God she had once believed in, to put people in flesh, and then ask them to rise above it? What kind of mercy could there be in that, endowing creatures with so much weakness, charging them to be strong?

"Where is your pity, God?" She fell to the carpet, holding on to its softness as though there were compassion there.

A little stabbing sensation shot through her belly. She sat up, astonished. She felt beginnings. Movement. A stir. Was this it, then, leniency? Benevolence, after all?

"Betsy?" she whispered, holding herself. "Betsy?" Tears sprang to her eyes. So there was a God, after all. Betsy wasn't really gone. Betsy was coming back. Betsy was growing inside her.

NINETEEN

♦

Living on the edge made a man feel more alive. Knowing that at any moment the ground could collapse beneath him, the cliff branch he clung to pull away from the rock, the hand that grasped his as he swung out over the abyss let go, gave a man a great sense of immediacy. To be in Hong Kong at the start of the nineties was electrifying, in the true sense of the word: it galvanized a man, sprung him into action. Since there might be no tomorrow, today was full of meaning. There was no place James would rather have been, he told himself.

No one in the colony was aware that he actually had been disowned, that he would never bear the title he should have inherited. But whispers of the disgrace, funds missing from his father's bank, hastily replaced by Lord Bingham, had followed James across the many seas between England and China. In some cases, the rumors had preceded him, like letters of introduction, that accounted for such a bright, personable young man being in such difficulty in a city of scoundrels. It was one thing to behave like a rogue on an exotic island, where such actions were deemed usual. Quite another to have done it in England.

He was not proud of his shallowness. Living someplace else people accepted the lies they would have seen through at home. But he did grieve over the part of himself that was lost when his granny died, the only one in the world who'd loved him unconditionally, given him feelings of self-esteem layered like cream between the spoiling. As a child he imagined if a sweet-smelling woman could love him like that, he had to be one of the splendors of the world. When she died and left him all her money, his parents had turned away from him, his father taking it as a personal affront that a son of his was more endearing than he himself was to his own mother. James was offered no guidance on what to do with his inheritance; his father hoped he would squander it. That was exactly what he'd done, spending recklessly on women and amusement, both of which he took to, as they took to him. Massive as the amount had seemed in his eighteenth year, it was gone by the time he was thirty. He'd had no choice but to go to work for his father, and embezzle a little, his standard of living being higher than the wages paid him. He'd had every intention of paying it back, as he'd told his father. His father had said he could do that from Hong Kong.

Exiled, a man found out what his country was. James's heart really ached for England. Since his greatest gift was self-delusion, he'd convinced himself Hong Kong was his ideal setting, offering as it did a sea full of stylish sharks. He was an accomplished sailor, so fancied himself cutting an even more stylish swath through the infested waters. Only once in a while did he notice he didn't have a boat.

"You wouldn't really want me to come to California," he said to Claire, as they lay on the satin sheets she'd bought in Stanley Market. Judith was off on an assignment, so they spent a good deal of time in bed, on royal blue satin. Claire told him the sheets were the color of his eyes, the title of the song she'd written. The romanticism would have been an embarrassment for him but he thought the song quite good. Like Granny's outings to Harrod's, it gave him a positive sense of himself, especially when he looked in the mirror and saw how blue his eyes really were. And the sheets felt lovely on his skin. Unlike many of his confreres, he was a sensuous man, as aroused by foreplay and texture as women were, but only when he was controlling. So it was fine to have the smoothness of silk against his back, with the silkiness inside her against his penis.

"I'd ruin everything. I'd get restless and bored and start chasing after starlets."

"I wouldn't leave you the strength."

"It has nothing to do with strength. It has to do with weakness. I have one great character flaw: I haven't any."

"At least you're honest."

"Only with you." He could see even as he told her, that she did not believe him.

How amazing women were, so quick to fall in love that you could not help loving them a little, even while their eagerness made them less intriguing. There was something so girlish about Claire, so stubbornly innocent, that he almost never had the feeling she was older. Only the desperation that showed now and then, making her cling to him, weathered her. Only her neediness overrode how appealing she was. Only her obvious hunger to be the other half of a couple canceled out her conspicuous independence. Only the things that made women stupid undercut her wit, her talent, her ability to survive.

Still, because he was touched, without meaning to be, he tried to be straightforward with her. "I'm basically a dishonest man. The last thing I want is to care deeply about anyone."

"I don't believe you."

"You'd do well to." He stroked her hair, undercutting her reason even as he urged her to use it.

"You can't be that callous."

"It isn't callous. It's reality. Why do women always take as brutal what they don't want to hear?"

"Well, if you're honest only with me, you'd be a great success in Beverly Hills. Not many people tell the truth. You'd fit right in."

"That's your home ground, not mine."

"This isn't your home ground, and you're doing well here." Not only did Claire not want to hear the truth, she didn't particularly want to speak it. At least, not with respect to James. She saw him as he could be, as most women see the man with whom they are infatuated, and was sure if she convinced him he was strong, he would be. It was the same technique she had used with Charley. "Won't you think about coming?"

"That's all I'd do, is think about it."

"Is it because I'm older?"

"No. I don't even know how old you are."

"Good." They laughed. "Then why?"

"Because I'd spoil it for you. I always do. I'm a spoiler."

"You haven't spoiled anything for me."

"It's been only a few weeks. Give me time."

"It would be my pleasure."

He lifted her face to his. "You lovely lady," he said, and kissed her.

"What?" she said, against his mouth. "What what what what what?"

"You won't get me to say it. It would be unkind of me to say it."

"Why?"

"Because I'd hook you in."

"Don't you think I'm hooked?"

"Only by your feelings. Not mine." He saw how she was looking at him. "Don't even think it."

"What?"

"That you could change me."

"Why would I want to change you?"

"You'd think you were doing it for my happiness. Women always think they're doing things out of unselfishness."

"Why do men always say 'women always,' or, 'women never'? Why don't they say 'women sometimes,' and then only 'some women'?"

"Because you're all the same."

"Not true."

"Oh, yes it is." He turned her over. "I'll show you."

"He's come up with a terrific script," Henry told Louise, excitedly. They were in Henry's suite overlooking the harbor, fresh fruit set out on a table by the balcony, next to a bottle of champagne, unopened, that Go had sent with the script the night before. Not having lived long in Hollywood, Henry had read it immediately.

"How would you know it's terrific?"

"It's *Of Human Bondage*, reset in Hong Kong. A doctor, caught in an obsessive love. It'll give me a chance to show my full range."

"What range is that? From Submissive to Dominatrix?" Louise had not slept at all well the night before, between being pursued by a criminal and the Greek who said he was a Count, and wouldn't leave her alone. She had less patience than usual, especially about anything to do with Anthony Go.

"It isn't that kind of bondage. It's emotional bondage. Human bondage. From the Somerset Maugham novel. Don't you know it?"

"Do you?"

"Certainly. What do you think I did in between takes on those movies?"

"I assumed the same thing you were doing during."

"Nobody in porn has sex off camera. I *read*. I read *books*." She looked smaller for her indignation, her chest appearing even more boyish with the puff of pride that failed to inflate it. Her eyes, beautiful, flat and wide and black, flashed with righteous anger, as though there were enough things in her history to feel bad about, without adding ignorance.

Louise felt moved, in a comical way, at this suddenly revealed life of the mind. She remembered Marie Dressler on her way to dine in *Dinner at Eight*, tripping at Jean Harlow's saying she had read a book. It was not a movie Louise had been old enough to see in its first release—thank God there were still some of those—but she had seen it on cassette, and it was one of the wryest moments in cinema history. Now, here it was, being replayed in Henry's room. She could picture the little Cantonese porn star, off to fuck on film, carrying her book bag. "It's a very old-fashioned story," Louise cautioned.

"Not the way they've rewritten it. The roles are reversed. I would be playing the doctor. And instead of having a club foot, I'm a co-dependent. That makes if *very* today." She seemed to actually bustle, so busy were her movements as she opened the front of the bookcase. "Look, this is some of the literature." She handed Louise *Women Who Love Too Much*, *Women Men Love—Women Men Leave*, *Co-Dependency, Codependent No More*. "Go sent it over. It's probably pirated."

"And who would play Mildred? Johnny Wong?"

"As a male prostitute."

"Does he turn tricks with men or women?"

"Women. He works for an escort service. He's a drug-addicted alcoholic, and I'm obsessed with him. I could believe it. He is wonderful looking. My character could have come from a dysfunctional family. My real family would have been dysfunctional if they had had the time, if they hadn't been so busy scraping to stay alive."

"You're adorable."

"Yes, I know. But nobody knows how deep I go."

"Except your many co-stars."

"Please don't make easy sex jokes, Louise. The past is over. The past is always over, unless you're a true co-dependent and have to keep reliving it in every relationship."

"A drug-addicted alcoholic male hustler who does Tae Kwan Do." Louise shook her head. "I don't know if I could buy it."

"You don't have to buy it. All Asia will buy it, because he's Johnny Wong. The States will buy it because it's a hot topic, sexual obsession. And they've kept the physical stuff down. There's only one big scene where he kicks the shit out of somebody, and then it's for a valid emotional reason."

"Men are right. They never should have given us the vote."

"What does that mean?"

"It means you shouldn't have learned to read. It means I shouldn't have encouraged you to take acting lessons. I liked it better when you were an innocent slut, in the lobby of the Oriental in Bangkok, dating Harry Magic."

"I never *dated* him," said Henry. "We just co-starred."

There was a knock on the door. Louise went to open it. Clement Leslie stood in the doorway. "Well, Superintendent," Louise said.

"May I come in?"

"Of course. You know Miss Wu?"

"I haven't had the pleasure."

"You're one of the few in Hong Kong." She saw Henry's face. "I'm sorry. My mouth moves faster than my brain."

"Are you with the police?" Henry asked.

"I am." He sat down on the squarely stuffed sofa. "Actually, I wasn't expecting you to be here, Miss Felder."

"I can go."

"No, it's fortunate. I wanted to speak to you as well. Have you been talking with Anthony Go?"

"Only when I couldn't avoid it," said Louise.

"The word around is that you're representing him for films."

"I am not."

"She represents me," said Henry.

"And you're planning to do a film for Mr. Go?"

"She hasn't agreed to it yet," said Louise.

"It's nice how you cover for each other."

"Nobody's covering," said Louise. "It happens to be the truth."

"What exactly did you come to Hong Kong for, Miss Felder?"

"The waters."

"There are no waters."

"I was misinformed."

Clement smiled. "Humphrey Bogart. *Casablanca.*"

"You're a movie buff?"

"More than a buff, I'm afraid. A fanatic. The origin of *fan.*"

"Are you here as a movie fan?"

"I'm afraid I'm here in my official capacity. Didn't you come to Hong Kong specifically to do business with Anthony Go?"

"Certainly not!" said Louise. "I didn't even know who he was till I went on that yacht."

"Do you know a man named Harry Magic?"

"Who?"

"Harry Magic. An actor in porno films. Or a performer, I suppose I should say."

"Never heard of him," said Louise.

"And you?" He looked at Henry.

"I know him," she said.

"Do you know where he is?"

"I haven't seen him for years."

"Professionally?"

"In any capacity," Louise interjected.

"But I thought you never heard of him."

"I've been like a housemother to Henry since I found her. I know every man who's come into her life, for fun, or business. There's been no Harry Magic. Is that all, Superintendent?"

"Not nearly."

"I'm sorry, I don't know how it works in Hong Kong, but in the United States we have certain rights. And I don't think we care to speak with you anymore."

"I have nothing to hide," said Henry.

"We've seen that, dear."

"I asked you not to make those jokes."

"Sorry." Louise opened the door. "Superintendent?"

Clement got up from the couch. "Thank you for your hospitality."

"It's my pleasure," said Louise.

"Just a word of caution. Stay away from Anthony Go."

"I wish I could," said Louise.

Mornings, Kip buried herself in the various journals of the high-tech trade, charged herself with the hum of the PC, a kind of carnal buzz. The computer was all she had besides Peter that absorbed her completely. Getting her mind off him, it had become a substitute sexual partner, but one that, unlike her lover, gave her back something every time. Lost in the most recent issue of *Lightwave: The Journal of Fiber Optics*, she gave it the attention a voyeur would the centerfold of *Penthouse*. But when her mind shifted from its self-inflicted daze, she had the same feeling a masturbator would: loneliness.

She met her cousin, Henry Wu, for lunch in the cafeteria of the American Club, a fast food "joint," as Henry called it, a floor above the formal dining room. Henry had offered her the panoramic, many-coursed option downstairs, but Kip had only forty-five minutes for lunch. Besides, the club was sacrosanct to her, the only place she'd had the nerve to go where she didn't belong. To penetrate legitimately, with an invitation, rather unnerved her. She felt she would be less conspicuous at the lower-priced arm of the establishment.

"Still throwing yourself away on that snob?" Henry asked. They were sitting by a floor-to-ceiling window, overlooking boats stacking up in the harbor, the American fleet having anchored that morning. Henry had had a hard time getting through the pedestrian traffic, which was, for one of the few times in her experience, mainly a crush of Caucasians, young sailors on their pimpled way to Wanchai.

"I wish I could argue with you and say he wasn't a snob," said Kip.

"Why do you stay with him?"

"You sound like my brother."

"Chen isn't dumb. Just because he wears his hair freaky doesn't mean he has nothing inside his head. You, on the other hand, have beauty *and* brains. Why don't you use them?"

"I love him."

"You don't love him. You're caught." She handed Kip a book. "You're a woman who loves too much, a co-dependent."

"A what?"

"There's a lot of it going around. Read that. I have more for you when you're done."

"I don't even have time to catch up with my technical reading."

"This is more important. You've got to free yourself."

"I can't."

"Read the book."

Kip worried the noodles in her chicken salad with her fork, while all around them Europeans used chopsticks. "And suppose I was to get free. What would I do then?"

"Enjoy your freedom. Live life differently."

A blond woman with heavily kohled eyes sat down at the table next to them. She was joined by a spindly-looking Brit carrying a tray. Obediently, head down, he began setting food in front of her.

"Oh, God, you really expect me to eat that?" she asked him.

"Maggie, it's what you said you wanted."

"I can't imagine ever making love with anyone else," Kip said to Henry.

"He's twisted you into his way of thinking. Made you feel guilty, because basically the British believe sex is wrong."

"Do you think it's wrong?"

"Darling." Maggie leaned over. "We *all* think sex is wrong."

"Stay out of other people's conversations," the gray-faced man said.

"You stay out of mine, Nicholas." Maggie smiled at the two tiny Cantonese women. "This is us, the girls. We're all in it together. They can talk all they like about this being practically the twenty-first century, but we're still ruled by Queen Victoria."

"Maggie, be quiet. I'm sorry if she intruded."

"Don't you dare apologize for me. Stop being such a stick. You're just proof of my pudding. This is my once-beloved ex-husband Nicholas. I'm Maggie Evans." She held out her hand to Kip. "Haven't I seen you at Saint John's?"

"You've become Church of England?" Henry said, darkly. "You go there for him?"

"I like the cathedral," Kip said. "I go there for me."

"You want to belong with him. But you never will."

"How is Saint John's?" Maggie asked. "I don't go inside. Do you hear from God?"

"Let them eat their lunch."

"It's all right," said Henry. "We've finished."

"I haven't," said Kip. "I'd like some dessert."

"I'll get it for you." Henry was on her feet. "What do you want?"

"Ice cream."

"And a little stroking," said Maggie. "We all need a little stroking. It's just we're afraid to ask."

"Maggie be quiet."

"Maggie be quiet. Maggie be quiet. Is that like Jack be nimble? Be sure if you get this young man, dear, that you really want him. The worst thing about the English is once you manage to capture what is laughingly called their hearts, they stick to you like glue. It makes it very hard to pee."

"Must you be so disgusting? She's only a child."

"Do you find me disgusting? Are you only a child? How old *are* you?"

"Twenty-two."

"Was I ever twenty-two, Nicholas? Your memory's better than mine. Was I?"

"What's happening to you, Maggie?"

"Why, I thought you knew. I had a terrible loss. But it's all going to be fine. She's coming back, you see. Betsy's coming back. Go get me something else to eat, the last thing I want is a salad. Bring me something with loads of *calcium*. Teeth and bones are growing here." She patted her stomach. "Cheese. Pizza. That should do it. Have you ever been pregnant?"

"No," Kip said.

"For God's sake, leave her alone." Nicholas got up from the table.

"For God's sake I would. But for her sake, I won't. Do you want to marry this man?"

"Yes."

"You need a little luck. You ought to get a piece of jade." Maggie handed her a card. "Stop by and see me. I'll give you a good price."

"I don't wear jewelry."

"This isn't jewelry. It's jade. Full of mystery. Bringing good fortune. If it's authentic good fortune, you'll stop wanting to marry him. But if you insist, it will help you."

"You wouldn't do it if you had to do it over again?"

"Only to have my daughter. Do you believe in reincarnation?"

"No."

"I thought all Orientals believed in reincarnation."

"It depends on their religion."

"What are you?"

"I was Taoist. But now I'm Episcopal."

"Why?"

"I like the philosophy."

"What philosophy is that? Don't be too passionate?"

"Here's your ice cream," said Henry, coming back to the table. "Thank you."

"My husband is typical. Afraid of passion. Afraid of women. Most men are. You know what Falstaff said: 'They hate us youth.' Well, I say, they hate us bright. They hate us giving. They hate us loving."

"You really think that?"

"I *know* it."

"Are you still nattering away?" Nicholas set a pizza in front of Maggie. "You must forgive her."

"Why *must* she? What is there to forgive, except that I'm a woman? Something you find unforgivable." Maggie leapt to her feet, knocking the plate with the salad on the floor. "Forgive *me!*"

"Sit down."

"Why? So I don't make a spectacle of myself? Well, I've already been a spectacle! Photographed, set out on a sideboard like Auntie." She sat down. "The tiny little kinks of one of the kinkiest. Sentiment, who would have thought the old fart had such mush in him? In black and white. Worth a thousand words. So there's not much you can tell a policeman."

"What are you talking about?"

"Oh, good, lumpy cheese." She took a bite, kept talking. "They say they need us." A string of mozzarella pulled between her teeth and the wedge of pie. "Want us. Promise to care for us. But that's not what it's really about. It's about *them*." She chewed. "They don't really *want* women. They're just afraid to be without us."

"You're frightening her."

"Am I?"

"No," said Kip.

"All we have to do to get rid of them is to give them everything they need. All the love they hunger for. All the embraces they feel they were deprived of. Because when you love them, they know they've got you. That's when they get their revenge."

"Revenge on who?" Kip asked.

"Mother. Mother God. Aphrodite. Their teachers in school. All the women they think let them down. All the ones they fucked or wanted to fuck or were afraid to fuck."

"You poor woman," Nicholas said.

"I am not alone." Maggie took another bite.

"I have to go back to work," said Kip, getting up. "It was very..." She hesitated.

"What? Nice? Don't say it was nice to meet me, because I'm sure it wasn't."

"Unsettling might be better," said Nicholas.

"That's what we all need, is to be unsettled. I'm glad it wasn't nice. 'Nice' in Shakespeare's time meant foolish. I'm not so sure it's changed all that much. Or that we have. I wanted to be an actress once. Aren't you an actress?" she said to Henry. "I'm sure I've seen you in something."

"Yes."

"Was it Shakespeare?"

"No."

"I didn't think so." She smiled. "I think you were in a film or three with an acquaintance of mine. Harry Magic. Am I right?"

"Yes."

"I never forget a face. Or certain other things either, though of course it doesn't show even though your skirt is *very* short."

"You'll be late," Henry said, pushing Kip with her elbow.

"You will come to my boutique, yes? Both of you. Don't forget, *carina mia*. Jade will do the trick, if you insist on the trick being done."

"Thank you," said Kip. "Goodbye." She smiled at Maggie in a friendly way, but not too friendly, puzzled by the woman.

"Ciao, goodbye," said Maggie. She looked at her plate. "This is excellent pizza, Nicholas. You're really good to me when people are watching."

"Poor Maggie," he said, tears in his eyes.

"Oh, don't be so judgmental, my once darling. It'll pass. You know it will. I always get unstrung when I'm preggers."

TWENTY

◆

According to Passport Central, Harry Magic had left the country twelve times in the previous year, traveling under his real name of Roy Gaiquin. He had returned, for what appeared to Clement as the last time, three months before. No record was found of a subsequent departure.

There was a kind of terrible relief in its coming together in a dark way, the Black's Link murder. Somehow, Clement's quixotic wish that the murderers not be Cantonese did not extend to scum. The girl who had tumbled from the Albany balcony, Wendy Lu, seemed to be the last innocent involved.

"Wendy worked as Harry's maid," said the young man who had been with her that night at 1997. He was being questioned at Central Station by Clement, with a juvenile officer present. Clement could never tell exactly how old these people were. Their skin was so unlined, even as they passed into middle and sometimes old age, that he considered it a wise precaution to have the proper division member present, in case the boy turned out to be a minor.

"And they were lovers?" Clement asked.

"Who knows." The boy shrugged.

"She mentioned an old boyfriend. Was that Harry?"

"Could have been. Wendy was good about keeping secrets. Most of the time."

There was something about the way he said that that troubled Clement. "Did you mind that he had been her boyfriend?"

"I didn't know the guy. The Albany isn't exactly in my league."

"Was he there the night she fell?"

"I dunno."

"You didn't go with her?"

"No."

"Did she tell you she was meeting somebody?"

"No. Not even you."

"And you let her go up there alone, at that hour, in the dark?"

"Is that what police do now? Arrest you for not being polite?"

"I just find it curious that you'd let your girlfriend go off like that, and not worry she might be in some kind of danger."

"Hey, we're all in danger. The Chinese are coming. Didn't you hear?"

The realtor who had sold Harry's home on Lantau Island, Natalie Winsome, was an Australian woman in her early thirties, Clement guessed from her hair and body and arms, though he couldn't tell her age either, from her face. There were already deep crow's feet at the corners of her eyes, and heavy expression lines between nose and mouth, as if she had deliberately been working against the Australian image of easygoing. Natalie frowned even when she said things that didn't seem particularly troubling. "I got an excellent price for his Lantau house."

"Why did he want to sell?"

"Why do people want to sell? It's time to move on. He also got rid of his art collection at auction. But he kept one of his Warhols, and left it in the study, as part of the deal."

"Was he hurting for money?"

"Not to my knowledge. He bought an apartment in San Francisco. Very pricey, but he paid all cash."

"What about his place at the Albany?"

"He said he might put it on the market when he resettled."

"He was moving permanently to San Francisco?"

"I think he would have liked to think in terms of permanence. He looked ill."

The doorman at the Albany confirmed that Magic had been hospitalized a few months before, supposedly with the flu. The doctor's office address was in a leather-bound diary at the side of Harry's bed.

It was in a remote part of Kowloon on Hammer Hill Road, out behind the Golden Harvest movie studio, in a small building that doubled as an infirmary. "What was his illness really?" Clement asked.

The doctor was a small man, intense. He had specified proudly at meeting Clement that he was Shanghainese. There went with the self-introduction the snobbery those from that province had, carrying with it the understanding, especially among their own kind, that they were better educated, with higher intuitive abilities in science, as well as the arts and finance. "You saw the records. It was flu."

"And you kept him here?"

"That was his wish. He didn't like big hospitals."

"How long have you been in Hong Kong?"

"Four years."

"I understand in China homosexuals are treated with electric shocks to discourage erotic thoughts."

"It is regarded as mental illness. Their families are very upset. Some of them are ready to commit suicide. When they are cured, they cry tears of gratitude."

"You hold to that line, even though you fled?"

"I fled the politics. Not the medicine."

"How do you regard homosexuality?"

"I've never known a homosexual. It's a Western problem."

"Like AIDS?"

"You could say that."

"Where is Harry Magic now?"

"I have no idea. I haven't seen him since he left here."

"No follow-up appointments, when the man was deathly ill?"

"He wasn't deathly ill. He had the flu."

*   *   *

After he left the doctor's office, Clement called Anthony Go. "When was the last time Harry Magic did a film for you?"

"I know no Harry Magic. I have not been in the film business until now."

"You distributed his pornos. He had a drawer full of chips from the Paradise Casino in Macau. *Your* casino."

"My operations are all quite legitimate."

"And have been, ever since you were a teenager, and joined the Triads. And mixed your blood with chicken blood. And your blood with the blood of other Triads. Do you still do that, or is everyone a little more careful about mixing blood these days?"

"I have a busy day," said Go.

"Meet me for lunch."

"I have a number of appointments."

"Consider it necessary for your survival," said Clement.

The Mandarin Grill was already crowded, a few minutes after noon. It was a quiet kind of crowding, impeccable, as the restaurant itself was, tan ceiling fretted with bamboo, square copper lamps glistening, copper over the barbecue. Conversation hummed at an unintrusive level, bubbling like the fish tank set into the wall. A quietly erotic ballet was taking place in the water, between a tiger fish, striped yellow and black, and a parrot fish, green with a red triangle curving back from its eye, and a red dorsal fin. A languid clown fish played with a white circled baby octopus, all of them moving in such slow motion it became as sensual as the food, and what was happening between Claire's thighs.

James's hand was on the silky skin of her inner leg, underneath the table. That he should touch her in public, and at lunchtime, concealed though the gesture was, fueled her own heat. She was hardly able to breathe. All the time he smiled in his most boyish way, deceiving the rest of the room with his innocence. Giving the finger to the world, as it were, while he fingered her.

It was wantonness on a level she had never permitted herself—not just what he was doing, but what he inspired in her, what he made her want to do. She had only suspected what carnality was in her. Charley had been so clean, in every sense of the word, showering several times daily, saving their lovemaking for bed. He had relished her passion, even while making jokes about it. But she'd always felt a little guilty at how lascivious she really was, at what she was moved to do to him, and wanted him to do to her. Most of it they'd done, but always with a little disclaimer in the corner of her brain because they were longtime partners, and sex in marriage was not only sacred, but a little boring.

Now here was James, unabashedly a rake, by his own proclamation. Touching her in ways and places that would have mortified Charley, mortified Claire in her ladylike portion, but made crazy and joyful the girl in her, the chubby adolescent who had never had a boyfriend, much less a lover. Here in the middle of the Mandarin Grill were all the hillsides she had never rolled on, the lakes she had never been fondled beside. So along with arousing her, he was opening old wounds and healing them, shoring her up from the inside.

His hand was exploring the lace of her panties now, moving over pubic hair, artfully separating lower lips while the hand above the table stroked her facial ones. He turned the fingers on her mouth over, and gentled the ridges on her lips with the tops of his nails. "You're feeling very lovely today," he said, sliding onto her point with his middle finger.

His fingers were square at their tops, nails carefully manicured and buffed, a squarish shape to them as well, a wide disc of light pink, white at the tip, conspicuously pale against the sun-browned hand. It was a big hand, but strangely smaller than the wrist and arm it was attached to, his forearm bulging, like in some cartoon of Popeye. She had felt a strange knell of recognition the first time she'd seen his forearm, remembering her son when he was still an infant, and Charley had pulled up the sleeve of his Doctor Dentons, exposing an outrageously outsized forearm, saying all that was missing was a tattoo of an anchor. She'd wondered if the tenderness she felt for James could be because he reminded her of her son. But there was nothing maternal about what she was feeling now.

She could not speak. She felt as open-mouthed and mute, unblinking as the Ahi tuna laid out on the island table below, flown that morning from Japan, next to the red snapper pulled an hour before from the sea. All of it was artfully arranged on cabbage leaves and flowers, opening as she was. Tilted straw baskets eased golden peppers and artichokes onto the display, in between giant abalone shells iridescent with mother-of-pearl. "Why do they call it mother-of-pearl?" her daughter had asked her on a long-ago beach. "Why don't they call it mother-of-colors?"

Her children. She hadn't even thought much about her children. She had talked to them almost daily, but from a distance that was more than the distance between them, all her affection in fervent reserve for James. She could still manage to observe the setting she was in, but the one she had left eluded her. It was as if the pain would not exist if she didn't focus on the place where it had happened. So even as James stroked her and she bit her tongue not to cry out in pleasure, she noted how radiant it all looked, the chefs in spotless white toques grilling steaks on the brazier, the raw table edged with brass, picking up the metal tints of railings, and the dessert table a few feet away. The last was laid with crystal bowls filled with berries, six different kinds of chocolate cakes on silver-stemmed trays, fruits the shades of the tropics, pale green kiwi, sunset orange mangoes, three kinds of pudding, creme caramel, white cake, tarte Tatin. How base a sensualist was she, that she could see all this, feel all this, and not be ashamed or utter a word of caution?

He was rubbing her quickly now, speeding up his tempo, his laugh low-throated, mischievous, as her lips parted. She wanted very much to kiss him. Wanted to replay a gossip story of her youth, where Paulette Goddard had disappeared under the table at El Morocco and gone down on Erich Maria Remarque. Was that the stature lust gave a man, that Claire would have been willing to ruin herself for this boy who probably hadn't even read *Arch of Triumph*, much less written it?

She didn't care. She didn't care anymore what he was, or who he was, or if he was what he said he was. All she knew was what she felt. Even knowing it was only a feeling, and feelings were passing, could not keep her mind from coursing ahead to the next time this would happen between them. Making sure it did. She wanted to hold him past holding him. Keep him with her. Make him a part of her. So what was happening between her legs would happen between the covers of her life, that he would become a permanent part of her story, the melody of her song. Even as she saw how ludicrous sentimentality was, in view of where she was, and what he was doing, even as she perceived the bawdiness, the raunchiness, she wanted to lift the moment, and make it softhearted.

He stopped his motion for barely a second, greeting a big man in a safari suit coming up the steps to the second tier. "Superintendent!" He held out the hand that was not busy beneath the table. "Clement Leslie, this is Claire Black. Clement is a Superintendent of police."

She managed to nod.

"Won't you join us for a drink?" James said, resuming the stepped-up rhythm.

"Well, thank you. My appointment isn't here yet. I think I will."

He sat down, looked at Claire. Her eyes were very bright. "Claire Black. You're the American friend of Judith Taylor, aren't you?"

Claire nodded again.

"Is she still away?"

"She's in Beijing till Tuesday," James said for Claire, his eyes crinkling with mischief. He held up his free hand for the waiter.

"Barley water, please," Clement said.

"Barley water. I'm impressed. Don't you want a real drink?"

"Have to keep my wits about me."

"As do we all. That doesn't mean we can't drink. I assure you my wits have never been sharper than they are at this moment. Wouldn't you agree, my sweet?"

Claire smiled.

"You're looking very prosperous, James," Clement said.

"I am prosperous. Involved in a most exciting venture. Wouldn't you say it was exciting, Claire? A new group has taken twelve years of schooling and made it into a mass education resource. They're readying learning computers for the schools in China, so every student can go at his own pace. If a student misses a question, the computer forces him to a review section. The sharper students can move ahead. The brighter ones are challenged, the slow ones get more time. Doesn't that sound thrill . . . ing?" He extended the word, winking at Claire.

"And where does your prosperity come in?"

"I'm a principal stockholder."

Claire moaned. "I suppose you've put money in it, too," said Clement.

"Not actually," said James. "But Claire *has* been extremely encouraging."

"I see," said Clement, and wondered how much money she had given him. She was pretty enough, dark-eyed, and very alive-looking, but obviously older than James by twelve or fifteen years, although in the case of American women you could tell their age with only a little less difficulty than you could time-slot the Chinese. Especially if the women came from California, as Judith had told him this one did.

He imagined if she was a close friend of Judith's she had to be bright. Still, bright women fell in love with the wrong men. Right now she was all crimsoned, her face a forehead-to-throat blush, as if something that had been said had deeply embarrassed her. Was it the business about the Chinese computers? Was she chary of its not paying off, and James's being back in the difficulty he had been in since coming to Hong Kong? Expats in the colony knew a great deal about each other's affairs, even when they weren't policemen. So Clement was well aware of the whispers about James, the covered disgrace at home, the messages from his father to all major banks not to extend him credit. Still, he liked the young man, found him ingratiating, and rooted for him, since every day unlikelier people grew rich.

"Well, I wish you luck," said Clement to James, raising the glass of barley water the waiter had brought him.

"I'm having it," said James. "I'm having everything I wanted."

"So am I," said Claire, speaking, finally. "Actually, more."

A few tables away, Erica Thorr was also engaged in a play of hands, except that both hers were woven in between Lockwood's fingers. Their eyes were similarly caught, even as the waiter announced the specialties of the day, lobster fresh from the waters of Maine making no apparent impression. Regulars of the restaurant and the hotel were aware of what was happening. Just as news of financial disaster traveled through the community with dazzling speed, news of good luck in love was rapidly relayed. People in Hong Kong were nearly as addicted to romance as to incredible profit, both having a fantasy element. That these two handsome, fit, aloof people had found each other, and were collapsing into each other's irises, in the midst of lunch, fired the same unrealistic expectations a sudden fortune did. If it could happen to two, why not to many? Loneliness was a drug on the market, more available than drugs. Did the universe really provide a cure, if one were in the right place at the right time? And was Hong Kong the right place, just at the moment in history when the only thing certain it offered was uncertainty?

But Louise, sitting at the next table, seeing how they looked at each other, only felt more confused. She had let the Greek order her wine, although she rarely drank, allowing him to palaver on in the language she didn't understand, about how wonderful she was, which she knew was a lie, in whatever language. His feelings were clear to her, as obscured as the specific words were, puppylike behavior unmistakable as it was unexpected.

She had awakened that morning depressed. Sleep had never come easily to her. Her dreams, when she was conscious of their content, were racked with disappointment and betrayal. But now, in addition to the insecurity that troubled them, lurked an element of actual danger. *Lurked* was hardly the right word: knives split her throat, acid ate away her eyes, windows opened at perilous angles, as phantom hands thrust her toward the sill. In all the time she had represented heavyweights in Hollywood she had made it a policy never to see horror films. All the nightmares on Elm Street had had to take place without her. But since the confrontation with Anthony Go, her waking moments were edged with anxiety, her midnights razored into terrified wakefulness. She would bolt up in bed, covered with perspiration. And where through most of her life such moments had been filled with sorrow, at the realization she was alone, now there was relief.

In addition to the toll the night's sleeplessness had taken, she had read in the *South China Morning Post* that Elizabeth Taylor's home

in Puerto Vallarta was up for sale. Louise had spent some happy days
in the Casa Kimberly, as it was called. Partaking close up of the
world's sexiest romantic fantasy, Elizabeth and Richard Burton, she
had at least been able to believe in unbridled passion for other
people, conceived that the same thing might have happened to her
had she been coddled from childhood, rivetingly beautiful, with
violet eyes. Had there been another male diva, eloquent beyond the
ability of writers to put dialogue in his mouth, funny as gorgeous
men were hardly ever funny, striking and physically magnetic as his
mate. More so, really, the unexpected brain power combusting his
Welsh bravado into true fire. His was the most present male presence
Louise had experienced. She had understood and sympathized with
Elizabeth's protracted grieving, during the rest of his life and after
it, the sense of loss, that you could realize the big dream, and still
lose it. A curious consolation, that love brought more agonies to the
enviable than those who envied. But it seemed a sad landmark to
Louise now, in terms of real estate, and romance.

The Bridge of Sighs arching above the Mexican village street,
connecting the two houses belonging to the then Burtons, had
become, in its way, as tragic as the original it was modeled after. In
Venice, the covered bridge had marked the last glimpse prisoners
would have of the world, on their way into the cold and dark. To
Louise the copy seemed to mark the last glimpse those who believed
in glamour would have of great romance.

So she was deeply disconsolate. The Greek had sent a basket of
flowers with an invitation to lunch. Henry had insisted that she go.
Louise felt listless and victimized, wanting nothing more than to go
back to bed and pull the covers over her face, wait for her executioner
and hope that he came in the daylight instead of in her nightmares.
But in the end she had dressed and gone to meet the Count, as he
said he was. She believed him no more than she did her dreams,
including the good ones, which she challenged even as she dreamed
them, knowing they could not possibly be true. As even Elizabeth's
dream had turned out not to be true, real as it had seemed while the
world dreamed it with her.

Usually when Louise went somewhere with the Greek, which
she'd done for the past few days, since he'd refused to take no for an

answer—though it was the only Greek word she knew—there was someone in his retinue who'd served as translator. Today they were alone, except for the quietly contained crowd. It made her uneasy, since the Greek was all over her with his eyes, and a little with his hands, touching her elbow, her wrist, all of it respectful, a lot of it seemingly unintentional, as he handed her the menu, opened her napkin and offered it to her, his pale green eyes cowlike as he assiduously avoided setting it on her lap.

He was, she supposed, in his white-haired, imposing-nosed way, a fine-looking man, if a little short for her. But as her mother had said of Louise's long-ago pursuer, Harry Bell, he was very tall when he stood on his money. Did this Bassia really have money? Money had never been the end-all for Louise, especially once she had started to make it, at which point people started offering her everything free. The privileged of the world, who needed nothing, she had begun to understand, were the ones who received the gifts, eager and hungry as suckarounds were to be in their favor. So plays and books and limousine rides and trips to exotic climes had been Louise's from the moment she no longer thirsted for them. Once your cup ranneth over, all of life was a wine steward, toadying attendance.

Now, besides the *things* she no longer wanted, was this man she hadn't even gone after, who showed absolutely no signs of being disinterested in her. All she had ever had were men who misprized her, who'd used her and thrown her away. She was not prepared for or receptive to a courtship she hadn't initiated. Especially as it seemed to have nothing base or self-serving as its motive. Except, of course, if he was, as she suspected, setting her up. "What are you really after, my alleged Count?" she asked him now, trying to x-ray the seeming desire in his eyes, see what lay behind them. "You've never had a blond loudmouth past her prime, right?"

"Right," he repeated, and beamed at her.

"Any zillionaire could have a twenty-two-year-old showgirl with giant breasts. But you want to be original. Correct?"

"Correct." He stumbled over the word, steadied it with her hand, moving it to his lips, not quite looking in her eyes.

Several tables away, Louise could see Claire, in profile, so caught by her young companion she hadn't even noticed Louise's presence. There was that to be glad about, at least, that she wasn't coming over. Louise had already said to Claire all she had to say. Nor did she want to deal with this new element of Claire's being involved with a younger man. It was embarrassing to Louise what women put themselves through, how grateful they were for male attention, how little they cared about what people thought.

Louise turned her attention to the little snatches of conversation she could hear between Erica Thorr and her mogul. "I'm revising our travel plans," Lockwood was saying. "We'll go by way of the Andes. Fly from L.A. to Lima, spend the night at the Cezar Hotel in Miraflores. Fly by Fawcett Airlines to Iquitos, Peru. Hire a boat that will take us to some shacks that sit on sticks on the river where the pink dolphins are. And macaws and parrots. Then we'll make love on a pink dolphin."

To her surprise, Louise could actually feel her heart beating. What was the matter with these people? Didn't they know the Casa Kimberly was up for sale? And at a reduced price, because nothing was worth what it had been anymore. Not Mexico, not great love.

"But you have to see the Andes," he was saying. "Twenty thousand feet high, snow-capped mountains, close as they are to the equator, almost on top of it, and still white with snow. And over the crest, the Rain Forest. Stretching like a carpet for hours. With the silver Amazon snaking through . . ."

"Probably you've been reading *Lear's* magazine." Louise turned back to the Count. "You've discovered the mystique that age is beauty. That wrinkles are hot. You understand the basic emptiness and frustration of young women who are unlined, and can't get old fast enough. Right?"

"Right," said the Count, and placed a diamond bracelet on her wrist.

"What is this?" asked Louise. "What are you trying to do to me?" She got to her feet, and burst into tears. "Stop trying to kid me!" Throwing the bracelet on the table, she rushed from the Grill.

*   *   *

When she came out of the stall in the ladies' room, blowing her nose, Claire was coming in. "Shit!" said Louise, and went back inside, locking the door.

"It's a pleasure to see you, too," Claire said. "Are you all right?"

"I have something in my eye," said Louise.

"I do that all the time. I know how to get rid of it."

"You do?" Louise opened the door.

"Pull the lid all the way down, and spit three times."

Louise smiled. "I remember that. My mother taught that to me, along with how inadequate I was. How are you?"

"Happy." She went inside the stall, and closed the door.

"Well, I hope it lasts. He's very pretty."

"And bright."

"Don't sell me. Your life is your own." She went to the sink and washed water into her eyes. "Do you think men cry in the men's room? Or is it only us who think to save ourselves some steps by crying in the sink?"

"What are you sad about?"

"It's a dark day for romance. Elizabeth's house in Puerto Vallarta is up for sale. Well, I guess it's time we all stayed out of the sun." She dried her face, and started repairing her makeup. "Still, it's hard not to remember how lovely it was looking toasted. Radiant and brown, thinking enough sex in exotic places was the answer to everything."

"Maybe it is," said Claire, coming out of the stall. She started washing her hands at the next sink.

"Still believe a dashing companion is all the protection you need?"

"I do."

"Better stay out of the sun, anyway. Too many harmful rays. But what days they were, weren't they, when we were so hopeful, and ignorant. The present pales by comparison, to the time we bought into the fantasies. The one where we walked hand in hand, tanned, into the sunset. Nobody figured on goodbye, or lovers dying, or the sun causing wrinkles."

"You want to have lunch with us?"

"No, thanks. I'm here with a purported Count. Who's your guy?"

"His name is James Bingham. English."

"I would hope so. How old is he?"

"Thirty-four."

"I'm not saying anything."

"I don't feel much older than that myself."

"Is he successful?"

"He's a darling man."

"I was afraid of that," said Louise. "Not enough for you."

"Maybe you're jealous."

"No maybe about it." She started rolling mascara onto her eyelashes, with a thick black brush. "This is all clumpy and clotted."

"I have some I could let you use." Claire opened her purse.

"Never mind. I don't want anything of yours. You're too generous. There's nothing I can do for you, so stop offering me things."

"It's only mascara."

"No it isn't. It's friendship. Affection. Things I can't return. Not on the level you demand them."

"You don't really know me anymore," Claire said, bristling. "We haven't been friends for a long time."

"People don't change. They just become more who they are. And I don't have time for you, or the Greek."

"Greek?"

"The so-called Count. I can't figure out what he really wants."

"Maybe he really likes you."

"How could anybody really like me? I'm over the hill, and the hill wasn't that full of flowers to begin with. Why would anybody want a woman our age, when the woods are full of nymphet sweeties?"

"Maybe some men are smart."

"If they were that smart, they would have been born women, so they could experience the full range of human suffering. Well"—she snapped shut her purse, and turned—"how do I look?"

"You look very well. But I like you better with a tan."

"I like us all better with a tan. Poor Elizabeth. It's the end of the world."

Louise decided to go straight back to her room. She did not for a moment believe anything about the Greek, including that he might actually care about her, so she owed him nothing, not even a polite goodbye. Love was a raincoat people held on their laps, to hide the dirty things they did in the dark. Anthony Go was obviously even more perverted than he seemed, getting the "Count" to pretend an infatuation, to torment her at a deeper level than the one he promised.

She pressed the elevator button to go up. The doors opened. Anthony Go stepped out.

"Don't think I'm not on to you," she said. "I know you set me up. Not enough, cockroaches in my chicken salad. Getting me caught in zippers. Threatening me with acid in my face."

"Did he do all that?" asked Clement Leslie, standing by the door of the Grill.

"Superintendent," said Go, smiling pleasantly. "I'm sorry if I kept you waiting."

Clement turned to Louise. "What has he done exactly?"

"Miss Felder is overwrought."

"You bet I am. Why did you send that supposed millionaire to pretend he loves me? What kind of pervert are you? Why don't you just kill me, the way you said you would?"

"Would you like to make an official complaint?" asked Clement.

"Did you?"

"I don't think this is the place to discuss this."

"Just tell me if you did."

"Did what?"

"Set me up to have my heart broken?"

"I have no idea what you're talking about."

"If there's one thing I can't handle it's an innocent criminal. Slime. I have half a mind to make an official complaint."

"That's what it would take," said Go. "Half a mind."

"Don't let him intimidate you," said Clement.

"Ha!" said Louise, and started to go into the elevator.

"Moment!" cried the Greek, running out of the restaurant, amazingly fast on his feet for a short man. He caught Louise by her hand, pulled her from the elevator, fell to his knees, started babbling.

"Does anyone here speak Greek?" she asked.

"He's asking you to forgive him," said Clement.

Go looked impressed. "How do you know Greek?"

"Two years in Cyprus in the army."

"A man of many parts," said Go. "One must never underestimate you."

"He didn't mean to offend you," said Clement, translating.

"What woman wouldn't be offended at being offered expensive jewelry," she said. "I think I'm losing my mind."

"He says he loves you."

"What bullshit. How do you say 'bullshit' in Greek?"

Clement told her. The Count stood up and slapped his face, started raging at him.

"What's he saying?"

"He will cut out my tongue if I ever say another word like that to such a great lady."

"It's my fault he hit you. Forgive me."

"Not necessary. You forgive him. He'll do anything," Clement translated. The Count was kissing her hand now, talking against the pulse in her wrist. "He says he knows the reason you were so offended is that he offered you an expensive gift without making it clear he wants to marry you."

"You twisted swine," she said to Anthony Go.

"I don't even know the man."

"Do you know him?" she asked the Count.

Clement translated, pointing to Go. The Count shook his head.

"Then this isn't a setup?"

"He appears to be serious. I would say very serious."

"You're a policeman. How do we run a check on him?"

"Do you know who he is?" asked Clement.

"Is he in show business?"

"Not exactly. He's one of the six richest men in the world."

"Excuse me," said Louise. She got into the elevator, waiting until the doors were closed before she started screaming.

TWENTY-ONE

◆

Clement was outside Judith's office on the day she returned. He managed to look as though the meeting were accidental. The daily phone calls to her secretary to find out if she had come back had stopped a few days before, when he had gotten information from James Bingham as to her whereabouts and expected day of reentry. A friend at the airport had alerted him, as requested, when her name appeared on the arrival list from Beijing, China Air. Clement tried to make his reaction seem interested but diffident, as though she were a suspect in some not very exciting crime.

That he was actually standing in a doorway, tailing her wrong way round, that was to say anticipating her arrival, would have given him pause, had he not been so busy constructing the moment. He stood at half-tilt, as though on his way somewhere, leonine head slightly angled out of the arcade that marked the entryway, ready to take on the rain, which had started falling before dawn that morning. He had been there since eight o'clock, early for him. But not as early as it had been in the days when he was drinking. Already he looked on them with nostalgia, the resentment that had characterized the first days of his abstinence having evolved into a kind of awe that he had been able to stop without backsliding. Added to that was an affection for Judith, a different layer from his attraction to her, an absolute fondness that she had gotten him to quit. It didn't occur to him that he had stopped himself, revenge having always been his best motivator. The initial drying-out had been a kind of "I'll show her." Now, he couldn't wait to. Longed to parade for her his surprising self-discipline. He had also moderated his beard, letting his barber trim away the grizzled woolliness of it, so that it came to its own neat conclusions, much as he had done. All in all he understood that she had tamed him, or wanted to think she had, investing her with sufficient interest to go to the trouble of caring. He felt rather like a schoolboy, something he did not particularly bridle at. His schoolboy years, as he remembered them, had been quite driven, his wish to be of service prematurely rampant. So he'd been a little too dedicated, too devoted and serious, with almost no silliness, no flutters in the heart. It pleased him to feel them now.

Still, he knew that she was the adversary, that this thing between men and women was basically a game, not always friendly. So he couldn't seem to be waiting for her. Policemen were actors when they needed to be, able to cloak their eyes. So he nearly managed to hide how glad he was to see her.

"Clement . . ." She was on her way into the arcade, umbrella half-closed, collapsed, little sparkles of rain clinging to the black nylon. Beads of moisture shone on the ends of her reddish hair, wisping it into curls, twirling her into a kind of puckish innocence, giving the lie to the shrewdness in her eyes.

"What a surprise," he said, as though it were, as though he hadn't monitored her steps, listening to them coming, like an Indian, ear to the ground. "I thought you were still away." His voice was not quite as good at deceit as his eyes could be. He heard the falseness. But she didn't know him as well as he knew himself, so perhaps he was managing to fool her.

"I've got a lot to catch up on. Forgive me." She started to move past him.

He sensed a light perfume, clean, crisp, made fresher by the rain. He had never noticed fragrance on her before, her no-nonsense attitude seeming to extend even to her smell, as though she wished to do nothing to enhance what she was, in any way that could seem misleading. "A new perfume?"

"An oil," she said, looking pleased, surprised he would notice. "One of my informants gave it to me. I've been in Beijing."

"How is it?"

"Tougher than ever. They're clamping down on study abroad for their students, so they won't be infected with democracy."

"What's the situation there with AIDS?"

"According to the government there isn't any."

"Homosexuality is a disease of the West."

"Exactly," she said. "A disease they cure in China."

"With electric shocks."

"Not always. They offer the alternative approach of herbal medicines that induce vomiting."

"That ought to reduce your erotic thoughts."

"Not to mention your ardor."

"Maybe I should try it," said Clement.

"Excuse me?"

"Can you have dinner?"

"I'm just too far behind."

"Maybe I could help bring you up to date."

"I don't think so."

"I haven't had a drink since the last time we were together."

"Good for you," she said.

"Good for *you*," said Clement.

"I don't want the credit."

"Whether or not you do, it's yours. Besides, I'm very close."

"To what?"

"The answer. Black's Link."

"And you'd tell me?"

"Just enough."

"Enough to what?"

"Get us to dessert."

In the end, of course, she agreed to meet him. He was a bit ashamed of himself, even while he rationalized that she was trustworthy, planned to charge her with revealing nothing until the criminals were arrested and brought to trial. Assured himself that *Elan* magazine never printed speculation. But the inarguable truth was he was using what he knew, or believed he knew, as a lure. Information was the best aphrodisiac for a journalist, more powerful than the powder of the rhino horn, still being peddled in Taiwan, in spite of the government ban on rhinoceros products. Was he any better than merchants who sold them, or businessmen expecting the rhinos to become extinct, stockpiling Asian and African horns, now bringing forty thousand U.S. a kilo? Was there any difference between his setting aside a bit of his integrity to interest her, and the medicine shops in Taipei openly selling the horns, believed to be good for lowering fevers and raising erotic longings? Was the rhinoceros any more an endangered species than the romantic man?

Morality aside, as men always put morality aside, no matter how moral they were, when it came to the heart, or a part of the body more base, he was very ebullient. Now to the certainty that he was close to a solution, was added the fillip of courtship. He would bring her roses, in the guise of revelation.

Knowing he was seeing her that evening energized his day, stimulated him to tie up a few more threads. Anthony Go had been no help at all, sticking to his story that he had not known Harry Magic, unwavering in his declaration that he'd had no prior connection with films. Little as Clement trusted Go, something about the pride with which he spoke of his new venture, the film he was preparing for Johnny Wong and Henry Wu, convinced him, at least for the time being, sending him off in another direction. If Anthony Go wasn't the link here between all the elements tying the crime to pornography, he needed to find out who was. The episode at the Mandarin, with Erica Thorr being filmed in the pool, had turned out to be innocent enough, in its way. But there was too much that was far from innocent involved in the rest of it.

He returned to the Albany. Usually the first forty-eight hours after a crime was committed had the case won or lost. There had been a raft of experts at Black's Link, taking soil samples, pieces of wood, checking flora, looking for traces of clothing, seeds, twigs, anything to be able to tie in a suspect later on. But at Harry Magic's apartment, there had been no need to bring in the Advanced Technology Unit. What little evidence there seemed to be at the crime scene had been taken to them. Nothing had been out of place. Except for the shred of fabric from Wendy Lu's skirt on the railing of the balcony, there'd been no signs of a crime, if salacious pictures in silver frames weren't counted outside the law. Technically, he supposed, there was nothing illegal about them, since pornography in Hong Kong was charged the same as prostitution. Just as one woman working alone was not an offense, but two women made it a brothel, so did one copy of the obscene go unpunished, but possessing more than one made it a crime.

Magic's apartment had been routinely dusted for fingerprints. Wendy Lu's had been all over everything, including the headboard of the bed and glasses that had been washed. But there was precious little else the police had been able to do. After Black's Link there'd been all sorts of follow-up: checking out sexual offenders, finding out what vehicles had been seen in the area. But the posh Albany, with its swimming pool, squash courts, sauna, and the most senior member of the Legislative Council in the penthouse, not to mention the ex–Attorney General of Hong Kong, offered little in the way of possible suspects who were casual visitors. According to the night doorman, no one had been around who didn't belong there at the time of Wendy's death.

The day doorman backed him up. He was Cantonese, about twenty. "We all knew Wendy. She had permission to be here. She worked for Mr. Magic. She had a key. She went up in the elevator alone that night. Mr. Magic was not in his apartment. He's away."

"Couldn't he have come back without your seeing him?"

"There's no way into the building except through the main entrance, or the locked garage. I would have seen him."

"You're on day duty."

"I was working on the elevator that night. I have just been promoted to doorman."

He looked very proud about it, prideful as young Cantonese always seemed prideful, but with a little extra, as though the gold-striped navy blue uniform was more than that of a doorman, and there was a community responsibility involved here. Clement supposed, in a way, there was, considering the stature of tenants in the building. Porno star aside.

"How long has Magic been gone?"

"A *long* time. Months. He doesn't even pick up his mail. A registered letter came yesterday. I had to sign for it."

"Registered letter?"

"From the police."

"Let me see it."

It was from the North Point Police Station, advising the owner of the cited vehicle that it had been towed from the street where it had been parked too long, that such notice had been sent and ignored. There was an overdue fine for the towing. As the vehicle had gone unclaimed for two months, it was to be auctioned the following Wednesday, unless the owner acted promptly.

"Ah, yes," said the young sergeant at the police pound a little dreamily, looking at the letter. "My Silver Cloud."

"*Your* Silver Cloud?" Clement said.

"Had my eye on it since it got brought in. Never know when a thing will go cheap."

"What would you do with a Silver Cloud?" They started to walk across the gray-graveled lot toward the rows of cars, a kind of elephant burial ground for vehicles.

"Same as the fellow who owned it before me. Show off. He must be pretty peculiar not to have come for it."

"Maybe he can't," Clement said. "This the car?" It was bright pink.

"Not many Rolls-Royces here. This is the one."

"You have a key?"

"No."

Clement reached into his belt, pulled out the Slim Jim his policeman friend in San Francisco had given him. He jammed it into the space between door and window.

"Try not to damage it," the young sergeant said, proprietarily.

There was a box on the front seat, filled with a dozen smaller boxes, covered with Chinese characters. In each small box was a vial, filled with what Clement guessed was one cc of clear liquid.

"Morphine?"

"Don't know," Clement said. "You read Chinese?"

"I'm the last Englishman in my division." There was more resignation than bragging in the statement, as though he knew he had answered the wrong advertisement, that he should have thought ahead to 1997, and realized there wouldn't be a job for him then, like other Brits who'd been too smart to join.

Only two English words were on the packet. "Injectie Tricosanthin," Clement read, aloud. In the pocket of the door by the driver's seat was a piece of paper, with a list of telephone numbers, all of them U.S. area code 415. "San Francisco."

He called his friend, the cop he'd been visiting during the earthquake. "I'd like you to find out what these numbers are."

"It's the middle of the night," said his friend.

"Call me when it's a decent hour your time, and you can wake *me*." He hung up the phone and went to see Dao Tsim.

Dao studied the characters through a magnifying glass. "It gives dosage and warnings. Some kind of experimental drug. Must be administered by a physician. Highly toxic if improperly used. Will terminate pregnancy. Must be used before sixty days after missed cycle."

"An abortion drug?"

"So it would seem."

"Grandfather?" Chen stuck his head in the doorway. The dinosaur back that had spiked up the center of his skull had given way to a moderated Mohawk. "Did you see a video cassette?"

"You left it in the bathroom."

"Thanks."

"What's the movie, Chen?"

" 'Lo, Superintendent. *Funny Face.*"

"One of his best. Can I have it when you're finished?"

"It's not mine to lend. The guys in the club . . ."

"How come you never ask me over anymore?"

Chen avoided his eyes. "The rest of the members kind of figure the British aren't interested in the same things we're interested in."

"You mean, the Brits aren't interested in Hong Kong."

"Something like that."

"You ought to know better. Certainly about me."

Chen looked at him, and a flicker of a smile started at the corner of his mouth. "That's right, I should. I'll ask him if I can lend it to you."

"Nice boy," Clement said when he was gone.

"I am grateful you look beyond appearances. I myself have been worried about him. What will happen to my great-grandchildren?"

"How's Kip doing?"

"The same. Not smart to pursue a love where only one is in love."

"Are you talking to me?"

"Why are you really here, Clement? You can read Chinese."

"Not Mandarin."

"You know many who do. Police. Technicians. Why come to me? Is she back?"

"I can't fool you."

"What about yourself? Can you fool yourself?"

"Is it going to go anywhere? Shall we toss the sticks?"

"We already tossed the sticks. The quality of your passage is up to you."

"I don't want to be disappointed," Clement said.

"Then don't have expectations," said Dao Tsim.

"My *Fung shui* man has advised me not to have expectations," Clement said. They were in One Harbour Road, the restaurant of the Grand Hyatt Hotel, looking at Kowloon, the same floor-to-ceiling windowed spectacle the Regent offered from the other side. Somehow even though the view of Hong Kong was more striking, by virtue of buildings with aluminum cladding, mirrored skyscrapers, there was such drama to the restaurant itself that the vistas seemed matched. Black marble columns arched like swans toward the thirty-two-foot ceilings. Fountains flowed, arced slender bursts of water against shimmering lights. It was such a graceful setting—so sexy, he would have welcomed Judith's saying now in her journalese—that he could not help thinking it would have some effect on her. In spite of Dao's warning.

"Did he tell you about the Bank of China building?" Judith was as crisp in her questions as she was in her manner of dress. Rust linen jacket with a slight puff at the shoulder added a subtle femininity to tailored black skirt and white blouse, the soldierly uniform she seemed to sport in places where she knew her laundry would get done.

"What about it?"

"It's got bad *Fung shui*, according to the locals. The high antennae on the top of the building points directly at the eye of the dragon on the mountain, piercing it. A sign of economic disaster for Hong Kong, when the Chinese come."

"Maybe they'll be different by 1997."

"And maybe I. M. Pei should have thought about good *Fung shui*. He *is* Chinese. I don't care how important an architect you are, there isn't a major building on the island, American, British, or Japanese, that hasn't brought in its *Fung shui* man. Back to the mountain, face to the sea. How could he have overlooked it?"

"Maybe he was being practical."

"Everyone in Hong Kong is practical. They're still superstitious."

"Are you?"

"Of course. Especially about Hong Kong. I want it to stay Hong Kong."

"You missed a couple of parades while you were away. The Student Union. The Hong Kong Alliance. They're not too pleased about the new Basic Law."

"How many marched?"

"About three thousand students, a thousand from the Alliance."

"A far cry from the million who marched after Tiananmen Square."

"Protests aren't pragmatic," Clement said. "Hong Kong is nothing but pragmatic. They have to get back to business, earning money so they can get out."

"It's worse than that," Judith said. "The Chinese are cynical. They figure they can get away with it, that the world will forget. And they're right."

"We won't forget."

"Maybe not you. But people who want to do business with them will. Sure, it seems to be a whole new planet, at least three quarters of it. But the name of the game is still economics."

"I missed you," Clement said, smiling.

"Tell me more about the case." Outside the wall of windows sampans glided into the dusk, a brightly bulbed ferry coursed toward the pier at Wanchai. On the plate in front of Judith giant shrimp lay butterflied in an arrangement presenting them like a flower, paper-thin cucumber slices, seeds removed, the heart of the blossom. But none of it seemed to capture her full attention, as respectfully as she ate, as carefully as she chewed.

"You know what I know."

"Was this Wendy Lu pregnant?"

"The autopsy didn't show that."

"Then what was Harry Magic doing with an abortion drug? Especially as abortions are so easy to get here."

"The police pathologist says that drug is also being used experimentally for cancer therapy in China. Apparently it goes after what they call macrophages, the infected cells. Kills them, the way chemotherapy does."

"You think he has cancer?"

"Maybe something like it. Maybe something worse." He paused. "I think he has AIDS. I think this whole thing, starting with Black's Link, is connected to pornography. The awful way the couple was killed, like in a snuff film. Wendy Lu being thrown from the balcony of Harry Magic's apartment. His being a porno star . . ."

"But what's it got to do with AIDS?"

"I'm not sure. Some kind of cover-up, maybe. Trying to hide the fact that it's a world plague now. That it's come to Hong Kong. Bad for the brothels."

Music coursed through the restaurant, amplified gently on hidden speakers, tasty piano, the neat simplicity of George Shearing. Melody seemed to rise and fall as the fountain did, a sound show with a video of water and lights. "I'd rather be talking to you of pretty things," Clement said.

"Pretty things don't sell magazines."

"You're not going to print it?"

"I gave you my word."

"Then why do we have to think in terms of selling magazines?"

"Because that's my job."

"But this isn't work time."

"It is for me. Pretty much every waking moment of my life is work time."

"That's not very healthy."

"Well, maybe they'll come up with a drug for that one. To attack the workaholic macrophages."

"There's already a drug to counter those."

"Really?"

"Rhino horn."

She smiled. "You really think aphrodisiacs work?"

"I know they do. Bad luck for the rhino. Good luck for me."

"What do you mean?"

"I put some in your soup, when you went to call the office."

"You're kidding, of course."

"Well, we'll find out. I hope you're not angry. I figured if the CIA could put acid in people's drinks, I could put rhino horn in your miso."

"I know you're joking."

"We'll see."

He kissed her in the elevator going up to her apartment. She had already made noises about how tired she was, and Claire's being in the apartment, preparing him for not being able to ask him in. So he kissed her in the elevator, as a very young man would have done, more patient than a very young man, the urgency contained. "Do you feel it?" he whispered against her lips, which were softly responsive.

"Feel what?"

"The rhino horn."

"I'm not a good subject. A hypnotist told me that once. I don't like giving up control."

"Then take it," he said, and kissed her, more fervently this time.

The doors to the elevator opened. Kip stood outside, her face streaked with tears. "Oh, excuse me. I pushed the wrong button. Superintendent," she said, surprised, seeing who it was.

"If you go," came an Englishman's voice, "you needn't come back."

"How are you, Kip?"

"Never better."

"And take this damn trash with you," cried the unseen man, as a book came hurtling into the hall. "Give it back to your whore cousin. Tell her to stay out of my life."

"I saw your grandfather this afternoon," Clement said. "He's very concerned."

"Well, as you see, there's absolutely no reason to be." She did a little half bow and smiled, as the doors to the elevator closed.

"I really am tired," Judith said, outside her door.

"I understand." He put his hand inside her jacket, touched her breast.

"Obviously you don't."

"Obviously I do. As long as I let you talk, and listen to what you say as if you meant it, we're going to make no progress."

"I mean what I say."

"Maybe you think you do. What's in my hand tells me different." He rolled his palm against her nipple, felt it stiffen.

"Only a very boorish man would force himself on a woman."

"Good. I'm tired of being civilized."

"Then I guess you'd better come in."

Claire and James were in the living room of Judith's apartment, Claire smoothing her skirt, as if they too had been interrupted. It seemed to Clement an evening of interruptions, as though every time he made little inroads with Judith, there was a detour. In spite of his avowed wish not to be civilized, he was, chatting pleasantly with Bingham about his planned trip to Bangkok, asking the polite little questions about the weather this time of year and proposed hotels, the kind of busy chat English people tossed at each other, filling the air with words even while they were saying nothing.

"I really have to go to bed," Judith said, after some minutes.

"I feel exactly the same way," said Clement.

"Why don't you call me tomorrow?"

"Why don't I tuck you in?"

"I have to pack," said Claire. "James, help me pick out what I should take."

"Why don't you take me?" Judith said. "I love Thailand."

"Oh, to be Thailand," said Clement.

"Call me tomorrow," said Judith, and, kissing him lightly, showed him the door.

He did not imagine for a moment this was a light romance anymore. He could hardly fall asleep for thinking about her. When he finally dropped off, he dreamed of her, opening the blouse he had touched, astounding himself with the size of her breasts, deceptive in such a small woman, burrowing his head between them, licking a path to her nipples, roseate brown, and full as he suckled them. He took his swollen penis, rubbing it in her cleavage, pressing her breasts from the outside, creating a velvety channel to pump himself through, a soft pipeline. It was the first erotic dream he was aware of having since he was a boy. Like a boy he was also ashamed, even while he was dreaming, knowing he was dreaming: it was not a proper dream for a young gentleman, especially one who was no longer young.

But he was spared the mortification of coming in his sleep, as a boy would, the telephone blasting him out of his salaciously soporific state. He picked up the receiver, and mumbled his number.

"Am I waking you up?" asked his friend, the policeman in San Francisco.

"You certainly are."

"Then we're even. I have that information for you."

"Let me get a pencil."

"The first number is 'Project Inform.' It's an AIDS hot line. There's a whole bunch of organizations here that advocate counter-medicine, getting experimental drugs out, telling people to use what's unapproved. There are 'Buyer's Clubs' where you can get them. You find out where they are through something called 'Healing Alternatives.' That's another number on his list. The third number is one of the buyer's clubs. I went over and checked it out. It's at 1748 Market Street, right by Kwan Yin, an herbal medicine outlet. They've got a thing they're selling to AIDS victims now called 'Compound Q.' Apparently very toxic. Has to be administered by a doctor who knows the protocol. A lot of people have died."

"How is it given?"

"IV. But it's got to be slow, and it's got to be carefully observed. A lot of allergic reactions, apparently, swollen esophagus, stopped breathing. Some reported cases of dementia. They've got a drug that's supposed to counter that called decadrone, that you have to take in advance. Those poor bastards.

"Apparently this Compound Q goes after the affected cells. But you can't have fewer than a hundred normal T cells. That's why people have been dying. They're already too weak to handle it."

"What's the normal number?"

"Eight to twelve hundred in a healthy person who's HIV negative. You get familiar with this stuff when you live in San Francisco, unfortunately. Whether or not you want to be, you get knowledgeable."

"What's the dosage for this Compound Q?"

"One cc. Two doses right away, then once a month. The last number you gave me is an outfit called 'Gene Laboratory.' They're working on their own version of Compound Q, but they're very careful to say it's strictly in the experimental stage. The FDA has just approved its use on an experimental basis, but these things take a long time to be freely available, so there's still a lot of black market action. The original was apparently developed in China."

"Tricosanthin," said Clement.

"That's right. Tricosanthin. How'd you know?"

So now he could stop dreaming about Judith, and dream about Harry Magic. Somewhere at the bottom of Victoria Harbor, maybe, with bricks for shoes. Dead of natural causes, probably, if this new horror show of a plague could be called natural. Unless he'd been killed by Anthony Go, because of what he knew. Could he have been witness to the Black's Link murder, involved, as it was being filmed? Or had his wasted body just been spirited away, to spare the colony embarrassment? All Clement could be relatively certain of was that Magic was dead. If he'd been alive, he would never have left the Compound Q in the car. If he'd been too sick to get the medicine himself, he would have sent someone for it. Was ready to move to San Francisco where AIDS drugs were more available. Where a doctor would administer them with compassion, not like the little doctor in the private hospital, humiliated that such a thing could happen to someone Chinese.

Poor Harry Magic. What kind of world was it turning into, all the good set aside, when people were ashamed not of how a man lived, but how he died.

BOOK FOUR

◆

EXOTIC PLACES

TWENTY-TWO

◆

People who complain about traffic have probably never been to Bangkok," Claire said. She and James were in a taxi outside the Dusit Thani Hotel, waiting for the light to change, a wait which had already encompassed ten minutes. It seemed to Claire not so much a stop as an encampment. She could see the couple in the cab stalled in the next lane, watched them quarrel and reconcile, kiss, and quarrel again. "Probably two people side by side in different taxis here could meet, fall in love, get married and divorced by the time the light changed," she observed.

James laughed, but not very cheerfully. She wondered if the irritation she perceived behind his merriment was simply the stress of the traffic, or that her joke was badly timed, because he was afraid she wanted to marry him.

She thought she did. The feelings he elicited in her went deeper than their relationship. He connected her to a place in herself that was filled with ardor, complete, the way she and Charley had been. So it was the emotion she was in love with, and confused with James. If love was blind, neediness was deaf and mute, and a little crippled. Being used to an open heart, able to trust and give and receive with no caution, she wanted to be that way again. Free, in captivity.

Caught by the fantasy, she fathomed little of the truth. He was handsome, he was charming, he was witty; they were in Bangkok.

As the reality of the traffic was a nightmare, they were on their way to the dream: a room that looked out on the river Chao Phraya. James had made a reservation at the Oriental Hotel, which countless addicts of romance and travel considered the finest in the world. So Claire thought all that was needed for the dream to come true was for the light to change.

Eventually it did. She felt practically whisked the rest of the way, so effortless did the journey seem in comparison to what it had been. The taxi beeped through alleyways, along tiny streets clogged with more vendors than cars, selling T-shirts and watches and what James advised her were the addresses of younger sisters, unless boys were the customer's preference, in which case the whereabouts of parlors that featured younger brothers were offered.

All of this he spoke about matter-of-factly, as if sex had nothing to do with love, and was really a commodity, which she could not believe he believed. It was part of his wit, she was sure, his subtle sense of irony. Having spent so many years living in Beverly Hills, believing people who didn't mean what they said, she now could not believe those who did. Especially when they said what she didn't want to hear.

The taxi turned into a curved driveway, sloping slightly upward from the poverty a few feet away from it, lifting them as though in a magical coach to a transformed world. Doormen in gold-braided, spotless white uniforms greeted them, taking their luggage, helping Claire from the back of the cab, passing her into the glassed-in opulence of the lobby. Giant carved teak temple bells hung in clusters of four, close to the ceiling. Antique desks and stiff-backed chairs were set formally out on gray rugs covering the marble floor, as though awaiting the return of Somerset Maugham. In a line of straight chairs facing the front door four businessmen, in dark suits and ties, sat like obedient elderly schoolboys, briefcases at their black-socked, sensible-shoed feet, reading the *Asian Wall Street Journal* and the *Bangkok Post.*

It was a passage so abrupt from the clamor and the dirt and the heat outside, it dizzied Claire. Certain times in her life she had passed from panic to tranquility, a transition brought about by nothing she could put her finger on, a dubbing from some generous, invisible sword. Like love that surprised, unexpected, it was with her awhile before she recognized it, at which point she tried to hold on to it, and it vanished. That was the feeling in her now.

"Let me have your passport," James said, "I'll register us."

Her stomach knotted, as it had on the plane when she covered the year of her birth as they filled out the landing cards. All along she had told herself it didn't matter how much older she was, that she was older at all. But that self-delusion had been enhanced by James's not knowing exactly how old she was. "I'll register myself," she said.

They started toward the concierge's desk. Someone called out James's name. A pale, ascetic-looking blond man stood at the cashier's window, hand raised in greeting. "Roger," James said, unenthusiastically.

He made no attempt to introduce Claire, so she moved away. A terrible heat suffused her, worse than what had been outside. It seemed clear to her that he had been embarrassed, distressed, at what she could only assume was a young contemporary's seeing him with an older woman. "I'll be outside," she said, but not so loud that she was sure he could hear.

On the veranda next to the river, salmon bougainvillea curved around a base of fantasy lights, black iron flowers inset with bulbs arcing beneath a central light, like a congregation paying homage to a priest. In the branches of the tree, sparrows hid, as though from the putt-putty noise of the boats on the river, while on black iron stems holding the lights, bolder birds played. Above the white balustrade, a lone butterfly fluttered. Like her own soul? Claire wondered. How presumptuous she was, how self-aggrandizing, pretending to herself that she had a soul, and one with such substance, when what she was really was vain and trivial. Fleeing because she was ashamed of being older.

"Why did you run away?" James was beside her.

"You seemed embarrassed to be with me."

"You great soft lump." He squeezed her neck. "I just don't like that fellow."

"Who is he?"

"Nobody interesting. Someone I worked with in London. Didn't I half enjoy being able to tell him about my stock."

She felt a moment of pleasure that so much good was happening for him, then wondered if it would mean he could do without her. How shallow women were in their desperation.

Water taxis went by, long narrow boats that stopped at the landing of the hotel, carrying their populous burdens up the Chao Phraya River. The current was muddy, streaked with leafy green water hyacinths growing as seaweed would in oceans. Boats carved from teak with facing rows of benches transported saffron-robed monks. At the next table on the terrace, a woman with a golfer's face leaned on a bony elbow, discoursing on silk, the cigarette in her hand streaming smoke over her words, too much sun and her habit having stained her the color of a tobacco leaf. By the turquoise waters of the rectangular swimming pool, tourists baked, their conversation filled with planned excursions to the Emerald Buddha.

"It's so beautiful here," said Claire.

"It's you who are beautiful." James touched her very tenderly, as though he had read all the doubts in her mind.

When she had been younger than everyone else, youngest in her class, youngest in her group, the quickness of her mind elevating her to a circle of acceptance her emotions never could, no man had paid her compliments. That she might have become actually beautiful, that James might be paying her a tribute that was justified, was nothing she could think or accept. Instead, all she felt was gratitude that he would be so kind, panic that he might go away. "Why can't it just keep being like this?"

"Why can't you take it for what it is?"

"What is it? If you say 'an interlude,' I'll throw you in the river."

"An episode then. A little respite from reality."

"But it *is* reality."

"No, it's not, my sweet." He pointed to the angled roofs across the river, the cloudless sky. "It's a postcard."

"Then it can keep being a postcard. It can be a series of postcards. A string of them, for as long as . . . as long as . . ."

"That's right," he said, when she hesitated. "Sometime we have to go home."

*   *   *

Their room had a wall of windows looking down at the river and the bright blue pool. Pink azaleas flocked the windowbox outside. In the room were three different vases filled with tropical flowers, mauve and lavender and white, the colors of the furniture and rugs. Everything was soft tones but the bright fruits set out on a plate, pomelo, a sturdier, more succulent variation of pink grapefruit that resisted the teeth, exploding against the tongue, lichee nuts, melon and mango. Bellman and stewards rapped on the door, presenting their cards, pressing offers of service. James hurried them away.

He laid her on the bed, and took off her clothes, sat on his haunches between her legs and spread her like the petals of an orchid, trailing his fingers slowly along her delicate folds. She was more stirred by that tender exploration than all the rubbing of genitals. And she began to understand what she really hungered for was skin, the solace of flesh, the warmth of simply touching. He studied her nether lips through heavy lids, looked so carefully she could feel his eyes, soft and subtle as his fingers. He took what seemed an infinity, not so much teasing as shifting her into gear, soothing her into wakefulness. And he murmured sounds that were less than words, and more than words. Little rivulets of contentment flowed from his lips, honeyed hums of pleasure that counterpointed her sighs. He drove her gently with his voice, as she moaned, spurring her on, lauding her for her passion, the love of life that twisted beneath his fingers. And then he covered her with his mouth, sealed her with his tongue. She screamed with ecstasy, shattered by a moment so complete she forgot that this was all there was to be, and didn't care.

Until it was over, when she whispered, "Why won't you come home with me?"

"Because it's only home to you. I don't belong there."

"You could if you wanted to. It's because you don't love me."

"Of course I love you," he said, after a long moment. "How could I help but love you?"

"How do I know you're not lying?"

They laughed.

*　　*　　*

For days laid out, like fruit on a plate, they laughed. Taking the boat trip up the river to Ayutthaya, the ancient capital of Siam, they laughed, in between lunching at a table crowded with other tourists, finding places on the boat where no one else was, to kiss. She climbed to the prow of the ship, next to the striped flag of Thailand. He took pictures of her. She took pictures of him taking pictures of her. And they laughed.

In Ayutthaya, they toured the temples with the group, pausing to stand for a moment in the shade of a giant banyan tree. In the garden of the temple, they left the tour, as he signaled her to fall behind. After everyone was gone, he lifted a chain that barred them from going any farther, and led her to a closed-off path. Picking a flower for her hair, he set it among the strands, touched her lips, then backed off and took another picture.

He moved around the garden, kneeling, snapping pictures of reclining Buddhas, sitting Buddhas, while she watched him from her perch, on a giant Buddha palm. She heard the whirr of his camera as the roll finished. He came toward her, winding, stood in front of her, raised her to her feet, and kissed her. "Turn around."

"Are you crazy? What if someone comes?"

"Exactly my intention," he said, lifting her skirt. And they laughed.

"What would Buddha say?"

"As long as we didn't hurt anybody, I'm sure he would say it was fine." His hands were on her breasts, and he was inside her.

"Leave the flower," he said, when it was over.

For seven days, they made love, and laughed, exploring gilt-roofed temples, climbing pyramids set with pieces of porcelain plates. They ate fruit carved into flowers, watermelons sculptured into giant roses, papayas whittled into leaves. They hung temple doors and the toes of the colossal Reclining Buddha with fragrant flowers fashioned by native hands into beaded wreaths. Everything was art. Marketplaces offered vegetables arranged on great metal pans like exotic terrain, mountains of purple eggplant tumbling into hills of cucumbers, white radishes, turnips. Banana leaves held five colors of tiny chilies, bright green peas rolled from their shells, mounds of yellow and red tomatoes. Even the fish, dried and shredded, was laid on newspapers like a mosaic, to match the mosaics on the temple walls.

And there was shrimp, hot spicy beef, mysterious omelets, curries. And in the morning, six kinds of honey, some dark with a heavy molasses overlay, some light, with the taste of orange blossoms. Twelve kinds of bread.

And there was Patpong, the long, neon-lit red-light district, a solid street of cafés where gorgeous young girls with magnificent breasts danced naked, made love to Coke bottles, blew smoke rings from their vaginas. "I have to get out of here," Claire said. "It's too sad."

"Not for them," James told her, as they walked down the street. "It's just a way to make money. You don't understand poverty."

"I understand women."

"You understand women like you. Not everyone puts their heart in it."

"What about you?" she asked, against his chest, in the moonlit darkness of their room. "Do you put your heart in it?"

"Why do you ask so many questions?"

"Because I want the answers."

"No, you don't. You want the answer you want. You think if you ask often enough, you'll get it."

"Aren't you happy?"

"Of course I am."

"Why couldn't it continue?"

"Because life is when the holiday is over."

"It doesn't have to be."

"You're such a little girl. You want everybody to live happily ever after."

"No, I don't," Claire said. "I just want them to live."

The great annual Festival of Lights, *Loy Krathong*, was held on the evening of the full moon of the twelfth lunar month, coinciding with their visit. It was Thailand's greatest celebration, but as far as Claire was concerned, it was happening just for her.

Now she was convinced, or had convinced herself, it was not just she who had a romantic heart. Ahead of them lay a night consecrated just to wishes. Everyone in Bangkok was making a *krathong*, banana leaf covering polyurethane, lotus-shaped mosaics fashioned from thousands of tiny flowers, topped with lanterns, candles and incense, to light and set afloat as offerings to the Goddess of the River, and the Lord Buddha. And love. Claire was sure they had to wish for love. For all the poverty and illness and spiritual longing in evidence around her, she was sure what everyone really wanted was love.

All over Thailand, except for the areas swollen with floods, there was joyful preparation, the measured work of gifted hands. Bad luck was supposed to be given to the river, floating it away. Claire was already filled with the mythology, court stories of ancient Siam, a lady-in-waiting who created a *krathong* so magnificent she caught the eye of the King. Lovers used the night to forecast the future of their relationships: if their *krathongs* were carried down the river side by side, so would they be. If they drifted apart, it was an omen.

There was a wish to be made by moonlight for each of them, Claire and James. A wish to celebrate the November moon. Moonlight, candlelight, starlight. How could he resist her? Where did he have to go, really? Deluded as she was by her passion for him, she could still see the trouble he was in. She was only infatuated, not unaware. She could feel how empty his life and his heart really were. All around him she sensed the specters of women who hadn't given him enough, or seen him as the prize he was, except for the grandmother who'd died too soon. Why couldn't Claire make up for all the rest, covering him with the affection and caring he deserved? Wasn't that the job of women, really, to shore up the crumbling walls of men's confidence, to make them feel as whole as they only pretended to be? Certainly the world had changed, women's roles had changed, Claire at the forefront of the changes, without meaning to be. But wasn't the heart still the center, and weren't women's hearts stronger, maybe because they had less strain on them, but mostly because they were more open?

Without telling James, she bought two *krathongs*, one for herself, and one for him. She made a wish on his that he would wish for her.

He'd seemed very pleased with himself all during their stay, making reservations in all the best and most expensive places, the good fortune he'd come into with his stock having unleashed on him a show of generosity that bordered on flamboyance. He was buying gifts for Claire, clothes for himself, lavishly tipping everyone in the hotel. "Outstanding!" he would say to the bellman bringing them their daily offering of fruit. "Excellent service!" he said to the concierge. "I congratulate you on your staff." All of it seemed a euphoric balm to him, this chance to once more tread through the avenues of privilege, overdoing. It seemed to Claire a little prodigal, but she said nothing, seeing how happy it made him, being extravagant.

The full moon rose in the darkening sky above the terrace where they dined, the opulent section of the river alongside the hotel. Children were already swimming in the polluted waters, river urchins waiting for the first *krathongs*, hoping to help float them safely on their way in exchange for coins. A trio of saffron-robed monks made their way upstream in a water taxi, heads bowed in meditation, while from the restaurant across the way came the bell-like music of the dance.

"What a country this is," James said. He was looking particularly elegant, having bought himself an expensive blue silk shirt, greatly overpriced, which took some doing in Bangkok, where clothes were still reasonable, as they no longer were in Hong Kong. The collar was soft, open at the neck, framing his cleft chin and jaw as though with a ribbon, giving him the prize for masculine beauty. "All the contrasts of the human spirit. Caught between its love of pleasure, and its hope of God."

"No reason we can't combine both, is there?" Claire asked.

"No reason *you* can't."

"I'm not that different from you."

"Of course you are. You're a great sentimental lump."

"I don't know why you'd say that." She reached underneath the table, and lifted the two *krathongs*, presenting him with his.

He smiled, with an edge of tolerance.

From the lobby came the sound of stringed instruments, as the parade of hotel employees, beautiful young dark-eyed women, bare-shouldered, in vibrant silks, jeweled scarves, and golden coronets marched beside the stewards bearing their giant *krathongs*. Orchids twisted high into parapets of castles, blossoms rose into minarets, dancing goddesses arched, reaching for the god Siva. Each *krathong*, like the women who had made it, was more dazzling than the next.

"Shall we follow?" James asked, and, lifting up his *krathong*, moved after the parade, toward the river.

"You see, you're just as excited about it as I am," she said, hurrying behind him, carrying her offering.

"No reason not to get into the spirit. I suppose you'll want to make a wish."

"I've already made it." The sound of stringed instruments whined across the water. On the other side, lights outlined the shapes of temples, tiny white bulbs danced through the branches of trees.

She set hers on the dock, and lit a match, moving it toward the candle. Dark-eyed, thin-armed children, ragged clothes floating around them, waited in the water to receive her *krathong*. "I wish—"

"I thought you already made it."

"I wish that James would want it too." She knelt and, reaching over the edge, set her *krathong* in the water.

"You are hopeless," James said, lighting his candle, setting it beside hers.

The children floated them away from the dock, moved them into the stream of *krathongs* candlelighting the darkness of the water, like illuminated lotuses on a pond. "Now, if they stay together..." Claire started to say.

He touched her hand. There was in the gesture at once a reassurance, and a tender halting. They both already knew what she wanted to say, had said too often already.

She watched the two *krathongs* float away from the dock, not breathing. A motorboat went by. The waves lapped over and put the candles out.

"Not to worry," he said, kindly. "It doesn't mean a thing." His arm was around her now, lovingly, as if he would vanquish the disappointment, argue with it, since it was not destiny's job to rid her of expectations, but his own.

"I say, James!" The voice was whining and familiar. They turned and saw Roger, the young Brit who had been in the lobby the day of their arrival. "I see you're taking this thing quite seriously."

"I enjoy participating in local customs," James said.

"Well, maybe one of those floating things can turn your luck around. I certainly hope so. What a let-down, yes?"

"I beg your pardon?"

"I read about that China computer business. Rotten break."

"What?"

"The educational system you told me about. Your stock. Didn't you see this morning's *Journal*?"

"We're on holiday," Claire said coldly.

"There was a huge announcement about China using this new computer system for education, just as you said. But it's not the one from your company. They lost the bid."

"Don't be ridiculous," said James. "They probably just used a different name."

"Not at all. A totally different group got the contract. Japanese. There's a great brouhaha about it. The stock's absolutely plummeted."

"I've got to call Hong Kong," James said, blanching. "Excuse me."

"But the fireworks . . ." Claire said.

"You watch them. I'll see you in the room."

She turned back to the river, sick to her spirit. All around her were the beauties of a great celebration; all she could feel was her own sense of loss. Hers were the lights that went out, with James's. How could she rejoice? The water was aglow with the blaze of hundreds of candles, none of them hers. The air was alilt with music and laughter and songs, none of them hers. Suddenly the sky was flashing with fireworks, streaking arcs and circles and spheres of silver and green. Trailing stars across the moon, showering lovers on the shore. None of them hers. None of them hers. None of them hers.

TWENTY-THREE

♦

Well, maybe Biff hadn't had enough influence at the goddamned Mandarin Hotel to find out Erica Thorr's room number, but he certainly had connections in the good old U.S. of A. He'd gotten information about her passport through a friend in the State Department. She hadn't even had a passport before the one that carried her to Hong Kong. So sophisticated as she looked, and high as her nose was in the air, she was no world traveler, that much was obvious. Knowing now that her city of origin was Philadelphia, Biff had run a credit check on her there through a buddy at Wanamaker's and discovered she didn't have any. Not even a bad rating. *No* plastic. None at all.

So where had the clothes come from, and the jewelry, and the airfare? He had friends in high places, literally, when it came to the airlines. All of them owed him something. He'd found out she'd traveled Cathay Pacific in early October. Her ticket had been charged to a Biddy Rittenhauser.

"You any relation to Bill?" he asked Biddy on the telephone, after he'd introduced himself, not telling her what he wanted, but being Texas gracious enough to get her to talk to him.

"He's my ex-husband," she said coldly. "Is that what this call is about? Because if you want to discuss anything about Bill, you should call his fiancée. She'll be glad to talk to you right after her two o'clock feeding."

"No, ma'am. That's not why I'm calling. You know a woman named Erica Thorr?"

There was a pause. "Yes, I do. Is anything wrong?"

"Well, that depends, ma'am. She must be a very good friend of yours, for you to have paid for her ticket."

"It was a loan," Biddy said. "Is she saying I paid for her?"

"It's not so much what she's saying, as how she's acting, ma'am. It just seemed peculiar to me that a woman of your obvious breeding would associate with someone of that type."

"What exactly is she doing?"

"Well, to begin with, she's hanging around with a slime who's a fallout from the Drexel Burnham disaster." That intelligence had been a little easier to nail down. The least he was determined to do in exchange for that brutal handshake was to ruin the bastard's reputation. "A junk bond junkie. Sort of a contemporary Robin Hood. Robbing the rich to give to the rich. Mostly himself."

"Isn't that just good business?"

"He's about to be indicted, Mrs. Rittenhauser." That part of it wasn't public yet, but Biff had made a lot of phone calls to move things in that direction, including several to Hong Kong where the news hadn't traveled yet. Lockwood Alexander hadn't known whose hand he was grasping. Wrestling Biff to the floor like a wimp, mistaking him for a punk without strength or influence. It would turn out to be a very costly victory, that little *mano a mano*, or Biff didn't understand the games he had learned in Texas.

"What's your stake in this?" Biddy was asking.

"Stake, ma'am? I have no stake. I just don't like those who take advantage of innocent people. It fires me up."

Glass and aluminum clad, the HongKong and Shanghai Banking Corporation towered above Queens Road, Central, like some futuristic robot diplomat, five welcoming smiles on its metal face. Rising forty-seven floors above the street, descending four below, the HongKong

Bank, as it was more usually known, captured daylight by means of a mirrored external sunscoop that followed the sun around. The ground floor was a public plaza, an amenity that gave the bank an extra 20 percent of area, besides its million square feet. Inside a spectacular atrium ascended, 170 feet high, through all eleven levels up to the giant mirrors, reflecting natural sunlight down onto the main floor of the bank, adding light as carefully as sound was managed through acoustical engineering. The building was considered a miracle of high-tech architectural design. The only thing more impressive than the glass and light and air, the crossed metal bands, the suspended groups of floors, was the power contained therein.

The higher floors were guarded with a not-very-veiled secrecy, secretaries closing the flanks, security guards monitoring the walkways that led to the elevators up to the executive floors, their guns making conspicuous bulges beneath their jackets.

A basic snobbism percolated through the operation. Three in-house master chefs performed their culinary magic just for the employees. The bank was too good for a bank. Too good for a kingdom, really, in its own estimation. Like the lightweight movable panels throughout, floated the conviction that rudeness was defensible when couched in the very best language: the arrogance of those who assumed that flawless manners excused one from a basic sense of decency.

There were touches of brightness splashing the black and silver in and out trays, the same fire red as the cardigan sweaters secretaries wore. Wells Fargo bronze sculptured coaches, six horses and driver, sat around on tables. Occasional palm trees softened the coldness, filtered the silence from silver to green. But mostly the decor spoke of the cleansing effect of money, which, when concentrated enough, gleaming out of enough glass and metallic lines and angles, served as a kind of balm.

For Lockwood Alexander, the HongKong Bank was a high-tech afterlife, raising his spirits, reinforcing his new assurance that there were unanticipated chances. The air of stylish independence that the architects of the bank had put into play became a part of his own bearing as he stepped onto one of a pair of escalators cutting through a curved, glazed floor up the main banking hall. In the plaza below, Filipino *amahs* celebrated their half day, chattering in the protecting vaulted shadow, crickets that had hummed through his burgeoning romance.

That he could even think in terms of that word surprised him. Like most of his confreres he had always been interested in action, not feelings. As his comparatively young life had been one of extraordinary gain, which in America was the highest form of action, he had seldom stopped to note what his emotions were. Living on adrenaline, as high rollers in business did, he responded to fear, excitement, anger. The tender passions had rarely come into his frame of reference. The very fact that he could pigeonhole passion, think of it in terms of a frame of reference, had been an indication of where the man was coming from.

But not anymore. Erica was in his life, and he was in hers. It was an extravagance he had never considered possible. The closest he had come to love had been possessiveness and jealousy, both of which he had suffered in good measure with the two ex-wives who were now riding out their settlements and alimony. To be experiencing such resonance, fullness of heart, the wish to make things perfect for her, was so unaccustomed as to make him feel drunk, which, in a way, he supposed he was. Almost drunk enough to forget why he'd come to Hong Kong.

He had wanted to tell Erica everything in the beginning, but she hadn't wanted to hear. No past, no history, she'd said. No confessions. Lockwood was not a dishonest man, no matter what the government was planning to allege. He'd wanted to present his demons. Longed to tell her what trouble he was in, what darkness there was on his spirit, how desperate he felt. But a man listened when a woman said she didn't want to know about the past, especially if the past had shadows that were about to swallow him. Particularly since he'd come to Hong Kong for a final fling, before packing it in.

Not that he was a coward. Not that he was guilty. But the trouble with RICO, the Racketeer Influence and Corrupt Organizations law, was that it didn't need to get to court to ruin a man. He was presumed guilty until proven innocent, his assets frozen, reputation irreparably damaged. The stigma of being compared to Al Capone, for the likes of whom the law had been enacted, was enough to destroy a man like Lockwood. The publicity alone, when the indictment was brought against him, a few weeks down the line, would obliterate everything he'd taken his professional life to build.

Pride was his spine. Pride was behind the way he looked at the world, watching how the world looked at him. All that had mattered to him was the pride he'd had in the way he did business. That was what his life was about. At least it had been that way before he met Erica. Business wasn't just the American dream, it was also the American stomach: a man digested his food well because he was succeeding. They were about to kill him, kill his image, kill his business. Though he was sure he would be proven innocent of any criminal intent or actual wrongdoing, he had not been able to imagine living through the humiliation. Like the Japanese, he believed that the greatest degradation that could happen to a man was to go on trial. Who could go comfortably through hostile scrutiny, the garbage of his life picked over, and come out looking good, smelling clean? A Japanese man had to settle a case on the courthouse steps, or, quite often, committed hara-kiri. That was why Lockwood had come to Hong Kong. That was what he meant to do, before he met Erica.

His was a white-collar crime, if it was a crime at all, but they would accord him treatment appropriate for a mafioso. So he had determined to have one last expensive hurrah, encamping in the Mandarin for a final self-indulgence, the self-indulgence he had never before permitted himself, so busy was he succeeding. The things he knew he would be accused of, insider trading, shorting the market, were winked at by most traders. But he hadn't been able to think of dealing with the mortification. So he had come to Hong Kong to die, as earlier followers of poesy had made their last stop Naples. The last great rush a man needed to experience.

And then he'd met Erica. Felt more than the will to live, felt the urgency of life. The understanding, finally, what life was about: a sense of connection not just with someone else but with someone who connected you to yourself. Who could make you feel you were back in business, on every level. Including the one he would embark on in this meeting.

So his mood was euphoric, his faith in the future restored. More than restored, generated for the first time. He was not a man who'd dealt in terms of faith, but always overriding doubt. This was a new beginning for him.

He made his way up toward the mast towers, high-speed elevators stopping at five intermediate levels, so programmed by the building's architects, to provide a more sociable way of moving through the various zones. Forcing visitors to take escalators, circulating them through areas designed to seem like microcosms of cosmopolitan villages. Because Lockwood's prospects seemed so alive to him, he was unaccustomedly enjoying the visual adventure. Ordinarily he would have clenched his teeth at not being zoomed directly to where he was going. All his adult life had been about being driven, fixed on his destination. Finally, he was enjoying the journey.

In the elevator, lights ran across the control board, flashing the prices on the Hong Kong stock exchange index, partly controlled by the bank. He noted how cool the building was, a different kind of coolness from that brought on by most of the air-conditioning in Hong Kong. Less chill in the air than comfort. "That is because we use sea water," said the Scot who greeted him outside the elevator, ushering him into an executive suite. "We bring it in from the harbor through a specially built tunnel." He pointed to the bay as he spoke, through a wall made completely of glass, flooding the room with hazy golden light, the special glow of Asia. "It all contributes to energy effectiveness."

"Energy effectiveness . . ." Lockwood let the phrase hang in the air as he sat down. He could feel renewed confidence, along with the cool. Nobody knew yet what trouble he was in; by the time they did, he was convinced he would be out of it. "Energy effectiveness is part of the technological brilliance the company I came to talk to you about has to offer."

The Scot consulted the proposal on the table. "Millennium Technology?"

"It's a good name for the outfit. They're worth much more than we can get them for."

"The price?"

"Three billion would take it."

"And the market value?"

"About a billion and a half. They've got the answer to cleaning up nuclear waste. Forty years we've been covering that one up. Everybody knows it's there, and nobody can fix it. But this company can. My group is ready to put up a billion."

"So you're asking two billion from us?"

"It won't be long till you get it back. You have assets of fifty."

"Fifty-four," the Scot said, smiling. "We've had some recent good investments."

"This one will be better."

The Scot closed his eyes, moved his fingertips under his nose in a church-and-steeple gesture. "It sounds most interesting."

"More than interesting. Good for the world as well as the investors."

"I had heard that about you. That you are active in trying to save various ecosystems. Admirable."

"Not really. It's selfish. I'd like to breathe. I'd like to stay alive." Hearing the words now, he realized how much he did. He sat up straighter in the chair. "I'd like my children to be able to enjoy their planet."

"How many do you have?"

"None yet. But I've found the woman to remedy that."

"Congratulations."

"A little early." Lockwood smiled. "But soon."

"All this sounds promising."

"To me, too." Lockwood grinned. He was not a man who smiled easily. A great portion of his success was due to having an expression not easily read. But his facial muscles were out of control, happiness moving them to anarchy. He could not stop smiling.

"What doesn't sound so good . . . is a law we understand you have in your country. Some organization called RICO."

"RICO?" Lockwood tried to conceal his shock that the news had reached Hong Kong.

"We have watched you for a number of years, admired your success. But our bank has a reputation to uphold." He stood and offered his hand. "We wish you good luck in finding your financing."

"What I want to know. . . what all of us in the Syndicate want to know, is why you've wasted your time, the clothes we bought you, the jewels we loaned you, the hotel room we're paying for, and *that* body, on some son of a bitch who's going to jail." In spite of being just slightly over five feet tall, Biddy Rittenhauser was a formidable woman, the muscles missing from her body seemingly relocated in the square of her jaw, which her ex-husband had compared to a snapping turtle's. There was nothing turtlelike about her move-ments, however: they were staccato and filled with energy as she paced the hotel room, in spite of the jet lag she should have had. Her lids were also far from the heavy, slow ones of a tortoise, wide open, the eyes behind them trained on Erica like a searchlight. But Biddy's head was still in Philadelphia, twelve hours behind, so every once in a while it would nod, like a puppet's on a loose string, before she jolted it to attention.

"I don't understand what you're saying," Erica said.

"Why did we think you were so bright?" Biddy lit a cigarette with short, snapping motions, blowing the smoke out of her finely carved nostrils, which plastic surgeons had used as their ideal several generations before, for those who had not been born with such a nose. "Were we so impressed by how you looked, we confused it with brains?"

"I went to college," said Erica, angrily.

"And did what with it? Got a job at a country club."

"Not all of us had ex-husbands who could pop for a membership."

"That's right." She paced, inhaling, blowing smoke out through her nostrils. "But we were ready to fix that. Set you up like no one's ever been set up. And out of all the heavyweights who pass through Hong Kong, you come up with this loser."

"He's anything but a loser."

"What's your idea of winning? The best cell at San Quentin?

We've got seven futures at stake here. Eight, if you count yours. You owe us a ton of money. You made a deal."

"I'll pay you back."

"With what? How much do you think he'll have left when the government finishes with him, when his lawyers finish with him? You were supposed to find a rich husband. Cut your losses *now*. Before you get more involved with this man."

"I couldn't get more involved."

"Based on what? Sex? Sex is passing. People get older, people get bored."

"It's not like that with us."

"Of course not. Just like it wasn't like that with any of us and the men we married. Just like we weren't crazy to believe that because we gave them the best years of our lives, and a few of the worst, the bastards wouldn't dump us for a teenybopper."

"They're not called teenyboppers anymore."

"You don't have to show me that I'm out of it! If I want to feel out of it, I can talk to my children."

Time had not been kind to Biddy. Skin that had been soft enough for Pond's ads when she was seventeen, and a highly publicized debutante, had cracked in a lot of places. Like many women of her class, she was too vain to consider the vanity of having her face lifted, especially since she had once been the model for how ordinary people wished they looked. She was still thin, in a way that had seemed enviable in high school, when she had been the only one able to eat all the Ritz crackers and cheese she wanted, without gaining an ounce. But her thinness looked washboardy in middle age, reinforced in that slatted illusion by the dress she wore, gray challis, a light, costly wool that did nothing to make women look softer than they were, or, in Biddy's case, weren't. She still wore her hair as she had in college, parted on the left, held just to the right of the opposite temple with a flat barrette. But her dark hair had grown somewhat thinner and was streaked with gray, which she was also too proud, in a way she thought humble, to alter.

But the unkindest cut of all was the nickname she had permitted to stick. Invited, really, telling them at Miss Porter's that that was what they should call her. It had seemed a wry joke when she was the cutest one in high school, as distant as she was at the time from being a biddy. But it had become self-fulfilling prophecy.

"I don't believe what you told me about Lockwood," Erica said. "He's the finest man I've ever known."

"Well, I don't doubt that. How many princes can you meet, being a locker-room attendant?"

Erica's great green-yellow eyes narrowed, and her lips, thin to begin with, tightened into an angry slit. She was still in her bathrobe, her hair wet from the shower, freshly shampooed and hanging straight, so she looked very much the little girl she felt in Biddy's presence. "I'm sorry if my place in life doesn't meet with your approval."

"I don't give a shit about your place in life. That was about to change. This isn't just an investment for us. It's your big chance. Don't throw it away."

"I love him."

"Oh, come on." Biddy flopped down on the bed, kicked her shoes off, stretched her feet on the spread, dropped her cigarette into a vase of drobidium orchids. It sizzled. "I've been flying for twenty hours. It makes it easy to get nauseous."

"I didn't believe in it either. But miracles can happen."

"Bring me the wastebasket," Biddy said. She lifted herself on her elbows. "He's going to jail."

"For what?"

"For what men do. For what all our husbands did, only they were too smart to get caught, hiding their money in secret accounts, so not only couldn't the government find them, our lawyers couldn't either. But he's not even in their league. He's not even *cleverly* dishonest."

"What I love most," Erica said hotly, "is your sense of outrage. Your shining example. You think it's any better, what you ladies in the Syndicate were trying to put over?"

"You bet," said Biddy, and fell asleep.

Erica dressed, and waited for his call. No matter what he had done, she knew she would forgive him, that there was nothing to forgive him for really. It was business. What she didn't know was whether he could forgive her. How could any man excuse a woman who'd been as manipulative and scheming as she had been, weaving a web, with the help of seven bitter spiders. She was worse than the high-priced whore he'd brought the Texan to his knees for suggesting she was.

She spoke softly when the phone rang, so Biddy wouldn't wake up. She met Lockwood in the lobby.

They took the ferry to Kowloon, stood by the open window looking out at the water. They turned toward each other. "I have something to tell you," they said, together.

TWENTY-FOUR

◆

Having always been a realist, Judith was finally starting to participate in and cherish fantasy. Returning from China, she understood how essential to the spirit and body luxury was. A hot bath, after her spartan sojourn in Beijing, had become like lover's arms after a lifetime of celibacy. She was using bubble bath and sweet-smelling oils, considering as staples what she had once categorized as profligate. For anything to bloom, she saw now, it needed the option of excess. The grayness of China, the silent resignation of the people, the swarm of bicycles with joyless riders, had made her hunger for splash, the noisiness of Hong Kong, the happy depravity of pink Rolls-Royces. She had hardly been able to wait to get back to a place where she could spend too much money.

In the same way, she was starting to comprehend that exotic places were not necessarily of foreign nature or character, as the strict dictionary definition would have had it. Claire had paraded that by her before leaving for Bangkok, trying to spell out for herself what exactly Judith had meant by "exotic places," and her assertion that James was only for those. Nor were they necessarily strange, or glamorous, both of which adjectives would have applied to Beverly Hills, giving Claire the sanction to take him there. Exotic places, Judith was beginning to feel now, were anywhere you felt alive, where you couldn't wait to get up in the morning because something unexpected might happen.

What was most unexpected for her was how happy she had felt at seeing Clement again. She supposed that was sort of a fringe effect of her other perceptions, that what she had considered fat and extraneous might be essential, that delicious was basic, that the soul had appetites the body could feed, in the right setting. She had quietly rejoiced at how interested he was, how open, after all the diffidence of China, the deliberate inscrutability. A touch had never felt more like a touch than after such cold distance, personal, political, social. Perhaps, as once the message had been that the truth would set you free, so much monitoring of truth had made her desperate for real communication.

So when Clement called now, she didn't put him off, no matter how busy she was, how backed up the pile of papers on her desk, how many unreturned phone calls there were in the message tray by her computer. He had gotten the number of her private line without her giving it to him, an ingenuity she might once have bristled at. In spite of his role as policeman she had not liked the idea of his being able to police too much about her. But now she was pleased when the phone rang, knowing it was either him or some very hot story she was authorized to get on, since no one else had that number but New York.

"I need you to come with me for some legwork on the Black's Link case," he was saying. "I got a tip. A call from a restaurant. Come with me."

"Seducer." She noted a certain playfulness in her language to him now, a flirtation that had not been there before. It was the kind of thing you could get away with with men when you weren't really interested. She wondered if it was as comfortable for them when you were.

"I wish," he said. "It's only lunch. But it is the best restaurant in Kowloon."

"There were four of them," said the maître d'. He was a Cantonese, in his forties. "They were young boys. One of them very young.

Under sixteen maybe. The biggest one was boasting he had had a white girl, and it didn't . . ." His eyes moved to Judith, and he hesitated.

"It's all right," said Clement. "She's a journalist. She doesn't take anything personally."

They had ordered their lunch: simple, easy-to-prepare dishes that were for the proprietor a form of fast food. McDonald's had opened just down the street, creating a certain awe and anxiety in the neighborhood. Better restaurants, which this one was, had made a point of asserting that there was no substitute for quality, an American phrase that had traveled not quite as well as the hamburger franchise. Still, the chef had learned to speed up his procedure, and the waiters were already asking customers how much time they had, before recommending dishes.

"He said . . ." The maître d' avoided looking at Judith. "It didn't seem any different. Or better."

"And they were flashing a student identity card?"

"Yes. Saying they should offer it for sale. That any identity papers were better than what Hong Kong Belongers had. They were very noisy. Drunk, maybe, the older ones. They kept handing out tips to the waiters. Showing off."

"You have any idea what their names were? Where they lived?"

"Around here, I think. One of them said he passed this place all the time, but this was the first chance he'd had to eat here. The first time he'd had enough money. He said he'd just gotten a promotion."

"Did you see the picture on the student identity card?"

"Not close. Not well. But they were waving it around. There was a girl's picture on it. Gweilo. Blond.

"Then, this morning one of the waiters came and asked me if I could cash this for him." He handed Clement a chip. It was a hundred-dollar gambling chip from the Paradise Casino in Macau.

"So they had access to Harry Magic's apartment," Clement said.

He was walking with Judith on Nathan Road, his hand eased informally through her arm, a casual gesture that no longer felt so casual to Judith. She had made too much of a point of physically distancing herself from him in the beginning for him not to be noticing how receptive she was now. She was starting to feel in his presence as she did on the occasional Sunday night—oh, maybe, once or twice a year—when she caught up, the story was finished, or dead, and she could make a phone call she didn't have to make. How enviable her career had to seem, she realized, everyone imagining she was flouncing around to all these exciting places, when in reality her life was a series of hotel rooms and planes and computers and faxes. "Exotic" was starting to seem to her to be a picket fence. Well, not really. That was a little extreme, even for one who was going noticeably soft. Maybe just a comfortable place that she felt was really her own, where she could put fresh flowers, and her feet up, close to someone else's.

"How can you be sure they had access?" she asked Clement.

"These boys were too young to gamble, to go to the casinos in Macau by themselves. They must have taken the chips from the cache I found in Harry Magic's drawer. Whoever was in there with Wendy. Whoever threw her off the balcony."

"And the same person was definitely on Black's Link?"

"She told me I was looking for her boyfriend. I don't think he killed her because he didn't like her shoes. Although they were, as you ladies say, a bit much." He moved her away from the curb, closer to the window of the shop they were passing, nodding in the direction of the bright array of shoes set on Lucite stands, arranged in a kind of dance, some of them balletic, others splay-footed, as though the invisible inhabitants of the window were at a party. "You'd look good in those. Second from the left."

"They're frivolous," Judith said.

"Sometimes frivolous is sensible."

"True. But it's enough I took a long lunch. Don't get me started window-shopping. I've lived here almost a decade and managed not to get hooked."

"Then you're missing the fun," Clement said. "You're missing one of the great joys of life in Hong Kong."

"Not the only one," Judith said, and, kissing him quickly, ducked into a taxicab.

*   *   *

"This is herbal tea for the kidneys," Dao said, pouring. "Sex comes from the kidneys."

In the next room, the old woman waxed the floors, grumbling.

"Maybe you should give some to her," Clement said.

"I don't want to encourage her."

"But you want to encourage me?"

"You have to be clear. Confusion also comes from the kidneys." He put the cup in front of Clement. "Be very sure what you want from Judith. What you want from yourself. This will cleanse your confusion."

The old woman got up from the floor, rubbing her knees, bringing her rag and the can of polish to Dao, her steps measured and obviously pained. She started speaking rapidly in Mandarin, a dialect Clement did not understand well. But there was no mistaking the complaint in her tone, the annoyance in her words.

"Nobody asks her to keep the floors polished," Dao said, his usually peaceful expression beleaguered. "Why do they do what you don't ask them to do, and then complain how hard it is?"

"You're the wise man. I only try to solve crimes, not the puzzle of women."

"So the murderers are young? And Cantonese?"

"It looks that way," said Clement sadly. "These boys had a Gweilo's student identity card. They bragged about having a white woman. They tipped with chips from Harry Magic's apartment, where Wendy Lu was murdered. She said I was looking for her old boyfriend. He was probably one of them."

The old woman shook her rag in Dao's face, her words rapid-fire and whining. Dao pushed her hand aside, and softly spoke language Clement grasped to be not as gentle as the tone. "It's because of Chen's hobby," Dao explained. "She says she cannot keep the floors bright because of his hobby. I tell her to forget the floors. She tells me to get him to forget about his hobby. She understands no more about young boys than she does about old men."

"What hobby?"

"His dancing."

"I didn't know he danced."

"He's quite good at it," said Dao. *"Tit ta wu."*

"A Chinese dance?"

"No. I just don't know the word in English."

The old woman put the rag to her nose, and started to weep. "Oh, dear," said Dao. "What shall I do?"

"Get him to stop his *tit ta wu,* whatever it is. Or put your arm around her. That's all she really wants, is comfort."

Dao took his liver-spotted hand, and put it on her shoulder. He sighed. "Wouldn't it be nice if that was all they really wanted."

The Veranda Room in the Peninsula Hotel was a long, elegant restaurant that once had had a view of the harbor. Now it overlooked the new Space Museum. Much of the Kowloon side seemed as though the architects of the territory deliberately had chosen to block with their vision of the future what was beautiful about the present. Erica tried not to do the same.

She ate her lunch pretending to taste it, looked into Lockwood's eyes hoping they would stay as loving as they were, as grayly blue, free from judgment. But there was no way he wouldn't despise what she had done.

She hardly heard what he said about the trouble he was in. Her mind was racing ahead to how exactly she could tell him without his hating her. Vaguely she got a sense of the government being after him, tying up his assets, planning to conduct a trial that, even if he managed to be acquitted, would ruin him. None of it seemed that terrible to her, being only business. The Syndicate had given her a good education in how businessmen behaved, and the truth was, they didn't. That was what made it business. People did what would profit them. Women in love were supposed to be different.

He finished talking. He waited. She saw he was expecting some reaction. His features were tight, a slight grimace at the corners of his mouth, as though he were getting ready to wince when she spoke her disdain.

"Why did you come to Hong Kong if you're in so much trouble?" she asked him.

"To have a last holiday. The one I'd always been too busy to
have."

"Before you went to jail?"

"Before I went out the window."

"Oh, my darling." She took his hand, turned it, and kissed his
palm, pressed it to her cheek. "Nothing's that bad."

"What did you want to tell me?"

She hesitated. "You've been set up."

"I don't understand."

"Seven women. Seven corporate wives, whose husbands dumped
them, got together and bankrolled me for this trip. I was supposed
to nail a rich husband, and they were going to share in the profits.
I'm a leveraged buyout." She averted her eyes as she spoke, so she
wouldn't see the contempt in his.

To her astonishment, he started laughing.

Maggie took the ferry to Lantau Island to pray for her baby. Because
of the miracle that she was sure was bringing Betsy back to her,
Maggie had decided to forgive God. But not so much that she could
go back to Saint John's. The minister seemed a good man but he was
caught in his orthodoxy, and would probably try to shake her
conviction that there was reincarnation, that the baby inside her was
the one she has lost.

So she crossed the water, which was, in itself, a kind of a
rebirth, on her way to hills and forests and wilds, temples that
housed her new belief that a soul returned. The day was gray and
overcast, puffy white clouds making inroads on the steel of the sky.
In the distance, hills loomed in dark metal tones, echoing the colors
above them. She stood at the rail, dressed in baptismal white, a
collar of thick wire wound with hot pink satin around her throat,
matching her neon pink earrings, so though she might appear
virginal, God would recognize her.

The sea was a grayish green, quietly turbulent. All the way to
Lantau she spoke to Betsy, without speaking aloud, describing the
wonder of the day, dull as was its disguise. A whole new school of
thinking had arisen since the first time Maggie gave birth, believing

that a baby was in tune with its mother from conception time. So the sooner she spoke to her, she was convinced, the closer would be their tie, the more alive the child would be. Betsy had been so bright the first time, her eyes luminous from the moment they could focus. Maggie had chatted her up from babyhood, as if she were even then the sociable creature she was to become. Bright and ready for witty exchanges, even in her teens.

Well, this time, she would not only be lovely and cheerful, but go very deep. They had never really explored each other's thinking, the mother assuming there would be plenty of time when the daughter got older, which of course, she hadn't had a chance to do, the daughter probably figuring there was not that much her mother would understand. Otherwise surely she would have come to her, opened her heart, told Maggie how needy she felt, how desperate for someone to lean on, so she wouldn't have to go to the Peak and be murdered.

Well, all that was behind them now. They were doing it again, right this time. The wind had changed. The prow of the ship headed for the quiet lagoon that was the entrance to Lantau Island. The beach was edged with two- and three-story apartment buildings, the shore bright with fishing boats returned from their morning catch. One last stubborn mantle of leaden haze clung to the highest hill. But as the hill sloped into a valley to the east, there were patches of sapphire. Cornflower blue, actually, the color of Betsy's eyes. Maggie wondered what color the eyes would be this time, which of the many men she'd been with had fathered her baby. Oh, she could hardly wait to begin buying the layette, so she could dress her, spoil her all over again, but this time with too much attention. Never letting her wander off on her own, or with someone who couldn't protect her.

Maggie stopped for lunch at Charlie Tong Fuk Store, making sure that her belly would not have a sour moment. The two-storied, blue-shuttered wooden building had a canopied veranda, covering two tables, serving as a restaurant. Little lights, unlit, were strung to the sides of the umbrellas, awaiting some festivity. She ordered prawns, which Betsy loved, and ate without appetite.

"Well, hello." A smiling, white-shirted, Bermuda-shorted Englishman stopped his bicycle at the entrance to the restaurant.

"Ciao. Goodbye. You're too late."

"Beg pardon?"

"I'm not in the market. Case closed. Position filled."

"You work here?"

"I'm eating my lunch."

"Mind if I join you?"

"I told you. I'm not interested. You should have come along six weeks ago when the job was still open."

"What job was that?"

"Planter. Tiller of the soiled."

"You're not being very hospitable to a countryman far from home." He got off his bicycle, and stood beside her table.

He was a nice-looking man, Maggie could not help noting, his legs strong and muscular, covered with a light brownish down. Ordinarily she might have found him attractive, if it hadn't been for her new conviction, and the slight nausea she felt. She hoped Betsy wasn't going to do that again, give her morning sickness. "I have no need to be hospitable, since I neither welcome you, nor care what happens to you."

"How rude."

"I think it's honest. So often we act only out of our needs and desires, but fortunately I no longer have those."

"No desires?" He sat down.

"Well, I do have one. I wish you would go away."

"But here we are, in this out-of-the-way place, and we have the good luck to meet . . ."

"How do you know it's good luck?"

"I've been feeling lonely."

"Are you staying in Hong Kong?"

He nodded.

"There's a million bars with a million girls. The phone book is full of escort services and massage parlors."

"I'm looking for something different. Companionship. Conversation."

"Excuse me. I have to throw up." She got to the bathroom just in time.

*   *   *

When she got back, he was gone. She took a taxi up a winding hill that led to the Buddhist temple. A water buffalo rooted among the succulents by the side of the road, his black nose stained with sand and dust. Trees splayed midway up their gray-brown trunks offered forked visions of the trees beyond. A Buddhist shrine on the edge of a hill framed mountains to the west, while, in its shadow, an orange-robed, shaven-haired monk meditated.

"Oh, isn't it good to be alive, Betsy!" Maggie said. "Aren't we going to have fun."

The taxi driver said something in Cantonese. "No, it's all right. I'm not talking to you. I'm talking to my little girl who's in my belly. Are you Buddhist? You understand the principles. A soul unfulfilled, and all that, having to come back. We have to come back till we get it right, isn't that how it works? Betsy didn't have a chance to get it right. That wasn't her fault, it was mine. But God is merciful sometimes. So he's giving us both another chance. Baby," she said, patting her belly, repeating the word in Cantonese.

He grinned, and looked at her in the rearview mirror, repeating the word.

"Right," she said. "One of the few words of yours I know. Not very farsighted of me, really, living here all these years and not learning your language. Can you forgive me? Is forgiveness Buddhist? Or is it only we Christians who are stuck with that one?"

"Baby," he said, again, and giggled.

"Why are you laughing? Is it because you know the stork doesn't bring babies, and you think sex is dirty? Or is it only we Christians who are stuck with that one?"

In front of the steps to the temple, two great black iron tubs sat filled with incense burning in sand. Maggie took a whiff of it: the sweet scent of hyacinths, Betsy's favorite flower. White balustrades bordered the concrete stairway, up to the carved orange wood of the temple's double doors, each door set with curving twin ovals of glass on the top half, miniature repetitions below. Scrolled writing in gold on lapis lazuli fronted the gold-painted roof. And everywhere were flowers, potted roses, white spider mums, pools afloat with lotuses, scarlet against the water.

"But it's me!" She pointed. "A lotus. Out of the mud! Redemption!"

In the center hall, a great gold Buddha rose out of a carved gold lotus, the air around him hung with thick gold ribbon lengths, edged in royal blue, embroidered with scarlet lotuses. It seemed so generous, the temple giving Maggie back her personal theme. The poetry of her own imagination: lotuses. Coming back at her from every direction, assaulting her with the truth of what she hoped for, that there was a plan, a design, not only to art, but to the universe, a beneficent mind behind it. The realization came to her in gold-leafed fragments, lotuses, crashing against her eyes, battering her mind. "Oh, thank You, thank You, thank You," she cried out, and fell to her knees weeping.

Maybe what God had really wanted was a Prodigal Daughter. Sailing into the soft light of dusk, with the sun passing behind the once-again thickening clouds, turning the waveless sea silver, Maggie felt such a rush of love for what was above her, and what was inside her, she could hardly contain her joy. She blew a kiss to the sky.

"Well, I'm glad you have some affection in you," a man said.

She turned and saw the Englishman who'd been on the bicycle, standing on the deck behind her. "Ciao, hello," she said, grudgingly.

"You could open a school, you know. How to kill a conversation. Get rid of a man no matter how attractive he finds you. 'I have to throw up,'" he quoted. "That *will* do it."

"I did have to throw up."

"I heard that was the best restaurant in Lantau. The safest place to eat."

"It is. It was."

"What made you ill?"

"It's the most natural thing in the world. I'm pregnant."

"How old are you?"

"None of your bloody business."

"Look, I'm not trying to insult you. You're extremely attractive. But I'm a gynecologist. Have you seen your doctor?"

"I don't have to. I'm perfectly healthy."

"Then you don't know for sure?"

"Of course I know. I've been through this before. I recognize the symptoms."

"But it could be something else. Something dangerous. At your age . . ."

"I happen to be very young at heart."

"I have no doubt of it. But spirit and body are separate things."

"Not if you're lucky," Maggie said, smiling. Her expression changed to anger. "I've had enough of your arrogance. Your sureness that *you* are in charge."

"Me?"

"All of you. I *know* who's in charge." She turned her back to him. "Go away."

"Very well. But do yourself a kindness. See your doctor."

"Thank you for your solicitousness," she said.

The lounge of the Holiday Inn in Kowloon was featuring a singer who was a Helen Reddy soundalike, which struck Louise as particularly funny since she considered Helen Reddy a Helen Reddy soundalike. Still, for one of the few times in her life, Louise did not make a crack, even though the Count wouldn't have understood it. He seemed so happy to have brought her there, to this place he imagined would make her feel at home, decorated like the lounges in Las Vegas, with palm fronds and brass spittoons, and people that looked like hoods.

The singer was Chinese. She had her hair cut short, in the manner of Helen Reddy when she had first become a star, asserting that she was Woman. The Chinese girl wore satin pants and a beaded, loose top, overbeaded with silver leaves. Silver leafed earrings hung from her lobes to her shoulders. She held a hand mike close to her heavily glossed lips with her right hand, stretching out her left toward the audience, making little wiggling motions with her fingers, as if she would draw them closer. For Louise, who had never cared much for women singers, except for Eydie and Barbra, and who had little nostalgia for any performer who had been in her life and left it, besides Mama Cass, sitting in a lounge—any lounge—listening to either the original or a clone was an ordeal.

But she tried to look pleased, because the Count was such a sweetheart. He beamed, actually beamed, at how hard he had had to work to dig up this performer. "It wasn't easy to find her," Stefan said, translating the Count's Greek.

"I can imagine," said Louise. She sipped on her Perrier and smiled through the glass at the Count.

She considered it all unbelievable. Once she had bedded one of Hollywood's leading movie stars, a man she had worshiped as a teenager. In the middle of it, she had looked up and seen who it was drilling away, the famous face inches away from hers. And she had shrieked his name as a line of fans waiting outside a premier would have screamed it, as the realization struck her that it was really *him*! So if she hadn't been able to believe *that*, how could she believe this? Especially as *that* had been the stuff that teenage dreams were made of, and still disappointed.

Fantasy had come true for her and was still hollow. How could she even begin to deal with one that, with all her nerve, she hadn't had the nerve to have? There was nothing Princess Grace about her, nothing to command the attention of this Croesus. She hadn't even made an effort to attract him. After a lifetime of trying so hard, and frightening away every man who mattered, how was it possible that with no effort at all she had magnetized this swarthy little knight?

The truth was, he wasn't even so little. His eyes were on a level with hers and he looked into them with embarrassing intensity. His shoulders were twice as wide as Louise's. He seemed as though he could take her in his arms and actually come between her and whatever it was she was afraid of, which, in this case, was a powerful man who genuinely seemed to want her. She hadn't even let him kiss her, fearful of its being a disappointment. All too much for her, really. She mistrusted the situation, and mistrusted him, even though a number of people had checked him out, and found he was what the gossip said. But mostly she mistrusted herself, because she'd always thought she knew what she wanted, and been crestfallen after she got it. Now, like icing on a cake she hadn't ordered, came this incredible reality.

The singer struck out with her next number, piercing nasality cutting through the air, left hand beckoning the audience to come into her heart, or possibly her massage parlor. The lounge of the Holiday Inn, Kowloon, Louise thought, appraising. Who would have though that the tacky could be facsimiled everywhere, with such flawless attention to detail? Why had poor Cass died before any of them knew how wide the world would become, how many places there would be to book a performer, offering the illusion that only steps away was the Main Room? Headlining. The Big Time. Or in Cass's case, a return to the big time. Cruel tongues had wagged she had died of a ham sandwich, choking in her hotel room in London. But Louise knew full well Cass had died of the same thing they were all dying of: loneliness.

"You like?" the Count asked in struggling English.

"She sounds very much like Helen Reddy," said Louise.

Stefan told him. The Count nodded enthusiastically, grinning. "He thought you would enjoy hearing a true American-style singer," Stefan translated.

She started to say that Reddy was Australian, but thought better of it. Good God, she was starting to think twice. Was she getting discretion, at too long last? Or was it a sign that her life was coming to a close, a symptom that she was losing it, like a sudden sweet smell with no physical source was a warning of a possible brain tumor.

As if the thought of such an aroma could create it, a sudden powerful wash of male cologne invaded her nose. "Good evening," said Anthony Go.

"Go away. I don't like crooks."

"I am not a crook."

"You should come to the States and say that. You could end up President."

"Your mouth is too sharp for your own good."

"As opposed to the good of the Triads?"

"You have been listening to stupid tales."

"I didn't think they're so stupid," said Louise. "They sound pretty heavyweight to me. Secret societies going back to the seventeenth century, trying to restore the Ming dynasty. Shedding their patriotism, getting involved in blackmail and drug dealing, gambling, vice, protection . . . Get me Brandon Tartikoff on the phone, I can sell it as a miniseries. What time is it in L.A.? Is that a cellular phone in your pocket, or are you just glad to see me?"

"You are a most irritating woman," said Go.

"Still, you do want me to represent you, right? Maybe we can get Johnny Wong to play you. What's the story of your life?"

"That is not your business," said Go.

"How can I have a client when I don't really know about him? We tell each other everything in Hollywood. I mean everything. A hundred thousand Triad members, right?"

"Do you have some affection for this woman?" Anthony Go asked Bassia.

Stefan translated.

Bassia covered his heart with both hands and spoke passionate words. Stefan started to translate. Go held up his hand. "I understood," he said. "Tell him if he genuinely cares, he will try and help her avert a tragedy."

"Tragedy?" asked Stefan.

"All the money in the world cannot protect someone who is intent on self-destruction."

"I am not intent on self-destruction," said Louise, defiantly. "I just think it would make a good miniseries."

"Because this man marries you, does not mean you will have a shield."

"I haven't said I'd marry him. Although it *is* a temptation if you promise you'll come to the wedding."

"It would not excuse you from the obligation we've discussed."

"What obligation?"

"To represent my company."

"Which company is that? Sun Yee On? 14K? Wo Sing Wo?"

"Where did you get these names?" said Go, tight-lipped.

"Well, it wasn't *Daily Variety*."

"You are looking for a knife in your throat."

"That sounds almost like a threat. Did that sound like a threat to you, my would-be darling?" She touched the Count's hand. He picked hers up, and kissed it.

"Perhaps it is not so much that you are brave, as that you are brazen," said Anthony Go. "Perhaps you are not clever, but foolish. Perhaps you do not really know what is waiting for you."

"That's right, I don't. Nobody does. All I know is what's been so far, and it's enough. I'm not afraid of anything you can do to me. There's only one thing I'm afraid of."

"What's that?" said Go.

"Being a sucker," she said, looking into the face of the green-eyed man who stared at her with such adoration, trying not to sound as afraid as she really was.

TWENTY-FIVE

◆

What amazed Kip was not how different all cultures were, with respect to women, but how much the same. Before Henry gave her all the *Women Who Love Too Much* and co-dependent books, to help her work through her problems with Peter, she would have imagined that her guilt and shame were because she was a traditional Chinese woman, from a good family. As gentle as Dao Tsim was, as wise, as nonjudgmental, he still felt it did her dishonor to be living with a man, as her brother Chen did. That Peter degraded Kip was nothing her great-grandfather was privy to, or, she was sure, suspected. But still Dao suffered, just because she was not married to her lover. As she suffered. As all women suffered who did not have control of their lives. She understood that now, from the books she had read, and wondered why women with half a brain didn't use them.

She had smiled at first at the reams of material Henry had given her, knowing her cousin was guileless, in spite of the movies she had made. The books themselves had been a great surprise to Kip, and no small comfort. She had imagined she was very much alone.

It made her feel alone to love a man who was so unloving, giving her sensations of abandonment even when she was with him. Her desperation for him, her need for the love she was sure only he could provide, and one day would, if she held on tightly enough,

343

gave him enough of what he wanted, made her willing to sacrifice all personal dignity.

There were, apparently, women like her all over America, partners of drug addicts and alcoholics, or those caught in some other form of addictive behavior—though she could find no specific case history of an American man who liked little girls in schoolclothes. Still, Kip was sure Peter had sprung from that same well of self-loathing that characterized addictive men. More than enlightening her, it made her uncomfortable to understand she was only one of a vast army of women caught in a destructive relationship.

As her glass-blower uncle could fire a phoenix from a ten-inch length of silicate, so could a woman make art from her capacity to feel what someone else was feeling. But to surrender to it, she understood now, was spiritual suicide. And Kip, for one, had decided to live.

That was to say, she'd decided to live, provided she could get through the afternoon. Peter's mother was coming to tea.

"You do know how to make tea?" his mother had said to her on the telephone.

It was a terribly awkward conversation to begin with. Peter had taken the usual route English people took with each other: avoiding direct contact until it was absolutely necessary. He had handed the phone to Kip, as one would to a precocious child, telling them to say hello to a relative, showing off the fact that they could even speak. Kip's hand had shaken as she took the phone. There was only the exchange of hello, before his mother announced she was coming to tea. As if Kip hadn't known. As if she hadn't been preparing for weeks, laying in countless blends, pulling cups and kettles and saucers and pretty plates together to please her.

"Yes, of course I know how to make tea, Mrs. Sansome."

"Good."

"I look forward to meeting you."

"Really?"

"Till this afternoon, then."

"This afternoon."

"Goodbye." Kip hung up the phone. "She certainly does everything she can to make it easier," she said to Peter.

"You're being oversensitive."

"I heard her voice."

"That's just her English reserve."

"You don't have to tell me about English reserve. You never show what you really feel except when you're coming."

"Well, that's the proper time to let go."

"Your mother only relaxes when she has orgasm?"

"Oh, Mother doesn't do that. Well-bred Englishwomen don't."

All through the day at work, Kip prepared, inside herself. Having studied so carefully the difference between relationship addiction and intimacy, she imagined if she dealt with Peter and his mother as if the love affair she was having was really a *love* affair, and not some sordid interaction, it would become a love affair. As life imitated art, couldn't love imitate what was artful? Couldn't things change when people did? They were still both young enough to change their behavior, especially now that she was aware of the mistakes she had been making, giving up her freedom to him, acting not from will but compulsion. Having to be with him, instead of wanting to be with him, needing him to love her at all costs. But the cost was too high. She realized that, finally, having made the decision to use her reason, now that she understood how many women were without it.

"Thank you for the books," she said to Henry, returning them to her cousin's suite at the Mandarin.

"Were they helpful?"

"I'll know this afternoon. Peter's mother is coming to tea."

"Have you met her?"

"Only on the phone. She hates me."

"She doesn't hate *you*. *They* just hate *us*. No master loves a slave."

"You know that from books?"

"I know that from bondage movies."

"She loves Peter because he's emotionally unavailable," Henry said to Louise, looking around the suite, filled with flowers. "There's a whole breed of women that only get into affairs with men who have to withhold, who can't give them real support."

"That's all the men there are," said Louise, chewing her lips.

"What about the Greek?"

"How can I believe him? He says he loves me." Louise paced her room.

"That's beautiful," Henry said. She was dressed for an interview slated that afternoon with the *South China Morning Post*, which was going to photograph her and Johnny Wong in their martial arts garb, in Henry's case fuchsia, an innovation that Johnny himself had decided on, combining, he said, athleticism with her strident sexuality.

"Beautiful? I think it's bizarre. Things like this don't happen."

"It's happening," Henry said.

"I'm not making it up?"

"You aren't making these up." Henry made her way from flower arrangement to flower arrangement, touching the stalks of tiger lilies, cymbidium orchids. Tropical flowers that flushed out the centerpieces of the great hotels of the world filled the room. Stalks of blossoming white quince from ports where the season was spring, haliconia from Hawaii, the bamboo-stalked reddish-pink flower that looked like a cooked lobster claw, obake anthurium, heartshaped, with its penislike center, and red and pink ginger.

"What am I going to do?" Louise said.

"Do you love him?"

"How do I know? How could I possibly tell? I haven't even let him kiss me. I saw this Shirley Temple movie when I was a little girl, where she's poor and she wakes up and she's surrounded with food and beautiful clothes and toys and everything she's always wanted. I loved the movie so much I didn't know if I saw it, or dreamed it.

"Then I grew up, sort of, and I got all the things I ever dreamed of, even the things I didn't dream of. I had the friends and the clothes and the trips to places where everyone wanted to go, and dinner conversations with people everyone wanted to be with, and I ended up—God, can you believe it?—still lonely and more than occasionally bored.

"So I stopped even dreaming of what I was dreaming of, because it all seemed like such a put-on. I mean, unless you're starving, and have Shirley Temple's innocence, and life doesn't last more than the two hours it takes to run the movie or dream the dream, everything wears thin.

"I mean I've been in the great restaurants, and the great villas, and even some of the great beds. And it all ends up food and shelter and fucks."

"Forgive me if I don't cry for you," Henry said.

"I don't cry for myself. Please don't misunderstand me. I know how lucky I am. Too lucky. I'm a fake. I'm lead. I don't deserve to have the life I'm having."

"Is that why you're trying to end it?"

"End it?"

"Spitting in the face of Anthony Go."

"Well, I haven't really spit. It's just hard not to talk back. So much of my life has been deals and gossip, it's fun to get my teeth into a little real drama."

"As long as you have teeth. It's my theory you're trying to commit suicide."

"Really? How very Inger Stevens. I know. You don't know who she was."

"No, I don't."

"There are annals of them. These beautiful Hollywood women who did themselves in. Starting with Carole Landis, Gia Scala. All of them light-eyed and gorgeous and thin. Marilyn Monroe."

"I know who she was."

"Then she didn't die in vain. But I don't think I really want to die, do I? I just don't want it to come up empty."

"What?"

"All of it. Waking up and finding the clothes and the food and the toys, and the little music boxes with crystal ponies and ballerinas that dance on pointe. And then it turns out to be a dream, and you never even really saw the movie."

"I don't understand."

"I don't want to be let down again. I've gotten everything I hoped for and a lot of things I didn't and it's all been disappointing.

I just couldn't stand it if the big one was a fizzle. I've loved people, and they don't even call you themselves when they fire you: they have their secretaries do it. I couldn't stand for that to happen with Pericles."

"Who?"

"The Count. He actually has a first name. Pericles." She picked up a card that lay by a tub of flowers. "I love you. Pericles." Another. "I worship you. Pericles." She walked to the huge standing vase by the balcony, overlooking the Star Ferry terminal across the way. "You are the moon. Pericles." Louise looked up, and her face was actually soft. "What if that changes? What if I let him have me, and he's a turncoat, like everyone else in the world, and he doesn't even tell me himself? I just get a call from Stefan, telling me it's over."

"Love isn't like that. Give it a shot. What do you have to lose?"

"The illusion," said Louise. "I just have one left. That it all would have been different if someone really loved me. That everything that felt vacant and painful would have changed if there was someone who really cared to share it with me. What if I let him come into my life, and he does, and takes over. And then, it isn't really the answer at all. All it is, is having to share your closet space."

"What if it turns out like you never even dared to hope it would, and everything's great?"

"You think that could happen?"

"Stranger things have," said Henry.

"Not to me," said Louise. "But then I've never done it on a trapeze."

All the way back from Bangkok, James gripped the arms of his seat, knuckles white, face pale, lips slightly edged with blue. Claire knew better than to talk to him. She was feeling ill herself. The bright glow of infatuation had been diminished into gray by the reality of loss. His loss would be hers. The children's. She was responsible for them, and she hadn't really considered their needs and futures at all. Only James's. And her own, she realized, covered with shame. Never in his life had Charley been able to provide for his family as well as he'd wanted. Only with his death, and the insurance that came from it, was there any real security. She had gambled Charley's blood on this young man who sat beside her.

How much had he risked? How much had it cost him besides the loan she'd underwritten? All the questions she wanted to ask, she couldn't begin to ask, because that would involve getting at the truth, and truth had never been an issue between them. What had been involved was fantasy: his, that he could be what he wanted, rich, a spendthrift, catered to in a part of the world where all that seemed to count was dazzle; hers, that nothing mattered but love. And not even love exchanged, but love that a woman felt for a man.

As for James, his fall from grace, or what he considered grace, was swifter than if the plane had fallen from the sky. When he got back to Hong Kong, he wished it had. The offices of his cohorts with the computer scheme were empty. Drawers were pulled open, their contents scattered. Someone had taken the phones. Nothing was left but the lines, curling across the carpet.

"It couldn't be plainer," Kenneth said, when James got to his office. "The stock is worthless. Bottom fell out. I don't blame them for running away."

"How could that happen? They showed me their prospectus. They showed me their computers, demonstrated the software."

"And a good idea it was, too. I don't think they were making it up. Not a total scam. It just wasn't a done deal. They didn't have it in their pocket. Or maybe they thought they had it, and the Chinese got a better one with the Japanese. Everybody does, you know." He rubbed his palm over the top of his head, as though flattening the hair he didn't have anymore. A line of sweat beaded his forehead. "The Chinese *are* traders."

"I can't believe it. What am I going to do?"

"I hope you're going to muddle through. But I do wish you'd listened to me, and not insisted on margining more. You owe us four million."

"How long have I got?"

"No time at all. I've been covering you for the last three days, ever since the stock collapsed. Uppingham and the old school tie notwithstanding, I do have partners here."

"I also owe the bank," James said.

"Well, I trust you'll have some sense of priorities," said Kenneth, and showed him the door.

The home of Anthony Go was considered high-tech traditional. Though he had the input neither of I. M. Pei, nor Foster Associates, the architects of the HongKong Bank, it was, after all, a part of the world where the counterfeit oftentimes looked better than the original, and even those who'd designed the original could have been fooled into thinking they themselves had done the copy. Such was the case with the Villa Victorious, which cantilevered the side of a cliff overlooking Repulse Bay, its structure as striking as the banks it made no overt claim to resemble.

There were clear views of the water and the yachts below from everywhere in the house, with its four-leveled floors virtually column free. Tubular steel columns connected by haunched beams rose on either side. Glass and aluminum clad, the structure offered the boaters below their most spectacular gaping spot, making their yachts seem trifling and unluxurious, and an afternoon at sea not as glamorous as a day on land.

It was quite a trick, good *Fung shui* notwithstanding. With the infatuation there was in Hong Kong with the American skyscraper, for all the arcades and atriums, waterfalls that sided escalators, free-falling fountains that bubbled and arced behind open-slatted stairways, no one had managed to facsimile the feeling in a home before, making a skyscraper out of a four-story house, using the cliff into which it was built as an illusion of height, the sea that gently brushed the shore below its visual floor. Just beside the road that led down to the villa was a roof garden, and inside, a pool with a frosted glass canopy that opened mechanically to let in the sun, should the bathers desire it, which they seldom did, being mostly Chinese. On the side of the building fronting the road was a membrane glass skin that added to the veneer of perfect coolness.

Several prominent architects had been interviewed for the job, the best of them commissioned to draw up plans. But ultimately Go had given the assignment to a member of his own organization, who'd been put through Harvard by the Triads, a young designer who knew how to take orders, as well as originate, and steal.

The house appeared in a double-page spread in the *Hong Kong Tatler*, one of the few real estate features that was simply a bird preening its feathers, and not offering up an estate for sale. Directly on the following page was a property listing in France, a layout that would have been appropriate to an article in *Town and Country*, which it rather more resembled than a solicitation, with the heading "An Englishman's Home Is His French Château." It included photos of gardens, well-appointed sitting room in the guest cottage, vineyard, dining room, and bougainvillea-bedecked exterior, the price at "around" 2.5 million pounds. On the page after that was a straightforward advertisement for a block of seven houses in Gloucester Gate, Regents Park, London, where few could imagine they were actually going to relocate, 1997 or no, though the grass did look very green in the picture.

The renowned British real estate agency in the South of France that was handling the sale of the château, according to the *Tatler*, was headed by Fiona Capulet, direct descendant of the Capulet who established the firm in 1842, the year the British came to Hong Kong. She was seen on the page opposite in an unrelated advertisement trying on a necklace of Kutchinsky jewels, gold with huge ruby pendant, depicted in red, herself sketched in a black and white ink, long neck arched gracefully backward, deep-set eyes closed, lips slightly parted as if something besides the necklace was dangling against her. She was also in full color in the flesh on Anthony Go's living room couch, stretched out, showing her fine legs to their best advantage, along with a brochure of the estate of the soon-to-be-divorced wife of an overpublicized Los Angeles litigator, who, after a lifetime of too-high fees, was bankrupt. At least that's what he'd maintained to his wife's divorce attorney. The asking price for their Bel Air mansion was nine million dollars. As the area had run out of relatives of the Shah, Fiona had advised the wife that the best market would be the Orient.

"I'm not really interested in Los Angeles as a base," said Anthony Go. "I'm thinking San Francisco."

A steward appeared at the entrance to the atrium that sided the living room, and bowed apologetically, speaking in Cantonese. "I don't want to see him now," Go answered.

"Please." Fiona got up from the couch. "Don't let me interfere. I really should be going."

"Will you come back for dinner? I'll have my driver pick you up at seven."

"I'm not sure," Fiona said. "I must concentrate on this sale. That *is* why I came."

"All things are possible with flexibility."

"All things?"

"All things. I will send my car for you at seven."

When she had left, the steward showed in James Bingham. He did not seem any longer the dashing young Brit. In spite of the freshness of his shirt, there was a tired look, even about his clothes.

"I was wondering when you'd show up," said Go. "Although your timing could have been a little better."

"Look, I've had a turn of bad luck," James said.

"Luck? Four million on margin at Rumis, Peterson, plus the original bank loan that your American lady guaranteed. Not to mention all you spent in Bangkok. I don't call that luck. I call that bad planning."

James blanched. "Well, since you seem to know everything, maybe you'd like to tell me what to do."

"Make yourself at home, Mr. Bingham," Go said.

Kip had bought eighteen kinds of teas, seven Chinese, two Indian, nine English. She had set them out in an assortment of delicate flower-painted bowls, leaves and herbs intermixed as Dao Tsim had taught her, for the medicinal teas, flavorful varieties of English and Indian, their heavy scents rising to flood the living room she shared with Peter. She'd opened the drapes wide before leaving for work that morning, letting in a full day's worth of light, to dispel the darkness she could already feel moving in on her with the visitation. The room was a little overheated from the sun's rays, and she wondered if she'd made a mistake, sacrificing coolness for what she hoped would be illumination.

"Shall we have a little quickie before Mum arrives?" Peter asked her, his hands on her breasts from behind, as she sorted out the tea.

"She'll be here any minute," Kip said.

"Wouldn't take more than that. Nobody says *you* have to be satisfied." He laughed.

"Are you laughing to make me think you're joking?"

"I *was* joking."

"A good way to let yourself off the hook, trying to pass it off as humor. The truth is, you're totally self-centered. My satisfaction means nothing to you."

"Quite right," he said. "So do you want to fuck?"

The doorbell rang. "Why don't you fuck your mother?"

"She wouldn't be any good," said Peter, and went to answer the door.

There was the sound of exchanged English affection from the hallway, controlled enthusiastic murmurs, modulated, of how well everyone looked, how fit everyone was, how no one had really changed except that the son had grown better looking. And then they were in the living room.

She was larger than Kip had expected. She was a great virago of a woman, standing several inches taller than Peter, her chest expansive, her ribs looking nipped, as though she was wearing an old-fashioned wire corset under the green-and-white printed dress, a regulation design from Number 10 Dowdy street, as fashion people had referred to Mrs. Thatcher's address.

"Mother mine," he said, expansively. "This is Kip."

"How do you do," said Gertrude Sansome. Her smile was inordinately wide, like the brim of her hat, which fell about her graying brown hair like the eaves of a house that had been neglected.

"I'm happy to meet you." Kip took the large hand, hoping her own wasn't sweating, that the lie of what she had just said wasn't imprinted on her palm.

"Here we have the entire history of tea." Peter indicated the table Kip had so carefully arranged with its exotic assortments. "How many from China, Kip?"

"Seven." She ran off the varieties, pointing them out as she spoke and his mother pretended to listen. The piercing gray eyes were not anywhere near the bowls, but x-raying Kip, for subtlety, deceit, manipulation, seduction. All the qualities Kip knew Gertrude suspected she had, most of which Kip would have given her own eyes for, to actually possess. "And these from India, and these . . . British, though of course, the best of them are actually from Ceylon."

"We call it Sri Lanka, now," said Gertrude, and sat.

"Yes, I am aware of that. But I always wanted to go to Ceylon. They have moonstones on the beach. The air is heavy with the scent of cinnamon. From the time I was a little girl I dreamed of going there with someone I loved."

"Really," said Gertrude, with an overlay of tolerance. "Well, after a while, even the most exotic locale becomes quite humdrum, and what you long for is the simplicity of home."

"Still, *Ceylon* has a much more romantic sound than *Sri Lanka*," Kip said.

"I don't think of tea as connected with romance," Gertrude said.

"Yet you British are so . . . attached to it."

"Well, it's civilized, dear. Civilized is so much more lasting than passion."

"I'm not sure of that," Kip said, brewing. "The sun seems to be setting on the Empire, but it never sets on love."

"You didn't tell me she was a philosopher, Peter."

"She's been studying for the occasion," he said, tolerantly.

"Really? What have you been studying, dear?"

"Books."

"Books?" Gertrude repeated. "Confucius?"

"American books. About people who come from dysfunctional homes, that leave them incapable of having healthy relationships."

"Why is it that all American subjects have a tendency to sound like they could use a good dose of salts?" asked Gertrude, and laughed, a rather constipated laugh that sounded as if she herself could use one.

"I'm afraid Kip's cousin has introduced her to some rather silly thinking."

"I don't think it's silly. Americans are healthy because they don't try to sweep things under the carpet. Whatever else you can say about them, they want to have happy lives."

"Everyone wants to have happy lives," said Gertrude. "You have parents, dear?"

"Everyone has parents."

"I mean, are they still alive?"

"I don't know. My mother followed my father into China when my brother was a baby. We never heard from them."

"How sad. You must have felt quite abandoned."

"We have a very loving great-grandfather who raised us," Kip said. "And I often think it is better to have been abandoned than be in the power of parents who do not know how to give love. Who never show affection."

Gertrude waited a moment before speaking. "What's that cinnamony tea you're brewing there?"

"That's from Ceylon," said Kip. "Sri Lanka. Milk?"

"Lemon."

"Sugar?"

"It smells quite . . . sweet enough."

"A rose by any other name," said Peter.

Gertrude beamed.

"Isn't he clever," said Kip, and handed Gertrude a cup.

"Exceedingly clever," said Gertrude. "A young man like that could have any life he wanted."

"He seems to want this one," said Kip.

"That's now. But when his divorce comes through . . . well, his father and I have been talking, and we think that Peter should come back to England. Alone. What with the uncertainty here and the enormity of what he has to offer—"

"You've seen him naked, then?"

" . . . after all," she continued as though she hadn't really heard what was said. "He understands finance, he's well traveled . . . well-spoken . . ."

"He can quote Shakespeare," said Kip.

"Exactly. The doors would open anywhere for a man like that. But not if he has too much luggage."

"According to these books," said Kip, "most of the luggage people carry is emotional luggage."

"Emotions are not that important," said Gertrude.

"I guess if you've never had any," said Kip. "Sort of like orgasms."

Gertrude sipped her tea again.

"Peter tells me you've never had one."

The tea seemed to catch in Gertrude's throat. A small stream of it came out of her nose. She blotted it with her napkin.

"You don't know what you're missing," said Kip.

Gertrude turned and looked at her son, steely-eyed. "It's one thing to ask your mother to come help you out of a difficult situation," she said. "Quite another to expose her to this filth."

"You think *this* is filth," said Kip. "What would you say about a woman who made her son feel so guilty about masturbating that he's emotionally arrested, caught in a time when he had fantasies about schoolgirls?"

Gertrude set down her cup. "He *never* masturbated!" she said. "How dare you even use that word. Our house was a *clean* house!"

"You made him wash his hands afterwards?"

"He didn't have to wash his hands!" Gertrude stood. "I tied them. I caught him once, and that was all it took for him to learn. Just once, twenty-four hours, with his hands tied behind his back. He never did it again!"

"Well, you must be really proud," said Kip. "I guess it's lucky that he only wants to eat brassieres."

Gertrude started for the door. "How could you subject me to this, Peter?"

"At least he hasn't handcuffed you to the headboard," Kip said, and lifting a plate, held it out to her. "Ginger cake?"

"I'll see you at the hotel," said Gertrude, and left.

"I could break you in half," said Peter.

"You already have. You didn't have to bring in your troops. This isn't the Falklands."

"Cheeky bitch!" He raised his hand. "No. No. I won't let you do that to me. I won't let you move me to violence."

"That'll make you a bigger man than your mother." Her voice was shaking. She started to clear the teas.

"I want you out of here."

"Don't worry. I'm gone." She saw what she was doing, the habit of tidying stronger than her anger and her sorrow. With a sweep of her arm, she clattered the cups to the floor.

"Now look what you've done! Clean that up!"

"You clean it up!" she shouted. "I'm going to pack!"

She was halfway through filling her second suitcase when he appeared in the doorway. "Are you really going?"

She didn't answer.

"It was good for a while, though," he said softly. "We both know that . . ."

She kept on packing, not speaking, not looking at him.

"Will you keep in touch?"

No answer.

"Well, then, would you at least leave your underwear?"

TWENTY-SIX

♦

Oh, how Maggie disliked doctors, with their infuriating certainty they knew more than you did. Only once in her life had she had a man of medicine who listened to her, noting her symptoms as she described them, and then telling her what was wrong was exactly what she'd thought it was. "How do you know?" she'd asked him. "Because you told me," he'd said. She'd loved him very much, right on the spot, but unfortunately she'd been too young at the time, and unflirtatious, to give herself to him that minute. Hong Kong being transient, he'd moved away. She would never find him, much as she loved him in memory. Besides, she had no time for that now. Once the baby was born, it would be her whole life. No more men. No more jade either. She had put out feelers to see what she could get for her business. She was impressed. It surprised her, in spite of her success, to find out how high the price might be. She just adored businessmen, they were so greedy.

She supposed that doctors were greedy in their own way, somehow more offensive, cloaked in their mantle of doing good. Still, it had to be hard, she thought, in a wash of compassion, to be part of a "healing art," that was neither an art nor necessarily healing. All they could do was try to fix whatever was wrong. Like being a mechanic with tools that worked only if the car was in good shape.

Well, she was in fine shape, no matter what this young fool

who was examining her said. "How long have you had this cough?"
he was asking her.

"I don't know," she said. "It's not important."

"It's a nasty cough."

"Then I won't be nice to it." She figured him to be in his early
thirties. All her life doctors had been older, making her feel
protected and young. Now they had the audacity to be juveniles.

"Step on the scale, please," the puppy was saying.

"I hate all this."

"You've lost a lot of weight."

"I haven't been hungry. I've been too excited. Not many women
at my age are lucky enough to get pregnant."

"I don't know of any once they're on estrogen."

"Dr. Rogers said I was perimenopausal. I remember it quite
well. It was right before he retired. Not *exactly* menopausal. Peri. I
made him define it."

"Please get up on the table," he said.

She did. He put her feet in the stirrups.

"What are your other symptoms?"

"Sometimes I get so tired," she said, trying to distract herself
from what was always a humiliation, even when the doctor liked you
and was kind.

"Is it fatigue, or weariness?"

"Aren't they the same?"

"Fatigue is when you exert yourself, and get tired. Weariness is
a general feeling. Even when you wake up in the morning, you're
tired."

"Well, I guess you could say I've got both. But, of course, I
have been through an ordeal." She could feel the harsh intrusion of
the metal. "Be careful. Don't do anything to hurt her. She hasn't had
an easy time."

"You can get dressed now," he said, when he was finished.

"Well? Are you satisfied?"

"No," he said.

"Well, just don't think *I'm* going to satisfy you."

"Mrs. Evans, I don't think you quite understand me. There's
something wrong."

"That's a very negative view. I think childbirth is the most natural thing in the world."

"So do I. But not at your age. It isn't happening."

"Don't be ridiculous. Betsy's inside me. I've felt her move."

"Betsy?"

"My daughter who was murdered. So cruel." She started to cry. "They did such disgusting things to her."

"I'm sorry."

"Well, don't be sorry," she said angrily. "Everybody's always so fucking sorry, but sorry doesn't fix anything."

He gave her some tranquilizers which she knew she wouldn't take, because they might hurt the baby. He told her to call him in two days when they'd have the result of the blood test. She could hardly wait, so he could see how wrong he was. Still, when the day came, she forgot to call him. She wasn't feeling at all well, and he was no one she cared to tell that to.

But he called her. "I'd like you to come into the office."

"I don't feel like seeing you. You can deliver my baby when it's time, and *that* is a concession."

"I'm afraid I've something unpleasant to tell you. You'd best come in."

"You can tell me on the phone."

"You insist?"

"I insist."

"You're HIV positive."

"Does that mean it's a boy?" asked Maggie, alarmed, bitterly disappointed. She had already started buying the layette, and it was pink.

"It means you have the AIDS virus," he said.

Sometimes, it seemed to Maggie, everything in Hong Kong was in cages. The tenements looked to her like cages, rising in furrowed metal sheets, floor after floor, congested even from a distance, the only bright color the laundry that hung from their tight, small windows. Birds in their bamboo houses never seemed to be singing. Pigs roped and crisscrossed, trussed to poles, in bamboo cages no bigger than they were, crumpled hooves beneath them, patiently waited for slaughter.

Maggie did not intend to be like them. She wandered Hong Kong in a kind of dreaming, still not comprehending what the doctor had said, exactly, but knowing it was over. Not just life, but Betsy. When she had been young the first time—all there was to be now—Betsy had loved the Tiger Balm Gardens. Maggie herself had never really liked them, finding the murals, and the huge plaster animals, painted in strident colors, grotesque, frightening. But she owed one more trip there to Betsy.

The punishments of hell were depicted on the walls, at the top of the steps, guts being pulled from adulterers, tongues of those who'd lied being cut in two. Above it sat the Goddess of Mercy, white-painted plaster face benignly indifferent, eyes closed. How humorous life was, with its illusion there was mercy, how striped with irony and symbolism. To the goddess's right knelt Jade Lady, whose job was to carry out the mercy.

Flat painted tortoises lay against hideous bright blue rock. Sickening greens marked the backs of giant plaster toads. Maggie felt so ill she was concerned she might collapse, and not be dead, trapped in this maze of horrors that tourists thought wonderful. There beneath a tiger scaling a pagoda, was the wedding of a rabbit and a pig. Animals with breasts, dressed in Chinese dresses, white-faced plaster dogs in light blue suits beat drums for the wedding. "Symbolic," read the legend at its base, "of the truth that things that did not seem to belong together sometimes did, when ordained by Heaven."

Heaven. What a joke. Tiger Balm Gardens, indeed. Where was the unguent for the spirit? Where was the reward for those who believed in the mysteries, hoping to soothe their souls? History was striped with the blood of the martyrs, strung with the intestines of the Saint Sebastians, innards pulled out slowly on a wheel. Did they really believe that crap about heaven in their agonies?

Well, Maggie didn't. Not the afterlife, or this one. The earth was foul, and she was foul, and her daughter was rotting in the ground. And that was all there was. Death was in her belly, not a baby.

The huge plaster statues seemed to move and murmur; the wedding became a parade, as the animals turned to jeer her. She could hear the cackling of the cock, the mewing of the sheep, spreading scandal about her. Well, what could they say that wasn't true? Still, how pitiless of them to join in this caterwauling. She despised them. They were worse than people. Why had Betsy loved it here?

"*Stop it!*" she screamed at them, with their overblown, overwide eyes staring down at her. "I know a few things about you, too!"

A group of Japanese tourists turned to stare. Their silent censure was no more painful than the animals' noisy one. "I see no reason to put up with any of you creatures," she cried, and stumbled back down the entrance.

She hailed a cab. "*Yan Yuen Shek,*" she said, in Cantonese. "Another of my daughter's favorite places," she went on when she was settled in the taxi, as though the driver understood her, as though anyone understood. "Lover's Rock. She so enjoyed stories of love. Lovers reunited. Lovers abandoned. Of course, we've all been abandoned by our lovers. In my case, every one of them, including God. I did think God was going to be the great one, *carino*, but he's as bad as the rest. He never calls."

The path she climbed to get to the rock was green with moss and fanning leaves of fern. By comparison, the rock seemed even starker than it was. It rose nine meters tall, listing slightly to the left, wider at its base, a separate thrust of stone its shaft.

It was grayish brown, sandstone and shale, base brightened with red prayer paint, crevices ashen with incense that had burned out, as her hopes had. Little rolled-up fortunes were stuffed into its crannies, talismans and paper prayers, stubs of red sticks, remnants of the good luck symbols sold by the hawkers below, flogging changes of luck to the lovelorn.

But as it was not one of those days prescribed on the lunar calendar as fortunate for offering prayers, Maggie was alone there. "Ciao, hello," she said to the cloudless blue sky, "I'm willing to give you one more chance."

Just over the edge of the cliff was a cluster of high rises, semicircled around the Royal Hong Kong Jockey Club, its track manicured and green. Happy Valley. How cruel the world was, giving people such illusions.

Still, if reality wasn't merciful, couldn't she be? Couldn't she be like Jade Lady, and carry out the kindness the world seemed to withhold? Couldn't she feel some compassion for the Creator, realize if she was so disappointed, how brokenhearted He must be?

She fell to her knees. "Oh, God, please, can't we forgive each other?" Tears fell from her eyes. "If you won't give me back Betsy, at least give me back You."

She waited in the silence. From far away came the noise of jackhammers. She could hear the laughter of children, the clamor of traffic far below. And from somewhere she couldn't quite locate came a sound she couldn't identify. Then she realized it was a scream, and, as she fell into the chasm below, that it was coming from her.

With the suicide of Maggie Evans, the Black's Link case was in the headlines again. Obviously, went the accusatory stories, the unsatisfactory police investigation had driven the poor woman mad. There was more pressure on Clement from higher places than he was already putting on himself. Still, there was a part of him that managed to feel lighthearted, close as he felt he was getting to some real interaction with Judith.

"The sky is falling," he said to her on the phone. "Most of it on my head. So before it's too late, I think we ought to do it."

"Do what?"

"*Tit ta wu,*" he said, smiling.

"I don't tap-dance."

"What?"

"That's Mandarin for *tap-dance.*"

"I'll call you later," he said, and hung up the phone. He had to sit there for a minute. His brain was in a blender. That's what Chen had been doing: tap-dancing. The turbulence in Clement's brain moved to his belly, and he felt sick. "You wouldn't be able to find them," Dao had said, "even if they were right in front of your eyes." As even a psychic wouldn't know when the answer was in his own house.

* * *

"How long has Chen been tap-dancing?" he asked Dao Tsim. He was afraid he already knew. Probably had for a while, but hadn't wanted to hear even inside his own head, wanting the villains to be the Bad Guys. Anthony Go.

"Since he got his new shoes," said Dao. "Would you like some tea?"

"I didn't come here for tea. What new shoes?"

"The ones with the metal. They make the sound. And the marks on the floors."

"May I see his room?"

The shoes lay on the floor of Chen's closet: black and white spectators in the style of Fred Astaire, taps on the heels and toes. Clement knew without checking where the shoes had come from. But the lab confirmed from the print on the insole, as unmistakable as a fingerprint, that they were the ones that had been taken from the feet of David Palmer-Smith.

What James described as their final outing took place at the Casablanca. There was a mockery of its forced romanticism now. Claire could see how broken he was, how drained of blood and easy charm. The palm trees looked metallic, the busboys in their fezzes looked foolish, as she felt. The club was nearly deserted; what had seemed before a kind of public privacy, giddily erotic, virtually empty except for them, which she had taken that first time as a gift from the universe, now looked more like what it was: a seedy setting where not many people came because they didn't want to throw away money.

"Why our final outing?" she asked him, fearful, in spite of her understanding that it was almost over, and right for it to be over.

"I can't keep looking at you, with your sweet, trusting face. I feel such a fool."

"Don't worry about the bank loan. I'll be all right." She wondered if she would. If she could face her broker without his saying "I told you so." If she could make the money back by the time the children needed it for college. If there was really an afterlife, as she had always hoped, from which Charley was watching her, so disappointed, because whatever else she had been, she had never been stupid.

"I've taken care of it. It's been repaid." He didn't look comfortable or pleased with that news.

They were dancing, in a way. He moved her listlessly around the floor with a touch she supposed was meant to be tender, to the slow music. But the real music between them had already stopped, and she knew that. It was like watching the spasms of legs that were moving when a person was already dead.

"Where did you get the money?" He was very pale, thin-lipped. She had never noticed how lacking in character his mouth really was, so intent had she been on having it on hers. "You didn't ask Anthony Go?"

"You don't understand this city. It's not even dog eat dog. It's people eat dog. And people eat people."

"I don't see it that way." She was fierce in her attachment to the island now. She couldn't let go of everything, not all at once. "I love it here."

"That's because you have no malice in you. People see you and they know you're not going to steal their money or business or their ideas. That's why you feel welcome here. But it isn't like that for others."

"You can make it what you want it to be."

"No, I can't," he said angrily. "Most people can't. You try to make everybody so special. Because you love somebody, you see them as extraordinary. But they're not. They're just people doing the best they can. In my case, not very well."

"You'll change it," she said, as she had always said to Charley. As she'd always said to everybody she cared about, imagining she could alter circumstances and people's character, when really all she could change was herself. And that she'd been too stubborn, or frightened, to do.

"Not now. Not anymore. I belong to Anthony Go."

"You belong to yourself." She was amazed that she could say that, much less think it, when, only a few hours before, she'd thought he belonged to her.

*   *   *

Clement needed only one day of putting Chen under surveillance to see who his contacts were, before rounding up all four boys. One of them was the doorman at the Albany, working as elevator man the night of Wendy Lu's murder. So it all came together as neatly as a cracked heart.

It was the rule, when a minor was brought into the station for questioning, that a relative or guardian had to be present. So Clement had no choice but to have Dao Tsim. Because Chen was so young, whatever the outcome, he would not be sent to jail, but "detained under Her Majesty's pleasure." Certain phrases caught in Clement's head now, made him slightly queasy, because of the anguish he felt. Her Majesty's pleasure. The richest woman in the world, her salary just increased 9 percent by the government, to $160 thousand U.S., a day. Much as he loved his Queen, much as he still felt honored to serve her, there was something askew that her pleasure couldn't include a little help for Hong Kong.

His distress was intensified by his having to bring Dao Tsim to the station house. To have to inflict pain on the old man he loved, to force him to be present for Chen's questioning, made the situation ranker than it was.

"Forgive me," said Clement, as Dao Tsim was escorted in. He looked frail now, as he never had in his soft-lit rooms, the flat yellow paint of the station house walls echoing from his countenance.

"You must do what you must do," Dao Tsim said.

The four suspects had been sequestered from each other, Chen, the doorman, and two other twenty-year-olds. They were all identified by the disc jockey of Hot Gossip as having been seen frequently with David Palmer-Smith. The maître d' of the King Wu restaurant said they were the four who'd been at dinner, flashing the girl's student identity card, tipping with chips from the casino in Macau.

"We were all in the same club," Chen said to his interrogators. His eyes nervously sought out those of his great-grandfather, but Dao Tsim's lids were heavy, nearly closed, his head turned away. "We watched old movies together. Fred Astaire." He looked younger than his years, the glowing red *Fung shui* light on the altar behind him doing nothing to mellow the harshness of the room, with its hard-slatted wooden chairs.

"David Palmer-Smith was in the club?" asked the sergeant.

"He was the head of it," Chen said.

"Where were you on October fifth?"

"What day was that?"

"A Wednesday."

"I don't remember."

"Were you with Horace Lin, Ng Yuen, and Harold Ko?" He gave the names of the other three arrested.

"I might have been. Sometimes we hung out on Wednesday."

"And that Wednesday?"

"It's a long time ago to remember."

"Not if you were doing something you didn't always do."

"Tell the truth," said Dao Tsim. "Whatever you have done, it can only be made worse by lies." He could hardly sit straight in the unforgiving chair, proud as his posture had always been, energized as he'd always felt by connection to the earth and sky, as if nature and spirit ran a direct route through his spine. Now he knew how old he really was, joy sapped from him, with his strength. There was a sickness in his belly, ringing in his ears. He could barely hear the questions or the answers.

"Did you see David Palmer-Smith and Betsy Evans that Wednesday?" the sergeant was asking.

"Yes."

"Where?"

"Underneath the banyan tree. Making love."

"What were you doing there?"

"Watching." Chen looked angry suddenly, the black eyes narrowing. "He always acted so much the gentleman. Up the Empire! Up Fred Astaire. Good manners. Style. Grace. That was all that mattered, he said.

"But he was no better than the rest of them. They have no shame, the British. He used her the way that pig Englishman uses Kip."

"What happened?"

Chen started to sob. His words were indistinguishable now to Dao Tsim, but he didn't have to hear. He could see. It was as if he had been transported to the awful scene itself, was witnessing it with Chen's eyes. He saw the other three boys, leering through the bushes, erections pulling at their pants. And then Horace took out a gun, ran out and surprised them, held it to David's head while Ng held Betsy down, and Harold had her. Then they changed places. All the while David was pleading, and Betsy was crying, but they held their hands over her mouth so she couldn't scream.

When it was over, David still had an erection. Horace laughed at that. He put the gun to Betsy's head, and forced her to suck David's penis. When he came, Harold held her nose, pushed her head down, wouldn't let her breathe. She gagged, and he choked her.

David struggled and screamed. But they held him down, covered his mouth. Horace laughed again, and picked up the pencil that lay by the books, and shoved it in David's eye. Hammered it in with the butt of his gun.

The scream of the murdered boy ripped at Dao's heart. He toppled from the chair.

"Oh, God," Clement said, and fell to his knees beside Dao, touched his face, reached for the pulse that he knew was no longer there.

"I have an assistant. Andrew." Clement looked at Judith. The afternoon sun streamed through the French doors to her balcony, giving him an excuse to squint, so his eyes wouldn't seem so swollen. "Youngish man. Says he'd like your job. Reporting the news, but not having to dirty his hands in it. I know what he means."

The door to Judith's workroom was open. Claire was in there on the telephone.

"Sometimes I get involved," Judith said, reaching as though to touch him. But he sat very far away on the couch.

"You were right all along. Not just a murder. Perversion. Crime. But a burst dream."

"Like the bubble of Southern California, at the end of the sixties," Judith said. "Everything was going to be golden and easy in the sun. But the flower children lost their petals. What we got was Charlie Manson. And everything turned dark."

"All we had to do was look for the dream that exploded here. We found it." Tears filled his eyes. "Those beautiful children, dead. Maggie Evans dead. Wendy Lu . . ."

"The elevator boy at the Albany killed her?"

"He knew she was going to tell me who I was after. He was her old boyfriend. He met her when she went to work for Harry Magic."

"What about Harry Magic?"

"I'm sure he's dead. Somebody probably dumped his body so people wouldn't know this plague had hit Hong Kong." He took a deep breath, which seemed to choke him. "And now, Dao Tsim . . ."

"You've got to stop blaming yourself."

"It was my fault he came to the station."

"It's the law."

"I'm the law." He put his head in his hands. "I need a drink."

Judith waited for him to say, "but I won't have one." He didn't. She went to the bar and reluctantly started to pour him a whiskey, good training as a hostess overcoming her sadness that he was drinking again. "How odd. I have twice the amount of booze I had before I went away."

"I bought it for you," said Claire, coming out of the workroom.

"It's like 'The Shoemaker and the Elves,'" Judith said. "I turn my back, and everything's taken care of. You ought to stay here another month. My whole life would be in order."

"I've been here long enough. Too long. How would you define adventure, Judith?"

She took a moment to think. "Heading off into the unknown." Judith handed Clement his drink. "Not really knowing what you're getting into. Putting yourself at risk. But it's very positive."

"Then I have to leave, while it still is."

"I have to go myself." Clement was on his feet. "I've got to get back to headquarters."

"And I have some stuff to finish at the office." Judith smiled, hopeful. "Shall we have dinner later, the three of us?"

"I'll call you," Clement said.

She tried to conceal the disappointment she could feel palpable on her face. Now it was she who was making the overtures, and he who was hedging, ducking out of the way. Was it always such a sorry game, this contest between men and women?

"Well, the condemned man ate a hearty breakfast," Lockwood said, wiping the linen napkin across his smiling mouth. "But then, who wouldn't with two such lovely ladies for company." He smiled particularly broadly at Biddy Rittenhauser, sitting on his left at the coffee shop, across from Erica. "I hope you don't mind my calling you a 'lady.'"

"I'm not a feminist," Biddy said. She was dressed in what she called her travel togs, the only thing cute about them her description. "Though I probably should have been, and then the son of a bitch wouldn't have screwed me."

"Not even in the beginning," Lockwood said, pouring Erica some more coffee. "So you're straight about what you have to do?"

"I have the banker's name. And your letter. You really think he'll give the money to me?"

"The Swiss are very fastidious. He has my instructions. I've called him to make sure."

"I'm very grateful," Biddy said. "Most men would have been mad."

"How could I be mad, when it's so funny? A shining example of American ingenuity. Besides, if it hadn't been for the seven of you, I wouldn't have found Erica. So I'm the one who's grateful."

"Still, it's a lot of money."

"Better you than the IRS," Lockwood said. After all, when they put a lock on his funds, they could also lock up Switzerland. Secret bank accounts notwithstanding, when the whistles blew on Marcos and Kashoggi, the Swiss had come forward with place and numbers. He was just as glad, gladder, really, to give it to the girls.

"You're really convinced I should do this?" asked Louise. Six Chinese were in her room, pinning and basting and folding the creamy beige lace dress onto her body, a convocation of worker bees around the queen.

"Absolutely," said Henry, grinning.

"You think this is off-white enough? You sure I shouldn't wear charcoal?"

"You look lovely. You really do."

"I still don't understand why he wants me. He doesn't get what I say."

"Maybe that's why. All he picks up on is your energy. Your *joie de vivre.*"

"My *what?*"

"Your joy of life."

"I know what it means. I just didn't know that was what I had. After twenty-five years in Los Angeles, I thought I had joy of death."

"Well, as Tennessee Williams said, 'The opposite of death is desire.' "

"Mike Nichols said the opposite of death is room service. I could deal with that. The desire part sort of scares me. What if Pericles turns out to be a dud?"

"What if he doesn't?" asked Henry, smiling.

"I have this passionate recollection of *Wuthering Heights.* 'Love's uneaten bread.' " Louise rolled her eyes skyward. "Laurence Olivier. I know you don't know who he is, but he was the finest actor of our time, my time anyway. And they're so much in love, Cathy and Heathcliff, and they never do it. And the housekeeper talks about 'love's uneaten bread.'

"I'm so afraid that's what my life will turn out to be. 'Love's uneaten bread.' "

"Maybe you'll get a surprise," said Henry. "Maybe it will be a feast."

"Don't hold your breath," said Louise, holding hers while the dressmakers pinned the bodice.

"I am so sorry about your great-grandfather," Ernest said, leaning in from the next cubicle at Wolf, Simpson & Co.

"Thank you," said Kip.

"What are you going to do?"

"I don't know."

"Would you like to have dinner?"

"Not tonight," she said. "But maybe soon."

"Good," he said, and smiled. "Would you like to have it here or in Australia?"

Now it was Judith who waited outside Clement's office, not even pretending that running into him would be a coincidence. "You didn't call," she said, as he came out of Central Police Station.

"I didn't know what to say."

"What about 'Let's have dinner'?"

"Not much point, is there?"

She fell into step beside him, and tried not to let her anxiety sound in her breathing. Her chest felt tight.

"You were right from the beginning," Clement said. "You're smarter than I am. No point in either of us looking for a relationship. We have things to do."

"But . . ."

"You were patient with me. I appreciate that. I must have seemed very foolish."

"Not foolish at all. You make a lot of sense."

"Not as much as you make. It's tough to be sentimental and nostalgic in this kind of world. Thank you for making me see." He hailed a cab, opened the door as it stopped alongside them. "You don't mind if I don't see you home?"

"I mind a lot," she said.

He smiled. "I'll call you sometime."

"You do that," she said, as he slammed the door. She sat back against the seat and watched him disappear into the crowd. "Or I'll call you, and then you can really run."

The yacht of Pericles Bassia anchored in the harbor at sunset, at which time the wedding ceremony was performed.

"I keep waiting for my alarm to go off," Louise said to the judge.

"Just say I do," said her bridesmaid, Henry Wu.

"I do," said Louise.

The judge pronounced them man and wife. Pericles looked at her with so much joy, his green eyes misted over.

"I'm really very nervous about this," Louise said. And then he kissed her. Expertly and sweetly. "Well, well, well," Louise said. "Well, well, well."

"I wish you every happiness." Anthony Go held out his hand.

"I hope you mean that," said Louise, shaking it. "I wanted you here so you could be a part of that happiness. I never expected my life to work out. Now that it seems to be doing that, I'd really like to be around to take it in."

"As long as you follow through, there's no reason you won't be."

"Follow through how?"

"I expect you to take care of my deals."

"Mr. Go, I don't think you understand. You know the joke about the man who cleaned up after the elephants in the circus? And someone asked him why he didn't quit, and he said, 'What? And give up show business?' Mr. Go, I am out of show business. I've cleaned up after elephants for most of my life, and the worst of it is, they don't even say thank you. So I am gone. Away. Free and clear, Willie. I am going to be a simple Greek billionaire housewife."

"You won't be able to stay away from it."

"Watch me."

"I intend to," said Anthony Go.

"Goodbye." Lockwood and Erica waved Biddy off, as she headed for the Departure Lounge.

"Now us." He put his arm around Erica. "We better check in."

"Going where?"

"Home, of course. To face the music."

"Are you crazy, when we could have the music of Brazil?" She touched her fingers to the back of his neck, and pulled him toward her for a kiss. "At gate twenty-one is a plane to Rio de Janeiro," she said against his mouth.

He pulled away slightly. "I don't want it to look like I ran away. I didn't do anything wrong."

"You said yourself you couldn't prove that. Even if you did, you'd be ruined. And the jury would hate you for making all that money. You'd go to jail.

"Of course, I'd wait for you. But by the time you got out, we'd be old and they would have cut down the Rain Forest. It's going at the rate of an acre a second the latest report says. We have to save it."

"You really think we can?"

"Of course. First we take a luggage cart. Then we check into Linea Aeronaves. Then we fly to Rio. Then we make love on the Justice Department."

"Sounds good to me." He grinned.

"I'll really miss you," James said to Claire, in the Departure Lounge.

"Not for long." She looked at his handsome, chiseled face. Just as Judith said, *beau*. Good Judith, who always saw things as they were. He was only for exotic places. "You ought to go someplace else. Get a fresh start."

"I'm afraid Anthony Go wouldn't look kindly on my leaving."

"You might be surprised." She stood on tiptoe and kissed him, as the loudspeaker announced her flight.

"Maybe you'll meet him on the plane. The man who really deserves you."

"Maybe I will, and maybe I won't. But it's been a lot of fun. A lovely interlude."

"You don't mind that that's all it is?"

"That's all anything is," said Claire.

And then she was on the plane. Adventure. "Heading into the unknown; not really knowing what you're getting into," Judith had said. "But very positive." With all the people Claire had asked to define *adventure*, she hadn't asked herself. Adventure. Something you couldn't be afraid to have on your own. Something it was maybe more exciting to have on your own.

She looked around to see if by chance there was the same flight attendant as on the trip over. But it was just another pert, cheerful-faced young woman, who perhaps might become friends with her, by the time the plane got to Los Angeles. But no one her life depended on.

Because there wasn't anybody her life depended on.